TEMPEST

TEMPEST

Christina Savage

A DELL BOOK

Published by
Dell Publishing Co., Inc.
1 Dag Hammarskjold Plaza
New York, New York 10017

Dell ® TM 681510, Dell Publishing Co., Inc.

Printed in the United States of America

TEMPEST

PROLOGUE

Snowflakes hissed against the locomotive like spent souls spinning into hell. Black smoke rising from the funneled stack presaged the coming night to the six short, wooden passenger cars it covered. Steam from a hundred loose fittings wrapped the legs of well-wishers come to wave good-bye in fleeting wet warmth as the conductor bellowed and stepped aboard, swung his lamp, and closed the door against the cold wind. And at last, the whistle shrieked over the ominous, exciting thud of pistons driving the great wheels and the squeal of iron on iron in the excruciatingly slow transition from dead stop to barely moving.

No one had come to wave good-bye to the woman who settled into the third seat in the second car. Lines of weariness marred her strong, sensuous face and made her look older than her twenty years. White gold hair with the merest miraculous hint of auburn, untamed by pins and ribbons, spilled from underneath her wool bonnet and cascaded down her neck and shoulders like a sunrise. Heavily dressed against the cold, only her face was visible. Only later, when the stoves at either end of the drafty car chased the heaviest chill from the air, did she remove her scarf and open her coat to reveal a heavy, dark green velvet dress that couldn't totally disguise the delicate, sweet curves of her body.

Wind-driven snow rushed by outside the window. The woman stared slightly up and to her right at the swaying lantern. A drummer seated across the aisle buried himself in a newspaper and tried not to look at her. Two seats ahead, unnoticed by her, a small boy peered over the back of his seat. The lantern swayed, the stoves glowed a bright, almost useless red, the wheels underneath went *clunkety-clunk, clunkety-clunk*. The sound faded when the train went over a trestle, then returned in full force, reflected upward by the frozen ground.

"Tickets, please."

The woman looked up to see a thin wisp of a man wearing his uniform like an ill-fitting sack stitched with brass buttons that lent the ensemble a military air. "I beg your pardon?" she said.

"Conductor, ma'am." He held out his hand. "Tickets, please."

"Oh. Yes." Fingers stiff with cold, she loosened the drawstrings on her purse, extracted a packet, and handed it to him.

"Ahem," the conductor said importantly. He licked his thumb, flicked through the clipped papers, and read off the names of more than a dozen cities. "All the way from Vicksburg," he remarked officiously, wagging his head. "Quite a trip for a young lady alone. Meridian, Corinth, lay over in Chattanooga. Knoxville, Lynchburg, Charlottesville, lay over in Washington. Baltimore, Philadelphia, lay over in New York." His punch clicked rapidly. "I'll punch you through to Providence. If this storm don't get worse and delay us, you'll be able to stretch your legs there tomorrow morning sometime. Knock on wood."

"I expect the worst."

The conductor tilted the ticket to the light and read aloud. "Celia Rose Bartlett. Well, Miss Bartlett," he said, not unkindly, "it's not right one so young and pretty should expect the worst. Wisdom is supposed to come when your teeth go." He smiled at her, revealing an assortment of crooked teeth, and handed back her tickets. "New man'll pick you up in Providence and see you through to Boston. If I was you, I'd just make the best of a bad situation and get plenty of sleep. Might be easier if you was to move closer to the stove. I'm sure the gentleman there now would give you his seat."

"I'm doing just fine, thank you. Will we be stopping somewhere where I can buy something hot to eat or drink?"

"Miss Hattie has a stand with coffee and cakes and such in Providence, but other'n that I'm afraid not. Weather like this, I keep a kettle goin' up front. If you've tea in that hamper I'll be glad to give you some hot water."

"Coffee and cakes will do," Celia said, stuffing her tickets back into her purse and ready to end the conversation. "And now if you don't mind?"

"Certainly. I can take a hint, ma'am." The conductor squinted through his pince-nez, stared at her red-rimmed, pale blue eyes. "Yessir, show me a barn with the side caved in, and I'll show you a near-sighted mule."

Celia wasn't sure she knew what that meant, but the conductor obviously enjoyed his wit for he threw back his head and laughed as he moved on. Alone again with her thoughts, Celia sagged back against the hard seat and closed her eyes, then, as abruptly, sat up. Four hundred miles to Boston. At an average of less than twenty miles an hour, with possible delays for the storm as well as scheduled stops, the night and most of the next day stretched ahead of her. If she didn't want to go mad with boredom, she'd have to keep busy. The facing seat, thankfully unoccupied, held her hamper with a replenished supply of bread, cheese, jam, and other foodstuffs any seasoned traveler carried, her hatbox, one of her carpetbags, a muff she had bought in Washington, and an assortment of papers, magazines, and books she had brought to while away the time. One newspaper in particular drew her interest. She had seen it in New York and bought it on the strength of the banner headline. "Mississippi Secedes!" it said. "Second State Withdraws from Union."

Celia stared at the black, grave message, slowly read the account as if in a dream, then leaned back and closed her eyes. Mississippi had seceded. Her father had spoken for the Vicksburg delegation, which opposed secession. "I vote for reason," he was quoted, "and against bloodshed. For surely, gentlemen, if reason fail, blood will be shed." The reporter noted that the majority of the convention cheered and then, the Vicksburg delegation's sentiments notwithstanding, passed the resolution that removed the state from the Union.

South Carolina, then Mississippi. That others would follow was a foregone conclusion. The long, slow pressure that had been building for years between the industrial, non-slave North and agricultural, slaveowning South was, with the Republican Lincoln's election, on the verge of eruption. Civil war, once a term to be whispered fearfully, was now spoken of openly and regarded as a reasonable alternative to the North's unabashed trampling of the South's rights and sensibilities, not to speak of its very economic life. The country from Maine to Mississippi was seething with partisan anger. Normally rational men, whipped into a frenzy by demagogues and self-appointed patriots, had taken leave of their senses. War loomed on the horizon. And if war came, Celia would find herself far from father and friends in what amounted to virtually a foreign land. For a moment she considered getting off the train in Providence, wiring ahead to Boston that she wouldn't be arriving after all, and catching the next train back south. But that course was closed to her, she knew. She had left with only the most perfunctory of excuses, left a confused and worried father as well as a disheartened suitor, to puzzle over her decision to visit her aunt in Boston. As a result, her life had been set loose on a tangent that would take her far from the world in which she had grown up. There could be no return. Not after what had happened.

A minute ago, an age ago. Only three weeks? Not quite. Three weeks less two days. Not nearly long enough to forget the shame or come to grips with the guilt that haunted her every moment. Worst of all, there was nothing she could do. Nothing, nothing, nothing, except, perhaps, to try to explain. Not to her father, certainly, for the knowledge would kill him. Nor to Rafe, for he would kill Micah and perhaps be killed himself in the attempt. To herself, then. For no one else would ever know. With weighted movements, she opened her carpetbag, removed diary, pen, and stoppered vial of ink.

> January 11, 1861
>
> Today is the ninth day since I departed Vicksburg. Will this interminable journey never end? I left New York this afternoon and am cooped in yet another draughty, rumbling box that, like the others, carries me ever and drearily northward.
>
> Eighteen days and some few hours have passed since my ordeal, and still I cannot fathom that it happened to me, that it was I who lay there so powerless. One reads and hears of such things—the poor young plantation Negress's violation is common—but the horror one feels at such accounts is nothing compared to the actual experience. Such degradation corrodes the soul worse than I ever could have imagined in my wildest nightmares. All pride, all honor is destroyed. One is left with nothing but shame and, no matter how wrongly that I should feel it or how hard I have tried to dispel it with these writings during these past two weeks, an overpowering sense of guilt.
>
> I understand the shame, understand the feeling of having been touched by something evil and filthy. But the guilt? I am not guilty! I refuse to be made to feel guilty! And yet I feel guilt. If I could only find the words, the damned, cursed words that evade me so persistently . . .

The train rumbled over the frozen countryside. Across the aisle, the man reading the newspaper had fallen asleep and snored. The little boy two seats ahead had disappeared. Celia sat alone and wrote and wept. Ahead, the whistle screamed for her while, painfully, she reached into branded memory, and found the words.

The past began with a poem.

> Wings across the moon
> As swift, my thoughts return to you
> Return again, again so true
> I wake from sleep too soon, so soon.
>
> In night's dire and blackest fire
> Whose forge is rarely bested

Our hearts, in separation, tested
Are founded to be of pure desire.

We are the doves of light
Who soar on airy streams.
But on the winds of dreams
We are the hawks of night.

PART I

CHAPTER 1

Celia Rose Bartlett carefully folded the poem, placed it in a small wooden jewel box, which held all her most cherished mementos, and went back to fixing her hair. Her fingers moved automatically, twisting, patting, pinning, as she recited yet again from memory the lines of the poem. Arriving six months after Rafe left to go to sea in one of her father's ships to learn the practical side of the shipping business, the poem had been part of the first letter she had received from him. That had been a year ago, she remembered. A year less one day, for the letter had been delivered to her on the day before Christmas, 1859. In all her life she could remember receiving but one present more perfect—and that had been two weeks ago when she answered the door and saw Rafe, home to Vicksburg after a year-long voyage on one of her father's ships trading in the Caribbean. Only her father's presence kept her from throwing herself in his arms and weeping for pure delight.

He had come home just in time to call a halt to parental machinations to marry Celia to Rafe's older brother, Micah. Celia had seen it coming six months earlier. Hal, her father, and Nathaniel, Rafe and Micah's father, had been close friends for years in spite of their differences of opinion regarding slavery. The campaign to join the two families started in earnest within a week of the time Celia first noted the subtle changes in the two older men's attitudes around her. Nathaniel became even more courtly and solicitous than usual. Her father began turning every dinner conversation to what a catch Micah would make some lucky girl. Micah, the firstborn, and in line to inherit the Lattimore fortune! Micah as fine-looking a man as could be found: big and strong, from good stock, and smart. Micah as headstrong and bull-headed as a man could be, but what young man worth his salt wasn't? Micah, the perfect mate, for he'd sowed his wild oats and gotten them all out of his system. And think of what good friends the Lattimores were—think of the future! The Bartlett shipping firm joined with the Lattimore land and cotton interests! There would be an alliance as powerful as any on the middle Mississippi! Such a union virtually assured future generations of a veritable kingdom over which they should exercise control.

There was, though, one overriding, overwhelming reason why Celia wanted nothing to do with the proposed scheme, and that was Rafe. One of Celia's earliest memories was of Rafe when she had been four, he eight: she had wanted to play, he had pushed her down and had run away. That barely recalled incident had set the tone for their relationship until, at thirteen, Celia had blossomed. Then and at last, Rafe had taken notice of her. In the painful three years that followed, she had watched him come and go with a maturity beyond her years, for she knew he would someday be hers. She was proved right at the annual Fourth of July picnic, in 1858, when Rafe took her aside and told her he had decided to accept her father's offer and join the Bartlett Shipping Company. He would be gone for some time, he said, but vowed his love and asked her to wait for him. It had been an easy promise for Celia to make and, though the time had hung heavily on her hands, as easy to keep.

The campaign to marry Micah had come as a surprise to Celia. Micah was seven years older than Celia and, beyond seeing her frequently at his house or hers, had never shown the slightest interest in her. That was fine, as far as Celia was concerned, for as time passed she had grown to dislike him more. The eldest Lattimore son's reputation as a womanizer, his frequent drinking bouts at Vicksburg Under the Hill, and his violent temper were ignored by her father. What became more important in Hal's eyes was his long and close friendship with Nathaniel. The two men had been partners once many years earlier, but when Hal found it increasingly difficult to reconcile slavery and profits, the partnership had been dissolved. Yet both men had lost their wives on the same day when the steamboat on which the women were traveling to Natchez sank. Both men had been involved in Vicksburg's politics and were jointly responsible for the municipal gas works, the first in the state. It was therefore natural for Hal and Nathaniel to seek a union between their two families.

Celia, on the other hand, could only avoid arguments, controversy, and Micah himself—and bide her time until Rafe returned. Now he had returned, had been home for two weeks, and still her father was singing the same tune. In praise of Micah Lattimore.

"Miss Celia!" Immelda, Celia's mulatto servant hurried into the room, and rushed to her mistress's side. "It's Mistuh Rafe. He's downstairs in the back an' says that he's got to see you."

"In the back, Immelda?" Celia asked, looking quizzically at the slight, coffee-colored woman in the mirror. "He just saw me in church. And will again for dinner tonight. Why ever?"

"He say Mistuh Micah comin' to propose, an' he got to talk to you first," she said, glancing nervously over her shoulder. "I told him I ain't gonna sneak him up the back stairs no way. No, sirree. It ain't proper. Just ain't proper. But he says to tell you anyways."

Celia blanched. "Micah's coming to propose?" she asked. Her fingers felt cold as she tied the top bow on her chemise. "Is . . . is Father here?"

"Yes'm. No'm. Him an' Mistuh Lattimore are due back any minute now, though. Mistuh Rafe says he reckons they just left to give Mistuh Micah time. An' if he comes in an' find that Mistuh Rafe up here? . . . Lawdie, but there ain't no tellin' what he'll do."

"Here. Help me into this," Celia ordered. "And then bring him on up."

Immelda held the top of her gown so Celia could slip her arms through the sleeves. "This room's a mess. Ain't no man ought to see a lady's room—"

"Immelda! Just get him, please. Let me worry about Father."

"If you say so," the mulatto said, edging toward the door. "Still an' all, you mark the time an' don't tarry long. It fine that you doin' the worryin', but Mistuh Hal's temper got long arms. They for sure stretch out to me if he find out—"

"Immelda!"

"Yes'm. I'm goin'."

"And then keep an eye out for Micah," Celia called after her. "Let me know when he gets here."

The mulatto disappeared down the hall. Fingers shaking, Celia pinched the green velvet to work the glass bead buttons through the eyelets, then turned once quickly in front of the mirror to check herself before hurrying to the window to make sure Micah hadn't arrived.

The front drive was still empty. Relieved, Celia rested her forehead against the glass. "We'll have to do something," she whispered. "I can't marry him. I just *can't!* Not Micah!"

"What about my brother?" a voice said from the doorway.

Celia whirled about. "Rafe! I can't marry him. We have to stop it!"

"We will. I promise that." Slim and wirily built, his face all tanned planes and angles, honed to sharpness by the sea, Rafe closed the door behind him and crossed the room to her. The emerald chips of his eyes glinted in the sunlight as he took her in his arms and lifted her close to him.

"Rafe?"

His kiss was ardent, almost bruising. Breathless, Celia thought she would melt, and cried out as his lips traced fire down her neck. "Rafe . . . Rafe . . ."

"I love you, Celia."

The words thrilled her more than any she could remember hearing. Eyes swimming, she leaned back from him and brushed the long waves of soft black hair from his face. "And I love you," she whispered, touching his cheek. "Oh, my God, how I do love you. What?"

Rafe had stiffened, abruptly stepped away from the window, and drew her with him. "Damn! So soon!" he hissed, moving to the side of the window and surreptitiously peering down.

"You shouldn't curse. He's your brother."

"And an unpredictable one, too. Only three days ago he was refusing to grant Father his wish and make an attempt at respectability. I thought . . ."

"It's just as much our fault. We should have told them."

"What? That you wanted to marry a sailor?"

"You're more than a sailor. You know that. Father wouldn't have taken you on if he hadn't had *some* plans for you."

"Maybe so. Nonetheless—"

"Nonetheless nonsense. You're a Lattimore. You're handsome and intelligent, a gentleman, if you will. And"—Celia wrapped her arms around his neck and kissed him—"I love you. Which should be enough for any father."

Rafe held her closely, and breathed the delicate sweetness of lilacs in her hair. Once before he had come to her room. Stolen up the rear stairs when her father was at church and the servants were gone. Then as now their kisses had fired such passion that only with the greatest of effort did they remain under control of themselves. "Hair like white gold spun by the light of the moon," he whispered softly. "Skin the soft texture of love itself, a figure full and ripe for love's caress . . ."

"Mmm. I wish I weren't so pretty. Then maybe Micah . . . Oh, dear!" Blushing, Celia covered her eyes.

Rafe laughed, lifted her face and kissed her nose. "Lady, there are those who would sashay with the devil himself to look as pretty as you do."

"I only meant that if I looked like this"—she squinted one eye, twisted her face, and managed to appear absolutely dreadful—"then Micah wouldn't be attracted in the slightest. Which would solve all our problems."

"You're forgetting one thing," Rafe corrected. "You look like that and I might lose interest, too."

"Why, you . . ."

Rafe laughed, ducked a playful swipe, and caught her wrist. "Uh-

uhh! Temper, temper. I love you for your sweet soul and personality, but a face like that?" He held her face in both hands, gently kissed her on the lips, then on each eye. "When a man thinks you are the most beautiful woman on God's green earth, that's the man you want to keep. Because he'll never, never forget how lucky he is."

Celia took his wrist and kissed the palm of his hand. "I don't want it to be luck, Rafe. Not between us." Her eyes shone with tears of happiness, and her voice was husky. "I'll be beautiful for you every minute of the day. Morning, noon, and night. Just let me be with you, is all. Anything else . . ."

Rafe held her, stroked her hair. "You will be. And I'll be with you." The sound of a door closing downstairs made him stop. "But first, there's a little matter of telling Micah. And our fathers." He held Celia at arm's length. "Do you remember the time when I dunked your pigtails in Johnny Tobler's inkwell?"

"You were terrible," Celia said, laughing. "Your father made you apologize to me and Daddy. Your face was so red I thought you'd pop."

"That's because it was one of the hardest things I ever had to do." He took a deep breath, let it out slowly. "Until now. This isn't going to be pleasant."

"But just think," Celia replied, coming back into his arms, "of the reward."

"I'll—"

But she was kissing him. A slow, languorous, mulled wine of a kiss that warmed him to the tips of his boots. Lost in the taste and feel of him, Celia's heart sang to the lines of his poem.

"We are the doves of light . . . we are the hawks of night."

"Why, it's Mistuh Micah!" Immelda exclaimed, standing aside as Rafe's older brother filled the doorway and crowded into the foyer.

"Where's Miss Bartlett?" Micah asked, entering like a storm cloud pregnant with thunder and lightning.

"Why, she's, uh . . . upstairs," Immelda stammered. "Gettin' dressed, I reckon. She wasn't expectin'—"

"Tell her I'm here," Micah ordered, tipsily pushing past her and heading for the formal parlor.

Immelda scooted ahead of him to get the door and wrinkled her nose at the strong smell of whiskey that followed in his wake.

"Something the matter?" Micah growled.

"No, suh. We ain't used this here room since about a month ago when the preacher come to call, is all. I'd best light a candle. This room ain't been aired for a week."

"Forget the candle," Micah snapped impatiently. "My father and Mr. Bartlett. Where are they?"

Immelda hovered in the doorway. "Out, suh. Left right after they got in from church. Said somethin' 'bout ridin' down to the river road by the docks."

"Good. Get Miss Bartlett, then."

"Yes, suh."

Swaying slightly, Micah stood alone in the center of the parlor, abruptly went to one of the windows, and drew back the curtains. "Down by the docks. Where I ought to be," he muttered to himself, fuzzily picturing one of Fancy Darren's girls, maybe the new redhead, trying out some of her French tricks on him. The notion made his skin tickle. Word was she kissed hot enough to melt a minié ball. The room whirled and he willed it steady. *Damn hangover*, he thought, stifling a belch. If he'd just eaten . . . Well, a man couldn't drink enough good whiskey, hangover or no. What he needed was a hair of the dog that bit him . . .

"Let's see . . ." A panel in a bookcase slid open at his touch. Micah removed a bottle of Kentucky bourbon and a glass, helped himself to a couple of fingers neat, and set the bottle on the mantel.

A fine thing, he grinned, raising the glass to himself in the mirror over the mantel. Thinking of Fancy's place and girls on the day he proposed. But then, why not? What the hell. They were all the same, when you turned them upside down. Maybe even a little more so, in Celia's case. A rare bit, indeed. Might even know a trick or two herself. Just proved you never could tell. All those years being more like a troublesome little sister, and then ending up his wife.

The whiskey smoothed out the raw edges and perked him up. Micah poured another couple of fingers, contemplated himself in the mirror once again. "Time you settled down, Micah, my boy," he said. "Least part of the time." It would be difficult at first, this gentlemanly business. Rafe managed it better, but then Rafe was a bit of a prig anyway. Always wearing his sense of pride and protocol like a captain his stripes. Still, Celia with her firm little body and sweet light gold hair wouldn't be that bad to come home to. In fact, if there was a prettier girl in all of Vicksburg, he hadn't seen her. In addition to which, of course, was her father's business. Hell, no telling how many ships the old man owned. A dozen? More? Lattimore cotton on what would be Lattimore ships before too much longer wasn't at all a bad deal. Cotton, ships, a beautiful wife, the best mistresses money could buy. "Celia, honey," he said, shifting his gaze to the silhouette of a young girl etched in gold leaf on a porcelain plate, "this looks like your lucky day!"

The fog in his brain was lifting. Pleased with himself, Micah reached for the whiskey bottle, missed, and knocked it off the mantel. Before he could catch it, it hit the hearth and smashed. The sickly smell of bourbon filled the room. Cursing, Micah knelt to pick up the pieces and yelled in pain as a glass splinter jabbed into his knee.

"God damn!" he howled, rising and swatting at his knee. "Son of a bitch!" he yelped when the blade of glass reappeared in the palm of his hand. He picked it out and threw it into the fireplace. "Immelda! Blast it all, where are you?" he bellowed, starting for the foyer. "Damn city's full of niggers and never one about when—" He stopped in midsentence, brought up short by the sight of Celia and Rafe descending the stairs arm in arm. "What the—?"

"Lawd, Mistuh Micah!" Immelda exclaimed, hurrying down the hall toward him and not yet seeing Celia and Rafe. "What in tarnation has happened? You look like the woebegones done took up your case for sure. An' your han' is cut an' bleedin'—"

"Shut up, Immelda." Micah's voice was dangerously hard. "I broke a bottle in there. Go clean it up," he snapped, stepping out of her way and motioning her into the parlor.

Immelda glanced over her shoulder, saw Rafe and Celia. "Yes, suh," she said, her voice sounding too loud. She backed a step, then another. "I best get rags an' such . . . Yes, suh. Rags an' . . ." Terrified, she spun and hurried back down the hall.

The silence was thick enough to be felt. The two brothers were a study in contrasts. Micah, his arms like cordwood bulging beneath the heavy fabric of his coat, was as thick as Rafe was slender. Micah's face was rounder, chunkier, and his eyes were black and shone with a keen and animal suspicion. Both brothers' hair was jet black, but Rafe's was long and Micah's was cut short enough to betray a shade of scalp. Where Rafe was clean shaven, Micah sported a luxurious mustache that curled down at the ends and made him look as if he wore a perpetual frown. "Well, well, well," Micah finally said. "And just what the hell do we have here?"

"A younger brother," Rafe said, warily. He stepped ahead of Celia, and stood on a level with Micah. "We need to talk, you and I."

"You aren't supposed to be here."

"Let's go into the conservatory. Celia, why don't you wait in—"

"No." Celia held her ground. "I'm sorry, Micah. It's a terrible time and way to tell you."

Micah ignored Celia, and glared at Rafe. "You were up in her room, weren't you? Up in her room!"

Rafe shrugged. "I had to get here ahead of you. Look, Micah. Celia and I have been talking about this for over a year. And when I got back and found out . . . Well, what with Christmas coming up and everything, there just didn't ever seem to be a good time to say anything. Besides, until three days ago you were acting as if you couldn't care less. I—we—figured we had plenty of time to tell Father and Hal, and you, too."

"Tell me what?" Micah asked in a monotone.

"That we're in love. And will get married as soon as my position is improved."

"Well, I'll be damned." Micah squeezed his eyes shut and shook his head as if to clear it. There it was again, ever since he could remember. Oh, they'd liked him well enough until little brother came along. How things did change then, though. Suddenly his mother had no time for him, and spent every waking minute with the squawling, puking, pissing newcomer. It was "be quiet, now, Micah" and "you're the *big* boy, Micah. Be nice to Rafe." It was "isn't Rafe darling?" and "isn't Rafe the spittin' image of his daddy?" and "such a sweet little boy!" It was Rafe smiling and laughing and sweet-talking all the time while Micah had to fight for every ounce of recognition until he finally gave up and figured what the hell. They thought he was rough and coarse and mean, he'd be every bit of it and more. And now, the final insult: Rafe taking his woman away from him while all the town watched and laughed. "Up in her room while I was down here waiting. Now doesn't that take the cake?" he said, wounded and dangerous. It wasn't love that was dashed, though. It was pride. His right hand raised slowly, and he pointed at Celia. "You and I are going to stand before the altar," he said, his finger stabbing the air like a knife. "And you, my back-stabbing brother, will have nothing to say about it."

"Back-stabbing?" Rafe asked. "I was gone for a year and a half. In all that time did you ever show any interest in Celia? No. Did she in you? No! There's been no—"

Micah grabbed Rafe by the collar of his coat and slammed him against the wall. "You," he snapped at Celia as she started toward him. "Not another step. And you, little brother." His voice trembled with rage and his fists bunched the fabric so tightly that one seam parted. "Two things. One, you're lucky I didn't put your head right through this wall. And two, something I want you to get straight. I'm firstborn around here. Lattimore Hall will be mine, the plantations will be mine. What I say goes. Now I've already let everyone know I'll be marrying Celia Bartlett. And I won't have folks laughing at me and saying she turned me down."

"That's precisely what I *am* doing," Celia broke in. "For heaven's sake, Micah, try to understand."

"Keep out of what doesn't concern you," Micah said, snarling. "This is between me and Rafe."

"Doesn't concern me?" Celia asked incredulously.

"Let loose, Micah," Rafe said evenly. His face was flushed as he strained to bring his temper under control.

"Let loose," Micah mimicked. "Or what, little—" He stopped abruptly, stiffened as the point of a knife pressed against his abdomen.

"It's called a snickersnee, brother. A little something I picked up in Martinique. It won't kill you, but you'll wish to hell it had for a few days."

Micah's face blanched. Slowly, carefully, he let Rafe go and stepped back.

"Almost impossible to take away from a man," Rafe said, holding up the knife. The handle was barely long enough to fit in a fist. The blade was a short triangle, less than an inch long, and honed to razor sharpness on both edges. "Maybe you'd better leave now. We'll talk later. With Father."

For a moment, Micah looked as if he'd attack anyway, but then evidently thought better. "Haven't heard the end of this, little brother," he said, sucking his wounded palm. "Not by a long shot. As for you—" He turned his attention to Celia. "You ought to be damn grateful I'm willing to take you. The whole town knows how the Bartletts stand. Soft on niggers, soft on states' rights. If trouble comes with the Abolitionists, certain folks will remember some of those letters your father wrote to the paper. Friends could get to be mighty scarce. Now you think on that."

"And we still live in a free country, in case *you*'ve forgotten," Celia retorted. "Father has as much right to express an opinion as anyone else. And if you or any of your cronies disapprove, I can offer only one suggestion. Live with it, Micah Lattimore."

"Easy, Celia," Rafe said, trying to calm her as well as Micah. "He's been drinking. We aren't accomplishing anything, and Micah is saying things he doesn't mean."

"The hell I am! Since when were you my keeper? Miss high-and-mighty thinks she is too good for me? We'll see. And as for you, little brother . . ." Micah let the threat hang unfinished, whirled on his heels, and leaving hat and walking stick behind, threw open the front door, and stalked out.

Celia cringed as the door banged against the coatrack, then slammed closed. Rafe got to the door in time to see Micah yell at Tobias, Immelda's husband, to leave the damned carriage alone. Tobias, black as a twig and about as thin, darted out of harm's way as Micah leaped onto the carriage seat and whipped his horse into a run. Rafe closed the door and rejoined Celia at the bottom of the stairs. "I'm sorry. Micah . . . His drinking drives Father to distraction. I suppose Father feels that getting Micah married to you would straighten him out."

"And my father agrees," Celia replied with a shudder. "Let's go where there's some light."

Rafe followed her into the sun parlor, a cheerfully appointed room with thickly cushioned, curved back chairs and purple hassocks and a woodstove warm with a comforting blaze bright behind the mica windows in the door. At the same time, Immelda, carrying a dustpan full of broken glass and dripping, reeking rags, poked her head through the connecting door to the kitchen. "Can I get you anything, Miss Celia?"

"Some tea perhaps, thank you, Immelda. You'd best put some fresh coffee on, too. And make it strong. I have a feeling Father is going to need it when he and Mr. Lattimore arrive."

A sudden draft moved the curtains. Celia, Rafe, and Immelda turned in unison in time to hear the front door slam closed. "Celia?" Hal Bartlett's voice rang out. "Celia!"

"Quickly with the coffee," Celia whispered to Immelda, who hurried out. "In here, Father!"

Hal Bartlett had started up the stairs, now retraced his steps and hurried to the rear of the house. "There you are," he said, giving Rafe a perfunctory nod and crossing to his daughter. "What in heaven's name is going on? Nathaniel and I just passed Micah driving his poor mare hell for leather down South Street. I had to pull out of the way to keep from being run down. Nathaniel took my carriage to chase him down. Is something wrong at Lattimore Hall?" The rotund, bewhiskered, feisty man did an about-face as it suddenly dawned on him who he'd greeted when he came in. "My God," he said, staring quizzically at Rafe. "What are you doing here, young man?"

"Making a mess of things, I'm afraid," Rafe said awkwardly, crossing to the window to look out at the garden in order not to have to stand face to face with the man who had been almost as close to him as his own father. "I'm afraid I've let matters get out of hand, sir."

"We both have," Celia chimed in.

"Will someone please tell me what is going on? You two are making no sense whatsoever."

"Yes, sir. No, sir." Rafe cleared his throat, took a deep breath, and plunged ahead. "Celia and I have talked of announcing an engagement."

"Precisely what was supposed to happen today," Hal said. "Only I return to find, I suspect, that nothing of the sort has transpired. And I'm darn near run down in the process." He looked from Rafe to his daughter. "I'd appreciate you telling me . . ." He trailed off as the sudden realization hit him. "Oh, no."

Celia rose from her chair, walked resolutely to Rafe's side, and took his arm in hers. "Rafe and I are in love, Father."

Hal stared dully at them, moved to a chair, and sat heavily. "Love?" he asked, as if he'd never heard the word before. "Oh, dear."

"We told Micah," Rafe added.

"Oh, dear! Oh, dear me."

"Yes, sir. We wanted to wait for a more propitious time to tell everyone, but events sort of got out of hand," Rafe explained apologetically. "I know Micah as the eldest stands to inherit the bulk of Father's estate should, God forbid, anything happen to Father, but I won't be a pauper by any means. And I think I have learned a great deal about all aspects of the shipping business—from the water up, so to speak—so I should be able to acquit myself well in any way you think . . . That is, sir, ah . . ." He was babbling, knew it, hated himself for it, and made himself stop. "What I'm trying to say, sir"—he took a deep breath—"is that I am certain I can do quite well by Celia, and ask you for her hand in marriage."

Hal rose, walked across the room, stood and stared at a sketch he had drawn of the sun setting behind a cypress swamp. Rafe and Celia watched him silently, followed as he returned to his favorite chair and eased himself down. Immelda entered from the side door, placed the coffee service on the table next to her master, and attracting as little attention to herself as possible, hurried back to the kitchen. Celia and Rafe heard Tobias ask, "What is happnin' in there?" only to be violently shushed by his wife.

"Father?" Celia finally asked, uncomfortable with his silence.

"I know this is a bit sudden, sir," Rafe began, "but—"

"On the contrary," Hal said and laughed brittlely, waving Rafe to silence. "Five minutes is quite enough time to reconsider my daughter's future. Good God, man!"

"Now, Father. Watch your nerves. Remember what Dr. Stewart—"

"Blast Dr. Stewart. What does he know? Now Tom Senior, there was a *real* doctor. Old enough to know what he was talking about. A man my age doesn't need a boy telling him what to do. Watch your temper, watch your cigars, watch your liquor. Hell's bells! You'd think I was ninety instead of fifty!"

"Tom isn't telling you anything different than Tom Senior did, Daddy, and you know it. Your heart simply isn't—"

"Heart? Heart? What the thunder does my heart have to do with you and Rafe? My God, wait until Nathaniel hears this. Why didn't you tell me?"

"I was going to," Celia tried to explain, "but I had to wait until Rafe got home, and then everything was so busy, and Micah never did say one word to make me even think that anything would really happen, and—"

"We hoped to avoid opposing either you or Father by waiting, sir, until it became evident Micah wasn't interested. Then, when I had something of substance to offer—"

"Substance! Precisely. Substance is what we've been talking about, damn it!" Hal grumbled, reached over to pour himself a cup of coffee. "Of course," he mused, "Micah is a little wild. But gossip," he amended quickly before they should think he had changed his mind, "has a way of stretching the truth. Especially when the truth is, shall we say, a trifle unsavory."

"I think I know Micah better than you, Mr. Bartlett, meaning no disrespect."

"Then you know how good Celia would be for him."

Rafe disengaged his arm from Celia's, and put it around her shoulder. "Is that really what you want, sir? Your daughter to be good for someone else?"

Hal stopped and let the honey spoon drop back into the jar. "What's that?" he asked softly.

"You heard me, sir."

They did make a handsome couple. Rafe, dark and hard, gentled by a sensitivity sorely lacking in Micah. Celia, golden and soft, a woman like the sky, capable of sweet summer days or turbulent storms. Capable of love's every season. Damn it, but why hadn't he noticed before? The two of them had grown up together, played together, gone to church together . . .

"Celia would be good for anyone," Rafe said. "But I mean to be good for her, sir. No man will ever love her more than I do."

"Well." Hal tapped his thumb on the arm of the chair. Not such a bad idea, really. Not when he thought it through. "I perceive you've learned more than seamanship during the last year, young man," he said, more for appearance' sake than anything else. "Impudence."

"I prefer to call it honesty, sir."

"The two are often one and the same," Hal said, waving aside any further response. He looked at his daughter, shook his head, and pursed his lips. "I'll give it some thought. I assume I'll be allowed a day or two to consider your proposal? Or do you intend to run off with him in the dead of night?"

Celia looked up at Rafe, slipped out from under his arm, and went to Hal. "Thank you, Father," she said, and eyes glowing, kissed him on the forehead. "Thank you very much."

"I did *not* give my permission. I said I would *consider* what you've said. I think you ought to give it careful thought as well." He patted Celia's hand, caught himself beaming, and forced his face into a frown. "As for you, young man, I suggest you hurry along and try to find your father, who is probably in much the same state as I. Worse, perhaps, if he's caught up to Micah."

"Yes, sir!" Rafe strode to Hal's chair, pumped his prospective father-in-law's hand. "I was just leaving. You won't regret this, sir. I promise—"

"Please, please, Rafe," Hal said, freeing his hand. "You don't have to—"

"I'll see him to the door," Celia interrupted, anxious to be alone with Rafe for a moment.

"He's been in and out of this house since he was a baby!" Hal roared. "Knows it as well as he knows his own! Ahhh!" He threw up his hands in mock disgust. "Have it your way. I'm only your father."

"And a dear one, too," Celia said with a musical laugh.

Hal watched them leave hand in hand, then reached for his coffee. "Love," he growled. "What in the world does love have to do with anything?" He sipped his coffee, winced at the bitter taste of the chicory Immelda added to it, and reached for the honey pot. "Micah will be furious, Nathaniel will want to know what happened, and I'm damned if I have an answer for either of them. Love, indeed!"

Hal was holding court with his emotions half an hour later when Immelda and Celia found him again in the same chair. Both women looked anxious.

"What is it now?" Hal asked, peering up from under his eyebrows. "Don't tell me you have a new revelation to spring on me."

"No," Celia said. "Just that Tom Stewart is here."

"So?" Hal asked. "That's cause for a furrowed brow?"

"He's in the garden, Mistuh Bartlett," Immelda explained. "Drove right on around back without stoppin'."

"You'd better come and see for yourself, Father. He isn't alone. Old Harmon is with him, and I think others as well."

"Two others," Immelda added. "An' they's hid inside his carriage."

Hal breathed in sharply. "Black?"

"Yassuh."

"Harmon knows about me, then?" Hal asked Immelda as he stood and crossed the parlor to her.

"Yassuh. But he like all the rest promise' not to say nothin'. He knows it'd be bad for you."

"I sincerely hope he knows, for all our sakes." His face was set in a serious look. "We'll certainly find out, won't we, Celia? I should prefer to speak with Tom alone, if you don't mind."

"Of course, Father."

"As usual, you know nothing of this call, Immelda?"

"Yassuh. She was in her room nappin' when Doctuh Tom come a'callin', an' didn't see or hear nothin'."

"Good. I'll let you know when all's clear."

Celia knew what was expected of her and dutifully ran up the stairs to her room, where she always waited when Negroes involved in the Underground Railroad arrived at the house. Then Hal followed Immelda out the back way to the garden where Tom Stewart's closed carriage waited out of sight from the front of the house.

Tom Stewart, Jr., had read for medicine with his father and had later taken over his father's extensive practice when two years earlier the elder Stewart drowned during a night crossing of the Mississippi to deliver the baby of a plantation owner's wife. Though he was not yet thirty, a zest for good food had given young Tom a paunch that strained the buttons of his vest. Normally as cheerful as his father had been dour, his round face was now devoid of its usual good-natured smile, and his shoulders spoke eloquently of the same tension that appeared in his eyes. Old Harmon, the Stewarts' long-time family servant, fidgeted nervously behind his master.

"Tom! This is a surprise," Hal said, shaking the physician's hand. "No one here is sick, I'd better tell you right off. And Harmon. Good to see you."

"Yessir, Mr. Bartlett. Good to see you, too," the servant replied, unable to meet Hal's gaze.

"I need to talk to you, Hal," Tom mumbled, impatient with the amenities.

"Of course." Before Tom could stop him, Hal stepped around him and opened the carriage door. Inside, two young Negroes, a boy and girl not even out of their teens, cowered in the far corner. Both were dressed in simple cotton shirts and trousers, the dress of field hands. Hal smiled at them in an unsuccessful attempt to put them at ease and closed the door again. "Perhaps we should go inside to talk," Hal said to Tom. "Immelda, bring some of your cookies out to Harmon and these others. We'll be in the sun parlor."

Hal led the doctor into the parlor and offered him one of the wicker chairs. "Tea or coffee?"

"Nothing, thank you," Tom said, preferring to pace rather than sit.

The older man sat and let Tom pace for a moment. "I have a very good brandy. But you know that."

"I have a problem," Tom blurted. "You were, of course, much closer to my father, and I have no right to presume on that friendship, but . . . but . . ."

"You didn't drive over here to beat about the bush, young man. It is true I was your father's friend. I also held him in great esteem. That affection and respect has been transferred to his son." Hal chuckled. "No matter if I do rail at you from time to time for some of your new-fangled ideas."

Tom blushed and looked away a moment. "Thank you, sir."

"So what's the problem? And why have you brought Harmon and those other Negroes here?"

"The boy is Harmon's grandson, Calder. Annie is Calder's wife."

"I'm listening," Hal prompted when no more information seemed to be forthcoming.

"Annie and Calder are owned by the Kirbys."

"Yes." Once started, Tom overcame his initial uneasiness. Calmer, he took the chair Hal had offered, sat back, and folded his hands in his lap. "But they have suffered some losses and are selling off some of their property in order not to lose everything." He leaned forward to emphasize what followed. "They sold Annie to Zebus Hutchin."

"My God!" Hal breathed. "The breeder over in Meridian?"

"The same. And Calder would remain at the Kirbys'. I sewed up Calder's foot when he cut it with an ax last year. Two nights ago, he and Annie showed up in my kitchen."

"Runaways," Hal finished.

"Yes," Tom said. "Now I believe that a man's property is a personal thing, and no one has the right to steal it from him. But Zebus Hutchin? Sweet Jesus! I couldn't send them back. Not to the likes of that miserable scoundrel."

Hal shook his head in agreement, waited for Tom to go on, and apprehensive of the answer he knew he'd receive asked, "So why bring them here?"

Tom appeared embarrassed. "Because I know that you're a member of the railroad," he said in little more than a whisper.

"Oh? What makes you think—"

"The Underground Railroad. You've been smuggling slaves to the North for the past year." Emboldened, he stared at the older man. "Harmon told me all about it—about you."

The two men stared at each other in silence for a long moment. Hal weighed the advisability of denying complicity and of admitting that he was indeed involved. Tom had the good sense to remain silent. At last, unable to let the two young Negroes be separated, much less countenance the girl's sale to the most notorious breeder in that part of the country, Hal rose from his chair and walked to the kitchen door just as Immelda was starting out with a platter of cookies and a pitcher of milk. "There's been a change of plans, Immelda," he said softly. "You may take those down to the room in the cellar. Bring the boy and girl down there, too. They'll be spending a night or two."

Immelda glanced past Hal's shoulder in horror that he should address her in front of Tom. "You mean . . . uh . . ."

"Yes. That is precisely what I mean." Hal smiled, lightly touched Immelda on her arm. "Don't worry. Dr. Stewart is a friend. I trust," he added, turning back to Tom as Immelda ran to the side door.

"I'm as guilty as you are now," Tom said with a wan smile, "so you needn't fear your trust will be misplaced."

"Guilt is an unworthy foundation for trust." Hal clapped Tom on the shoulder, then hurried to the window so he could look out into the backyard. "But never mind. I believe there's something deeper there, something more admirable." He gestured for Tom to join him. "A touch of humanity, perhaps, for the most downtrodden souls on the face of the earth."

Outside, two frightened figures jumped down from the carriage and, following Immelda, scurried to the cellar door and disappeared into the darkness below. "Perhaps," Tom sighed, turning away from the sight. "But I never guessed I'd take such a benign generality and turn it into such an extreme particular."

"These are extreme times," Hal replied, moving away from the window. "Come. Some of that brandy now?" He poured two snifters without waiting for an answer. "I do hope I don't presume on our friendship by asking you to keep what you have learned to yourself."

Tom raised his glass, touched Hal's, and drank. "Learned?" he asked with a grin. "Did I learn something? Seriously, though. I'd never given much of this any thought before. How ever do you—"

"Don't ask," Hal interrupted, holding up a hand, "and I shan't have to lie."

"Uh, yes. Of course." Sobered, Tom stared into his brandy. In truth, he didn't want to know any more than he already knew. It was enough to get these children off his conscience. He considered himself a practical, law-abiding man, but the thought of consigning any human being to Zebus Hutchin . . . He shuddered and drew himself up. No sense getting sentimental, he scolded himself. Once, just this one time, and he'd never again let Harmon or anyone else talk him into sticking his neck out so far. "You're right," he went on gruffly. "Better that I don't know, especially since I don't even believe that what you're doing is right. In addition, it's outright dangerous and hardly fits my prescription for a man with a bad heart."

Hal Bartlett didn't smile. "I'll tell you something, Tom. Every man, woman, or child who passes through my house to be taken to the next stop, every one is an Annie or a Calder—to me. And no matter the state of my heart, I sleep soundly at night. So you see," he finished, not unkindly, "it does, however, fit *my* prescription for a man with a conscience."

Vicksburg Under the Hill was no worse nor better than any of a hundred other second cities scattered throughout the South where the more gaudy vices were kept segregated from the proper arenas of life. The city within a city was a conglomeration of low ugly buildings that fronted Levee on the south side of Vicksburg. Weathered clapboard, hand-hewn timber, dull mud brick colors predominated with a smattering of garishly lurid primary colors that assaulted the eyes in the same way as the smells and sounds of the area assaulted the nose and ears. The squalid structures stood cheek to jowl, crowding one another to the base of and part way up River Hill. Here lived the dregs of society. Along narrow cobblestone and mud alleys crisscrossing randomly to eventually empty out onto Levee once again congregated the gamblers, the dance hall girls, the prostitutes, and the customers.

Always the customers. Here was the haunt where a man could drink and fight to his heart's content. Here a man could sin in peace and, bruises and blotches hidden from the everyday world of business and family, not have to confess it to a soul. For convenience and propriety's sake, he could forget he even knew the way until the secret urge struck the next time. And the next time and the time after that. Vicksburg Under the Hill was tolerated because the city fathers did not expect individual men—themselves and their sons included—to be more perfect than mankind at large, and because it kept the riffraff off the streets where their ladies walked.

Micah followed what for him had become a well-worn path to Vicksburg Under the Hill and Fancy Darren's, where he had been a frequent visitor since his sixteenth birthday when, already six feet tall but yet to fill out, he had been instructed in the delights of the flesh by the town's most famous and prosperous prostitute. The two, an unlikely pair on the surface but bound by an insatiable lust for each other, had soon become great friends as well as bedmates, a relationship that had lasted over the intervening years. Micah had, as a matter-of-fact, spent half the night before there, leaving only in time for a few hours' sleep prior to church and his ill-fated call on Celia. Now, still shaking with rage, he beat on the locked door, cupped his hands against the glass, and looked into the front parlor. The place was empty. One lantern cast a feeble light over the red swag curtains and fringed drapes. Crystal stemware glimmered softly inside an open cabinet against the back wall. Plush overstuffed chairs and loveseats with needlepoint serpents sat like dark, heavy shadows. At last, a second light appeared. "We're not open," a voice called.

Micah beat again on the door. "It's me," he yelled. "Micah. Lemme in, damn it, Fancy!"

Footsteps, the rattle of a chain, and the squeak of a bolt. The door opened a crack. "Jesus, Micah. It's the middle of the night."

"It's one in the afternoon," Micah said, pushing in.

"Like I said. The middle of the night. I have to sleep some time. So does everyone else. Besides, you just left."

"I left seven hours ago. You want me to take my business somewhere else?"

"No, no. Of course not, honey. What the hell. C'mon in since you're here." Fancy locked the door and leaned wearily against it. Waked from a deep sleep, she looked the worse for wear in the dim light. Her face was stripped of the usual heavy veneer of rouge and shadowing. Her eyes were widely spaced and large, the soft liquid brown of a doe's, only not nearly as innocent. Her hair, uncoiffed, hung in dark brown tangles down her back. She wore a faded, nondescript and shapeless flannel gown that contrasted sharply to her workaday bright colors but in no way concealed her main attributes, abnormally large breasts and a derriere to match. "So my Romeo returns," she finally said with a yawn. "What can I get you?"

Micah wished he'd never bragged about the fortune he was going to marry into. "A drink," he said, subdued. "Anything."

"That's all?"

"A quiet place to think."

Fancy's laugh was deep and husky. She waved an arm. "You got that, my friend. Quiet as a tomb." She led the way across the room to the bar, poured him a drink, and handed him the glass. "Wakin'-up whiskey. It's too good to gulp, so don't."

Micah flopped in one of the overstuffed chairs, sipped and didn't gulp, as ordered. Fancy sat opposite him and nursed a cup of cold coffee. "You don't look like a man who just got engaged," she said. "I thought—"

"I said a quiet place," Micah interrupted harshly, standing abruptly. He paced across the room once, then again before stopping in front of Fancy. "You're right. This place is like a tomb without people in it. Makes me nervous. Isn't there somewhere else?"

Fancy hadn't won the respect and business of Vicksburg's landed gentry by being slow-witted or insensitive. Keenly aware of moods, she recognized now that Micah was in a dangerous frame of mind and on the raw edge of violence. Rising, she took his arm and led the way out a side door. "Lady likes to get away from where she works all the time," she said. "You know how many hours a day I spend in that parlor? Too damned many. A touch of home does the heart good."

"Where we going?" Micah asked suspiciously.

"Where you haven't been before," Fancy said, opening another door and preceding him into a large, sunlit room.

"Jesus!" Micah swore, impressed. At least sixteen by twenty, the room was carpeted with thick, gaily colored rag rugs. A great brass bed, covers and quilts all tumbled about, gleamed brightly against one wall. The rest of the furniture was slim and fragile and elegant, totally unlike that in the rest of the bordello. An exquisite desk of French design sat against the wall opposite the bed. Micah walked slowly around the room, inspected a painting of a waterfall, and stopped by the desk. "Who the hell do you know to write to?" he asked.

"Lincoln," Fancy quipped, shoving papers into a pile which she hid in a drawer. "He wants me to come to his inaugural ball."

"I'll bet he does," Micah snorted, at the same time flopping down on her bed and grabbing a decanter from the bedside stand. "You keep glasses in here?"

Fancy took a pair of snifters from an intricately turned four-shelved whatnot and brought them to the bed. "This is my room, Micah, not a crib, and I don't like mud on my sheets. Take off your boots," she snapped, taking the decanter from him. She poured, waited for Micah's boots to hit the floor, and handed him one of the snifters. "This stuff isn't for customers, and I didn't invite you in here as a customer. So don't act like one."

"Yes, ma'am," Micah said with a lewd wink. He leaned back against the pillows, swirled the amber liquid around in the snifter, inhaled, and blinked back the tears. "Ooosh!" he gasped. "I'm supposed to drink this? What the devil is it?"

"The devil's own, just like me," Fancy said, laughing. "You've drunk worse." She sipped slowly, savored the taste, and watched Micah out of the corner of her eye. "What is it now, Micah?" she suddenly asked, as though apropos of nothing. "Ten years? Eleven? I remember the first day you came in my place. A boy born to trouble but with a man's way of satisfying a woman." She patted his leg. "I broke you in, remember? Sort of makes us family."

"The hell it does."

"You know, I like you even if I can't figure out why. Maybe because we're gonna be neighbors in hell. That make sense?"

"Fancy, you must wake up drunk," Micah said with a snort of disgust.

"Nope. Stone cold sober, just like I went to bed. You've never seen me drunk, Micah. And never will." Her hand rested lightly on his leg, and she avoided looking at him, even indirectly. "You want to tell me?"

The muscles in his thigh tightened. Fancy heard him swallow. "Celia Bartlett, didn't you say? Everybody knows her." Fancy's voice was low and soothing, a balm to wounded pride. "Soft and sweet to make a proper wife. Pretty as can be." She shrugged. "Or something of the sort. A lady who'd make it worth your while to settle down and stop wasting yourself on old crows like me."

Micah's snifter hit the bedside stand and snapped at the stem. In one fluid movement his hand caught Fancy by the throat and pushed her back across his knees. His skull hammering, his eyes closed to slits, he leaned over her and choked her into the quilt. "I wish you were her right now. I'd show brother Rafe a thing or two. My gentlemanly brother and his darling Celia! If you were her . . ."

He let go and flopped back against the pillows. Gasping for air, Fancy rolled away from him, down his legs, and off the bottom of the bed.

"But you're not," Micah went on wistfully. "You're just a whore, and Rafe wouldn't think twice about you. Just a whore and he likes his women pure and lily-white." A drunken smile crossed his face and he laughed insanely. "Sorry, Fancy, but Rafe wouldn't be caught dead with an old punch pot like you. Pure and lily-white. Just like Celia. A pair of sweet little lambikins"—his voice had been rising and falling almost melodically, now turned ugly and flat and harsh—"in the bed I was supposed to be in!"

Knees on the floor, elbows on the bed, Fancy rested her forehead in her palms and breathed deeply. She had miscalculated, had pulled the wrong string, and the results had nearly been fatal. Micah was in a far more dangerous mood than she had thought. Evidently jilted for a younger brother, he'd turned ugly mean. Not that that was anything new for a lady of Fancy's profession. She'd seen more ugly drunks than she cared to even try to count, knew how they were so twisted inside that hate poured out of them like water out of a bucket. And she'd let one into her room. Actually invited him in. *Getting old, Fancy girl,* she thought, pasting a smile on her face and rising as if nothing had happened. *Losing your touch, girl.* She got two clean snifters from the whatnot. Drink would make him worse or put him to sleep. She bet on sleep and, years of experience guiding her, deftly began pulling the right strings.

"Goody-two-shoes, Micah," she purred, pouring new drinks and sitting next to him again. "Neither one of 'em are in your class. What'a you care?" She pressed the snifter into Micah's hand. "Kinda sad when you think of it. Neither one of'em'll know what to do or how to do it."

Micah sat up, tossed off half his drink. "What to or how . . ." He sniggered. "I like it. Like it, Fancy."

He was mellowing. Fancy laughed with him, let her hand slide up the inside of his thigh.

The last of the brandy disappeared and an idea took shape in Micah's besotted, pride-racked brain. "Don't know what to do or how to do it!" he gasped. "Poor little Celia. No one to instruct her. Well, what's a brother for? A man to shoulder his brother's burden, by God!"

Mouth wide open, lips curled back in a feral grimace, stomach heaving, he fell back on the pillows and laughed until the tears rolled down his cheeks. And Fancy shuddered.

"And you didn't recognize him?" Celia asked.

"No, ma'am," Immelda replied with a shake of her head. "A little white boy. Looked like he come from down around the docks, maybe."

Celia studied the crinkled slip of paper and the shaky, almost illegible, scrawled note. "Am in carriage on way to your father's Levee

Street warehouse. Use side entrance on Felicity. Urgent you meet me there alone soon as possible. Rafe."

Almost four thirty. The afternoon had been a shambles. First there was the confrontation with Micah and all the attendant unpleasantness. Next the arrival of Tom Stewart and the fear that her father's nocturnal activities had been discovered. What a relief it had been when, at Immelda's signal, she ran downstairs to learn that all was well, that instead of another confrontation, Tom Stewart himself had brought Harmon's grandchildren to be smuggled to safety. Thank heaven, he had not arrived when Micah or Rafe or, for that matter, anyone else was about. The engagement dinner, originally set for three, had been postponed until seven in order to give Nathaniel time to patch up a very ticklish situation. Celia stared out the window. The sky was clear, the sun low in the southwest. Lord only knew what had happened in the four hours since she had seen Rafe. Some new development regarding their engagement, obviously. Something important enough that he couldn't talk about it at her house or his.

"Have Tobias hitch Daisy to my sulky, Immelda," she said, deciding abruptly to obey the summons. "And then fetch my coat."

"You ain't goin' out alone *this* late in the day," Immelda protested.

"Do as I say, please. I don't wish to argue."

"Yes, ma'am. But your papa—"

"Is asleep. Let's leave him that way."

"He gonna be powerful displeased."

"I'll be back in an hour," Celia promised, sounding much more certain than she felt. "He'll sleep that much longer and never know I left. Unless," she added pointedly, "someone tells him. Which I trust—?"

"I still don't like it!" Immelda huffed. "Ain't no reason why that boy can't come—"

"Immelda!"

"Yes'm. I'm goin'. Daisy an' the sulky . . ."

It was one of those perfect Mississippi winter days. The sky was a bright blue dotted with lumbering cumulus clouds. The air was warm and balmy, an unpredictable treat so close to Christmas. Vicksburg, as Celia drove out the drive and turned her mare down Crawford, looked fresh and clean and new, as if it had been placed there the day before. The city was best seen by an outsider from the river, but Celia, born and raised there, needed no such perspective. A hundred scenes so well known she barely noted them passed by as she rode. The sky spiked by the cupola of the courthouse and the spire of St. Paul's church; Duff Green's house, four gleaming white stories tall and trimmed with ironwork; and the red brick convent of the Sisters of

Mercy. A hundred stores packed with food and goods for the forty-five hundred inhabitants of the bustling river city. Carriagemakers, gunsmiths, apothecaries, jewelers, tailors, haberdashers, dressmakers, bookbinders—all flourished on the uphill downhill streets and lanes and thoroughfares.

There was much more, of course. Rolling hills and cobblestoned streets and tall magnolias and a myriad of flowers are picturesque, but only the trappings of a city. Behind the scenes, driving the giant mechanism of humanity and commerce, was an industrial and agricultural and shipping complex that not only determined the financial makeup of the city but affected the countryside for miles around. Factories produced farm implements, steam engines, carriages, firearms, and saddles. Wholesale grocers, commission merchants, and cotton brokers bought and sold. The railroads connecting Vicksburg to the rest of the south to the east and to Louisiana and Texas to the west gave the city access to millions of square miles of rich farmland and timberland and thousands of people who needed goods.

More than anything else, though, Vicksburg drew its life blood from the great Mississippi. Steamboats from St. Louis and Natchez and New Orleans arrived with iron ingots, newsprint, and yard goods, left with cotton and food and manufactured goods. Steamboats brought people and ideas from around the world. Steamboats opened Vicksburg, gave it a character and flamboyancy and vitality that inland cities only rarely enjoyed. Steamboats made agricultural and commercial empires possible, and so brought to Vicksburg the fortunes that led to a genteel society, an aristocracy of men and women of distinction and good breeding.

At the moment Celia was preoccupied with just what Rafe wanted to discuss with her and why he should make the strange request that she meet him at the warehouse. Felicity was a wide alley off Levee Street. Normally choked with teams and drays loading and unloading, it was now deserted save for a single horse and carriage waiting at the hitching rail outside the office at the corner of the two-story brick building. Celia guided Daisy to a stop next to the carriage and noted that the building's side door was cracked open. "Rafe?" she called. "Rafe! Are you in there?"

No answer. Perturbed, Celia jumped down, tied Daisy next to the other horse, a bay gelding she recognized as one of the pair the Lattimores had driven to church that morning. The door opened wide at her touch. "Rafe?"

The interior was empty, stern, and dingy, a drab alignment of desks and shelves and filing cabinets, a far cry from a proper place in which to meet one's beloved. A door opposite the street door opened to darkness.

No sign of anyone. No hint, no indication, no suggestion that she was expected. *He might have waited where I could find him,* Celia thought, briefly angered and then, in turn, intensely worried. Barely breathing, she zigzagged around desks and wastebaskets and paused at the door.

"Rafe?" she whispered loudly.

The warehouse swallowed the sound. Celia slipped through the door and flattened her back against the wall. "Rafe? Where are you?"

Stacks of baled cotton stretched away from the dim light at the door to an inky darkness at the far end of the warehouse. The silence was absolute. Only when her eyes had grown accustomed to the dark did she detect the soft glow of a lantern somewhere near the center of the cavernous room.

And still silence. It didn't make sense. A trick or game? But why? If he was . . . Her heart was hammering, her breath shallow. "Rafe Lattimore, if you don't speak up right this minute, I'm leaving. Do you hear me? I mean it."

The piled bales soaked up her voice, made it sound tiny and hollow. Terrified, Celia whirled and started out the door, only to stop when she heard a low groan from the approximate direction of the lantern glow.

"Rafe?" He was hurt. Hurt! "Rafe!" she screamed, blindly running forward, groping her way through the maze of stored cotton, blundering into bales, half tripping over broken boards and tangled piles of waste until, suddenly, she emerged in an open rectangle walled in by more towering bales and lit by a single lantern. A dirty mattress with filthy ticking poking out of tears in the fabric lay in the center of the cleared space.

Celia stopped and choked back a scream. No one. Not a soul. And still the silence, overpowering, ringing in her ears.

"Rafe?" she whispered in a tiny, terrified voice.

"Here," came the answer from behind her.

It was not Rafe's voice, and there was no one to hear her scream, or help her when the hand caught her by the throat and threw her down to the mattress.

CHAPTER 2

Thursday night dragged on interminably. Friday morning dawned gray and glum. The snow had stopped but drifts across the tracks slowed the train's progress. The station at Providence was bleak and virtually lifeless except for Miss Hattie who, as the conductor had promised, was on hand with an urn of steaming hot coffee, a tray of neat little cakes, and a smile bright enough to defeat any blizzard.

Celia's nest, the facing seats piled with boxes, magazines, carpetbag, hamper—everything she had bought on the way or brought with her from Vicksburg with the exception of one trunk which was in the baggage car—seemed almost like home when she returned. Cheered by the exercise, fresh air, and Miss Hattie's chatter, Celia watched the last of Rhode Island give way to Massachusetts. For the first time in a week, the clouds parted. Bright sunshine sparkled on a snow-and-ice landscape broken by the blacks, browns, and grays of winter-dormant trees and the occasional dark green of conifers. They were actually running ahead of schedule and expected to reach Boston before dark. And would have, had ice not torn up a section of rail outside Canton. There was nothing to be done about it. Celia and the rest of the disgruntled passengers were forced to sit and wait, watch the clouds move in once again, and listen to the sharp, metallic ring of picks and mauls as the crew labored to replace the brittle, snapped cast iron rail.

The longer the delay lasted, the darker Celia's mood became. Depressed, she nibbled bread and cheese from her food hamper and took out her diary to read over the past week's entries. Each word, each sentence, each paragraph seemed weighted. The tone, the message was one of unrelieved anguish and despair. Celia, the sweet and pure, the guardian of the chaste treasure of her body for Rafe. Celia, the ravaged, soiled, and shamed, despoiled and ruined, and without recourse. Celia, the frightened, terrified beyond measure that Micah's seed should spring to life in her.

Most of all, Celia, the helpless. Micah's revenge had been diabolically perfect. How, after all, could she retaliate? What could she do or say? Her father had already had one heart attack and his health was precarious at best. Were he to learn that the man he had almost forced his daughter to marry had raped her, he could well suffer a second, final attack. As for Rafe, he was lost to her. She could marry him, true, but on their wedding night he would know. And if he forced her to tell him, the repercussions would be horrible. Rafe and Micah would fight. Her father would learn the truth after all. Nathaniel, too, would know. A scandal of such proportions would be impossible to keep secret. Servants would tell other servants, and the story would spread like wildfire.

I must somehow forget, she had written. *I must seek a new life. I am dead to Rafe, as he must be to me.*

"Bawww-ston! Station is Bawww-ston!"

The conductor's sonorous cry jerked her out of her long reverie. Slowly, Celia closed the slim volume and tucked it into the top of her carpetbag. The train was swaying alarmingly as it rumbled over a bridge. Smeared lights showed dimly through the window streaked with soot-blackened ice. Celia sighed and rested her head against the seat. Boston. The journey was over. Behind her, almost half a continent away, she had left wondering friends, a puzzled father, and the man she loved with all her heart but from whom she had run away with no more than a perfunctory note of hastily contrived and empty explanation. Ahead, still indiscernible in the glow that lit the sky, was her aunt's house, seclusion, and time to clear her mind and set her course. She had made the only decision possible under the circumstances.

The train slowed. The other passengers were stirring, retrieving bags from the rack overhead, bundling children in coats and mufflers, stuffing stray articles into bags and boxes. Celia busied herself dismantling her little nest. Magazines and newspapers she stuffed into her carpetbag until it was so full it wouldn't close properly. She slid her muff far up on her left arm, draped her extra scarf around her neck, buttoned her coat, and checked to make sure she had her gloves. No sooner had she arranged everything than the brakes squealed and the car jerked to a halt.

"Bawww-ston!" the conductor bawled again, opening the door and letting in a blast of Arctic air. "Watch your step!"

It was as if a dam had broken. Hushed expectancy became pandemonium. "Grandma, Grandma!" a child shrieked. "I see her!"

"George, Andrew, Roberta Benton, you get back right now and help carry these bags!" Three children halted in midflight, turned as one, and pounded back down the aisle.

Loaded with bags and sacks and parcels and extra clothes, quite normal people grew to bloated proportions. Elbows protruded. The edge of a box, jammed into a fellow passenger's back, became a dangerous weapon. A fat woman carrying a Pekinese was given a wide berth out of respect for her snarling, snapping pug-faced burden. Celia took time to arrange everything in one load, ducked the point of an umbrella, and stepped sideways into the aisle.

"Slow down. Don't push!" the conductor bellowed unheeded from the front of the car.

"Mama! Mama!"

"Jimmy, you watch that stove! Jimmy!"

"—Take that damned mutt's head off, he nips at me again, lady!"

A whistle from the train on the next track rent the air. Bells clanged. The little dog yapped and was answered by the shrill neigh of an unseen horse.

Somehow Celia found herself outside the car. A hand on her arm helped her down the steps to the platform. The great roofed-over shed reeked with smoke and rang with echoes. Relatives called to each other and dodged through the milling crowd on the narrow platform. A cruel wind whipped between the cars, lifted hats and skirts alike, and sifted soot and snow on the throng. Celia pushed toward the station through the uncertain light, under swaying lanterns hung from the roof supports, past pots of burning coal where workers warmed their hands between tasks.

"Celia? Celia Bartlett! Yoo-hoo! Over here!"

"Aunt Nan? Where *are* you?"

A handsome middle-aged woman, bundled in furs and with one ungloved, ringed hand held high, forged through the crowd and wrapped Celia in a motherly embrace. "My dear, my dear!" she fussed, eyes bright with tears of happiness as she held her niece at arm's length and inspected her. "I couldn't believe my eyes when I received your wire. Celia coming to visit! Oh, how happy that made me, especially with all this horrid talk of war." A half frown wrinkled her forehead. "If only Hal had come with you, but he's *so* stubborn that . . . Listen to me." The smile returned and she hugged Celia again. "I'm quite happy enough that *you* have come, my dear."

Aunt Nan smelled of lilac water and wool and fur and just a hint, Celia thought, of maple. Her voice recalled warm memories of summer reunions which, save for the past three years, had alternated between Boston and Vicksburg for as long as she could remember.

"And how you've grown!" Nan gushed on. "My goodness. Three and a half *years* since I've seen you. You must tell me how everyone . . . Oh, but just listen to me! Here you are freezing and tired and, my heavens, what is the world coming to? All these porters and not a one to help you with your luggage. Not a one. What *is* the world coming to?"

Celia laughed at her aunt's irrepressible energy. Here she was, at eight o'clock at night in the middle of January, standing on a sooty, trash-strewn station platform, and positively aglow with good cheer and radiating safety and respite. "Oh, Aunt Nan, I'm happy to see you, too," she cried, at the same time trying to wipe the freezing tears from her cheeks with her shoulder. "And here I am crying like a baby!"

"Why don't you let me take some of that?" a rather stern-looking, slightly built, and dapper young man asked from her side.

Celia squinted as if she sensed she should recognize him. "I'm sorry, but . . ."

"My heavens, it hasn't been all that long," Nan hooted. "Don't you remember your cousin, my dear?"

"Anthony?" Celia asked haltingly. "Is it really you?"

"I am hurt and chagrined," the fair-skinned young man said, doffing his top hat. The wind whipped his thick red hair into immediate disarray.

"A mustache?" Celia exclaimed. "And sideburns and those clothes! I swear, sir," she added with exaggerated coyness, "you've turned into quite the gentleman."

"And you the most elegant of ladies," Anthony replied. "Here. Let me take that carpetbag. Porter? Porter! Over here, please," he shouted, signaling an elderly Negro, wearing three thicknesses of clothes to keep out the chill. "Follow us if you will," Anthony ordered peremptorily, loading the old man with everything Celia had been carrying, and topping off the pile with the carpetbag. "That's it?" he asked Celia.

"Oh, my God. My trunk! I forgot all about it. It's in the baggage car."

"Don't worry. Go on and start," Anthony ordered, taking over. He drew his wallet from his breast pocket and extracted a bill. "I'll have a word with the baggage clerk. He'll keep it in a safe place until I can send a man around in the morning. If I don't catch up with you by the front door, wait for me there."

Anthony dove into the crowd and disappeared. Celia and Nan, with the old Negro in tow, worked their way down the platform toward the station itself. "Where's Uncle Phillip?" Celia asked, half running to keep up with Nan.

"In Washington at the War Department," Nan answered proudly. "At Mr. Lincoln's request, no less. You've just missed him. He left last Friday."

"At least Anthony's here. It's a frightening time to be left alone."

"We're very hopeful." A knot of students barred the way. Nan pushed through the rear ranks. "Please excuse us. Will you excuse us, *please?*" A small corridor opened, through which she led Celia and the porter.

"I've never seen it like this," Celia shouted over the din.

"Weather," Nan replied leaning to talk right into her niece's ear. "They've had a real blizzard north of here and everything has been delayed. Wait until you see inside. Half of everyone there is spending the night, I suspect, poor souls. You're lucky the tracks are still clear south, and you made it through."

A wave of warm air washed over them when they entered the main station. Celia almost gagged, so thick was the smell of humanity. Bawling babies, running children, shouting men and women. Nan picked the easiest route possible, zigged and zagged through the seething masses. "You keeping up?" she called over her shoulder to Celia.

"I think so," Celia shouted. She caught sight of Anthony out of the corner of her eye, turned to wave to him. "If I can just— Oh!" Celia jumped aside, barely missed being run down by another porter who, so overloaded he couldn't see ahead of himself, collided with the old Negro. Bags and boxes flew across the floor. Clothes and papers and food spilled.

"For heaven's sake, be careful, man!" Anthony scolded, hurrying up behind them.

"I'm sorry, suh, but I couldn't get outa his way, no suh," the old Negro apologized, scrambling to pick up the mess.

Celia, Nan, Anthony, the old black, the other porter, and half a dozen others scurried about grabbing spilled articles, trying to get them back to their rightful owners. "This wouldn't have happened in the first place if you'd watched where you were going," Anthony snapped at the poor porter who, embarrassed, was already piled so high again he couldn't see. "And you, sir," he added, exchanging a handful of clothes for a handful of papers with the passenger who had hired the offending porter, "might have squandered an extra tip and not loaded down one man to the point where he's a hazard to others."

The fellow glared, but offered no rebuttal, and led his man off. Anthony returned to Celia's side. "Mother may disapprove, but there's only one way to handle these matters. Have you got everything?"

"I think so," Celia answered faintly.

"Poor dear, you look exhausted," Nan said, taking her arm. "Do we have to stand here all night, Anthony?"

"Sorry." Anthony took one last look around, stuffed a handful of papers he was carrying into the carpetbag, and led the way to the glass-paneled doors that opened onto the circular drive in front of the station.

Celia clung to Nan and fought to keep from passing out. The heat was making her nauseous. Faces and noses and mouths blurred against an amber-colored background of smoky light. Voices rose and fell in waves of meaningless noise. "There now," she heard Nan say as they pushed through the doors. "Watch your step. There's ice out here."

The fresh air was delicious, clearing her head almost immediately. Celia blinked, breathed deeply. "I don't remember anything like this," she said, leaning against her aunt. "Nothing remotely like it."

"Naylor!" Anthony called. "Ho, Naylor!"

A coach with rear seat enclosed and driver's perch sheltered beneath an overhanging roof left a line of similar conveyances, approached quickly, and halted in smart fashion. Anthony helped Celia and his mother into the coach while Naylor and the porter loaded Celia's luggage into the rear, then tipped the porter and climbed in. "Home in half an hour, Cousin," he said, sandwiching Celia between him and his mother. "Heloise has promised that there'll be hot food waiting for you." He tapped the silver hilt of his cane against the roof as the carriage rocked gently under Naylor's weight, then pulled a flask from his coat pocket as they pulled out into the drive. "Meanwhile . . ."

"Son?" Nan asked sharply.

"Just something to take away the chill, Mother," Anthony replied, holding out the flask for Celia. "Here you go, Cousin. It's . . . Well, I'll be. She's asleep!"

"Poor dear," Nan said. "She must be exhausted. Such a long journey. Why on earth did Hal let her travel unescorted?"

"Probably because she insisted on it," Anthony said with a chuckle. "It hasn't been so long that I've forgotten how Celia had a knack of getting her way when she wanted it badly enough." He took off his scarf, folded it neatly, and placed it over the side of her head like a small blanket. "Well, she's among family now."

A demon was loose in Celia's mind, and the nightmare it spawned made rest a jeering mockery. Twist and turn as she might, she could neither wake nor escape. The muscles in her legs twitched, but she could not run. Her arms jerked about, but fraily, like the rag arms of dolls. Her throat convulsed, but the scream was choked off inside her.

Micah Lattimore stood. He was finished, his brute lust at last given way to stuporous inebriation. Celia lay upon the mattress, pushed beyond the brink of screaming where only quiet terror remains, the sullen, silent aftermath of degradation and torment.

Micah stroked himself to wipe the residue of seed and blood—her blood—from his organ. He hitched his trousers to his waist and shrugged the suspenders over his shoulders. He buttoned his shirt, taking his time as if each methodical action were a discourse in contempt. When his vision clouded for a moment and the warehouse started a slow spin, he steadied himself against a cotton bale and closed his eyes. When the world straightened a little, he opened them again. Celia had not moved. She lay with her skirt bunched to her waist and her legs spread. He had taken her savagely, thrusting himself into her virginity, rending the maiden's veil of flesh, hurting her, and enjoying every second. Her screams had only increased his pleasure.

"Now you're ready for little brother," Micah slurred, wiping at his mouth with his sleeve. "All broke in. Tenderized, like a piece of meat should be." His laugh was a harsh, ugly noise that had nothing to do with humor. " 'Course, too bad he likes his meat fresh, but . . . it's time he learned nothin's perfect. And if you tell, I'll claim it was your idea, that you wrote the note and come to meet me. Don't matter how stupid that sounds. Folks'll believe it. They always do." He started to leave, bumped into a bale, and stopped. "But naw, you won't tell. Be like cuttin' your own throat far as Rafe's concerned, wouldn't it? Not to speak of what it would do to Hal and that weak heart of his."

Celia moaned and tried to cover herself.

Micah laughed at her, unbuttoned his fly, and voided himself against one of the bales. "Come to think of it," he added, stepping aside from the stream that ran across the floor toward the mattress, "go ahead and bust your lily-white reputation. The way your father's been carrying on in the paper, there's folks who'll think you got what you deserved." Finished, he looked down at himself hardening again, then grinned and, instead of leaving, stepped toward her, kneeled at her side, and reached for her, his pawlike hands groping . . .

"No, no, no!"

Jaws clenched, teeth grating, skin stretched drumhead-tight over her face. Image of oil lamp, yellow smear of light streaking across her vision. Hands on her, touching, digging, clawing. Obscene moisture, a slippery wetness . . .

"Nooooo!"

"Ceci. It's me. It's Anthony! Wake up!"

Celia's eyes flew open to see a figure leaning over her. Dream and reality mixed confusingly, she held her hands in front of her face when the figure's arm reached out.

"It's me, Ceci," the figure said, simultaneously turning up the wick on the lantern. "Anthony. It's Anthony. You've been having a nightmare."

The light increased and the bedroom swam into focus. She was in Boston. In the same guest room she'd slept in so many times before. Burled walnut armoire with beveled glass mirror. Nightstand with marble top, pitcher, and basin. Heavily cushioned armchairs. Lamps with peacocks on the glass bowls, flickering in vibrant orange relief. Lush green curtains parting to reveal a sliver of snow and frost-decorated windows. All was peaceful and serene. Warm air vented from the fireplace downstairs lent a cloistered ambience to the atmosphere of wealth and New England propriety. The howling blizzard outside, kept at bay by the solid old house, made the inside seem even cosier and safer.

Anthony had been sitting close by, dozing in an easy chair drawn up to the bed. As the wick rose, the room brightened further. Anthony twisted and sat on the edge of the bed. "Pretty bad?" he asked.

"What are you doing here?" she asked, peering at the clock on the mantel. "It's two o'clock in the morning."

"I know. Everyone has gone to bed. I was on my way, too, when I heard you call out. I peeked in, and you were sound asleep but twisting and turning."

"I don't understand," Celia said, wiping the perspiration from her forehead and nose. "You mean you've been . . . watching me?"

Anthony blushed, ran a hand through his red curls, and rubbed the back of his neck. "Not all the time. I fell asleep."

"Listening to me?"

"I . . . well, I thought you might need someone. That is, if the dreams were—"

"Why ever should I need anyone?" Celia asked, fighting down a sinking feeling and trying desperately to retain her composure. Had she done more than simply cry out? Said something specific? "I appreciate your concern, of course, but this is . . . this is most *unlike* you, Anthony."

"I know." Anthony jumped to his feet, walked nervously away from the bed, and returned. "When all those papers from your carpetbag were strewn about at the station," he said, sounding absolutely miserable, "I shoved one item in my pocket and forgot about it in the general rush. Then when I was taking off my coat . . ." He trailed off, reached into his pocket, and took out Celia's diary, which he handed silently to her.

"My God," Celia whispered aghast. He had read it! Knew everything.

"My Ceci, dear Ceci," Anthony stammered. "Forgive me."

The shame, the guilt, the stomach-churning terror. The secret she had sworn to keep had slipped loose. The nightmare could no longer be contained and spilled from her in burning tears. One after another, choked sobs spasmodically wracked her body as she drew her knees up under the covers and buried her face in the pillow.

"I'm sorry," Anthony whispered, his pain almost as great as hers. Crying himself, he put his arms around her and held her tenderly. "I'm so sorry, Ceci. I'm so, so sorry."

The clock's casing gleamed like a brass eye from the shadows. Four bells, tiny in the early morning stillness, chimed. Celia leaned against the pillows and looked at Anthony in the chair by the bed. She had been talking for over an hour and a half. The upper edge of her sheet was damp from her tears. She felt better, though, relieved to have shared the horror rather than walk around with the poison filling her every thought. Talking did help.

But not for Anthony, because a torch-lit Southern night still lived in his memory. He had been twelve, visiting his aunt and uncle in Vicksburg, and had sneaked out of the house to join some boys from town to watch what they described as a lark, but was, instead, the flogging, castration, and lynching of a black man. Nine years later, the scene was still etched indelibly on his mind. Anthony listened to and read with wholehearted approbation the speeches of the Abolitionist leaders, and shared their fervent belief that slavery was an abomination in the sight of God. At the same time, protected by his father's wealth, he assumed that everyone who disagreed with him—Southerners especially—conformed to the evil stereotype of the inhuman, bloodthirsty slavemaster. That he himself treated servants no less harshly than many a slaveowner and that the vast majority of men and women in the South neither owned slaves nor endorsed slavery made no impression on him, for he was so far gone in zealotry that he was blind to these truths. "They'll pay one day," he finally said, his face distorted in rage.

"It was only one man," Celia replied.

"No, it isn't. It's an attitude shared by all of them. It's the Southern character personified. They are slaveowners and brutes. The sooner the blight left by their kind on the land is stamped out, the better."

Celia closed her eyes and yawned hugely. "I can't believe that.

What about Father, for example? Oh, I'm tired. For the first time since . . ." She yawned again and, unable to stop, a third time. "Anyway, I'm glad I have a prying cousin."

Anthony colored, reached out, and patted her hand. "You mean a great deal to me. To all of us." He stood and kissed her on the forehead. "I was errant, but what's done is done. Don't worry. You're safe here. Ahhh." He yawned twice, shook his head. "It's catching. I'd better go to bed before I fall asleep on the floor. See you in the morning?" he asked, already halfway to the door.

"Of course. Anthony?"

"Yes?"

Celia was looking at her hands, at last looked up at him with a sad look in her eyes and a tiny, wistful smile on her lips. "Thank you for listening."

"I'm a good listener. It's one of my chief points." He grinned and fought another yawn. "I don't know what comes next, but whatever, let me know and I'll do my best to help. All right?"

"All right."

"Promise?"

"What comes next is sleep," Celia said with a little laugh, and then more seriously, "Tomorrow I suppose I'll try to talk Aunt Nan into letting me stay at Shoreside. Boston holds too many people for me right now."

"Mother likes company, but I'll see that she agrees." He paused uncertainly. "Do you want her . . . that is, should I tell her—"

"No. What has happened is between you and me. The truth would only upset her, and most assuredly reach Father's ears. Which would kill him."

Anthony nodded understandingly. "Not a word, then," he promised, and let himself out.

Celia felt drained. Still, one more act was required of her. Wincing as her bare feet touched the cold wood floor, she climbed out of bed, poured some water from the bedside pitcher into the bowl, and set the pitcher aside. Next she removed the shade from the lantern and, using a washcloth as a holder, lifted off the chimney. At last, ripping pages from her diary, she set them afire and watched them burn one by one until she reached the day before Micah's terrible deed. Only then, when the nightmare was reduced to curled and brittle ash that floated on the water, did she reassemble the lamp, turn it down, and climb back into bed, there to sleep restlessly and dream of a love and a life forever lost.

CHAPTER 3

In April dark and cold memories, like winter snow and ice, shrink from the coming sun's warming rays. In April pain lessens as spring rediscovers life's purpose in the quickening soil and sends shoots and buds to seek the light. In April routines of winter are disrupted and discarded, and a dizzy prescription of joy looses the grateful heart.

In April it is difficult to hate.

Boston had indeed proved too oppressive, and Celia had sought an early escape. The Rutledges' Shoreside estate was tantalizingly close, yet remote enough, given the season, for Celia to find the peace and quiet she hoped would soothe her troubled state. At first Nan had objected. Winter, she proclaimed, forgetting the untold thousands around the world which lived year-round near the ocean, was no time to live at the shore. Celia had persisted, though, and Nan, sensing that the crisis that had driven her niece north was deeper than had at first appeared, relented. A week later, the first day of February, Naylor hitched the horses to the sleigh and drove Celia the twelve miles to the shore.

Phillip Rutledge's law practice, in addition to placing him high in Republican circles, had made it possible for him to acquire the very private and elegant Shoreside estate. Celia had spent summers there in the past, but never had she visited in the winter, and never had she appreciated it more. Shoreside was everything she had hoped for. Except for the servants—a staff of four kept busy making sure every one of the twenty rooms was prepared for instant occupancy—she was alone. There, over parquet floors and amid gleaming brass and glittering chandeliers and the soft, polished glow of fine furniture, she was free to retreat into a shell of her own making, to lick her wounds, and to take stock. She had been mauled: she had fled. She had lost the man she loved for reasons she had expounded to herself a hundred times. She was aware that she could no longer expect any of the things she had been brought up to expect. She was being forced, if she wanted to survive, to wipe clean the slate of her life and start anew.

At first she let emptiness rule. Letters from Rafe, confused and questioning, she burned without answering. Those from her father, she read, but with little interest. The seashore in winter was the perfect place for emptiness. Gray sea, roiling chaotically but featureless, gray sky, a mirror for her thoughts. She slept, she dressed, she ate, she bundled up and walked the beach, she ate, and slept again. And finally, when all emotion was emptied out of her, she calmly contemplated suicide. There was a skiff. She would row well out into the bay and then fall overboard. Lightly clothed as she'd be, the frigid bay waters would kill her before any rescue attempt could possibly succeed. With this in mind, three nights later she crept out of the house and in her gown sat in the boat until her hands and feet were numb. And then, she didn't know why, got up and went back to bed and slept, for the first time since the rape, like a baby. The next morning, having descended to the depths, she began the long climb out to recovery.

From then on Celia took pleasure in the pattern of the days. She rose to a simple continental breakfast of muffins and jam, tea and fresh cream. After breakfast, no matter what the weather, she walked, sometimes along the beach, sometimes to Hatten's Bluff, a small fishing village two miles to the north. Lunch she took in the kitchen with the servants, where the talk was of boats and fishing and cooking and raising children. Afternoons she napped and read, on the porch when the sun was out and the wind was down, in front of the fire when the weather was bad. Dinner she ate alone, always with candles, in the formal dining room. Later, she sat in front of the fire with Herman, the great beautiful tiger tomcat who really owned the house, and read herself to sleep.

Three times during February and March Nan came to visit for a day or two. Then there was pleasant conversation, during which Nan tried to entice Celia to return to Boston and Celia dexterously skirted her reasons for coming north and for wanting to stay at Shoreside. Twice Anthony spent a weekend with her. She had always thought of Anthony as a brother and, secure that her secret was safe with him, welcomed his company. Each time he came, they sat by the hearth and talked late into the night trading childhood memories or arguing about current events, for Anthony was increasingly caught up in the patriotic fervor sweeping the North. Slowly but steadily, Celia felt herself healing.

The beach, so somber in February, began to come to life near the end of March, and by the end of April, the grays and blacks and dull beiges of winter had given way to the brighter hues of spring. The bright green of daffodil and hyacinth shoots and the pale pinks and faint blue-whites of crocuses sparked the artfully arranged driftwood garden that separated house from beach. Lichen dappled the rocks away from the water's edge with deep greens and purples. Shells of orange and opal and the deepest jet black jewelled the sand. And the bay itself turned now blue as ice, now green as emerald—the color of Rafe's eyes, Celia thought—and spilled fulgent dots and streaks of foam on the shining sand.

Celia had waked early, at the moment when the sun rose out of the Atlantic. Anthony had sent word that he was coming for a visit and that he'd leave around ten Saturday morning for Shoreside. He couldn't have picked a better time—Celia had been alone for almost three weeks and felt the need for company—or a better day. The sky was clear over an azure and white-capped bay. The breeze was stiff and chilly, but clean with the fresh salt tang of thousands of miles of untainted ocean. Out of the wind, the sun was warm and the temperature had climbed into the fifties.

Growing impatient as eleven o'clock came and went, Celia stood at the front parlor window and watched the waves. Overhead, sea gulls whirled and dipped, posed motionless for breathtaking seconds. Shore birds scurried about the beach in their never-ending search for food. Far in the distance, a patch of white edged over the horizon. A sailing ship, Celia thought, rising uselessly on her tiptoes in an attempt to see it better. Bound for who knew where? But to be on it! There was the ultimate escape. Or was it? Of course not, she realized, for no matter how far she ran, she could never stop loving Rafe. No matter what lengths she took to escape her dreams, she could never forget the horror of Micah raping her. At least, she repeated to herself, shaking off the melancholy, she had not become pregnant.

"Miss Bartlett?" The downstairs girl, the daughter of a fisherman in Hatten's Bluff, knocked on the door to attract Celia's attention.

"Yes?"

"Carriage comin', miss. Terrible fast. Cook says it's Mr. Rutledge."

"Thank you, Deirdre. Tell cook we'll want some lunch in an hour or so. Something warm, I should think."

"Yes, ma'am."

And so he had arrived at last. Celia hurried out to the porch in time to see the familiar black-and-gold carriage drawn by matched bays wheel around the corner of the house and, horses blowing furiously, careen up the semicircular drive. "Celia!" Anthony shouted, hauling the team up short as the outdoor man came at a run to meet him. "Have you heard?"

"That you're late? Yes."

"Hello, Charles. A rubdown and water only, please," Anthony ordered, handing over the reins and climbing down. "And check the horse's right rear. I think the shoe's loose or has picked up a stone. I'll be leaving this afternoon instead of staying the night as planned."

The wind flapped his overcoat around his legs, ruffled his hair that in the bright sun looked so flamelike. In truth, Celia thought, descending the steps to greet him, Anthony was a man afire. "What took you so long?" she asked, as he came bounding up the walk.

"Aha! News. Great things afoot. You haven't heard, I can tell."

"What on earth are you babbling about, Anthony?" Celia squeezed his hands, and kissed him on the cheek. "Oh, I'm sure you'll tell me in good time. Will you have something to drink? Or wait for lunch?"

"Neither. I can't be still." His face split by a wide grin, he took her hand and led her toward the water. "Let's walk. I don't think I could stand being cooped up."

"Wait a minute!" Celia said, laughing. "Let me get a wrap before I freeze."

"What?" Anthony looked surprised, as if he'd forgotten the wind. "Oh. Yes. It is breezy, isn't it? Don't take too long."

Celia ran up the steps and into the house, grabbed a large woolen shawl, and hurried back out. "I'm glad you came," she said, a little breathless. "I was getting lonely. Which way? Along the beach? You haven't told me your news."

"Yes." Only a moment earlier so ebullient, Anthony had just realized that what was marvelous news to him might be bad news for Celia. Suddenly unsure of himself, he turned and began to walk crisply toward the water. "Well . . ."

Celia was forced into a near run in order to keep up. Preferring leisurely walks, she gave up after a few quick steps, stopped, and folded her arms while Anthony continued on ahead. She heard him start to speak, saw him turn and discover she was no longer at his side. "Something wrong?" he asked.

"Not really," Celia replied. "I just don't feel like racing. We have all day, don't you know."

Anthony blushed, walked back to her, and took her arm. "I'm sorry. I have wonderful news. Well, perhaps not *that* wonderful, considering. Dreadful but wonderful might be more like it."

"If you don't tell me this minute, Anthony, I'm returning to the house and you can continue alone. All the way to Boston if you prefer. Which, at the pace you started off at, you'll reach in an hour or two."

"I'm sorry, Ceci." Anthony took both her hands. "It was all so wonderful, and then I remembered that, well, you being from Mississippi and all . . ." Regard for her feelings couldn't dampen his enthusiasm completely, and his eyes danced with undisguised glee. "It's war! War at last."

Celia stared at him in disbelief. "I don't understand you," she said, her voice a bare whisper.

"It's true. Listen to me. The damn slavers attacked Fort Sumter yesterday morning. The bombardment began at four thirty in the morning and is still going on, according to the wires. Or was, when I left Boston."

"They couldn't have," Celia stammered. "Why, that's . . . that's . . ."

"Of course. War. There's no way the fort can hold out. Only a hundred or so men inside. It's a terrible price to pay, but the slavers fired first. Lincoln will issue a call for volunteers within a few days. Father helped draw up the documents last week. Seventy-five thousand men to march south and punish the rascals once and for all."

"Dear Lord!"

"Yes. Dear indeed. And on our side! What holier cause than to put an end to treasonous rebellion and the godless institution of slavery? It is a time for greatness, Ceci. It's a time to stand for goodness, and for what is right. Think of the opportunity!"

"An opportunity to be a fool or a corpse," Celia said, appalled. "Or both."

"You exaggerate," Anthony replied, undismayed by her lack of enthusiasm. "We're talking about five states. Eight if Virginia, Tennessee, and North Carolina go out. And they call themselves a separate nation? The Confederate States of America? Really!" he scoffed. "A nation of slavers and tyrants. Any Christian and true American must see his duty clearly."

Celia wasn't so easily convinced. "My, my! Aren't we righteously indignant! Or is it indignantly righteous?" she asked sarcastically. "Be careful, Cousin. You're beginning to sound like a politician."

"So? Politicians helped get us in this mess. It will take better and wiser ones to get us out of it. Why *not* me as well as the next man? Congress is a mess! Once we've dealt with the Confederates, I'd like to—"

"You're only twenty-one, Anthony," Celia interrupted acidly. "You can't even be a Congressman until you're twenty-five. And I do wish you'd stop carrying on so. If you want to fight, if fighting will make you feel like a grown man doing important things, why don't you just say so and have done with it?"

"Look who's carrying on now," Anthony snorted. "You needn't sound so caustic. I am, after all, talking about punishing such wretches as Micah Lattimore."

"But that's preposterous," Celia protested.

Anthony remained steadfast. Nothing that had happened during the past three months of growing tension had changed Anthony's opinion of the South or Southerners. If anything, in fact, he had become even more zealous and virulent, more convinced of the righteousness of the cause. "Is it?" he asked.

"Yes. Because your blanket indictment overlooks men such as my father who owns no slaves, never for one moment believed in secession, and bears no animosity toward the North."

"Then let him come north," Anthony snapped, "and join us. Oh, Christ! I forgot." He fished a letter out of his pocket. "Mother told me to give you this. It arrived Thursday."

Celia recognized the handwriting of Nathaniel Lattimore, hurriedly broke the seal, and began to read.

"Honestly, Ceci," Anthony continued, "I fail to understand you. I should have thought you'd share my feelings. If any one person has cause . . ." He looked about and saw he was walking alone with nothing but space and incoming waves and sea gulls overhead for company. When he turned to look, Celia was standing near the water's edge. Her slippers and the hem of her dress were wet from a far-reaching wave and, her face white, she was staring at the letter. "Celia?" he asked, hurrying back to her side.

"It's Father," she said, her voice thick. "He was set upon in the street for his Abolitionist sentiments and for protesting the secession. A mob set fire to his warehouse. It was almost totally destroyed. There's talk, too, of confiscating whatever of his ships are in port. I can't imagine—"

"I told you," Anthony said, leading her away from the water. "He should come north. Is there a chance he will, now?"

Celia shook her head, bit her lower lip to keep from crying. "He can't," she said, dazed. "Father's . . . had another heart attack."

"I don't like it," Nan said testily. Busy arranging a centerpiece for the dining room table, she was speaking not of flowers but of Celia's impending journey home. "Not in the slightest. How do you know the trains are even making connections?"

"They are, Aunt Nan. They will be," Celia replied, pouring tea for the older woman. "I checked at the depot here and Anthony has wired New York and Philadelphia and Richmond."

"But Richmond is practically a foreign country now!" Nan wailed. It was true. Virginia had seceded the day before to become the sixth Confederate state. And while no actual declaration of war had been issued, it was clear a state of war existed between parent and child, between the Union that Abraham Lincoln was so determined to preserve and the Confederacy that the Rebels were equally determined to defend. "You're an Abolitionist's daughter. God only *knows* what they'll do to you."

"They won't do anything, Aunt Nan. Father was always careful not to let me get involved in any visible way." Her smile was wan. "Most people will think of me as that poor Bartlett girl—you know, the one whose father is an Abolitionist. A perfect saint, taking care of him like that in spite of his perfidy. I'll be fine, believe me."

"Be that as it may. It's still too far for a young and unattached lady to travel." Clearly distressed, Nan took Celia's hands and squeezed them tightly. "I beg of you, Celia Rose. Don't go. Stay with us where you'll be safe. Please?"

"I've made the journey before," Celia said, hugging Nan as if to reassure her. "The only danger I face is boredom, and I shall have enough worry to keep me from growing too bored."

"And there's nothing I can say to dissuade you?"

Celia shook her head. "I'm afraid not."

Nan sat slowly, stared at the arrangement she had worked so hard to make beautiful, and wondered to what avail. The whole country was talking about war. Men were arming themselves and marching. Men, women, and children would be driven out of their homes, would go hungry, and would be maimed. Would die. And she was arranging flowers. "Couldn't you wait a *few* more days?" she asked plaintively. "Until next week at least?"

"I've been here over three months, Aunt Nan," Celia said, staring out the window to a rain-blown street. "Father needs me. If I stayed here and he . . . he . . ." She trailed off, spun and, headed for the door. "I'd never forgive myself. I leave on Monday."

Alone at the table, Nan turned in time to catch a glimpse of brown cotton dress and chocolate-colored bows slip out the door. Angered, she rose and stalked toward the door, then stopped in the realization that Celia's departure was an act of preoccupation rather than rudeness. And who wouldn't be preoccupied, with one's father hovering between life and death, and a long journey filled with unknowns stretching ahead of her? If only Hal had taken her advice, Nan thought, and come north before it was too late. Life in Boston might be a touch more staid, but at least he would not be surrounded by men who hated him enough to attack his person and destroy his goods, and caught in some awful warfare. *Sell,* Nan pleaded mentally. *Sell everything and leave before you are buried there.*

On the porch, Celia retreated to the far side corner and curled up in the swing seat, out of the wind. Nathaniel's tone, she recognized as she reread his letter, was surprisingly conciliatory. He had been angry at first, he said, but upon reflection, he recalled all the conflicting thoughts that had pushed him one way and another when he was twenty, and decided that anger was not only useless but silly as well.

There was little news, he went on, that could be called good. Her father's beating, and the burning of his warehouse, had occurred on a Saturday morning, the twenty-third of March, the same day a letter of his expressing hope that the Southern hotheads would eschew oratory and demagoguery and concentrate instead on real efforts to maintain peace, however shaky, was printed in the *Citizen*. That night, drunk and fired by some of the same demagoguery he had denounced, a dozen so-called vigilantes had descended on the warehouse and set it to the torch. A half hour later, when Hal arrived, he was dragged from his carriage, forced to watch helplessly while his warehouse burned and his carriage was smashed, and then jeered mercilessly and pommeled by some of the more inebriated toughs before they were driven off by the town constabulary. The public derision and undisguised hatred had hurt more than the beating, Nathaniel explained. A week later, ignoring the signs of an impending attack and chafing under "young" Dr. Tom Stewart's ministrations, he collapsed at dinner and had been bedridden ever since. Nathaniel had talked to him briefly the next morning, Sunday, the thirty-first of March, the day the letter was dated, and Hal had asked him to inform Celia of what had happened and tell her he wished expressly that she remain in Boston.

Nathaniel was forced to conclude that he agreed with his old friend. There was an air of ugliness, of surly, seething anger in the South. Talk of war was ubiquitous and incessant. And though he was pro-slavery and totally opposed to the North imposing its will on the South, he also feared a war, for he was virtually certain it would be fought in the South.

As for everyone else, they were quite well. Immelda and Tobias, with Tom Stewart's help, were taking good care of Hal. Amelia Wharton had had her child, an eight-pound boy who was healthy as a switch. Rafe, after being talked out of following Celia north, had departed in late January for New Orleans, where he was to embark on another of Hal's ships and, as first mate, continue his education in the ways of the sea. Micah and Nathaniel had had a falling out that was, as far as Nathaniel could see, irrevocable, and Micah had left for parts unknown. As for himself, save for an occasional malarial attack, Nathaniel was in relatively good health and was, Celia could be assured, seeing to it that everything possible that could be done was being done to make her father comfortable and speed his recovery.

Celia refolded the letter and slipped it up her sleeve. Far from convincing her she should stay away, her father's admonition made her the more determined to return and stand at his side. Someone had to. Except for Nathaniel, Hal's peers were heeding the implicit warning to stay away from him. Others, people who had once looked up to and depended on him, had turned on him. They were men and women for whom he had done favors, had given jobs, and loaned money. Men at whose side he had stood in time of need, and never called in his accounts until he was certain they could afford to pay. And this was how they had treated him! One twenty-year-old woman certainly couldn't fight those who had destroyed his property and driven him to this new heart attack, but she could put herself between him and them and so, unless they had lost all sense of decency, shield him.

The drum of hoofbeats roused her from her trance. Celia stood and watched Anthony's coach pull to a stop under the front awning.

"Celia!" Anthony called, jumping down and holding the door. Behind him, a gentleman of perhaps thirty years, sporting heavy sideburns and a large, drooping mustache, stepped out. He was austerely attired in black, which was relieved only by his white shirt and a gold watch chain that stretched across his ample stomach. His mouth was set in a firm line that reflected a sober disposition. He was not without courtliness, however, for he walked quickly up the steps and bowed to kiss Celia's hand as Anthony introduced him.

"Captain Powell, I should like to introduce my cousin, Celia Bartlett. Celia, this is Ambrose Powell."

"Captain?" Celia asked with a pointed glance at his garb.

"The military is not always required to announce its presence with a uniform," Powell said, adding with a wink, "Besides, I'm a very new captain, and uniforms are difficult to come by on short notice. If you'll . . . ah . . . ah . . ." He bent almost double in a great sneeze, straightened, and dabbed at his nose with his handkerchief. "I'm afraid you'll have to pardon me. It's this blasted weather. I've been wet and cold all the way from New York."

"I took the liberty of wiring Ambrose and suggesting he visit if at all possible," Anthony explained. "Seeing as it's your last weekend with us, that is . . ." He trailed off, pursed his lips as he tried to figure out the best way to continue.

"Is there tea?" Powell asked, rescuing him. "Or brandy? A touch of brandy would do marvels for me."

"Of course," Anthony replied, excessively eager to please. "Either or both."

"Brandy, I think, if you'd be so kind."

Anthony started for the door and stopped in his tracks. "Will you join us, Celia?"

"I think . . ." Celia glanced at the lowering sky that threatened rain and decided that she'd mooned about enough and that company and conversation was just exactly what she needed to cheer her up. "Why, yes, gentlemen. Perhaps I will."

The three hurried inside. A warm fire in the front parlor took the chill from the air and quickly made them forget the wind that howled and pawed at the door. "Anthony tells me you're from Vicksburg," Powell said, sitting next to Celia on the couch.

Anthony handed Powell a brandy and gave Celia a small glass of the sherry she preferred. "Vicksburg, Mississippi," he said in an amusingly exaggerated drawl. "A genuine Southern girl, if I've ever seen one."

"Never one so charming," Powell said, raising his glass in salute.

"Nor so suspicious of flattery," Celia said, laughing, feeling better already. "I must warn you, sir. I shan't be taken in easily."

Anthony paled, but Powell laughed easily in return. "Then I won't try," he said, and adroitly changed the subject. "So tell me all about life in the South. Anthony tells me you're thinking of returning. Isn't that a little dangerous? I should think . . ."

They talked through the afternoon and dinner. Anthony seemed a trifle stiff and ill at ease and hung on every word as if a battle were at stake. Powell, on the other hand, was as good a listener as a conversationalist and never let the pace lag. Celia was charmed. Ages had passed, she was sure, since she had enjoyed herself so much, and she found herself quite taken with Powell. Only when the dessert dishes were being cleared away, though, was the subject of her father's complicity in the Underground Railroad broached, and though Powell applauded Hal's bravery to smuggle slaves to freedom, Celia found that once that particular wound was reopened, she had difficulty concentrating. At last she excused herself, and snatching a shawl from the hall tree, fled to the front porch.

The storm that had been threatening all day had hit at last. Lightning flared and thunder rolled over the city. Celia wrapped the shawl tightly around her, leaned against one of the porch posts, and stared into the darkness. Why, she asked herself. A beautiful afternoon and then, without warning, the overpowering sadness. Light spilled on the porch and disappeared as she heard the front door click closed. A second later Powell was at her side and leaned against the railing. Celia moved away, increasing the space between them.

"I'm afraid I must apologize," Powell said with a nervous laugh.

"Sir?"

"I have a terrible tendency to crowd people when it rains. You will laugh, but I am afraid of thunder. Ridiculous for a grown man, but the noise terrifies me."

Celia glanced at the sky, back to Powell. "That's understandable. I've known other . . . people . . ."

"It's the lightning, actually. Quite irrational, really, but I once saw a cow killed by lightning. Ever since . . . well . . ."

"Yet you remain here on the porch."

"The promise of enchanting company. That and . . ."

"And?" Celia asked when he stopped.

Powell's look was stern as he clutched the railing. "Only if I confront my fear can I ever hope to defeat my fear." The clouds pulsed with light. Some blocks to the north, three simultaneous bolts etched blue-white lines through the night. Powell shivered. "So far my theory has yet to produce the desired results. However, I trust that if I persist I shall one day have the satisfaction of seeing this old enemy of mine brought to his knees."

Celia's face flushed with sudden anger. What chance had her own father to conquer his enemies? What action could one man with a bad heart take against the rabble-rousers who assailed him? Did it matter that he was a man of honor? No. Did it matter that those same rabble-rousers claimed to be battling against outside interference in their own lives? No. Where were Vicksburg's upright citizens, those who insisted that laws be upheld—when it suited them? Nowhere to be found. And what, finally, short of standing at her father's side, could she do to right the monstrous wrong they had wreaked? Nothing. Nothing at all. Of course, if she were a man . . . Ah, but she wasn't, was she. "A worthy ambition, bringing one's enemies to their knees," she finally said, more to herself than to Powell. A trace of bitterness crept into her voice. "A satisfaction allowed only to men, I'm told."

"And denied women?" Powell asked, one eyebrow raised. He forced himself to relax, reached inside his coat, and took out a cigar. "And how did you reach that conclusion? I have always thought of women as, ultimately, the more powerful of the sexes. They do, after all, hold sway over the hearts and minds of men. I have never met a woman who could not bend a man to her will, if she tried hard enough."

Celia shook her head. "You give us too much credit, Mr. Powell. Women are powerless when it comes to issues of real importance."

"Such as?" Powell asked, opening his pocketknife and starting to hone it on the side of his hand.

"Vengeance, Mr. Powell. Avenging any great wrong." She seemed to withdraw into herself, to shrink back from the vision of her father that appeared in the lightning illuminated, wind-whipped branches of the maples lining the street. She shuddered, drew back, gripped the rail for support. "A woman can dissolve in tears, Mr. Powell," she said, barely audible against the hissing rain. "A woman can run and a woman can hide. A woman can hope to make the best of a bad situation. Nothing more."

The knife was sharp. Meticulously, Powell cut around the end of the cigar. "Perhaps. But a woman of courage and daring and deep desire can have a far greater effect than she realizes." The tip of the cigar removed, he dropped it in his coat pocket, wiped his pocketknife, and put it away. "A woman like yourself, Miss Bartlett."

A distant echo of thunder rolled over them. Celia turned slowly and drew her shawl more tightly around her. "Just exactly who are you, Mr. Powell?" she asked slowly.

"You are perceptive." Powell wet his forefinger in the runoff from the roof, carefully dampened the outer layer of tobacco. "My visit isn't an exercise in cordiality." His eyes met hers squarely. "I am here to provide you with an opportunity, Miss Bartlett. An opportunity to exact retribution."

"I don't know what you're talking about."

"Come, come. We're not children so let's not play childlike games," Powell said curtly. He had already decided, in light of the afternoon's long conversation, that it would be best to avoid any indication that his knowledge of her affairs extended beyond what she herself had told him. "You've spoken at length about your father's—and yours, I take it—beliefs regarding slavery and the treatment he's been subjected to by men he thought were friends. Beyond that, Anthony has hinted to me privately that there were other factors of a personal nature that he felt would make you receptive to my suggestions."

Suspicious, feeling trapped and not knowing what to do, Celia backed away from him. "I don't want to hear anymore of this. I don't know what Anthony told you, but—"

"Your uncertainty is all the more reason for me to continue," Powell interrupted. "Do you approve of the transgressions committed against you and your father?"

"Of course not, but—"

"And wouldn't you like to set things right?"

"I . . ." Near tears, she turned and fled to the far corner of the porch. "I don't know."

"You used the word vengeance."

"I spoke hastily—without thinking."

"Really?" Powell heard the front door open, turned in time to wave Anthony back into the house before Celia saw him. "Your father is gravely ill," he said, covering the soft click of the door closing. A new tone, that of sarcasm, tinged his voice. "Not exactly from natural causes. And you return merely to *care* for him? Will caring alone suffice? Will caring make sleeping any easier?"

Gray rain, a shroud of death. Her father gray and pale, his warehouse burned, his ships confiscated. "No," she whispered, eyes closed and head back.

Powell struck a match, held it under the end of his cigar until it caught and drew to his satisfaction. "I am a captain in a particular branch of the service, Miss Bartlett. You might say I assist in the gathering of information." He paused, blew smoke into the rain. "Virginia tobacco," he said, the non sequitur making Celia turn toward him with a quizzical look on her face. Powell held out the cigar. "Precious few of these in the days to come. It won't end with Fort Sumter, you know. It will spread like fire, how far and how long it will last is anyone's guess. There are those, your cousin is one, who optimistically think in terms of a quick, punitive raid or two, and then back to business as usual. There are others who are not so sanguine and are involved in planning for every possible contingency."

"And you," Celia said, every nerve taut, "are one of the others."

"I am." Powell gestured to a wicker chair. "Do you mind if I sit?"

"Of course not."

"Good." He sat, crossed his legs, considered his cigar and how to begin. "Vicksburg. A crucial city in what will soon be enemy territory —and I am sorry, believe me, that enemy is the term I am forced to use.

"Our strategy will be clear. So clear it can't be a secret to anyone, so I can discuss it without fear of compromise. The Mississippi is the key. South to the Gulf, north to the heart of America, it's an absolutely critical artery. He who would win this coming war must control the Mississippi, for the Mississippi splits the Confederacy and controls the whole central portion of the country. And he who would control the Mississippi must control Vicksburg. Every other city or strong point can be taken with relative ease. Every other city or strong point except Vicksburg. The bend in the river makes navigation slow and leaves ships vulnerable. The heights control every inch of water for over three miles. The land around it is inhospitable. Though those of us who think about these things have no doubt Vicksburg will fall, we also are realistic enough to understand that it will probably be the last to fall. And because the day it falls will be the first day of the beginning of the end of the war, it is in our—in everyone's—interest that it fall as soon as possible. To that end, every piece, every scrap of information we can get from inside the city will be of inestimable value." Powell leaned back in his chair and smiled up at Celia. "Which is why I am here."

"To spy!" How monstrously amusing! And dear cousin Anthony, so innocent, so well meaning, part and parcel of . . . "So that's why Anthony's been so evasive and ill at ease all afternoon. He brought you here specifically for this, didn't he?"

"Yes," Powell answered truthfully.

"But was ashamed to say so outright."

Powell considered the end of his cigar as he chose his words. "Your cousin is committed to our cause. He is also, unfortunately, a novice. Given time he will become more adroit in these matters."

"What matters? Asking people to spy on their own people?" Celia asked in disbelief.

"Your aunt is your people. Anthony is your people. I am your people, too, Miss Bartlett. We are all Americans."

"That is a sophistry," Celia snapped.

"Not at all. Eighty-six years ago all of us fought against a common—"

"Not *one* of us was alive eighty-six years ago," Celia hissed, stamping her foot. "We weren't even *born* then. You're asking me to spy on my own people! Why don't you just say so and have done with it?"

"Because . . . Very well," Powell said, holding up his hands to stop her. "I'm asking you to spy."

"Well!" Celia sat heavily in another chair and stared out into the rain. So there it was. The question spoken, waiting for an answer.

Her father had taught her to hate slavery. Now she must decide. What did she owe slavers? They had driven her father to what might yet prove to be his deathbed. They had raped her—perhaps there was some truth to Anthony's appraisal of Micah as a prototype—and stolen her future happiness. But to spy? Turn her back, in effect, on all the goodness that existed in spite of the very real evils? The thought was onerous. And yet . . . And yet what did she owe them? Loyalty to a system that was, at its core, rotten? Love to the many who had outraged her and her father? No and no again. Perhaps Powell was right after all. She was not powerless. She could exact retribution.

The wind fell off, the rain slowed. Powell waited patiently. Thoughts coiling around shifting images. Yes. No. Vengeance is mine, saith the Lord. *But why not mine, too?* Celia wondered. No. Yes. Two wrongs did not make a right. But to let wrongs go unchallenged? That was not right either. Later Celia could not have said how she arrived at her decision. She knew only that suddenly the idea caught her and swept her away. To spy! Here was vengeance, indeed. The idea was so bold, so daring, she could barely contain her excitement. "To spy," she said aloud, the very word sending chills up her spine.

"Yes."

She was a dark and lonely figure. A veritable Nathan Hale, who faced danger, even death, with icy calm and the famous words: "I regret that I have but one life to give for my country." She too had but one life to give—for her father who had been wronged, for herself, and for a cause that was just and righteous!

"Very well," she said, fate guiding her. "I accept. My answer is yes."

"What?" Powell said, not sure he had heard right.

Celia flashed him her most dazzling smile. "I said, yes. With two reservations."

Powell leaned forward expectantly. "Of course. What?"

"One, I can quit any time I please."

The captain nodded. "Easily agreed to. I couldn't stop you in any case."

"Good. And two?" She pointed to his cigar. "Get rid of that thing. It smells terrible in this rain."

Powell didn't even hesitate. "Time I gave the blasted things up anyway," he said, pitching the cigar into the rain and not even bothering to watch where it went. He stood and bowed almost formally. "A woman of courage and daring. I was right. Shall we go in?"

Celia rose, too. Her mind made up, all temerity had gone from her voice and her eyes glittered with excitement. "You mean that's it? Don't we have to make some sort of arrangements? New York or Washington or . . . or wherever is a far distance to come every time I have something to tell you?"

"Whoa!" Powell laughed, giving her his arm. "Before the evening is over, I'll arrange to meet your train in New York. We can talk more then, and I'll explain everything you need to know."

"But what happens when I get home?" Celia asked, not wanting to wait. "I can't just have people with Yankee accents walking up to my front door. Vicksburg isn't a big city like Boston or New York. Even a simple letter will be noticed, especially if it comes from somewhere in the North."

"You won't get any letters from us. And your name will never be used in any other form of contact we devise. At least not the name Celia Bartlett. We'll choose a new name for you, one that only a select few will know. A name that will suffice both as identification and password, should the need arise."

"You make it all sound terribly mysterious."

Powell laughed and patted her hand. "It's intended to. For your protection and ours. So . . . In we go. Think about it for a while. I allow you the prerogative of choice. But remember. Be sure to choose a name you'll recognize as directed to you and only you in any situation."

Celia stopped and removed her arm from his. Suddenly pensive, she moved to the top of the steps, wrapped her arms around and rested her cheek against the post. Everything was happening so fast. One second she felt as if she were soaring through the air, the next as if the weight of the world were pressing down on her. How could she indict all for the actions of a few? Nothing seemed to fit or make sense. Sorrow and guilt touched her, but she had been through all that before. And as for Rafe? Rafe was beyond the reach of her life. Their love had been foully murdered. Its remains were a cold ember in a dank and hollow earth. Their love . . .

"Wings across the moon," Celia whispered to herself. "We are the hawks of the night . . ."

She blinked back the tears, stared up at the lowering sky. Somewhere the sun was hidden. Maybe it would never be found.

"I have a name," she said aloud.

Already journeying, in her mind's eye, back to Vicksburg and a rendezvous with vengeance. What better name than the one spelled in the ashes of a butchered love. What better name . . .

"Hawkmoon."

PART II

CHAPTER 4

Two years of war. Two years of butchery at Bull Run and Hampton Roads and Fredericksburg and Shiloh, not to mention the countless meadows and fields and forest clearings and dry riverbeds where blood had been spilled and men had died. The Northern forces gobbled up peripheral cities where they could, and though plagued by Southern guerrilla fighters, occupied Tennessee. The Union navy controlled most of the Mississippi and had cut off the Confederacy from the rest of the world by a blockade that bottled up all but a trickle of vital shipping from Virginia to Texas.

The South hadn't worried at first. Its leaders thought that the North would exhaust itself in futile efforts to batter a wedge through the impenetrable heart of Dixie, and when they failed, give up, go home, and accept the sovereignty of the Confederate States of America. The plan might have worked had it not been for two flaws. First, the South underestimated the North's determination to keep the Union intact. Second, the North would simply not be exhausted. Even as it was, the plan worked well enough for the first two years. Under the brilliant military leadership of Robert E. Lee, Bedford Forrest, and Stonewall Jackson, the South compiled victory after victory. In the strategic long run, the victories were, though, empty. Backed by a vast industrial complex, mile upon square mile of fertile farmland, and a cohesive system of transportation that funneled men, supplies, and food where they were needed, the Union armies grew stronger and stronger, and never stopped coming.

The North was determined and inexhaustible: the South was determined but subject to the terrible mathematics of attrition. Every Confederate triumph was a Pyrrhic victory, for supplies and men—neither of which could easily be replenished—were diminished. To make matters worse and to seal the South's doom, England had refused to intercede on its behalf. The Confederate States of America were forced to stand—and fight—alone.

The war had reached a climax. In a desperate gamble to wrest peace through force of arms, to scare the Northern populace into seeking a truce, Robert E. Lee and his army of Northern Virginia was driving north into Pennsylvania. At the same time, in an extended campaign that had lasted a year, the Union's General Ulysses S. Grant was nearing his goal of reducing Vicksburg, opening the full length of the Mississippi to Union shipping, and dealing the South a mortal blow. Already he had crossed the Father of Waters with a Federal host of seventy thousand men, ravaged the countryside as far east as Jackson, and had doubled back to march his Yankee army toward Vicksburg. The war had been lapping at Vicksburg's shores for two years. Now it threatened to inundate the city they called the City of a Hundred Hills, the Jewel of the Mississippi.

So it came to pass, after two years of war, that the citizens of Vicksburg steeled themselves for their heroic role in the drama of a nation under arms. And so it came to pass, after two years of war, that the Confederacy stood on the brink of survival—or defeat.

There is no moon this night. The last, thin sliver sunk in the west two hours ago. Starlight is dissipated by very high, thin clouds. The cemetery lies deep in mist, out of which a gray mare and a gray-cloaked rider rise like a single wraith. The mist lies heaviest in the deep places. On higher ground, it writhes and flows like a living being in the marrow-colored light.

The rider doesn't concern herself with shadows here, but rides openly as if she has every right to do so. "Courier for Colonel Matterson," she murmurs when challenged by the forward guard. Taken for one of the many boy couriers crisscrossing the countryside, she is not questioned further.

The bluffs drop away gently to her right and to the east. Moving more cautiously now, she wraps the cloak tightly around her and seeks the shadows. The gray mare's hooves cut into the mist-hidden loess as she descends and leaves the heights behind. "Leaving," she will say if discovered past this point. "Leaving for safety." She wouldn't be the first. Many, many others have fled the beleaguered city.

The last light of Vicksburg disappears. She is well away into the country. Here the land changes. Here the earth is a dark chocolate that waits for plow and spade and spring sun and rain. And even though war's fiery chariot has seared the fields and rived the heart of the South, even though the land trembles to the tread of armies in attack or retreat, even though the nation has turned on itself and spilled the blood of its youth in great useless gouts, the land will not be denied. Those who serve it do so strangely in these difficult days, though. Instead of food to sustain the bodies of the men who fight, cotton is still king, for cotton will buy munitions and arms and, in the process, fill pockets with gold. The policy is madness, of course—starving men cannot eat cotton—but food would only be confiscated by the local troops and bring nothing in return. The young woman watches the virgin field and reflects for a moment on the waste and irony of war. Then chiding herself for relaxing her vigilance, she whispers gentle words to the gray mare, circles the Willis Plantation, and cuts across bare fields paralleling the Millsdale Road in order to miss the Cook and Edwards Plantations. Only one dog barks. No voices cry halt.

Ahead, the crossing of Millsdale and Bridgeport roads lies like a muddy X across the land. The girl eases the gray mare to a stop and dismounts to give the animal a short rest. "So far, so good," she says, her ears testing the dark.

The mare snorts softly and the girl tenses. What was that? The clamor of pursuit?

"No," she tells herself reassuringly. "Only a 'possum or coon rummaging through the brush."

And that? A rifle being cocked?

"No. Calm yourself." Only the mare's bit clicking against her teeth. Or that? A signal?

"Stop!" she orders herself, speaking aloud to ease the loneliness of the dark. "It's your imagination. No one saw you, no one is looking for you, no one knows you're here. Come," she adds in a whisper to the mare, and mounts. "There's little time. And it will all be over with shortly."

Confidently she urges the mare onto the road and heads east toward her rendezvous. She has nothing to fear. There is only one intruder afoot this night, here in the austere silence.

Hawkmoon.

Who has another name, but not tonight. Tonight, she is . . . Hawkmoon.

Nathaniel Lattimore never had believed that Rafe was dead. Not even when he received the note written by Admiral Stolt himself outlining the details of the discovery of the sunken ship Rafe had commanded did he believe. Never, in the face of incontrovertible proof, did he allow himself to falter in his faith. And now, vindicated by a note in Rafe's own hand, he waited on the docks for his son's return.

It was only right that he and Rafe be reunited. Only right. A man couldn't afford to let his son be taken from him, damn it. You raised them, taught them, and then had to watch them strike off on their own, leaving their fathers behind. Their fathers with their teeth going bad and food not tasting good any longer. With new aches and pains each day. With sleepless nights and ambling, featureless days. It was only fair that Rafe come back. Be different with him in the house again. Be damned good. Give a man a reason . . . He coughed, leaned on his cane until the spasms ceased, and he had spat another filmy splotch of phlegm into the muddy river.

"Mr. Lattimore," a man said, stepping out of the fog and striding onto the shell-splintered, patched pier.

Nathaniel turned and watched the intruder who encroached on his solitude. There was a little light, but he could make out the butternut coat and trousers of a Confederate officer. Nathaniel stared at and past the officer to the lights twinkling on the hillside that swept up from the docks. The mist gave each man a halo.

"You know me, sir," the officer said. "Phillip Laughton." Nathaniel blinked. "Ah, yes. Young Phillip."

"Twenty-three years old now, sir. And a captain."

"A captain, eh?"

"Yes, sir. With Vaughn's brigade, sir."

"My son, Rafe, was a captain, you know. Of a ship, of course."

"Yes, sir," Phillip said, wincing at the mention of Rafe's name. Eleven years earlier, when Phillip was fourteen, he and Rafe had been boyhood friends on a deer hunt when Phillip brought down but failed to kill a deer. Paralyzed, the wounded yearling buck stared up with wide brown eyes at the two boys standing over it. "Well?" Rafe had prompted when Phillip's hand had wavered. "I . . . can't," Phillip had stammered, unable to pull the trigger at such a close range. It was then, with the cruelty so natural to boys, that Rafe laughed and put the wounded beast out of its misery. Phillip had never been sure whether it was his own inadequacy or Rafe's laugh that had shattered their friendship. Only that, since that long ago afternoon, he had harbored an intense and brooding dislike for Rafe. Now that Rafe was dead, though, Phillip found it easy to be sympathetic toward his grief-stricken and understandably deranged father, "It's good to see you again, sir," he added courteously.

Laughton was respectful. Nathaniel liked that. A rare quality in the young these days. War was to blame. Made young men gruff and in a hurry with their manners. Not nearly as bad in the South, of course, as it was with the Yankees, they said. He'd heard all there was to hear about the Yankees. Armies of blue-coated scoundrels, the dregs of the big Northern cities, men conscripted from the mills and factories to be unleashed upon the South. Criminals, they were. Criminals and lotharios and brutes. Nathaniel stiffened, shut his eyes, and willed the pain in his arm to subside.

"Are you ill, Mr. Lattimore?"

"No," the older man said, exhaling softly. "No, I don't think so. Just the body remembering long after the last shot is fired and the war is over. I was in Mexico, you know. Helped storm Mexico City to bring Santa Anna to bay. Seventeen years ago. Long enough to forget most of it. The body remembers, though. Old wounds have a lasting effect and worsen as the years go by. So you're Phillip, eh?"

Laughton looked around, as if he hoped he might find an extra coat hanging nearby that he could drape around Nathaniel's shoulders. "It's chilling down here by the water, sir. The dampness. And this is off limits, Mr. Lattimore," he said gently. "There'll be business here tonight."

"I know that," Nathaniel snapped a little waspishly. "Why do you think I'm here?"

"Yes, sir." The captain looked pained, as if he didn't really enjoy his task. "Still and all, I'm afraid I'll have to ask you to leave."

"Leave? Leave? Now see here, young man . . ." Lattimore fumbled in a pocket beneath his coat and produced a carefully folded piece of paper which he waved under Laughton's nose. "You see this?"

Laughton squinted at it in the darkness.

"It's a pass. Signed by Brigadier General Louis Hebert, who's by God a personal friend of mine. Permission to meet the steamer *Bayou Belle* when she docks."

"*If* she docks, sir," Laughton pointed out, picking at his left ear. With the exception of the short stretch immediately below the bluffs at Vicksburg, the single remaining Confederate stronghold on the whole river, the Yankees owned the Mississippi. Only twice, in the last three months, had a rebel boat—this same *Bayou Belle*—slipped through the Union blockade and docked at the Old Landing. The chances of her doing so again were slim. "I wouldn't get my hopes too high."

Nathaniel seemed to sag, almost as if he'd been struck.

"But maybe this time," Laughton hurried on, mentally damning himself for being an inconsiderate fool. "Who knows? They say Snag Parken is the best pilot on the river. If anybody can bring her in, he will. So you've a pass, then." It was impossible to verify and probably didn't make that much difference anyway, really. "Well, sir, your word is good enough for me. I'll not bother with a light. No need to give some Yank sharpshooter a target. Just be sure to get out of the way when she ties up, 'cause there'll be about nine hundred men running back and forth trying to unload her before Porter's gunboats find her range." Rather peremptorily, Laughton took the old man's arm and led him to one side to a high piling where he could see what was happening without getting trampled. "Hope you don't mind my saying so, sir, but it seems like a hell of a chance you're taking, just to watch a boat come in. If a rifle ball doesn't get you, the grippe likely will."

"Are you going to be here?" Nathaniel asked. "When she docks?"

"Yes, sir. I'm in charge of off-loading."

Nathaniel's hand gripped the captain's sleeve. "Then you'll be aboard?"

"Yes, sir. The second she's tied."

"Find him, then. Find him and tell him where I am. So he won't miss me."

"Who?" Laughton asked.

"My son." Nathaniel pointed down river. "He's aboard. He's comin' home."

"Rafe?" Laughton shrank back. Old man Lattimore was crazier than he'd thought. "Rafe's de . . . that is, I thought he was . . . dead, sir."

"So did I." Nathaniel Lattimore's voice trembled with anticipation, and his eyes glistened in the wan light. "So did I."

The summons to meet with Major Powell, one of Grant's most capable Intelligence officers, had come as a surprise. Eight weeks had passed since Hawkmoon had last communicated with him, and she had thought herself miraculously relieved of a burden that had become increasingly onerous. At first she simply wasn't going to go, then decided that since there was nothing more to lose and everything to gain, she might as well. Powell had, after all, personally promised her—his courier's threats to the contrary notwithstanding—that she could stop whenever she wanted. Now she wanted to stop. And now Powell was close enough so she could tell him personally without fear of the courier's spite.

The gray mare held to a steady lope. Patches of sweat glistened on the animal's withers, chest, and neck. Hawkmoon sat her easily. Cool, for she had let the cowl fall from her head, she noted the well-known landmarks as they passed. The Bridgeport road was empty and had been for the last three miles. The plantations to either side were deserted save for the occasional dog that yapped at her mare's heels. Ahead, the hamlet of Hebron lay, probably deserted also. South and east of her, the Confederate Army lay dug in for the night. This ragged army, tired and worn from one defeat after another at Grant's hands, was all that lay between the Union armies and Vicksburg. And though Hawkmoon came from a Confederate city and those encamped defenders were Confederate forces, they would not meet. This time, for the last time, her rendezvous was with the men in blue.

The bridge over Clear Creek drummed resonantly under the mare's hooves. Hawkmoon kept on a mile, then another and a third, at last reined in to a walk at the edge of a shallow, frog-noisy bayou. Once again she stopped, dismounted, and reviewed her thoughts. She had been naive to think that spying would be romantic. She had done little more than send, through couriers who arrived at her house from time to time, general information about Vicksburg that she was sure any one of a dozen other people could have supplied, and probably better than she. Her father was not avenged; neither was she. She was unaware, she thought bitterly, of having furthered the cause of Abolitionism. In short, she had received nothing for her impulsive act but a sense of guilt for having lived a life of deceit. "I can live this lie no longer," she would say. "I have done little of consequence in the past, and I fail to see of what importance I can be in the future. In my thirst for vengeance I made a mistake. I beg of you, give me this little peace and release me as you promised you would."

The mare rested, cropped the deep, lush spring grass. When ten minutes had passed, Hawkmoon mounted again and turned the mare's head south. The road she followed was little more than a track next to the obsidian liquid black of the bayou. Hickory and sweetgum and yellow pine formed a gloom deeper than the night. The way was harder than it had been ten years ago when, as a child, she had visited the Silverhaus Plantation to spend summer weekends. Then it looked more like a boulevard than a dismal path through what amounted to a swamp. At least she no longer needed to ride with caution. A man had carried a message to her three nights earlier, told her that Powell wanted to meet in person at a place to be designated by her. Being expected, it was far better for her to approach openly than startle a sentry into shooting at her.

"That's far enough," a voice called from the side of the road.

Startled, Hawkmoon reined in the mare.

"Hold and identify yourself," a second voice, higher in register, ordered.

A tall shadow and a shorter one converged from either side of the trail. "What he means," the taller man explained in a deep voice, "is just who the hell are you?"

"Hawkmoon," the girl said simply. "I'm expected."

"The hell you say!"

"A woman!" the one with the high voice exclaimed. "It's a durned woman, Critus!"

"I can hear, you infernal buckbrain."

"You are pickets assigned to Major Powell's unit," Hawkmoon said. "You're—"

"Major Powell, eh? Reckon that gives you away right there, missy. Ain't no—"

"If you don't shut your mouth, Belknap, I'll have to help you," the one called Critus growled. He leveled his rifle at Hawkmoon. The bayonet was a tine of black iron filed to a brutal point.

"You're supposed to bring me to Major Powell," Hawkmoon went on angrily. "He expects me. I'm on urgent business and have no time to spare."

"Sure, sure," Critus snapped. "'Cept nobody said nothin' about no lady." He took a step closer to the gray mare. The woman was staring at him. He couldn't see her eyes, but he could feel them. He sniffed and cleared his throat. His rifle wavered. "Nothin' about no lady at all. Now why don't you just slide on down from that horse. Slow and easy so I can search you, and then we'll take you in, right enough."

"You fool!" the woman snapped.

"Not so much of one," Critus said adamantly, moving closer. "Belknap, you watch that side— Aaagh!"

Hawkmoon's boot had caught him squarely beneath the chin. Critus's head snapped back and he sat down in the road.

"Hey!" Belknap yelled, trying to dodge but then tumbling backward into the ditch when the mare slammed into him.

Horse and rider disappeared into the darkness. Belknap's rifle had flown into the underbrush. Critus's lay somewhere near him. Critus willed his arms to reach out for it. His fingers clawed at the ground, searching. Where the hell was it, he wondered. Where the hell was the damn gun? And then he slumped forward, unconscious. Across the way, Belknap struggled out of the ditch and staggered to his feet. His chest felt as if it had been caved in. Half expecting the devil's own demon henchman to come thundering back down the road at him, he looked around apprehensively. He was alone, though. Shaken but unharmed. The rumble of hoofbeats receded and the forest was quiet. Hawkmoon, he thought. Jee-sus! A woman! Who'd of thought it? Well, maybe she was the real thing. Lord knew she'd taken the two of them out pretty as one two three. Christ, but the old man would be pissed. Still and all . . .

Belknap staggered across the road and stared down at Critus, the regimental bully. Maybe it would be worth it after all, he thought, a grin of guilty pleasure spreading across his face. The tongue-lashing he'd get from Colonel Powell would be a small price to pay for the pleasure of telling this story.

Rafe Lattimore was very much alive, however much he risked remaining so while sipping the whiskey Captain Snag Parken had brought him. The two men stood together in the wheelhouse of the patched and repaired *Bayou Belle* as it plugged along at a meager four knots against the current. The engine was muffled with piled bags of corn flour and dried green peas. All lights were extinguished.

Snag Parken peered into the darkness ahead and cursed. "Well, shit! Here goes." He spun the wheel to starboard and rang for half speed, at the same time called out softly to a youth posted at the door. "Rough place ahead. We have to go in close. Spread the word to lay low and keep it down. The smoking lamp is out."

Rafe watched in silence. Thirteen years ago Snag Parken had first let Rafe ride in the pilot house high on the hurricane deck of a Mississippi stern wheeler. Now at twenty-five Rafe had come full circle and was on his way home again after two long years at sea, and wondering what he'd find when he got there.

"Durn river," Snag said between clenched teeth. "A month, especially in spring, is plenty enough to change it so's a man wouldn't recognize where he was half the time. Last time I was up this far was two months ago. Does make it difficult. Only way is to keep your ears open and hope to hell you hear enough." He rang the telegraph for three-quarter speed, turned slightly upstream. "Yank captain told me about this particular place without knowing who I was. Have to damned near go ashore to make it past, which I don't like 'cause, things being as they are, you can't win. You run with lights, and they find out who you are and do their damnedest to blast you out of the water. Run dark and they know right off something is funny and do their damnedest to blast you out of the water. Either way . . . God-damn bar!" The *Bayou Belle* swung close to shore. "Make this quarter mile and we can head out to the middle again. I hope."

"Hello, the steamer!" A voice called from the river bank.

"That sound like Reb or Yank to you, Rafe?"

"Yank."

"Me, too." Snag leaned out the window. "Hello, the shore!"

"How come you're runnin' dark? Identify yourself."

"I'm runnin' dark so some damn fool secesh don't shoot at me,"

Snag yelled back in what he imagined was a Northern accent. He winked at Rafe. "Identify *yourself!*"

"For sure I ain't the damned fool you think." The voice rose to a yell. "Fire, boys! Aim high an' try for the pilot house!"

Orange blossoms flared from the cypress-choked shoreline. "Hold your fire!" Snag shouted above the din of his crew. "Don't give 'em anything to aim for. We'll be past 'em in a minute!" One hand lay gently on the wheel, the other on the telegraph. "Beats hell out of them ironclads we sneaked by t'other night," he told Rafe, simultaneously laying the wheel hard to port and ringing for full steam.

The steamer slewed in a drift that seemed sure to bring it broadside against the shore. At the last moment the rudder caught and drove them straight along the line of trees. Gunfire at close hand flashed and identified individual soldiers. Minié balls caromed off metal fittings, thudded into wood and into the crates of biscuits and burlap sacks of smoked meat piled in a bulwark around the perimeter of the main deck. "Every damned foot of it, then," Rafe said, his voice tight with anger.

"What?"

"They really do own the whole river."

"Just about. Every once in a while you'll find a bunch of our boys, but mostly it's the Yanks. Lucky for us this is just a small party."

A ball whined through the glassless pilot house. Rafe flinched but stayed on his feet. "How the hell do you know that?"

"'Mount of lead in the air. See that shadow up ahead?"

"Yes."

"Our point. Past it and we run like hell for the middle again. And breathe a little easier."

"I'd breathe a little easier right now if we could return their fire."

"All right down there?" Snag shouted into the speaking tube.

"Red line and leaking like a sieve, but lookin' fine!" came back the weak, tinny answer.

"'Bout past. You can lay off the wood. Five more minutes of full steam and then give her a little rest." Snag acted as if no one had told him a rifle ball could hurt him. "Oh, a couple of nine pounders full of grape would be nice enough," he went on in reply to Rafe's comment. "Trouble is, the added weight would slow us down. Not much, but I like every inch I can get when I have to run by them ironclads. Just that many seconds less they got to unlimber and shoot at me. Object is to get where I'm going."

Another ball hummed past him and shattered an unlit oil lamp hanging close enough to Snag for the glass to fall on his shoulder. The slug had missed both of them by inches. Rafe glanced at the pilot. Snag was every bit as unperturbable as he remembered. "Good whiskey," Rafe said, raising the glass in his hand.

Snag grabbed the bottle and took a quick swig. "If you're lucky enough to live long enough to finish it."

"Maybe. But having that sloop turn turtle under me and surviving sun and thirst and hunger sort of convinced me the stars set a charm on my life."

A volley erupted from shore. One of the men on the deck below cried out. Lead and wood splinters filled the air in the pilot house. "God damn!" Snag shouted, dropping to his knees but keeping ahold of the wheel.

Rafe picked himself up off the deck and reached for the miraculously unbroken whiskey bottle with a shaking hand. "Of course, I could be wrong," he admitted with a sheepish grin.

Snag stood and gave the steamer just a pinch more port rudder. "Like to hear a man admit the error of his ways," he said, taking the bottle and drinking. "Like the old darkie said, 'Brave 'n stupid be two diff'rent things, massah.' They'll quit, now. We'll be out of range in a minute or two."

"You mind?" Rafe asked, pulling a revolver from his waistband.

"Be my guest."

Rafe waited for a muzzle flash, then fired five shots in quick succession into the darkness. His efforts were instantaneously rewarded with a yelp of pain and a string of Yankee curses that carried across the widening gap of water. A cheer, a great whoop and holler of exultation that normally follows a greater victory rose from the crew. Rafe braced one hip against a rail while the *Bayou Belle* slewed again, heading for deeper water, and busied himself reloading the cap and ball revolver. He had heard too few cheers since his return from the sea, and while the sound rang bravely in his ears, it also had a mournful character. Everyone said the Confederacy was winning the war, but to one who had returned from a four-month absence, it was difficult to agree. True, Lee was striking further north, all the way into Pennsylvania, and pushing Lincoln's Army of the Potomac out of the Southern states, but a bevy of contradictory facts told a more sober story. The Union Navy was becoming increasingly effective in enforcing its blockade of the Southern ports. Fewer and fewer blockade runners were successful, more and more of them—like Rafe—had been sunk, and replacements were rare. Europe had yawned in the new republic's face, and refused to commit itself to the South. More and more the lack of manufacturing in the deep South was becoming a factor. And last but not least, the Mississippi was virtually a Union river. The optimists had been adamant in their belief that Vicksburg would hold, that Johnston and Pemberton would drive Grant from his toehold, that the river would once more become a Southern waterway, but Rafe had had doubts after his reunion with Snag Parken.

"You want to go where?" the river pilot had asked, when they'd met clandestinely in a New Orleans dive.

"Home, Snag. Home after too long away. Two years of running all over the Caribbean is a long time. Do me good to get home for a while."

"Your daddy and brother still there?"

"Daddy is. Lord only knows what's happened to Micah. Probably off fighting somewhere. All the more reason to get home."

"Better chance of getting there on a horse, Captain," Snag had said, eyeing the mulatto dancing girl he'd come to watch. "It isn't exactly like the old days."

Rafe shook his head. He'd considered going overland, but was still weak from his ordeal and didn't think he could make the grueling, hazardous ride. "I'm a man of the water," he'd said simply. "You know that."

Snag had laughed a sour, bitter laugh. "Well, come along then. I leave New Orleans tomorrow and get upstream in another three, four days, depending on what kind of a load the boys have arranged. River's a dangerous place to be, though. Maybe we'll get there, maybe we won't. Maybe we won't even clear Red Corn Bayou. But if we do, maybe your luck'll hold long enough to get your daddy out before it's too late."

"Everyone says—"

"Everyone is full of shit, Rafe. They talk big but they haven't been there and they haven't seen Grant's army or Porter's navy. I have, and damned near didn't get back to tell the tale. You mark my word. Another month and Vicksburg'll be a Union town."

Rafe had bridled. "Then why are you going?" he'd asked.

The pilot thought about that while he downed his drink. "Because I might be wrong," he'd said finally. "I don't see how, but I might be. And small as that chance is, well . . . There just ain't nobody else left who knows Old Muddy the way I do, so I guess I'm elected." The river boat pilot paused and lined up his glass on a deep shadow a point off the port bow. "Same could be asked of you, Rafe. Why? Why're *you* goin' back?"

The question took Rafe by surprise. He hadn't thought much about going back to Vicksburg, just assumed that was where he was supposed to go and headed in that direction. So why, indeed? Everything he'd heard led him to believe Vicksburg was a doomed city. God knew there wasn't a ghost of a navy left there. Why, then?

His father was one answer, of course. Celia was another. But there was more to it than that. Vicksburg itself, to begin with, was in his bones. The way the sun rose over green hills to the east and set beyond the Mississippi to the west. The way the fog rolled in and the way the river swelled in the spring. In his mind he saw the docks crowded with ships loaded with trade goods from a thousand ports. He could almost hear the Negro ballads haunting the warm summer air. Vicksburg with its cobblestone streets rising and falling like waves of a frozen sea, and the smell of the streets, fresh and clean and exciting after a spring rain. The surrounding land—the plantations bustling with life, the quiet woods he'd hunted, the streams he'd fished, and the hills he'd climbed. And perhaps most of all, home—where he'd crawled and toddled and walked and grew through boyhood to young manhood, where he had learned to read and had become inspired by the sea and ships, so that no matter where he sailed later, the books and charts he'd pored over as a youth remained for him an integral part of that world, the port from whence all voyages began, at which all voyages ended.

"Vicksburg is home, I guess," he finally said with a deprecatory shrug that didn't fool Snag for one moment. And when home was threatened, any man who wanted to call himself a man hurried to protect it, no matter what the cost. "Can't just let the Yankees walk in unopposed," he added. "I imagine we'll keep them out somehow."

The next day they sneaked out of New Orleans and hiked overland to the secret Confederate hideaway camp on Red Corn Bayou. There, a friend of a friend saw to it that a message to Nathaniel Lattimore informing him of his son's continuing existence and plans to ride the *Bayou Belle* home was included in the courier packet to Vicksburg. Rafe ate and exercised to build up his strength, spent the first night trading yarns with Snag. The second day a year old letter from his father was given to him. The envelope was wrinkled and mud-stained. Someone had scrawled an artillery problem on its back. The letter itself, when Rafe found a quiet place to be alone, sounded like an echo from an era long gone. Johnston's standoff with Grant at Shiloh had infused the South with the spirit of victory. New Orleans in the south was still a Confederate city, as was Memphis in the north. Vicksburg hummed with activity. There was no mention of the disinherited Micah, but a long list of Rafe's friends who had marched off to the war and, too often, had been wounded or killed. His father's health was good except for the usual occasional malarial fever and a touch of depression over his old friend Hal Bartlett's continuing heart problems. Celia was still home, as he had reported in his last letter, and she had yet to give an explanation for her unannounced departure over a year ago. Neither had she taken a new beau. Most of her time was spent caring for her father, which kindness extended to Nathaniel as well, for she often tested his skill at checkers and, most Sundays, allowed him to escort her to church. Rafe had read those lines a dozen times and now, as the *Bayou Belle* neared Vicksburg, touched the pocket where the letter lay. Celia. Celia Bartlett, whom he loved and who had so precipitously and mysteriously dropped out of his life.

"Not long now," Snag said, pointing.

Rafe jerked back to the present and followed the pilot's finger. Eerily silent, like a sunken ship still sailing, a sun-bleached, broken pine angling from the water near the shoreline slid by them like a ghost. He had seen masts toppled the same way after an exchange of broadsides, only then there had been the stench of gunpowder and the groans and screams of dying men. "Hollow Point?" he asked with a shiver, trying to forget the haunting memory.

"None other."

Rafe ducked to get a better view of the sky. "Clouds are almost gone. Be more light than you counted on. Can we make it?"

"Make it and dock," Snag promised. He slapped the chart desk affectionately. "Old *Bayou* isn't as big as some, not as pretty as others, not as fast as most, but she by God gets the job done."

"No, not her. You, Snag. You're the one who gets the job done," Rafe said, raising his glass in a toast. "To the best pilot and teacher a man could ask for. May you continue your vital service to our holy cause in good health and well-being!"

"Hah!" Snag grumped, hiding his pleasure. He picked up the bottle, waved it in the air but didn't drink. "And to a damned fine blockade runner and scourge of the seas."

"Without a ship. And unlikely to get one, for that matter."

"Then you see how it is?"

"See how what is?" Rafe asked, confused.

"Being good is only half the game." Snag pointed. Far ahead, a tiny pinprick of light, the first sign of Vicksburg, shone like a star against the dark hills. "There she is. Vicksburg. We'll dock, all right. But as for leaving in one piece? . . ." The question hung ominously on the night-heavy river air. "That's a different matter, boy. A far different matter."

It was midnight and Colonel Ambrose Cutter Powell's stomach felt sour and burned from the bitter coffee he'd been drinking the better part of the night. That and disappointment. Hawkmoon had lied to the courier, it appeared, and wasn't coming. That was the trouble with amateurs. They started out willing enough, but then sooner or later began to feel guilty and fell by the wayside. Truth was, he wouldn't give a damn if this weren't the single most important campaign in the war. It was, though, and he needed every scrap of information he could get.

There was no sense in wasting time over what he couldn't control, though. No sense in crying over wet powder, as the revised saying went. If she didn't show, she didn't show. The only sensible path was to take a nap. If she hadn't arrived by two, he'd pack up, sneak back to his own lines, and make arrangements to deliver the letters to her father and the Vigilance Committee, as promised. This in mind, he extinguished the lantern, pulled the blanket from the window, and stretched out on the pallet he'd fixed for himself on the floor.

It was hard to relax. Open, his eyes looked like twin pools of whiteness floating in the night air. Nervous and jittery, he listened to the night sounds. A horse snorted outside his window. A boot scraped across the floor in the next room. A tin cup clanked dully against something. Frogs peeped and boomed in unceasing, mindless repetition only slightly less maddening than the constant whine of mosquitoes. Somewhere out there, insect bitten but implacable rebel patrols prowled the night, reconnoitering, probing, seeking contact with the enemy. Only by a fluke, the colonel thought, would they find his miniscule detachment. His fervent prayer was that his presence could go undetected while he got the information he sought and then got the hell out and back to his own lines.

The pallet was as hard as the floor and seemed bent on teaching his bones a lesson they wouldn't have needed only a year earlier. War did that to a man. Made him tired, wore him out. Aged him too fast. It was the pressure that wreaked the havoc. If he'd picked an easier line of work, supply, say, he wouldn't be stuck out in the middle of Mississippi running around behind Rebel lines. Slowly, muscle by muscle, he forced himself to relax. And just when he'd gotten to his stomach muscles, the door creaked open and the yellow glare of a lantern filled the room. "Dammit, man!" Powell hissed, bolting upright. "My window's open."

The door closed swiftly. In the dark again, Powell pulled on his boots, groped his way to the door, and let himself out. "What the hell do you mean, showing that light, Corporal?" he asked, closing the door behind him.

"Sorry, sir." His cheeks red, the corporal saluted. "Didn't know you'd turned in, sir. She's here."

Powell brightened. "Just a minute." He darted back into his room and emerged pulling on his tunic a moment later. "You sure it's her?"

"Believe so, sir. Called herself Hawkmoon like you said she would. She must have come in a different way than we figured, though. Either that or snuck by Critus and Belknap, 'cause she's alone. Said to give you this."

The corporal handed a folded piece of paper to the officer. Powell opened it and read the sweeping single word, "Hawkmoon," scrawled over the message he had sent her three nights earlier. "Good," he said, satisfied. "Where is she?"

"In the front room, sir."

"Good." Powell buttoned his tunic as he strode down the hall. "See to the woman's horse and tell Rutledge she's here. Where's Sergeant Vale?"

"In the living room with the woman, sir."

"Good. Get moving, Corporal." The colonel paused at the door to smooth what was left of his hair, then entered. Blankets had been hung over the windows to keep the light in and the room was hot and stuffy with the smell of cigar smoke, sweat, and a kerosene lamp. Sergeant Vale rose to attention as the door closed. Across the room, gray in the shadows, a cloaked figure waited. "Send out a relief for Critus and Belknap," the major snapped. "I want to know what's going on out there."

The sergeant waved a sloppy salute and withdrew immediately. Only then did Powell turn his attention to the woman. "Hawkmoon?"

"Major Powell?"

Powell pulled out a chair from the map table set in the center of the room. "Colonel Powell," he corrected. "At your service. We expected you earlier."

"I didn't know my schedule was that exact." The woman emerged from the shadows and, throwing back the cowl of her cape, approached the table. "You should consider yourself lucky that I'm here at all."

Powell stared openly as she removed her cloak and threw it across a chair. She was not tall. Five three or four, perhaps, but her legs looked long in tight lead gray breeches. Pert of hip, she was slim except where the beige shirt swelled over ample breasts that strained the light cotton garment. Powell tried to imagine those breasts. Firm with youth, he was sure, but soft and complimenting the creamy flesh of her neck and face, framed in long, tangled hair the color of a spring sunrise. Her eyes, a light, smoky topaz under dark lashes, were set above high cheek bones and, in the soft light, fixed him in place and read his interest with a perception that embarrassed him. "And so we meet again," he finally said. "It seems a long time."

"Less than two years," Hawkmoon said. "You were a captain then."

"So I was. One rises quickly these days." He held up one hand and closed his eyes. "Don't tell me. You wore a light green gown and a . . . what? Ah, yes. A cameo brooch. A necklace, but I don't recall of what."

"I don't have much time, Colonel Powell," Hawkmoon interrupted.

"Of course." Powell moved the lantern and arranged the creased and water-stained maps that covered the table with crude approximations of the surrounding countryside. "I don't know how much you know," he said, pointing to the topmost, "but this is what we look like now. Or yesterday, at least." A stubby finger moved across the map. "Here's the city of Jackson and our rear. This is a place called Champion Hill. I got word just after sundown that there'd been a fight there today. Pemberton got out with his skin, but not a lot more. He was pretty well routed."

"We heard," Hawkmoon said, her face hardening. She hadn't been looking at the maps at all, showed her disdain for them by turning her back on the table. "Everyone was very upset. That was, in part, what kept me."

"In part?" Powell asked.

"Yes. I very nearly didn't come at all. And only did at last in order to ask you in person to release me, as you promised you would."

Powell let one eyebrow rise in feigned shock. "Would you care to explain?"

"Explanations are . . . are difficult . . ."

"Try."

Hawkmoon took a deep breath and plunged in. "I can't go on living this lie!" she said as rehearsed. "You don't know what it's like. Those people are my friends. Men, women, and children alike, they are brave and deserve more than treachery from me."

"I see." Powell sat, looked up at her with a bemused expression on his face. "You seemed vitriolic enough—positive enough in your desire to help—when we met in Boston. You've been sending me information for a little over a year. And now, all of a sudden, you decide that—"

"Not suddenly. Not at all. I wanted to stop six months ago."

"Oh?" Powell asked, surprised. "And your vaunted Abolitionist views?"

"In spite of them, Colonel. Not because. General Lee himself was something of an Abolitionist, at least insofar as he personally didn't believe in slavery and had freed his slaves. Still, when Virginia was attacked, he rallied to the defense of his homeland. I'm doing no differently."

"Even if a little late in the game?"

"Even if," Hawkmoon admitted, her face reddening. "I was afraid. Father's heart attacks had incapacitated him and your courier threatened to denounce me to the Vigilance Committee. If Father had seen me . . ." She shuddered and wrapped her arms around herself as if the room suddenly had turned cold.

"Revealed as a spy and traitor?" Powell asked harshly. "Tarred and feathered and driven out of town? Maybe even hung from the gallows."

"You knew!" Hawkmoon said, aghast. "You promised me! You swore!"

"Of course I promised. Did you really expect otherwise?" The colonel's hands were flat on the table and he looked poised to come out of the chair at any moment. "Do you think this is a game we're playing? Do you think we're not utterly serious? Vicksburg is the lock that denies us the Mississippi. We mean to open that lock and you, my dear, are one of the keys we need. I had—and have—no intention of losing you just because your conscience has been pricked."

"But what difference can I possibly make?" Hawkmoon asked angrily. "Your own people say it's only a matter of days before the city falls."

"My own people have been saying that for a year," Powell said, "and still the river is blocked. So you'll pardon me if, for professional reasons, I remain pessimistic. Now, I have little time for this. So sit down and let's get to work."

Hawkmoon faced him defiantly. "And if I refuse?"

"That is your choice. But if you do, or if you lie to me and I find out, which, I assure you I will sooner or later, I promise you that the Vigilance Committee will learn of your role and your father . . ." He left the sentence unfinished. "How *is* your father's heart? I would hate to think of what the shock of such a disgrace would do to him, wouldn't you?"

"And you would go that far?" Hawkmoon asked contemptuously. "That far?"

"If need be," Powell answered flatly. "Yes."

"Then you have no sense of honor whatsoever," she spat, the loathing evident in her voice.

"On the contrary," Powell said dryly. "I have a well-developed sense of honor. Which tells me that the lives your information can save far outweigh your father's well-being."

"My father's well-being?" Hawkmoon's laughter was brittle, tinged with hysteria. "My father's well-being?" Her face was a furious, twisted mask in the lamplight as she leaned over the table. "Six weeks ago, my father was preparing to go to bed for the night when a shell from one of your Yankee gunboats exploded in the street. My father suffered his fourth and final heart attack from the shock. My father, sir, is dead."

Powell's face had turned white. "I didn't know . . . Please forgive me . . ."

"You didn't aim the gun or light the fuse. You can't be forgiven for something you didn't do. You see, Colonel, I've learned to narrow my hatred to focus it on the responsible party. Call it wisdom," she added bitterly.

"I don't mean that," Powell said contritely. "I mean—"

Hawkmoon's hand slapping the desk stopped him. "Don't say it. You're guilty enough for holding his life over my head. And that's something I won't forgive. Now, if you don't mind"—she straightened and reached for her cloak—"I'll be leaving. I hope you save a great many lives, Colonel Powell. And that you roast in hell."

The colonel swiveled in his chair and waited until she reached the door. "I *am* sorry about your father," he said quietly. "I'm sorry about a lot of things, most of which I can't do much if anything about."

"Contrition doesn't suit you, Colonel. May I go now, or will you have me shot in the back?"

"Where *will* you go? Back to Vicksburg?" Unable to meet her eyes, he spoke to a point high on the wall across the room. "The war continues. Men continue to die. I'll continue to do what I can. By tomorrow morning letters will be delivered to no less than three of the members of the Vigilance Committee. All the sordid history of our fine belle of Vicksburg will become common knowledge. Your home and property will no doubt be confiscated—there are always jackals waiting to pick up such morsels."

"You wouldn't . . ."

"Or do you plan to run?" he went on mercilessly. "Where? The Confederacy has an espionage branch, too, of course. We know some of their people. They'll know who you are and what you've been up to within two days. You can guess their reaction. Pilloried throughout the South, a pariah and outcast, who'd have you? Penniless and alone in a hostile land filled with soldiers all too willing to take in and use a beautiful woman, how far would you get? Need I say more?"

Hawkmoon's knees trembled under the onslaught, and she leaned against the closed door for support. The room spun and she felt she had been caught in a nightmare. She had convinced herself she was free, only to find she was more deeply mired than ever, and in her sudden confusion and fear could find no way out. The only noise in the room was the hiss of the lantern. Added, at last, was the sound of slow footsteps, a chair scraping the floor, and the creak of wood as Hawkmoon sat. "Why?" she asked faintly. "What would you gain?"

Powell's voice was cold and flat. "There are many others in your . . . position. Some will, inevitably and as you have, vacillate. But perhaps not, once they hear the story of Celia Bartlett, known as Hawkmoon."

"An example, then," Celia said dully. "I hope you're pleased with yourself."

"I am no more pleased with myself than you are. I am merely doing my job. Now let's get to work." Powell set some colored chips on the map and moved them toward a meandering line. "This is the Big Black River," he began anew as if nothing had happened. He arranged the dark chips across a line that ran through a hairpin bend in the river. "Pemberton, right across and blocking the road to Vicksburg, and"—the light chips were in disarray to the immediate east— "the Union forces moving up behind them. I suspect they'll look rather like this by morning." When he finished, the black chips lay across the road that led to Vicksburg, only ten miles to the west. To the east, facing them and cut off from flanking movements by heavy swamps, lay the Union armies.

"And?" Hawkmoon asked.

"Vicksburg *will* fall," Powell said confidently. "When and at what cost is precisely why I have had to be so ruthless with you. Here"—he indicated a spot some miles to the east and north—"is Sherman's Corps. We have two choices. Smash through Pemberton where he is, cross the river and march into Vicksburg, or give Sherman enough time to take Pemberton's army in a pincer action, and then march into Vicksburg. Anything you know will help. General Grant is losing patience and wants to get this over with."

Hawkmoon's hesitation was brief, but during it a thousand thoughts flashed through her mind. "The Bridgeport road is open," she finally said in little more than a whisper. She took the pencil from Powell and traced a line from Sherman's Corps to Vicksburg. "I just rode it and saw nothing of importance. General Pemberton is staking everything on holding the crossing over the Big Black until General Johnston can attack Grant's rear. That will take time, though, and I'm sure that if General Grant wants to wait, Sherman can get between Pemberton and Vicksburg without opposition."

"What kind of shape are those men in?"

Hawkmoon shrugged. "Tired. Discouraged. Hungry. They're trying to get food out there now, but no one's very optimistic. I heard someone say they'd just better hope that Grant didn't attack in the morning because they didn't think Pemberton could hold."

"Mmmm." Powell pulled a smaller scale map of the Big Black River sector out from under the large map. It showed the river, a road, bridge, and line of breastworks, but little else. "Anything you can fill in here?" he asked. "None of our people know the area very well."

"I . . . I'm not acquainted with that part of the country, I'm afraid," Hawkmoon said, a light frown playing over her face.

"That's strange." Powell turned the map so it faced her. "Because your father owned a plantation in precisely this spot some years ago, and you spent a great deal of your time as a child there."

Hawkmoon's mouth fell open. "How did you—?"

"It doesn't matter how I knew. Now, may we start again?" He nodded at the map. "I'd appreciate it if you'd fill in the blanks. And remember that I'll know within the next day or two how well you've done."

Trapped, unable to collect her thoughts sufficiently to defy him, Hawkmoon set to work. Drawing and shading, her hand moved rapidly. "Swamp here and here"—small marks denoting tufts of grass began to fill wide areas—"woodlands here, mostly second growth and hard to get through. These places"—rough boundary lines delineated large rectangles—"used to be open fields and still are, I imagine, except for here." She drew a jagged line that emerged from the forested area to the north, ran across a field, and paralleled another thick line marked, "Breastworks. Cotton bales covered with dirt?"

"This is a ravine," she continued. "Deep enough to hide men, wide enough for two wagons and teams abreast. Your men will probably find it in the morning anyway, but this might save them a little time. Anything else?" she added sarcastically.

Powell had half a hundred questions. Hawkmoon answered as best she could, spent a final fifteen minutes marking hospitals, churches, gun placements, munition and supply depots on a detailed map of Vicksburg that Powell produced. "I've captioned maps for you twice before," she said, finishing. "I can't imagine why you need a third. It's all I can think of."

"Again as a confirmation of what you sent us before and other reports as well. Confirmation is important, too. Don't worry." It was Powell's turn to sound sarcastic. "We'll use everything. Would you like some coffee?"

"I'm fine, thank you."

"Nonsense. You look all in."

"I don't want your damned coffee, Colonel. Don't you understand that?"

Powell sighed. "I'm the villain, Hawkmoon. Not my coffee." He took her by the arm and propelled her out the door. "I'm glad you suggested this place," he went on pleasantly, as if they were the best of friends. "It's nice to be inside a real house. To have at least one meal cooked on a stove." The smell of coffee and cooking food assailed their nostrils as they entered the kitchen of the deserted plantation house. "There's plenty to eat, if you wish."

Hawkmoon sank down at the table, let Powell get her a cup of coffee. "No food. I need to get back." She looked around the room and sighed wistfully. "This place was so alive and bright when the Silverhauses lived here. All the times I've sat right here in this kitchen. Manthy, their cook, used to give us cookies or rice pudding and tell us what sweet little girls we were. I loved those times so much, and now"—she shook her head sadly—"here I am doing everything I can to destroy them. Sometimes I wish I'd never . . ." She trailed off, stared glumly into her coffee.

"If wishes were horses, beggars would ride," Powell said, pulling out his watch and glancing at it. Almost one o'clock. Barely time to write the necessary reports and get them back so they would do some good in the morning.

Hawkmoon stared at him. Hatred flared momentarily in her eyes, but then faded in a dull wash of fatigue. "I could still just ride on, you know. Take my chances."

Powell nodded in agreement. "You're acquainted with the country. You might just make it. But to where, my dear?" He allowed himself a smile. "Nevertheless, I suggest you return," he said, more gently. "If it's any consolation, any further information I need and you supply will save lives. Many more than you think, perhaps. And now"—he rose—"it's late. I have a great deal to do before morning. If you don't mind, I'll turn you over to Sergeant Vale."

"Of course." Hawkmoon drained her cup and rose to face him.

"Oh, yes." Powell led the way to the door. "I forgot to tell you. You won't have to make this ride again." He could feel her perplexity as she followed him down the darkened hall and into the parlor to get her cloak. "You'll have help. One of my special agents. He's a Pinkerton man who'll do the dangerous work—be the courier—from now on. All you have to do is get him inside the city for the first time. The two of you can arrange your schedule and methods of meeting on the way back."

"I came alone," Hawkmoon hissed. "I'll return the same way, if you don't mind."

"But I do," a familiar voice drawled from a chair next to the fireplace. "Mind, that is."

"What?" Hawkmoon gasped. "What!"

A lanky, bearded figure of a man unfolded from the chair and stepped into the light. "Hello, Celia," he said, as naturally as if they'd seen each other only the day before. "It's been a long time."

"My God! Anthony! Is it really you? What are you *doing* here?"

"Why, the same as you, Cousin," came the laconic reply. "Spying."

CHAPTER 5

Unable to sleep yet unwilling to wake, Celia tried one side, then the next, rolled onto her stomach, and finally lay on her back and stared at the ceiling. Dreams had plagued her since she had fallen exhausted into bed four hours earlier, and had robbed her of much needed rest. At last, with the sun leaking around the heavy drapes that darkened her room, she resigned herself to the new day.

Still groggy, she tried to make sense of the events of the night before—the confrontation with Colonel Powell and her feelings of helplessness and defeat. And then Anthony's appearance. Dear Anthony! At first she had been overjoyed to see him, but joy had soon given way to trepidation. She recalled a gentler young man who had come to be closer to her than she imagined even a brother could be. Two years of war had changed him though, turned him into a cold and heartless fanatic capable of justifying the most onerous acts by the self-proclaimed righteousness of the cause he espoused. They talked, but only enough to fill in the sketchiest of histories of the past two years. His father and mother were now in France, where Phillip had been attached to the U.S. embassy for the past year. Anthony, incensed by the South's perfidy and even more confirmed in his Abolitionist fervor, had presented himself to the Pinkerton Agency and enrolled as a secret agent with the assignment of ferreting out Confederate sympathizers living in Boston and its environs. Later, as the war progressed, and because his Southern accent was impeccable, his assignments had taken him farther afield and into more dangerous locations. And now he was tackling Vicksburg. "And you?" he had asked.

Celia told Anthony about her father's death and the steadily deteriorating condition of Vicksburg, but was spared revealing further details when Powell, who was overseeing the breakup of the hastily contrived camp, suggested they be on their way. Two hours later, bone weary, she had led the way through the defenses and into the city, pointed out the shortest route to the waterfront, and after arranging where they should next meet, hurried to her own home and bed. Now, half awake, she wondered what quirk of fate had reunited her to her cousin.

Outside, the deep bass bell atop the Catholic church rang seven o'clock. Seconds later, as if timed on purpose, an explosion cut the fading reverberations. The first shell of the day landed. Admiral Porter and the Union's Mississippi Navy was greeting the morning in their own fashion. Celia—Hawkmoon but a few hours earlier—hoped no more shells overshot the waterfront for the next few moments, buried her head in the pillows, and tried to sort out her thoughts and emotions. Powell had frightened and angered her with his bald use of power and threats of blackmail. She could understand his reasoning and had to admit she probably would have done no less, but still she resented being placed in that sort of position.

Suddenly totally awake, Celia considered the problems posed by Anthony. A host of questions presented themselves. How much of his own man was he? Did his status as a Pinkerton agent give him any immunity from Powell, or was Powell's hold over him as complete as his hold over her? Had her initial impression of him as a fanatic been correct, and did she dare even consider trusting him? More immediately to the point was what would happen if Anthony were recognized? Five years had passed since he had last visited Vicksburg. He had changed a great deal in the interim, but even with his new beard there was a remote chance that he would be recognized. If so, what was her role then? To hide him? Or to help him escape? Or to ignore him and pretend shocked innocence?

Too many questions. No one, she least of all, knew what the next days would bring. Pemberton could hold at the Big Black. Johnston could wipe out Grant from the rear. Grant could roll through Pemberton and across the Big Black as easy as a sharp knife through a ripe watermelon. Vicksburg could be taken in as little as a day, could withstand a siege for an indeterminate time, and then be taken, or be spared forever. History would declare the result inevitable, but the only inevitability Celia could think of was that she was being forced to continue living the lie she had come to abhor with all her mind and soul.

The night before she had been confused, frightened, tired, and powerless in the face of Powell's threats. Now, in the cold light of dawn, those same threats were subject to a more rational analysis. Very well, then.

Denouncement to the Vigilance Committee was a real and very present danger, especially given Anthony's presence and his apparent willingness to act as Powell's eyes and ears. One word in the right place would set everything she feared in motion. Like father, like daughter, the patriots would cry and, though not hanging her—she feared death only in the worst of her fantasies—mercilessly strip her of what little wealth she still commanded and, tarring and feathering her, hound her out of town.

What would happen then was anyone's guess, and Powell's scenario was probably realistic. She would be a pariah and an outcast. Penniless and alone in a hostile land, she would be prey to the many men who, without a second thought, would use her to their own ends; that is, if she stayed in Vicksburg. Calmly, she considered her second option: of leaving Vicksburg on her own terms. The difficulties were immediately apparent but solvable. Like it or not—though the idea of abandoning her home, the people, and city she loved left her almost sick with fear—she would have to go.

The decision made, she calmly set about making her plans. The house she had to consider lost. Property in Vicksburg was changing hands at a rapid rate, but the possibility of Anthony learning she was selling her house and telling Powell was too great. No less the warehouse, which was, in any case, practically destroyed. The little money her father had kept in the bank might be gotten out, but the Confederate bills they would try to give her were daily decreasing in value. Which left her mother's jewels and her father's gold. The jewels—unfortunately few in number—posed little problem. They could be sewed into the lining of a garment. The gold was a different matter. Before his death her father had converted everything he could to gold; consequently, some twenty-five thousand dollars in twenty-dollar gold coins, almost a hundred pounds of gold in four twenty-five-pound heavy canvas sacks had been removed from his safe and hidden under a slate slab in the basement. But what was she supposed to do with a hundred pounds of gold? Impossible to hide, capable of inciting murderous greed in the mildest of men, the precious metal was an absolute necessity on one hand and a millstone around her neck on the other.

But if she took the gold, as she knew she must, where would she go? Due east was out of the question because of the Union Army. The Mississippi was an impossible barrier to the west. Downstream in a small boat might be possible, but she knew little of boats, and if she capsized, all was certainly lost. North and east she rejected immediately because that route led to the heart of the war-ravaged South. South and east would be her route then, she decided. Biloxi, Mobile, Pensacola. At any one of these ports, disguised and with some luck, she might catch a blockade runner and escape to England or France or, in a circuitous fashion, even Boston.

Or fairyland, she thought, temporarily discouraged by the miles and many obstacles she foresaw. *Steady,* she told herself. *If you falter now . . .*

What would she need? Maps, to begin with, which she would find in her father's library. Food and clothes and a method of carrying them, as well as the gold, would have to be procured, which meant at least two horses. Immelda and Tobias would have to be taken care of, and arrangements made so repercussions of her leaving should not affect them. All this would take time, too. A week or more perhaps. Very well, then, she decided. If possible, her last day in Vicksburg would be the next Sunday, May 24, at the earliest, the Sunday following, May 31, at the very latest.

The door to her room opened. Celia closed her eyes and pretended to be asleep. A board creaked. A moment later the curtain rings grated along the rods and light flooded the room.

"I knows you is awake, so you might as well quit tryin' to fool me. It's time to get up. Now hie you out of there."

Immelda's rich contralto voice was as warm as the sunshine that fell across Celia's face. She didn't want to get up. Didn't want to face the day. "Go 'way," she mumbled, and pulled the covers over her head.

"Oo-eee! Ain't you the high-falutin' one, though." Immelda moved around the room, picking up and straightening out. "You got to bathe —that horse smell like she be right here in the room with you—an' eat your breakfast. You got to dress an' go to church. You got to come back here an' load up for the picnic." Her voice faded as she left the room. "An' with all that, you ain't got time to lie abed."

Oh, Lord, Celia thought, stifling a yawn. The picnic. Only in Vicksburg, with a Union army knocking at the door, would they have the temerity to hold a picnic. It wasn't in a sense all that silly, though. The ability to lay aside travail was an indication of Vicksburg's inherent toughness. The city had been under pressure for almost a year. The weak and frail and frightened had left long ago, leaving behind those who, already stronger by nature, had become immured to danger. Besides, what could be more therapeutic than a show of derring-do? For that one afternoon, no matter what they faced, the greater share of Vicksburg's citizens would party and feast, place aside the noise of caisson and marching troops, the cough and bark of artillery, the moan of shells passing overhead and the jarring explosions that followed. For these few hours they would ignore the gun emplacements and pits that pocked the hills and bluffs, the unceasing movement of war materiel, the growing shortages of food and goods, the plain homespun clothes they had taken to wearing because the

Union blockade of the river had cut off their normal channel of supplies.

Celia pushed up on her elbows. The covers fell to her stomach to let the morning sun bathe her torso and set her hair aglow. Groaning—oh, Lord, how four hours on horseback made her ache—she eased her legs over the side and felt for her slippers. They weren't there. For a moment, she considered that ample reason to lie back down.

Immelda's finely wrought features poked through the door to the bathroom. "What's hot now ain't gonna stay that way," the black woman said. "You come on, now."

"I've decided today is Saturday, and I can sleep late. I'm going back to bed."

"Thou shall not blaspheme."

"Who's blaspheming?" Celia asked through a yawn.

"You are." Hands on hips, Immelda stood in the doorway and glowered at her mistress. "Changin' what the good Lord made, callin' His day somethin' other than His day is a powerful sin."

Celia sighed in exasperation. "I was joking, Immelda. For heaven's sake—"

"Nonetheless. Mistuh Lattimore'll be showin' up punctual at five to nine to take you to church, an' you know that is one ol' man that don't like to be kept late." Immelda turned on her heels and disappeared. The sound of a kettle raking across the stove top was followed by that of water being poured. "'Sides. It ain't ladylike."

"Ahhh." Celia made herself stand and pull on her robe. Her buttocks and the muscles along the inside of her thighs hurt the worst. "Remind me never to ride that far in one night again. I don't think I've ever been so sore. Do you know what, Immelda?" she asked, hobbling across the room and stopping in the door to massage her bottom. "You take all the fun out of being spoiled and pampered, that's what."

"Wasn't me that put the fun into it in the first place," the black woman said, pointing to the tub. "In you go. The heat'll take out the stiffness."

The high-walled enamel tub was filled with steaming hot water and the small wood-burning stove next to it showed a small purgatory through the mica windows in the door. Celia dropped her robe and tested the water with her toe. "Are you trying to cook me? Perhaps serve me up at the picnic? Add some dumplings and ladle me out to the hungry?"

"Well, there sure enough be plenty to poison the whole of Vicksburg." Immelda chuckled, catching Celia's hair as the young woman gingerly sank beneath the surface until the water lapped at her chin.

"You get your hair wet," she said, tying it in a rough bun, "and we'll never get it dry in time for church."

Celia felt the heat working on her bottom and thighs and groaned with pleasure. "That might be a good excuse. I don't think I want to get up from here. Ever."

"Don't want to, pish an' posh. You do what you got to do, girl." The black woman handed Celia a brush and a bar of soap. "An' no more complainin', hear? If Tobias could get up at three this mornin' to rub down an' feed and water that mare, you can for sure go to church." She started out and turned at the door. "What you want me to put out for you? That same ol' homespun?"

"Lord, no. Not today. I'm tired to the soul of feeling drab. Put out the pink. The one I brought back from New York."

Immelda clucked reproachfully. "People gonna talk."

"They talk anyway," Celia called after her. "It'll be nice to hear about something other than the war." She dropped the brush and soap and, luxuriating in the hot water, lay back and let the warmth leach the stiffness from her. "Anything but the war," she muttered drowsily. "Anything at all."

It was so peaceful. Immelda fussing about in the next room. A bird singing outside and now Tobias's accompaniment in a deep, plaintive bass as he worked in the backyard. The night before was little more than a dream, the war but a rumor to which none but a madman would give credence. "Mmmmm-mmm," Immelda said, breaking the charm as she picked up Celia's robe and hung it up before getting out a fresh towel. "You sure gonna look fetchin' in that dress. I mean, dresses is more fittin' for a young lady like you to wear. Not those old smelly men clothes."

"Everything has its place," Celia said and sighed, as if drugged by the heat.

"Just what I been sayin'. Things has their places an' can be out of place. Like you, carryin' on so. I never heard such things as a woman spyin' an' playin' these here foolish menfolk games."

A picture of Colonel Powell's face materialized on the inside of her eyelids. The lines were deeply shadowed in the dim light of the lantern, and his look was harsh and foreboding. She sat up abruptly and opened her eyes. Grateful to be freed of that image, she stared at the patterned paper covering the wall. "They aren't," she said.

Celia was staring so hard that Immelda was forced to look, too. She didn't see anything out of the ordinary. Only deep green leaves and multihued pansies. "Child?" she asked, her brows knotting in apprehension.

"They aren't," Celia repeated, blinking. "They aren't games, Immelda. I wish to God they were, though."

The black woman looked long and searchingly into her mistress's face. Her mistress, the little girl she had raised from the day her sweet Mama died so long ago. That in itself wasn't so uncommon. A good many black women had raised countless white children across the face of the South. What was rare was the fact that they had remained so close for so long, that the bond between them—far deeper and more profound for the day and age than was normal—had transcended the role of servant and mistress. The bond was friendship and, yes, even love and respect. The friendship, love, and respect of equals in an unequal time. "No," Immelda finally said. "I s'pose you're right. It's jus' that me and Tobias worries for you, Miss Celia. We knows you doin' what you thinks you gotta do, an' we don't mind helpin' where we can, but we still worries."

"I'm sorry for that," Celia replied honestly. "I wish—"

"An' now," Immelda interrupted, posing formidably with her arms crossed over her spare bosom, "I ain't listenin' to no more of your foolishness. I know what you about to say, but me and Tobias stayin' with you 'cause we wants to. You tell us we free, right? Your daddy give us papers an' such, right?"

"Yes. Of course."

"Well, free folk stay an' go where they choose. We here 'cause we *choose* to, just so!"

"Oh, Immelda." Celia reached from the tub, took one of the black woman's hands and held it. "I'm glad you stayed with me," she said huskily, wishing she could take Immelda and Tobias with her. "I'd be lonely in this old house all by myself. And I can't think of anyone else I'd rather be with."

Immelda squeezed Celia's hand and patted it affectionately. "An' so all's settled," she concluded with an emphatic nod. "An' time for the both of us to get crackin', too. I got Tobias to feed, an' that cookin' to do for the picnic, less'n you're gonna go empty-handed. Your breakfast'll be ready when you comes down. That an' the cocoa. I know how Mistuh Lattimore likes his cocoa of a Sunday mornin'." She started out. "Not much left, though."

Celia thought Immelda had left when she stuck her head back in through the doorway. "Honey, how many times we done had this same talk?"

"About three times too many, I guess," Celia said with a wry smile.

"Then let's not have it no more. We all of us do what we do, and that's the pig an' the poke of it."

Celia lay back a moment, then sighed and heaved herself out of the water to dry and dress. She stepped to the window, threw up the sash, and opened the shutters. The cool air felt refreshing on her still steaming body, and she came fully awake at last. Outside the day was well underway. Sounds muffled only seconds earlier were sharp and clear. Horses clip-clopped across the cobblestones. Wagon wheels rumbled. Below, the peacock and his three hens, her father's favorite animals, strutted about the backyard. Far to the east, a low rumble hinted of cannonades, and closer, from the river below and the overlooking bluffs, Union and Confederate gunners traded shots. Celia wrapped the towel around herself and craned her head out the window in time to see the wiggling arc of smoke from the fuse of a ball that sailed harmlessly past and, though falling far short of the trenches a mile and a half to the east, landed harmlessly in an empty lot on the next hillside. "How strange!" she thought. "Shells bursting about our ears, and we think it commonplace. I suppose if it gets much worse we too shall have to move to a cave. I hope not, though."

The bells began to ring again. Far across town, the Baptist church bells pealed their welcome and call to worship. Nearer, the Episcopalians joined in, followed by the Catholics' call for eight o'clock mass. In another hour, as the parishioners were leaving, the bells would ring again in an ecumenical arrangement with the Methodist church, whose tower had yet to be repaired, and whose new brass bells rested on the Union-held wharves in New Orleans.

An hour. Which meant she had less than that in which to get ready. Hurrying, Celia finished drying and began to dress. Mr. Lattimore hated to be kept waiting.

CHAPTER 6

He knew how the dream would end and so dreaded its beginning. The dream was only a year old, but during that year had visited him with maddening frequency. It was a strangely convoluted dream that began with the slow realization he was dreaming. The muscles in Tom Stewart's arms and legs and back tightened. A dry grating sound of grinding molars accompanied the tightening. Lately, sometimes, he whimpered, too.

He was sleeping on a floor. Exhausted, for he had worked hard the night before, he lay without moving until he became aware of the wetness underneath him. At first the wet was warm, but as it cooled and became uncomfortable, he slowly woke to find himself in a semi-darkened room. Always the same room. Always the distant bedlam of groans and piteous mewlings. Cursing, Tom rose on one elbow, then to a sitting position, and looked around to find himself in the center of a monstrous pile of amputated arms and legs, each of which oozed drops of blood that ran down the pile to form rivulets to feed the viscous lake of blood in which he lay. Whereupon he shrugged, stretched unconcernedly, went back to sleep, and then woke for real, panting and bathed in sweat. So it was on this Sunday morning when he fought the dream and lost and woke to reach for the bottle he had taken to keeping by the side of his bed. A moment later, Kentucky whiskey burning in his throat, he fell back, pulled the quilt over his head, and lay in the rose milky dimness while the whiskey went to work.

What peace he hoped to find under the covers quickly fled. He could smell Solange in the pillow next to him and in the empty mattress space beside him. The night before, lurking just outside his dream, she tried to waken him. Her hands were on his chest. Her lips, teeth, tongue—tools of an ardent gardener at work in a fallow field—worked across his stomach. She prodded him and nursed him, played and poked before growing desperate and retreating. Once lusty and alive, he lay alone next to her and knew that he had become a soggy lump of blood moist clay in which nothing grew. His roots were limp and powerless, rotting, lifeless . . .

One hand snaked out from underneath the quilt and snagged the bottle again. *Maybe tonight,* Solange, he thought, swallowing. *Maybe tonight.*

The whiskey cut the bitter, burned taste in his mouth. Suddenly determined, he threw back the covers and sat up, corked the bottle, and put it away. "But maybe not, too." Legs over the side. "You want so damned much. A house on a hill." He coughed, beat his chest with his fist, shook his head, blinked, and yawned. "Ten servants in place of the four we have to do the work of two. New clothes when there aren't any to be had. This and that and that and this, and on top of everything else, you want me to spurt life."

What was there about the day he was supposed to remember? Ah, yes. Moving day. A Union mortar boat had overshot the dock area and lobbed a cannon ball through the porch the day before and so the Stewarts were at least joining the lead of the hundreds of others who had moved to caves, responding to the sloppy marksmanship of Yankee gunners with the age-old adage of better safe than sorry. Tom stood and moved his arms in circles to get the blood circulating. "Moving into a cave. Burying ourselves. And out of this she wants life. Life from the reaper, but the man who wields the scythe has forgotten how to plant. Life indeed." The church bells clamored. Tom Stewart stripped off his nightgown and stood naked in the eight o'clock light.

"Missus Stewart waitin' for you downstairs, suh," a venerable white-haired Negro said from across the room.

Tom gave a start. He had not heard Harmon enter.

"She say to remind you of the picnic this noon, and that I should lay out the brown suit. It do look like a warm day comin', an' the brown be more comfortable."

"Mmmm." Tom stuck out his tongue, leaned closer to the mirror, and wished he hadn't. "I suppose. The brown will do nicely. My wife?"

"Yassuh. In the breakfast room."

"Or in a foul mood, which ever comes first," Tom muttered to himself. He slipped into the robe Harmon held for him and checked himself in the mirror. A heavyset, prematurely balding man with thick brown sideburns and a face creased from worry stared back at him. Tom Stewart had never considered himself handsome, but the past months had robbed him, he thought, of even that certain agreeable boyishness that tended to put patients at ease. Now his ravaged features looked stern and dour and foreboding, far older than his chronological thirty-two years. Children no longer offered to carry his bag.

The wonder is she still cares at all, he thought with a grimace, turning away from the mirror. Tom blamed the war for changing him so completely. Delicate and fine boned almost to fragility, and wanting to escape from a life with no secure tomorrow, Solange had latched onto a totally different man that day he had seen her strolling along Dauphin Street in New Orleans and offered her a ride in his carriage. He was smiling then, cheerful, bright, and witty. Devil-may-care, the matrons of Vicksburg called him. That night, when he went to the Cabaret Belle Heure where he saw her dance and sing, and when he sent his card back to her dressing room, she responded by visiting his table and spending every minute offstage at his side. Later, in the wee hours when the sky was pearl gray with morning light, he could not believe his good fortune when she accompanied him to breakfast and then home to his apartment. What followed was best done far from the eyes and ears of Vicksburg. Even in a day and age when single young men were allowed a great deal of latitude, Tom's conduct would have raised eyebrows, not to speak of the collective dander of the ladies of Vicksburg who didn't take kindly to one of their most eligible bachelors being snapped up by an outsider. Especially a worldly wise Frenchwoman, especially a cabaret singer and dancer. Dander be damned, though, a bewitched Tom had decided, and married Solange a week later, the day before he was scheduled to return home.

"And lived happily ever after," he said aloud, with a glance to the bedside cabinet where the whiskey bottle sat.

"Suh?" Harmon asked, pausing at the armoire.

"Nothing," Tom replied, shaking his head as if waking.

"You feelin' poorly, Doctuh Stewart?"

Tom steadied himself, stretched, and reached down to touch his toes. Discreetly, he slid the bottle underneath the bed. "Just fine, Harmon," he lied.

The old Negro pretended he didn't see the bottle to which he added watered-down whiskey every day, watched his master do the silly bouncing and dipping. "Well," he finally said, returning to his duties, "you the doctuh."

Tom grunted and pounded his stomach with his fists. "That's right." His stomach jiggled alarmingly. He looked distastefully at the expanding rolls of fat, then laughed at the ludicrousness of his situation. In the prime of life, supposedly. Damned good at his profession. Started out the day with whiskey to chase away the night. Couldn't get his pecker up for his wife, one of the most beautiful women in town. It was all so ludicrous he *had* to laugh. Either that or go completely mad. "That's right, Harmon," he repeated, monstrously amused. "I am the doctor."

Solange wasn't laughing. Crossing and recrossing the sun parlor, her shadow flitting across the rapidly cooling breakfast, she paced like a caged tigress. They didn't usually take breakfast in that room, but virtually all of the rest of the downstairs furniture had been moved to the cave where they'd take up residence later that afternoon. The idea of living underground was galling, but she couldn't stand the tension anymore. As if to reemphasize her fears, a double explosion from the river batteries rattled the windows. Solange flinched and hurried from the sun parlor, to continue her pacing in the empty dining room.

"Josey," Solange snapped, her voice cracking like a silk whip.

A dark face framed with kinky black hair appeared in the kitchen doorway. "Yes'm?"

"Where's Harmon?"

"Upstairs, ma'am. Fetchin' Dr. Tom like you told him, ma'am." Josey edged away from her mistress's wrath. "You don' mind, ma'am, I'se packin' this kitchen stuff, an' Zenia, she say dat I gots to keep movin' 'cause we—"

"*Très bien. Allez-vous-en!*" Solange ordered, in her anger reverting to French.

Josey, being new to the household, was ignorant of French, but not of wrath in its many guises. Relieved, she scurried out of harm's way and back to the kitchen.

Solange continued her pacing, and with it reviewed the catalogue of disillusion that had grown by leaps and bounds during the past year. When she had met, wooed, and won her husband two years earlier, she had been dazzled by his charm, impressed by his professional status, and convinced that he was her best chance yet to rise above the petty affairs that held others to the grubby level of existence to which she was so unfortunately accustomed. For the first year of her marriage, she did not question her judgment. Increasingly, during the second, she watched Tom Stewart's charm become a facade easily torn by the day-to-day routine of caring for the ill and, later, the maimed and dying. His professional status, while conferring respect on him, did not extend as fully to her as she would have expected had they lived in Europe. And his determination to rise socially had been the euphoric daydreaming of a man newly and hopelessly in love.

Rise, Solange sneered mentally. Rise, indeed. On all sides, the Bartletts, the Lattimores, the Caldervilles, the DuBois, the Laughtons, and others lived in large and gracious mansions that dominated the hilltops. And where did she live? On Locust Street between Grove and Clay, without a view of the river, on a flat narrow lot between two of the buckled, heaving apron slopes that gave Vicksburg, in this time of war, its strategic importance. The house was spacious, true, but Solange wasted no time in being grateful for what she had. She aspired to hilltops and was forced to settle for a valley nearly surrounded by humble dogtrot homes and shacks. She aspired to social preeminence and was forced to suffer the ignominious truth that she was not on every invitation list and that not every front door automatically opened to her. All the more infuriating, Tom Stewart was satisfied. When Solange railed at him, he replied that they lived comfortably and well, that their house, though not as ostentatious as some, was quite handsome and large enough in contrast to many. He enjoyed his friends, or more properly those who had not marched off to war. He did not aspire to greatness. His one cause was the furtherance of his country, the Confederate States of America; his one goal was to serve humanity to the best of his ability.

Solange could not bear his satisfaction, ascribe to his cause, nor share his goal. Solange had never been satisfied and had no use for either causes or goals unless they concerned her own personal well-being. Solange was, then, selfish as one who has known poverty and deprivation can be selfish: not out of meanness but out of fear. And though Solange thought she loved Tom, the truth was that she loved herself better, and her husband enjoyed her love only so long as he gratified her every need. Thus began the litany of his failures. Solange was hungry, and he was making her wait for breakfast. Solange was bored, and he was moving her to a cave. And worst of all, Solange ached miserably, and he hadn't made love to her for months.

"I'm sorry I'm late."

Solange froze and whirled at the sound of his voice. Wearing his robe, his hair still tousled from sleep, Tom stood in the doorway. Solange pointed dramatically to the breakfast table. "Breakfast is cold," she snapped. "Cold eggs, cold bacon, cold toast. The tea might still be lukewarm."

She was so beautiful. The sun streaming through the porch window fired her auburn hair. Her peignoir shifted alluringly when she moved and allowed glimpses of sensual contours—a hip, the slightly rounded abdomen, a crescent of breast, still taut at twenty-nine. "I'll enjoy it all the same," he said with a wry smile. "Really, Solange, it's only food. There's no reason to be so angry. We'll simply ask Zenia to heat it up or cook more."

"No, we won't. Zenia has the kitchen halfway dismantled. Or have you forgotten?"

"Of course not. I merely didn't think she'd moved so quickly. Speed isn't one of the attributes—" He paused and winced as the batteries along the river began exchanging cannonades with Union gunboats. "Well. Perhaps I'd just been asking the wrong way. When did this arrive?" he asked, sitting and picking up a letter propped against his coffee cup.

"Just after I came downstairs," Solange said, picking at her eggs, and pushing her plate back. "A soldier brought it. You're supposed to read it immediately."

"Damn! Wouldn't you know." He broke the seal and pulled out a sheet of paper. "Oh, Lord."

"What?" Solange asked, alarmed.

The *Bayou Belle* made it after all, and with the consignment of chloroform, dressings, and medicine that we requested. One of us must itemize and distribute them as we discussed the other day. I would ask Dr. Cline to do this, but a new batch of wounded came in last night, and he was hard at work until six this morning and is all in. Sorry if this interrupts any of your plans. Best to you and Mrs. Stewart.

Edgar T. Wharton

P.S. See that an extra case of chloroform gets to the Church Street hospital. They're about out after last night.

He handed the letter across the table to Solange. "I didn't ask for this," he said apologetically.

Solange read quickly, crumpled the paper, and threw it onto the plate with her uneaten eggs. "You said—"

"I know what I said, Solange. You don't need to tell me what I said. But an order is an order."

"Words, words, words. He *didn't* order you. He requested—"

"The same thing, as you well know." Tom poured tea for himself and started on his eggs.

"In other words, you won't be taking me to the picnic then," Solange said icily.

"I have no choice, damn it! You know what's happening out there. We don't even know how many men we have now, much less how many we'll have by tonight or tomorrow. There are certain responsibilities that take precedence . . ." There was no sense in going on. Nothing he said would make a difference. Tom sighed and turned to his eggs. "I'd better hurry, I suppose."

Solange's face was white. She gnawed on her lower lip and stared out the window at the carefully arranged rows of flowers bordering the lawn, beyond that to the street and the house across the street that blocked the view of the river. On the hilltop, there would be nothing to block the view. "Yes," she said bitterly. "Your *other* responsibilities —which take precedence in all things."

Tom stared at his toast. It was better than meeting her stare.

"Your last word then. You will not keep your promise?"

"What do you want, Solange?" he asked, angry at last. "You want me to let them lie there and die? You want me to let men bleed to death so I can go to a God-damn picnic?" Trembling with rage, he propped his elbows on the edge of the table and covered his face with his hands. "Very well," he finally said, the words muffled. "I'll try. Maybe I can speed things along and join you later. That's the best I can do."

Coldly, deliberately, Solange picked up her cup and poured her tea over her food. The thin brown liquid flowed beneath bridges of bacon, swirled around yellow islands of eggs, soaked into a soggy shoreline of buttered toast. Her chair scraped across the floor as she stood and stalked from the room, muttering in French as she left. Most of what she said was so much gibberish, but he understood one word. Bastard. Well, maybe he was, Tom thought, staring at her plate and losing his appetite. He tried his tea, but it left a tepid bitterness in his mouth. Giving up, he left the parlor, angled through the foyer, and was halfway up the stairs when her door slammed. "Solange!" he called, stopping outside the guest bedroom door. "Solange!"

"Go to your responsibilities, *allez-vous-en!*" her voice called back from within.

Tom gnawed at the inside of his mouth and reached the only decision he could make. "I'll look for you at the picnic," he said to the door. "Early afternoon. I'll be there, Solange."

The hall was empty. The rug, paintings, and furniture had been removed to the cave next door. Hurrying, he returned to his bedroom to find his bed stripped and Harmon, in his shirtsleeves, taking down the last of the paintings. Tom shrugged out of his robe. "Hot water first, Harmon, so I can shave. And then my black coat and trousers. The best, too."

Harmon set down the painting and glanced at the brown suit neatly arranged on the bed. "I already done laid out the brown, Doctuh. That black'll be too hot for wearin' out in the countryside. The black's for de hospital . . ." Harmon caught himself, was silenced by a stern glance from Tom, who knew precisely, after all the last terrible months, what the black suit was for.

Neither a sudden glimmer of reconciliation, nor the view of the city, nor curiosity alone led Solange to the balcony where she watched her husband's carriage roll past on its way to the work that, saving so many other lives, had taken so much of his and hers. It was nostalgia. Solange had been reading the works of a French poet, François du Monde, as he had called himself, a man of whom the world had not and never would hear. Poet, Parisian, starving scholar, and lover, he epitomized everything the adolescent Solange thought worthwhile in the scrubby, drab world she had once inhabited. Best of all, he loved to watch her dance. Solange was thirteen when he taught her the ways and joys of love, fifteen when he gave her a hand-printed copy of his poems, seventeen when he died of pneumonia in his garret, too poor to afford even the most meager and impotent medicines.

Bad food and worse wine had been more than good enough with François at her side. Without him, Solange recognized her life for what it was, a shabby, dreary existence eked out in sous and occasional francs, and a deadly procession of bistros and beds that led to an early old age and death. So it was that one year to the day after François' death she determined to climb into the light and stay there. She scrimped and saved and stole. She avoided sex, for sex inevitably brought the twin scourges of disease and pregnancy, not to speak of danger at the hands of degenerates. She read every newspaper she could lay her hands on and studied the occasional book that came her way. Carefully, she traveled to far parts of Paris to change sous to francs and francs to gold sovereigns. When two years had passed, she counted her savings and determined that, with care, she could afford the clothes and cosmetics and quarters that would give her the chance to snare a man of means. The only drawback was time. If she did not succeed in three months, she would once again be destitute.

Against all likelihood, she found a man, an American patron who, though married, brought her to America, taught her English, and set her up in her own apartment in New Orleans. When he died, there were two other men, and finally Tom Stewart, still young and full of life and with a future. Most of all, this gentle man stirred in her memories of older days and, for the first time in ten years since François' death, she was sure she had fallen in love. She did not understand at the time, of course, that the early stirrings of a war she cared nothing about carried a disease as deadly to Tom Stewart as the pneumonia had been to her beloved François.

The morning mist had burned off, the flowers were bright, the birds lovely in song. Tired from a sleepless night, worn from her emotional confrontation at the breakfast table, Solange leaned against the rail and let the sun soak into and warm her face and throat. No balcony, no sun tomorrow, she thought, the bitterness heavily tinged with relief. Dark but safe. But for how long? A day? A week? A month? Little more than a stone's throw away, the mouth of the cave they'd live in gaped in the side of the next hill to the west. She had been inside twice; once when the initial digging had been completed, once two days ago when Harmon and Lemuel started moving the rugs and furniture and clothes. Tom had urged her to spend more time there so the shock of underground life would not be quite so sharp, but . . .

She could not remember a time when she was not aware of a man's interest. Slowly, appearing unconcerned, she turned and looked down. Two wagons were passing. A man, his wife, and three children, dressed for church, walked along the side of the street. Two boys pushing a cart— And then she saw him.

The rider emerged from behind one of the wagons. Sagging in the saddle of a weary dun gelding, he wore dust-colored breeches, a gray shirt, and a butternut coat. A sweat-stained floppy flat-brimmed hat cast a shadowy mask over his face. No matter how tired he looked, no matter that she couldn't see his eyes, she knew he was staring at her because she could feel the warmth in her cheeks and loins, the faint tingling sensation in her fingertips.

"You want to wear the pink o' the white, Missus Stewart?" Zenia asked from the open door.

Mesmerized, Solange didn't hear her.

"Ah said—"

Solange stared as Zenia materialized at her side.

"Does you want to wear the pink o' the white?"

"Oh! The uh . . . white, I believe. Yes. The white."

"What you *lookin'* at, girl?" Zenia's eyes widened and she sniffed imperiously. "Humph! It's a no-good day now fo' sure, if that Micah Lattimore is ridin' back to town. Bad enough we gots Yankees all around without him, too. Best you get off'n this balcony, Missus Stewart," she said, stalking back inside. "That sort of man ain't fit fo' the likes of you to sashay in front of."

Fit or no, Solange couldn't resist a last look. Turning, her breath caught in her throat. Micah had reined in a little past the house and sat staring at her while he removed his coat. She had met him once shortly after she had arrived in Vicksburg and had found him handsome but, given her love for Tom at the time, uninteresting. The effect now was totally different. His shirt, a castoff perhaps, for it was too small for his chest, was open to the midriff and the sleeves were missing. Tanned almost as dark as a black man's, his arms were wiry and muscular. The hair on them, bleached white by the sun, made them appear to glow. He seemed to fill the street, to clog the air, with his presence.

"Solange Stewart."

Solange jerked as if slapped.

Micah swept his hat from his head. "I should have come back much sooner." His voice was deep and resonant. His face, unshaven for a week, was almost malevolently handsome. His hair was a black mane shot through with silver. His eyes glittered with a predatory icelike chill that sent shivers up Solange's spine. "Or never left at all."

Her mouth opened to say something, then closed. Her joints felt as if they were made of molasses. Slowly, Solange became aware that, with the sun at her back, her gown and peignoir were well-nigh transparent. More slowly yet, with Micah Lattimore's laughter nipping at her heels, she fled into the guest room. A moment later when, despite herself, she parted the curtains on the west window, he was already riding off. But even when he turned the corner onto Grove Street and disappeared, she had the distinct feeling he was still watching her. And that they would meet again.

CHAPTER 7

"Sure you won't change your mind and come with me?" Rafe asked, putting down his coffee cup.

"Of course I'm sure."

"Seems like you ought to. Prodigal son returned and all that."

"That's right. And have to listen to every old biddy there tell me, 'what a miracle,' and 'how the Lord has blessed you,' and 'how fine he looks, why the very flower of manhood,' and so on."

"Well?" Rafe asked.

"I'm not saying it isn't true, damn it," Nathaniel blustered. "Just that I don't want to listen. Some things a man needs to be quietly thankful for. No, you take your moment of glory."

"I'm not concerned about the glory, damn it. It's . . . well, it's . . . Celia," Rafe finally admitted. "She walked out on me, and I still don't know why. And I don't know whether I'm more worried about embarrassing her or me."

"Nonsense," Nathaniel snorted. "She'll be delighted." He paused, stared into the sun-dappled pattern on the tablecloth. There was more to say, to fit into that painful silence, but the truth—the real truth that except for Micah he alone knew—was too dangerous. If it weren't for Micah . . . Micah, who'd been such a beautiful child and then, while Nathaniel watched helplessly, had grown wild and undisciplined and downright cruel. Even now, banished and disinherited since the night he had boasted drunkenly to Nathaniel of raping Celia, enough of the evil that Micah spawned lingered to make him a liar by omission. Now, with that modicum of wisdom that comes with more than a half century on earth, Nathaniel was ready to shoulder some of the blame. But not all of it, damn it, he swore silently. Rafe was of his seed, too. Whatever had twisted Micah, in Rafe left strength and sense of purpose, left just enough of a reckless streak for him to be human but still a man of honor. No. There were no more answers now in the time it took the sunshine to travel half the width of a knife, than there had been in all the sleepless nights of knowing what had happened, but not what to do about it. There was only time to keep on to the next minute and hour and day.

"Penny," Rafe said, jolting Nathaniel back to awareness.

"Just gathering wool. Waste of time, I guess," Nathaniel said, moving the knife into the sun again. "No sense in holding what a woman said or did over two years ago against her. If you're still interested, go see her. You'll both have a thing or two to talk about after all this time."

"Maybe," Rafe said thoughtfully, remembering. Remembering the clandestine meetings. Remembering his argument with Micah. Remembering Celia's departure without a word of warning or explanation. "And maybe better if you came along. Easier, certainly." He looked up as the clock on the sideboard began to chime eight thirty. "At any rate, it'll be moot if I don't get on my way."

"No need to worry on that score. I'm always late. That way I miss the infernal singing. Can't stand the caterwauling. Give me a reading from the Good Book, threaten me with hell fire and perdition, and send me on my way," Nathaniel proclaimed.

"Sounds like good advice to me," Rafe said, unable to suppress a smile.

Nathaniel snorted. "Think that's funny, eh?"

"No, sir. I never thought hell fire and perdition was funny."

The older man peered over his glasses at his son. "Didn't tell you," he said, seemingly changing the subject. "I ran into Phillip Laughton on the docks last night. He's a captain now." Nathaniel well knew that Rafe and Phillip, for years and no known reason, had been politely but coolly at odds with each other. "Unlike some," he added impishly, "he's a polite young man. Courteous. Respectful."

Phillip Laughton. The name grated on Rafe's ears. Granted he had been cruel that afternoon they'd killed the deer, but Phillip had harbored the grudge for so long that Rafe finally had lost all respect for him. "Phillip always was courteous," he said, disguising sarcasm with a smile. "Does he still pick his ears?"

"I knew it!" Nathaniel exploded. His cheeks turned beet red beneath his sideburns and his fist crashed down on the table. Cups rattled. A fork jumped off a plate and clinked against a glass.

Recognizing his father's rage for the sham it was, Rafe laughed. "Well, he did," he said, teasing. "You've seen him yourself."

"Stop baiting me! Just because you've come back from the dead don't think you've earned special treatment around here. Not from me, by heaven."

"Carriage is out front, suh," one of the servants announced, poking his head through the door and saving Rafe from further castigation.

Rafe rose and dropped his napkin on the table. "We'll be back a little after church to take you to the picnic," he said, starting for the door and then turning to bow deeply. "Sir," he added, immediately holding up his hand to stop the blistering attack he could see coming. "All in fun, Father," he said. "I'm glad to be home. Very, *very* glad to be home."

Nathaniel watched him go, picked at a biscuit, then sat staring into space. The one son left to him, the one he thought surely dead, had come back. They'd talked until near dawn, slept a couple of hours, and then talked again. It was the best time Nathaniel could remember having in two years. Oh, there'd been work to keep him occupied. Plantations didn't run themselves, especially during the war when transportation, markets, and good foremen were hard to find. There'd been friends and a social life, too: church, politics, all the things a man did with his time. Most of all there'd been Hal, of course. He and Hal had been diametrically opposed on the slavery issue—their arguments had raged for hours on end—but the closest of friends, nonetheless. Hal's death six weeks earlier had left a void that would take a long time to fill.

Nathaniel hadn't realized how much conversation had meant to him and how much he'd missed it. Serious talk, banter, arguments waged fiercely over the most trivial point. Hours spent with cigars and brandy and, most of all, words and more words and more words. That was the best part of having a son. All those years of rearing a child. Baby talk, boy talk. The fickle, fey, callow arguments of a young man coming to terms with a large and complex world. And then the blooming! Once they'd been on their own for a while, tasted of life and death, got a few years behind them, then, by God, they suddenly became worth every penny and minute and worry and fear spent. Life held many and great pleasures, but none was so keen as the pleasure of sharing one's thoughts and ideas and humor with a son grown to manhood.

"One of the things you missed, Hal," Nathaniel muttered finishing the now cold coffee and wearily pushing away from the table. It had been a long night and he was tired, glad he had decided to forego the day's organized religion for a moment of quiet and solitary contemplation. Slowly, in deference to his rheumatism, he made his way across the dining room and to the second floor, then carefully up the narrow hardwood stairs to the cupola, an amber glass-enclosed cubicle thrusting up from the middle of the roof. A widow's walk ran the length of the peaked roof, but Nathaniel was uncertain of the railing. He was better off inside anyway, he thought, sitting on a dust-covered bench. Quieter inside. Warmer, too. Be nice if there were a little less dust, of course. He'd remind Hanna to get to that one of these days.

Bells and shells. God had to be on somebody's side. It only made sense. He counted. One, two, three, four, five, boom, seven, eight, nine. A strange way to ring the hour. He tugged his watch from his vest pocket. Inside the cover was a miniature silhouette, painted the week before she died, of his wife. He smiled at her, propped her against the window so she could see out, too, then gazed over the city to the horizon across the river, and beyond that to the distant blue of eternal space.

"Thank you, God," he said in the amber silence. "Thank you for bringing him home."

Sunday morning and an empty house. Celia wasn't yet used to the idea of her father's absence, still expected to hear him call, see him waiting at the table, or emerging from his room. Dressed and with nothing to do for the next few minutes, she wandered from her room into her father's upstairs study to open the curtains and bask quietly in the Sunday morning calm. The Union gunboats were out of sight around the bend in the river. Men were busy on the docks, as they would have been had the war never begun. Mockingbirds and jays squabbled over ownership of the garden. Nothing had changed, all was as all ever had been.

And yet it wasn't, of course. Innocence wasn't a quality one could recall at a whim. One could only pretend, and in that pretense hope to bury the past so completely that no ghosts could ever again rise to threaten the future. How that was to be accomplished, though, was no easy task. For just as time had dulled her thirst for vengeance and her father's and Rafe's deaths had removed the major reason for her fear of discovery, so had Anthony's surprising appearance awakened the past and necessitated a return to the dangerous game of spying. Anthony was, in short, a catalyst, a link to the past, to emotions best forgotten, to barely healed wounds that opened at a touch and festered anew.

The carefully constructed defenses weakened, the past flooded back. Secession, the outbreak of hostilities, the war brought to her very doorstep. Could two and a half years have passed so quickly? The days that led to the tedious journey north and the fateful meeting with Powell played out like a mural painted on glass that had been shattered. Unwillingly, yet unable to stop, Celia inspected each minute and gleaming shard. Here was Rafe, handsome and strong, with sensitive eyes that bored to the core of her soul, now impetuous, now tender, now awkward in his role of younger son defying father and older brother. Rafe the gentleman, gallant to a fault and perhaps too much the perfectionist, too much a stickler for form and tradition. And now, too, she thought sorrowfully, lost at sea, dead like so many others. At least he had died in blissful ignorance of his brother's perfidy. As had her father. He, too, she saw, not yet an invalid, still filled with life and the excitement of business, politics, friends, and family. Here, too, were those minor characters, friends and acquaintances from church and society, laughing as they visited and gossiped and dined in the social whirl that was life in a world without worry or disruption.

And then . . . And then, so abruptly, so suddenly, he was gone, and having foreseen the possibility of his death didn't lessen the shock. With his passing—she had heard his strangled call for help from the very spot in which she stood now—the study had seemed cold and empty, cursed with the unyielding darkness of death. Timidly, she glanced at his portrait, then quickly away. Downstairs would be brighter, gayer, fresher. The windows would be open to cool off the house, then closed at noon to trap the cool air. Downstairs, the sun parlor, the dining room, and the study would be cheerfully awash with sunlight and redolent with the perfume of Immelda's freshly baked Sunday morning cinnamon rolls.

The clock chimed. Old grandfather clock calling in solemn tones that filtered up the main stairway and permeated every nook and cranny of the second-story rooms. Quickly, Celia turned and, determined to be cheerful, swept out of the study. It was Sunday morning, at a quarter to nine. Nathaniel would be arriving any moment for his weekly rolls and hot chocolate. After church they would go to the picnic together and, in spite of whatever fate had in store for the massed armies to the east, celebrate their defiance of the Union and their confidence in their own strength and resilience. She had just stepped into the hall when she heard, reverberating through the house, Immelda's scream of terror.

CHAPTER 8

She had been betrayed! Anthony had been discovered and informed on her and the Vigilance Committee had come for her! Thoughtless, knees almost too weak to support her, she leaned against the wall at the top of the stairs. They would make short work of Anthony. As for her? . . . She had to escape, to flee. But where? Or how? On one of the fire ropes coiled in the bedrooms? If they'd broken into the house, surely they would have occupied the grounds, too. No. There was no escape. She had chosen her course and must now stand firm. The taste of fear was sharp, like copper, but gave her strength. Powell had been graphic enough. The ignominy of hot tar spilling over her body and feathers choking her. Lifelong friends turning against her with hatred and vituperation. In her mind's eye she pictured a noose and gallows, and herself facing death alone and fearlessly, like Marie Antoinette or Mary, Queen of Scots, head high, undaunted, her emotions hidden from the rabble.

"Then let them do their worst," she said aloud, picking up her skirt and starting down the stairs.

The foyer, wide and shadowed, dominated by a mammoth coatrack, was empty save for Immelda, who was pressed against the wall, her back straight against the papered plaster. Her mouth was frozen in an O, and she pointed with unsteady finger toward the sun parlor. Celia, thoroughly confused, glanced down the hall and glimpsed a flutter of shadow. "Don't worry, Immelda," she said, sounding much braver than she felt. "No harm will come to you or Tobias. This is something we should have expected a long time ago."

"You . . . you better see . . . for youse'f," Immelda whispered in a choked voice.

That they might arrest her was one thing, but to march in without the slightest regard for common civility and in the process frighten her servant was quite another. Celia squared her shoulders and, skirt flowing behind her, swept imperiously down the hall. "You have no right, gentlemen," she announced melodramatically as she entered the sun parlor, "to intru . . . Oh, my God!"

Rafe Lattimore was standing at the window and looking out at the garden. The sunlight melted around his shoulders and shone on his long, well-brushed hair. "But, you see, there's only one of me," he said, turning.

Celia froze in her tracks. "I . . . I didn't . . . Rafe?" Her hand fluttered to her lips and she had to steady herself against a chair to keep from falling. "Is that you?" she asked, unable to believe her eyes. "Is it *really* you?"

"Yes." His eyes glinted with an emerald light. His cheeks were tanned a dark bronze. He stared at her, drinking in the sight of her and then, smiling, walked toward her, bowed, and lightly kissed the back of her hand as proof of his existence. "I'm really me. And I hope you will accept this substitute for my father. He insisted I come alone, and I didn't argue overly long."

"Land sakes, Miss Celia!" Immelda said, bursting into the room and shying to one side just in case. "This man like to scare me to death. I opens the door an' there he is standin' on the porch. I thought the good Lawd had done gone an' signed my name in the heaven book for sure. I couldn't move. An' then he jes' walk right in an' say to tell you he's in the parlor an' I couldn't find my tongue to do nothin' but scream. Wasn't 'til you come in here I figgered there ain't no ghost who shows hisself in the light of day, 'cause night's the time for them poor souls to walk about, so it has to be Mr. Rafe. The onliest Mr. Rafe, alive an' in the flesh." Breathless, Immelda took a hesitant step forward and reached out a tentative hand to touch Rafe's sleeve. "You is alive, ain't you, Mr. Rafe?"

"I think so," Rafe said, laughing. "You'd better go reassure Tobias, though. I asked him to watch the carriage, but the last I looked he was holding the reins and staring off kind of sicklike."

"It's lucky he didn't just drop dead on the spot," Immelda said with a self-conscious laugh. Embarrassed, she edged toward the door. "I'll tell him things is right as rain. An' . . . an' well, jes' praise the Lawd you are home safe an' sound, Mr. Rafe."

"Thank you, Immelda. I appreciate that." He watched her leave, turned back to Celia. "And you?" he asked, plumbing the soft, smoky depths of her eyes for a trace of the love they had once shared.

Celia let go the chair, took two faltering steps, and sank on the couch.

"Are you all right?"

She nodded, watched blankly as he sat beside her. *My God*, she thought, her brain racing. *He's alive! Here and alive and looking just the same . . . no, not exactly the same.* Thin lines from salt wind and sea sun crinkled the skin around his eyes. An inch-long crescent scar was a streak of white fire across his cheekbone. Rather than marring his features, it hinted of mysterious and dangerous escapades, and made him look more attractive. "I . . . I don't know what to say," she stammered at last.

"Happy to see you. Glad you're alive. Thank God, you're safe. I missed you. Take me in your arms. Any of those will do." Rafe rested one arm along the back of the sofa, let two fingers brush her shoulder. "That is, if you are indeed happy to see me."

He was back. Alive! Come home to her! She could feel his touch, taste his lips on hers. And then, like ice water pouring over her, she remembered the touch of another man at another time. Two and a half years compressed into a single second, and she saw Micah standing in front of her. Micah, whose memory she had, if not forgotten, at least learned to control since he had disappeared from Vicksburg a little over a year earlier. Micah, whose name . . . whose name. . . .

Celia shuddered, put her hands to her cheeks, then over her ears. Not to keep out the sound, which came from within her, but in some muddled logic to keep it trapped inside her so Rafe wouldn't hear and learn the truth. Suddenly, all the old guilts and fears were sweeping over her and she was vulnerable again. There was no sense in fooling herself. She could no more have Rafe now than on that day when she left.

"Of course, I'm delighted. I mean, that is, we . . . missed you. . . ." The words sounded inane and empty, but she forced herself to go on. "We heard your ship had been lost," she said, control returning. "At first we hoped you'd be like so many others listed as missing or dead who showed up fighting somewhere else, but then word came that another ship had found the wreckage, but no survivors. Your father must be ecstatic."

Rafe smiled to hide the hollow feeling. Why was she so obviously taken aback, so shaken, so elated one moment, and so coolly reserved the next? The answer lay sometime in those few days before Christmas two years ago. Whatever had happened then to change her mind had, in the space of seconds, happened again. And whatever it was must have been cataclysmic to be so strongly felt even now. If he could only delve into that past and fathom its secrets, perhaps he could melt her reserve and find, once again, the woman who had professed her love and betrothed herself to him with each kiss and embrace. "He is. But no more than I am."

"Nor than I," Celia said warmly. After two years as Powell's agent, of hiding her real identity and feelings, playing a role was almost second nature to her. If she could dissimulate for all of Vicksburg for so long, surely she could present a cheerful and vivacious face to Rafe.

Once the need for control was recognized, it was easy to observe the social niceties. "But when?"

"Last night. On the *Bayou Belle*."

"Snag Parken's boat," Celia said and laughed. "Who else could get through? That was a sad day when he and Father parted company."

"About your father . . . I'm sorry, Celia."

"He had great plans for you. Hopes and aspirations, as he said once." Celia rose, walked to the mantel, and picked up a model of a centerboard schooner. "I think he would have wanted you to have this."

Rafe inspected the model. Each line, each spar and sail of the centerboard schooner had been recreated in exact miniature. "The *Dolphin*," he said, setting it on the table. Even the centerboard, rigged with tiny blocks, worked. "A fine ship. All seventy-eight feet of her. Not a better blockade runner in the gulf. You know, I loved this ship."

"I know," Celia said. "Or guessed, anyway."

"We were low in the water, not much freeboard, loaded with British rifles and locomotive parts, along with a pair of howitzers we'd picked up at the last minute in Jamaica. The night was overcast, and we were reaching across a southwest wind. The lookout didn't see the squall until the rain was on us." He paused and, remembering, tilted the model of the *Dolphin*. "She went right over. Both masts snapped. At the same time, I guess, one of the howitzers broke loose, and before anyone could do anything, she turned turtle with just the keel showing. Only two of us were on deck when it happened. The other eight were asleep below. I managed to swim out from under her—got this in the process—" He touched the scar on his cheek. "—but Johnny Crispin—"

"Oh, dear God!" Celia interjected. "Not Johnny!"

"But Johnny and the others never got out. Trapped in the lines? Stunned? Who knows? At any rate, we drifted apart during the night, and I washed up on an island off the coast of Florida the next afternoon." He shrugged. "It was mostly boring from then on. I lived off fruit, fish, and rain water collected in conch shells until an English bark found me, took me aboard, and then let me ashore on a Louisiana beach. I walked into New Orleans posing as a vagrant needing work and connected with Snag. And, here I am. Sitting in your parlor and about to escort you to church and a picnic."

Spellbound, Celia stared at him.

"But that's not important," Rafe went on, his voice softening. "What is important is that we're together again—" He paused as the clock began to chime.

"My goodness. I'll need my gloves and hat, Immelda," Celia called, grateful for the interruption and rising to break the moment of intimacy before it went on too long. She was in too much a state of shock, too unprepared, and needed time to think. "It's nine o'clock. We'll be late, and I'll be forced to entertain a host of glowering elders—"

"Father says it's your habit to arrive late to church every week," Rafe said, cutting her off.

"Please?" Celia begged. "This is all happening so fast, Rafe. One moment you're supposed to be dead, the next, here you are. I need a little time to absorb . . . it all." She let him take her hands as he rose, chose to look at them—her hands in his—instead of into his eyes. "Won't you understand?" she whispered.

"I'll try," Rafe said, drawing her to him and tilting her head with one finger under her chin. "But you'll need to understand, too. I never have stopped loving you, Celia."

Celia turned her head to avoid his kiss. "I have a special reason to attend church now," she said, bussing him on the cheek. "To thank God for His mercy in watching over you and bringing you, my dear friend, safely home."

Before Rafe could respond, she had broken free of his embrace and was walking to the door to meet Immelda. "Home," he repeated, disappointment bitter on his tongue. Ill at ease, he walked to the window and stared out. The whole concept of home had become foreign. Home was a place you recognized, but the city had changed. The hills were dotted with caves where the fainthearted lived to escape the shells that overshot the Confederate gun emplacements ranging a mile along the far side of the river. The docks were practically deserted because of the blockade. The city was seared where houses had burned. Other buildings showed the pockmarks left from shrapnel. Home was loved ones and friends, but of those there were precious few left. Most men his own age, as he had suspected and his father had confirmed, had gone to war: a goodly number were dead. Nathaniel himself had aged remarkably. His brother, Micah, had been disinherited and hadn't been seen for over a year. And Celia . . .

He turned, watched her adjust her hat and pull on her gloves. She too had changed, and much more than he had expected. She was, as the country folks said, deep as still water. She had become an enigma. A new personality, more complex, more deeply layered, hid the old he thought he had known so well. The way she stood, the way she talked, even the simple motions involved in pulling on her gloves, were different in a way that at once confounded him and made him all the more determined to solve the mystery she posed.

"Ready?" she asked, done at the mirror.

Rafe took her arm, escorted her to the carriage, and handed her in. If only he hadn't arrived at that moment, Celia thought. Another week, even, and she would have arranged her departure, and so avoid meeting and hurting him again. Powell could summon Hawkmoon all he wished because Hawkmoon and Celia Bartlett would have escaped from this world of subterfuge and evasion. He could tell the world she'd been a spy and she wouldn't care. The deeper secret, the one she could not reveal, would be safe. Sadly, she watched Rafe round the horses to take his place beside her. "Dear friend" had seemed so formal, yet what else was she to call him? She could not be his wife, dared not be his lover. Friend he was and friend he must remain for both their sakes. And if he seemed dissatisfied with such a description, so, curiously, was she.

Reverend Johann Lundquist, popular sentiment to the contrary, did not hold with war. A rock among the shifting sands of his congregation, he stolidly preached sermons of piety, peace, and prospects for the hereafter, and indeed, had planned such a sermon, a disquisition on the beatitudes, for this Sunday morning in May. They had sung the doxology, listened to the invocation, and sung the first hymn. They had read the scriptures, listened to Ella May Crispin sing her usual quavering solo, and had taken the collection. They had just begun to sing the second hymn when the rear doors opened and Celia and Rafe walked in and took their places in the Lattimore pew. Somehow, the hymn continued, though with many missed words in the third and fourth verses, which were unfamiliar. Lundquist sang as loudly as ever, never missing a beat, but his mind was on other matters. He had baptized Rafe, seen him grow from a child to a man. Rafe had been one of those children men take to. Smart and gutsy, he wasn't afraid to speak his mind or to hold his own in an argument, but never did so disrespectfully. The news of his death had been a blow to Lundquist, and his return to life and home was both a miracle and a sign. All the good ones had *not* been taken. God must surely be smiling on this one, and as surely on others and on the cause itself. After the hymn and the weekly announcements, he launched a sermon that was, for once, in total accord with his parishioners' sentiments.

Seldom had such heights of oratory been attained in Vicksburg. Forgotten was Lundquist's prepared script. Metaphors of victory set the rafters ringing. Samson defeated the Philistines with the jawbone of an ass. Trumpets felled the walls of Jericho. David's sling sang through the air, and the pebble he hurled dropped Goliath in his tracks. The Red Sea parted to let the Chosen People cross, then closed with a roar over the Egyptian horses and charioteers. On cue—no one could have planned better—a Union gunboat spoke from the river, engaged in an angry, momentary debate with a Confederate battery, and argued to a draw. One finger raised to heaven, his body rigid, Lundquist waited until the last rolling echo had faded.

The congregation sat spellbound. The cannonades that had become mere background accompaniment to their lives, that had symbolized their trials and many deprivations, took on meaning anew. "Thus speaketh our God!" Lundquist whispered in the deathlike calm that followed. "Thus . . . speaketh . . . our . . . angry . . . God! Lightning flashes from His fists and from His eyes! The heavens rumble and the earth quakes! Man, made in our angry God's image cannot, nay will not, allow himself to be tyrannized! Freedom is our cause, our holy cause, victory our sanctified goal! Out of this trial by fire and sword, out of these fulminous belchings of smoke and gunpowder, this new and sovereign nation, blessed by God, will rise triumphant from strife's forge, and all men will point and reverently bow their heads and say: Behold the shining South!"

Lundquist's voice rose in a thunderous oration that would leave him wet with perspiration and his audience quivering with religious and patriotic fervor. Beside her, Rafe listened raptly while Celia tried to match the words to her own emotions and then, her mind unable to cope with all the contradictions, gave up and focused on the sunlight streaming through the stained-glass windows. Amber for indecision. Pale green, shining, afraid to be hopeful. Red, the crimson of conflagration. Blue, the cool necessity of control. The colors rested on her skirt, bathed her gloved hands and bare wrists. The colors rippled like the surface of a pond. Patterns mingled, shifted, became isolated again, writhed with a life and turmoil of their own. The colors were her moods and emotions magnified. Carefully, coolly, thinking of blue, she scanned the rows in front of her, the blur of backs of heads and then, surreptitiously, out of the corner of her eye, the source of her sudden sense of disorder, the man she had once loved. True, she had loved with a girlish adulation born of an inexperienced heart, but the emotion had consumed her. And the girl lived still, she realized, within the woman, as youth is forever within, forever the wellspring nourishing and troubling maturity. The girl ached with desire, the woman counseled composure, for the woman knew that if he learned the truth . . .

"Let us pray."

Guiltily, Celia realized she'd missed the last few minutes, and quickly lowered her head.

"Our Father, we thank Thee for Thy anger, which is the reverse side of the golden coin of Thy love. We thank Thee for those You have returned to us, and pray that those others who Thou hast not, in Thy infinite wisdom, enfolded in Thy merciful arms, find their way back to this their home and these their loved ones. Give us courage, Father, in the days of travail that surely follow. Give us courage to stand against wrong and, at Thy side, live in freedom and peace and rectitude. We pray this in the name of Thy Son and our Redeemer, Jesus Christ, Amen."

One hundred heads rose as one. Footsteps running along the balcony were followed by the squeak of the pump handle and a whoosh of air into the organ. The sanctuary was charged with electricity, as during a storm. "Stand up, stand up for Jesus," Lundquist said, arms outstretched, his open hands bringing the congregation to its feet.

"Stand up, stand up for Jesus, ye soldiers of the cross. . . ."

One hundred voices filled the sanctuary, overpowered and drowned out the distant roar of the ten o'clock shelling.

"Lift high His royal banner, it must not suffer loss."

Rafe's baritone blended with her soprano. Celia sang as loudly as anyone, but her mind was elsewhere. Were men dying at that moment? What of the Big Black River? Did cannon and musket sing, too? Were the voices of the maimed in tune?

"From victory unto victory, His army He shall lee-ead. . . ."

All around her faces were shining, instilled with the spirit. The weak had fled, the strong remained, and were protected by the Lord. How could it be otherwise when the whole might of the Union had striven to take the city for over a year, and had not yet even reached its trenchworks? Their faith was their shield and their joy.

"Till every foe is vanquished, and Christ is Lord indeed!"

Filled to overflowing with the rapturous wave that swept through the congregation, Lundquist descended from the pulpit to make his way to the rear of the church where he would deliver the benediction. "To him that overcometh, a crown of life shall be. He with the King of Glory, shall reign eternally. A-men."

The sound lingered. An aura of pride and holy purpose suffused the sanctuary with a radiant glow that, through Lundquist's tears, blinded him. Suddenly, he was shaken with a great melancholy. He had succumbed. Carried away, he had been snared by the emotion of the moment, and preached, God preserve him, of the fiery, angry aspect of God he had tried so long to deny. Confused and saddened, he imagined their faces, full of hope he had given them, unwilling to foresee the hopelessness of strife he had fostered as surely as had he lifted a gun in anger. And they would praise him.

"Now," he intoned, arm raised, palm forward in the traditional gesture of benediction, "the Lord bless you and keep you: The Lord make his face to shine upon you, and be gracious to you: The Lord lift up his countenance upon you, and give you . . . peace. Amen." *Me, Lord,* he thought feverishly. *It is I, too, who needs thee.*

A buzz of conversation. Lundquist picked out the phrases as he watched the pews empty. "Best sermon he's ever—" "Rafe, boy! We thought you—" "I don't see how, with the picnic and everythng—" "She pinched me first so I just . . . Aw, Ma!" "Reverend Lundquist! I've never been so *inspired!*" They were on him, pumping his hand, beaming into his face. And he knew that if he conveyed his doubt, even hinted that he might have been wrong, he would lose them forever, so he smiled back and laughed and joked and played the role they so desperately wanted him to play.

Celia and Rafe, arm in arm, took their place in the crowded aisles and slow procession toward the rear of the church. Old friends and neighbors turned to exchange greetings. Children ducked underfoot in the rush to get outside first. Rafe was the center of attraction. The Lattimores had been members of the church since the newlywed Nathaniel and Leona had arrived in Vicksburg thirty-four years earlier, in 1828. The older members recalled the tragedy of their three firstborn dying before they were a year old. They remembered Micah's and Rafe's baptism and the uneasy relief each felt as those two boys lived and flourished. They remembered the ghastly tragedy of Leona's death, and followed each rise and fall of Lattimore fortunes. They gloried in the supposedly secret—such things are never really secret—rivalry between Rafe and Micah over Celia. They hypothesized shamelessly when Celia left both brothers without so much as a word, exclaimed with relish over Micah's expulsion from the family circle, and grieved over Rafe's apparent death. And so, when Rafe returned and appeared in church minus his father and with Celia on his arm, there were few who could refrain from approaching him.

Estelle Scott, once Leona's best friend, edged through the throng, caught his hand, and held it in both of hers. Overweight and heavily rouged, tears gleamed in her eyes. "We're so happy, Rafe, dear. So happy! If only Leona could be here . . ."

Norman Bailey, sixty and half crippled with the gout, grabbed his arm. "By damn!" he swore, forgetting where he was but not that Rafe had once shot a water moccasin just before it dropped on him from a tree. "By damn, by damn!"

Ella May Crispin, face white as her robe, pushed down the aisle against the tide and then, afraid to ask about her Johnny, fled through the pews and disappeared out the side door.

Celia tripped over Mr. Bailey's cane. By the time she recovered, Rafe had been pulled into another group and they were separated.

"Excuse me."

Suddenly, it was all too much. The morning, Rafe's appearance, the sermon, the bodies, the heat, the shifting lights pressing in on her from all sides. She was losing control. Faces blurred. Individual words disappeared and a low buzz took their place. She was perspiring heavily and her stomach felt bloated. Somehow, dizzily, holding onto the pews for support, she reached the end of the aisle where she leaned against the wall next to a soldier with one arm and a crutch in place of a missing leg. Blinking, she studied him. Once handsome, he now bore a vicious scar across his forehead and another where his upper lip and been. Stained-glass sunlight washed over him. As the press lessened and he took one hobbling step toward the door, multicolored shapes skidded over his tragic face and became a single crimson, bloody hue.

She could hardly breathe. The bodies around her radiated heat. She was burning. Her stomach heaved. Men like him . . . the Big Black River . . . Brave boys in blue and gray marching out to die, to rot in fallow fields. To, oh God, live on in ruined bodies, ruined faces, ruined lives . . .

And she had done her part. Pure little Celia Hawkmoon Bartlett had pulled the lanyard, thrust the bayonet, wielded the sword that slashed the living flesh!

Mouth open, breast heaving spasmodically, she could hear cannon roar and muskets fire and the wild and terror-filled shrieks of men enduring punctured bodies, suffering the obscene invasion of flesh by minié-ball or shrapnel or bayonet. A field of bloodied, muddy lumps twisted and heaved in a grotesque dance of death while overhead carrion birds wheeled and spiraled downward to the feast.

Her head was too heavy to hold up. The wall pushed her forward across a floor that had turned to a brown, shiny, wind tossed sea, upon which she could not balance. She was sinking, she was drowning.

"Excuse me."

"Why, Rafe Lattimore! I suppose now I'm going to have to pay you that five dollars . . ."

"Excuse me."

Drowning . . .

"Can't keep a good man dead, by golly!"

"Are you all right, Celia?"

Drowning . . .

"Rafe!"

The sharp pungency of smelling salts revived her with a start. Choking, feebly waving her hands to ward off the almost painful odor, she blinked and opened her eyes to see, swimming into focus, the gentle face of Frieda Lundquist and, behind her, Reverend Lundquist and Rafe.

"There, there," Mrs. Lundquist said, turning a cool, damp cloth that lay on Celia's brow. "Relax, my dear. You're in the manse. Rafe carried you in. We thought it best."

Celia pressed the cloth to her forehead and lay back weakly. She was lying on the sofa in the Lundquists' parlor. The last thing she remembered was the shiny brown floor pitching up to meet her. "I . . . I think I've recovered now, thank you," she managed, suppressing an instant of nausea.

"You gave us quite a scare," Rafe said, chuckling despite his obvious concern. "Next time you might try a milder tactic to rescue me."

"Rescue?" Celia asked, not understanding.

"From well-wishers. I saw you start to crumple, and had to fight my way to catch you before you hit the floor."

Lundquist clapped Rafe on the shoulder. "You should have seen him! He looked like a hound running right through a covey of quail." His eyes twinkled as he remembered the sight of the scattering women. "Flew away in all directions, by Bob! You put on quite a display. I haven't seen the like in . . . Well, I don't remember when."

"The people," Celia said, shuddering. "And the heat was so oppressive." She remembered a wounded soldier standing to one side and bathed in a cheerful light that had quite suddenly turned macabre and frightening. "I feel so foolish," she said, sitting up and suppressing the image.

"Nonsense," Lundquist exclaimed. "I almost fainted myself. Should have had the side doors open to permit a cross draft."

"Miz Lundquist?" a servant interrupted. "Here's that tea an' brandy."

"Oh, yes. Thank you, Melissa." Frieda smiled, took the cup, and handed it to Celia. "Here. Sip on this, dear. It'll perk you up."

"Fainting in public!" Celia said, reddening.

"Saving my hide, if you'd rather think of it that way," Rafe corrected, trying to make light of her embarrassment. "Those ladies were about to carry me off. I just hope you don't use it as an excuse to rob me of your company at the picnic."

Celia ducked her head to sip her tea. She hadn't thought of not going, but now that he had mentioned it, the idea was appealing. She needed time to think. The world was out of kilter, out of control. First Powell's ultimatum, then Anthony's appearance, now Rafe. The fainting spell was a plausible excuse. She could feign weakness and be free of his company long enough to come to grips with herself.

"I'll understand, of course, if you do," Rafe added softly, reaching out to touch her and then, remembering where he was, quickly withdrawing his hand.

She would have to decide. Going meant . . . For the second time since early that morning she remembered her decision to leave Vicksburg. Going meant two things, then: away forever and to the picnic. Rafe hadn't understood when she fled the first time. Running away again would be an even greater mystery and wound him even more deeply. Could she do that to him?

But what choice had she, really? He would be no less hurt than her father if he learned the truth about her. As for the picnic, was she so poor an artificer that she dared not go to a simple picnic? A week, perhaps two at the most, was all the time left her. After that, she would never see him again. She had loved him more deeply, more completely, than anyone in her whole life long, and would never see him again. Each second with him was torment, but each second with him was seeing him and hearing his voice and, however properly bestowed, feeling his touch. Each second was a memory she could keep and hold and cherish. No matter where she went, what she did, who she loved thereafter, no one could take those seconds from her. And no matter where Rafe went, what he did, who he loved thereafter, that part of him would be hers forever. Such tiny mementos were little enough to last a lifetime.

Their eyes met, touched, lingered. *Remember this*, Celia thought, tucking away the memory. *Remember how his eyes feel when they touch yours.*

"And leave you to the mercy of all those women?" she asked, smiling to mask the ineffable sadness that wrapped her. His eyes were so soft, and yet glittered like gems. "Why, I wouldn't think of it. Not for one"—hold on to each and every, this one—"second."

CHAPTER 9

Anthony Rutledge braced himself, balanced the hard-edged, wooden box of bandages that turned out to be heavier than he expected, and staggered out of the sand-bagged shed at the end of the pier. Straining, he negotiated the treacherously splintered planking and turned right to cross the narrow temporary bridge thrown up where Union shells had blown holes in the wharf at the same time a pair of men hurried past him in the opposite direction. Cautiously, his balance destroyed by the bouncing boards, he teetered on the edge of an unwanted bath in the muddy river, and then, startled by a shell exploding in the water some twenty yards to his right, jumped to the firmer footing of the main dock. While other dockworkers jeered at the Union batteries across the river, he scrambled for the line of wagons hidden for protection behind a long pile of cotton bales.

"Be careful, you," a stout middle-aged man with a medical corps insignia on his hat shouted as the man in front of Anthony stumbled and almost dropped a crate of chloroform.

The longshoreman turned into position for the man on the wagon to relieve him of his burden, cursed, and then thought better. A man never knew when he might find himself beneath the surgeon's knife. To which end, flatter the physician. "Yessir, Dr. Stewart. Sorry. Damned gravel is slippery."

"Very well," the doctor called back, grateful for the simple fact that the man was at least sober. "Take care, though. That chloroform is the kiss of an angel to a wounded man."

"I'll watch my step, sir," the longshoreman said, ducking back behind the bales as an explosion rocked the waterfront. "Jee-sus, that was close!"

"Hit anything?" Anthony asked, giving up his crate in turn.

"Looks like they got the boat again. Well, shit, here we go."

The cry of "Men on the lines!" came from the *Bayou Belle*. All night and morning long, while Snag Parken and his crew worked feverishly to patch the holes punched in their vessel during the unloading, other crews had pulled the steamboat back and forth along the dock to spoil the registry of the guns on the far bank of the Mississippi. That the tactic had worked so well was a miracle, Anthony thought sourly, running out on the pier and giving a hand.

"God-damn son-of-a-bitchin' no-neck, rump-sprung sons-a-God-damn bitches!" Parken cursed, appearing momentarily on deck and shouting orders to his crew. "They done it again! Get some timbers down there. What about them boilers? Who the hell—"

"That's fixed him," the dockworker said, panting, leaning forward into the line. "Damn thing's ninety-percent patch already. Hell, even if he does get that one stuffed, you couldn't get me on that boat. Where's he gonna go, anyway? Next best thing to slitting your own throat, far as I'm concerned."

Powdersmoke clung to their nostrils and burned their throats. The *Bayou Belle* tied up again, the two men ran down the pier and into the safety of the storage shed where they took their place at the end of the line and waited for a new load. "Ain't seen you before," the dockworker said. "Name's Trent."

"Ain't seen you neither," Anthony grunted noncommittally.

"Folks call me Jimmy," the man said, holding out his hand.

"Anthony Rutledge," Anthony said, one name as good as another and his own easier to remember.

"What brought you in?"

"In?"

"Into the city. I know the regulars. Been under the hill all my life. You're a new face. N'Orleans?"

"Naw," Anthony drawled in the slow Southern accent he'd picked up in his summers spent in Mississippi. "Had me a little farm just this side a' Jackson. Damn Yanks burned me out. Figure to go back soon as Pemberton whips ol' bluebelly Grant."

"If he does," Trent said, believing Anthony's story and thereby saving his own life.

"Will, I reckon," Anthony said, moving up in line and grunting as two quartermaster corps privates eased a load onto his back.

"Well, I hope it," Trent said. "Things is tough, though. Things is real—Jesus H! You sure this ain't meant for two men? Hell, I—"

Anthony didn't hear the rest. Out the door, he retraced his earlier steps and eased across the makeshift bridge. "Hurry up, men," the doctor called, his voice urgent. "Please hurry. We don't have all day."

Slip between the bales, wait in line to be unloaded, head back for the shed and another load. Anthony stuck to the pace and watched the line of men, hired hands and soldiers both, sidle past each other along the dock, antlike in procession, from shed to wagons and back, going about the mundane work of war. And all of them, he thought, amused, loyal Confederates. All save one.

Fancy Darren quit counting the days when she turned twenty-five. That had been over eight years ago, and life on Levee Street had been easier since then with such matters in their proper perspective. Time hadn't been particularly unkind to her, given the life of an Under the Hill lady. What few gray hairs had appeared she could pluck without anyone noting the loss. Her waist and hips had thickened, but only enough to give her a certain substantial solidity that most men liked anyway. Her breasts sagged a little, but gravity did that to a body. Gravity and overuse, so to speak, both of which were corrected by a corset that swelled her already impressive bosom to breathtaking proportions above the lace frills of her bodice. Her face, as well cared for as a carpenter's tools, was still pretty and unlined. All in all, she couldn't complain. Men still looked at her whenever she walked into a room, still mentally untied each bow, unsnapped each hook, and lusted after the heavenly delights of her bed and body.

Heaven had a healthy price, however, and not everyone gained entrance. Fancy could afford to pick and choose, and relegate the lusty rest to the stable of five girls she maintained. This morning, freshly bathed, rouged, and powdered, she greeted the day at an early eleven o'clock and sorted through the few customers, most of whom she recognized as holdovers from the night before. *Well, I'll be damned,* she thought, her gaze settling like a hot wrap around the broad-shouldered man standing at the bar. Pleased, she checked herself in the mirror and walked up behind him as he drank from a steaming cup and then took a bite from the quarter wheel of cheese kept out for those who felt the need of sustenance between rounds. "That cheese is expensive and hard to buy at that. It was supposed to last," she said, placing her hands on the shiny surface of the bar and staring at him in the mirror.

Micah looked up, showed his teeth, and cut another chunk off the wheel. Crumbs at the corners of his mouth were all that remained of the loaf of bread that had been set beside the cheese half an hour earlier. "Heard things were a little grim here, so I brought you a replacement," he said, jerking a thumb toward a pair of tow sacks to his left on the bar. "Even if I didn't, I always pay, don't I?"

Fancy nodded. He smelled of sweat and dust, neither of which were repulsive. At least not on Micah. "Didn't hear you come in. No tables wrecked, no chairs broken. No brawling, no teeth kicked out."

"It's Sunday." He refilled his cup from the pot the bartender had left him, reached over the edge of the bar and helped himself to another, which he filled for her. "Speaking of which, you're kind of busy for a Sunday, aren't you?"

"Times have changed, just in case you didn't notice."

"I noticed." Micah stared down her cleavage, invitingly deep, a chasm made to be filled with kisses, and wondered why his mind wandered. Over a year had slipped by since he'd spilled the beans to his father and had been kicked out. Fourteen months of evading the draft, of carrying mail and couriers' pouches, of living high on the hog one day and off pickled hocks the next, and every once in a while remembering Fancy, which was one of the primary reasons he'd agreed to deliver the mail to Vicksburg. Day and night for a week he'd looked forward to the romp they'd have. What he hadn't known was that he'd see the woman on the balcony.

Micah had rarely been so affected by a woman. Women came and went, were with him one day and gone the next, and what the hell. This one, though, exuded raw sensuality and lickerish whispers of unimagined delights. And that trick with the sun behind her! She was a woman to be had in the open air, the smell of crushed grass mingling with the scent of lovemaking, a breeze rushing over and between their bodies. He'd been tired and aching when he rode in, but she'd been a tonic to invigorate and revive him. Now, with the rumbling in his gut eased and half a pot of brandy laced coffee warming his vitals, all that waited to be satiated was his ardor.

"What do you think of the place?" Fancy asked, intruding on his thoughts.

Micah turned and rested his elbows on the bar. Like many others, especially those close to the waterfront where Union shells were more apt to land, Fancy had moved underground. The main room was spacious with curtained doors in the rear wall leading to the girls' bedrooms. The same bar he remembered from the old place ran along the north wall. Nearby, a real wooden door led to what Micah suspected was Fancy's room. As for the rest, the furnishings from the old place had been moved in lock, stock, barrel, and brass bed. "Lacks a river view," he grunted.

"Uh-huh. And nothing to see but Yankee gunboats. No, thank you. Keep your windows and your nine-pound shot. This may not be as grand, but when the shells come, it's as pretty as the pearly gates."

"And what would you know of pearly gates?" Micah snorted.

"Plenty. I had me a preacher just last night," Fancy said matter-of-factly. She moved closer, pressed her breasts against his arm, and slipped one hand inside his shirt. "No lasting power, for all his talk. I been thinkin' about you, Micah." Her voice changed, became deeper and huskier. "Not many men ever been able to satisfy me. You were one of them. One of the best."

"Yeah?" Micah asked, mentally comparing her to the Stewart woman. Solange. Dark red hair, not so jaded as Fancy, excitable, probably a woman to hold onto, one to make noises she meant, to thrash about wildly, to make demands, and to be wildly grateful. Doctor's wife or no, he wanted her. "Well, I always said that knowing what you want's important," he said, answering Fancy but at the same time talking to himself. "What about that picnic I heard about today?"

"Huh?" Fancy asked, confused by the shift in topics.

"You heard me. What about that picnic today?"

"Jesus Christ, Micah! I'm not talking about a picnic. I'm talking about you and me going—"

"What about the God-damn picnic, Fancy!" Micah snarled, grabbing her by the arm.

Fancy glared at him. "Lemme go, Micah."

Micah grinned and squeezed harder.

"Lemme . . ." She closed her eyes, gritted her teeth against the pain. "Okay. Okay," she finally gasped. "Just . . . let . . . go."

One of the patrons, alarmed by the ruckus, started to come to Fancy's aid.

"And why don't you just turn around, go back to wherever you were, and stick your head in a bottle," Micah said, stepping toward the intruder.

"It's all right, George," Fancy said, waving the young man off. "Just a friendly disagreement. Go on back. Have a drink on me." She rubbed her arm. "God a'mighty, Micah. You didn't have to—"

"I'm tired, Fancy. I've been riding all night and I'm not in the mood."

"The picnic," Fancy said hurriedly, "is to raise money for the cause. The ladies'll be taking off that linsey they've been wearing to show how patriotic they are and sashaying in their finery. Supposed to be food and contests and dancing. Everybody who's anybody's supposed to be there. A real big do."

"Invitations?" Micah asked.

"How the hell would I know? If there were, Fancy Darren wasn't on the list."

Micah considered that. A bath and some fresh clothes, he could get there by noon at the latest. His mind made up, he turned to the bar, opened one of the tow sacks, and took out a half wheel of cheese.

"Here's your cheese," he said, tying the bag shut again and slinging it over his shoulder.

Fancy couldn't remember when she'd been turned down. Livid, she grabbed the sack and jerked. "And just where the hell do you think you're going?" she asked, her bruised arm forgotten in her rage.

"Why, where you aren't wanted, Fancy. A picnic." A wide grin split his face as he clapped his hat on his head and turned to leave. "Like you said. Everybody who's anybody. And that's me. Oh, yeah," he said, pausing at the door before ducking out. "If I see any spare preachers, I'll send you one."

CHAPTER 10

Fragments of a day. And beneath the common sun, a small portion of earth. A rectangle perhaps three miles long from north to south, ten miles from east to west. To the west, the Mississippi and Vicksburg, to the east the Big Black River. In Kileen's Meadow, just north of Vicksburg, men and women and children gather to play and sing and eat and dance. Ten miles east, where the Big Black River horseshoes sluggishly through low, flat ground, stakes are being wagered in war's great gamble, the game of death. In the fragments of the day, two worlds coexist without touching.

At the Big Black, soldiers crack a last meal of hardtack, scrape chick-peas from their tin plates, and cast greedy eyes toward an extra cup of chicory coffee.

In Kileen's Meadow, the aroma of roast beef and pork mingles deliciously with that of amber lemon pies and golden apple cobblers bubbling sweetly through golden crusts. Whiskey jugs are unstopped and fresh bread is spread with dewberry jelly.

At the Big Black, where armies wait to outwait one another, men peer across the grim distance at other men who peer from rifle pits. All are afraid not to be brave, and all are wondering who is the most frightened.

In Kileen's Meadow, honey-lipped girls flirt and preen and vie to break the most hearts and young men watch in wonderment, hoping against hope each to own his true love. The young men ask themselves over and over who is the most frightened, the lady of my dreams or I . . . or I . . . or I.

One tenuous thread links both worlds: butchery.

In Kileen's Meadow, beef and pork will be butchered and carved.

At the Black River, men.

And now the fragments fall into place.

The banjo player was the first. An old black man alone in Kileen's Meadow, an old man of slavery bound for freedom, gray headed, and the white stubble on his cheeks like snow on coal.

The wind rustles the long grass carpeting the meadow, the birds sing of morning and springtime. The old man hears and stretches the strings just so, ear cocked to the twanging, buzzing, whining until each note is just right. As a man in the full vigor of youth he had made the girls giggle, made them sigh, made them beautiful as they smiled and twisted and jumped to the music he wrought. Now old and pink-gummed and with a cough that lasted from November to March, he found the notes that defied the passing years, the notes of memories, the melodies of past beauty and of past laughter. He closed his eyes and leaned back against a tree and let the music flow from his heart through his hands through his fingers through the strings and across the meadow to blend with the wind and the grass sounds and the birds. When he was finished playing for the flowers and himself, he selected a stump near the road from town and waited. Folks would be coming along soon. Some would throw coins his way. It wasn't the same as playing for the flowers or himself, but he would be the only one who knew that.

The colonel didn't have a name. At least not to the enlisted men. Or even to himself. He might have been a Harry or a Michael or a Paul or a Francis or any of a hundred others, but he wasn't. Not anymore. War had christened him with a name better than the one his mother had given him. Men called him Colonel. He loved his rank and his new name. He woke knowing he was a colonel. He breakfasted relishing the fact that he was a colonel. He was proud of his rank, thrilled when men snapped to attention and begged the colonel's pardon or requested the colonel's permission or agreed in any of a thousand ways with the colonel's opinion. He was proud of his uniform. He was doubly proud of the color, which was gray.

The colonel sat apart from the men in his command. When he was finished reading his maps and orders, when he had initialed the messages he had received and signed others he was sending, when he had assigned the artillery he commanded its targets, he left his adjutant to clean up the remaining details. Then the colonel climbed alone to the rise in the land behind the makeshift battlements that sheltered the Confederate Army. Just ten feet made all the difference in the world when it came to an unobstructed view. Ahead and to the east, on the other side of the Confederate breastworks and across low, wet ground, the Yankees waited. To the north, the Big Black itself and miles of thick swamp protected the Confederate left flank. The right flank was anchored on Gin Lake and more swamps. Fifteen hundred yards to the rear, horseshoeing south, the Big Black undulated slowly through soggy bottomland. A river at one's back was a disadvantage, of course, but could, with some rationalization, be turned into an advantage, for men who feel they are trapped fight with greater ferocity. Further to the west, ten miles behind him, Vicksburg lay hidden in a sea of spring green. His family lived in Vicksburg. Father, mother, two sisters, and one brother who would never walk right again after losing a leg at Shiloh. It was curious how things worked out. He'd be in the battle that sent General Grant and his Yanks packing and his family would be at the long-awaited town picnic his sisters had so greatly anticipated. That's all they could talk about on his last visit home.

"Fine day for a picnic," the colonel said aloud to no one in particular, and then unholstered his Starr revolver to recheck the loads and make sure the caps were dry. A crippled brother to revenge, a city to protect, a war to wage. He wouldn't have traded places with anyone.

Dust lifted from the road, coating white fences and fresh green gardens. Buckboards, surreys, carriages, and men on horseback formed a staggered, willy-nilly procession. Families walking to the side of the road trampled the tender spring thistle and scoured the underbrush for tiny tart berries. Slaves trudged along stoically, their hidden good humor geared to the hope for a changing future, not to speak of food aplenty to be sampled without master or mistress knowing the difference. Noise, like the dust from the road, lifted in a cacophony of hoofbeats and harness jingle, catcalls, laughter, and earnest speculation on just how devastating the Yankee defeat would be. The soprano appraisal of gowns and hats mingled with the basso jocularity of man-to-man joshing and the merriment of children wild and free, white and black playing together without pretense.

Five hundred, almost six hundred, on their way to Kileen's Meadow. With them, after discovering Nathaniel had left already, Celia and Rafe drove with an uneasy silence wedged between them. "We don't have to do this, you know," Rafe finally said, glancing at her. "If you're uncomfortable."

"Oh? And where might we go?"

A smile flirted with the corners of his mouth. "Somewhere else?"

"Oho!"

"Oho? And what exactly does 'oho' mean?"

Celia found herself staring at the sliver of white scar marring his cheek, jagged like the boundary on the hand-drawn map she'd revised for Powell barely ten hours earlier. "Somewhere alone?" she asked, pushing Hawkmoon from her mind.

"You said that, not me. I meant only that if you were feeling ill again, you might not want to face a whole crowd of people."

"I'm fine," Celia insisted. "And wouldn't miss being seen in the company of Vicksburg's most eligible bachelor for the world."

"Bachelor or ghost?" Rafe asked, only a little sarcastically.

"I don't understand."

Rafe stared down the lane at the carriages and wagons stretching on ahead, tried to decide if total honesty was the best policy, or if he should hedge. "I'd hoped . . . That is, after two years you'd tell . . ." He couldn't, still couldn't bring himself to ask point-blank. "I think I frighten you," he hedged.

"That's ridiculous. We've known each other for years. You don't frighten me at all."

"Really?"

"Of course not."

"Then why," Rafe asked pointedly, "do you sit so far away from me?"

Celia had been careful to keep an open space between them and now recognized, with Rafe's accusation, her motives. Perhaps she had been a little frightened of him. No, not him, she corrected herself silently. Of what his touch might lead to. "This impresses me as a proper distance," she said lamely.

"For strangers, yes."

Only a night ago she had been Hawkmoon, a night rider, a woman braving armies and rivers and capture. Now she balked at a matter of inches. Inches! Because . . . "What will people think?"

Rafe shrugged. "Maybe that you are happy to see me. Maybe more. But who cares?"

"I am happy to see you. If you still doubt that, then I suspect your island sojourn damaged your head."

"Ouch." Rafe winced, feigning hurt. "Still the same sharp tongue, I see."

"If you came back and found me very different, there wouldn't be much reason for us to be here together, would there?" Celia asked.

"No," Rafe admitted. "There wouldn't be. I never wanted you to be anything but the Celia you always were."

"Well, then?"

His eyes met and held hers. "One of the things you—we—were," he said softly, "was closer."

One week and she would be gone. So little time between now and then. A touch. The same touch she would carry with her, he, perhaps, would remember, too. Daring the distance, she shifted closer to him, inhaled sharply as their elbows and thighs touched, though so lightly.

"Hyaah!" Rafe yelled, popping the reins.

The mare broke into a trot. Momentarily off balance, Celia grabbed Rafe's arm for support. He did that on purpose, she thought angrily, and then realized, when she found that she didn't want to let go, that she didn't mind at all.

A half mile north of town, a winding ribbon of dirt road threading through the countryside branched off the Yazoo City Road. The silence, only a short time ago a wedge, had now become a mantle that wrapped about and isolated them from the general crowd. Driving slowly, the mare taking her pace from the carriage ahead, they rounded a swollen comb of land called Indian Mound, a constructed hill built Lord knew when or why. Nor did anyone care. Indian mounds made lovely spots for picnics or trysts, but beyond that history did not matter. Kileen's Meadow lay beyond the mound. Once in the open, Rafe pulled the mare out of line and alongside the carriage carrying Phillip Laughton and his fiancée, Gaillee Calder, a girl who had a reputation for hosting some of Vicksburg's most ostentatious parties which Celia, to keep her allegiance above suspicion, frequently attended. "Rafe Lattimore! Dry land becomes you," Laughton called. "It's good to see you. Sorry I missed you last night."

"Father hustled me off the minute I stepped ashore. Told me later you'd been there."

"Why, Celia Bartlett, you sneaky ol' thing!" Gaillee hooted, leaning forward to call across Phillip. "Just snatch yourself up one of the city's handsomest gentlemen before he's been home a day. Annie Slade said you were a mite slow, but you certainly put a stop to that kind of jabber." Gaillee fluttered a silk scarf before her cheeks, peeked at Rafe over the sheer pink ruffled edge, and laughed gaily. "Not even home a day."

"That mare of yours still as slow as she used to be?" Phillip called, unappreciative of his fiancée's flirting ways.

Rafe sighed inwardly. He was more than willing to end the long and meaningless rivalry between himself and Phillip, but Phillip simply wouldn't let him. "Only one way to find out," he called back, snapping the tip of his whip against the mare's rump.

The carriage shot ahead. Phillip shouted and cracked his whip, liberally punishing his own animal in an effort to counter Rafe's surprise move. "Phillip!" Gaillee squealed in terror.

"Are you out of your mind?" Celia hissed, clinging to Rafe's arm as the carriage swerved to avoid a buckboard that had pulled off the road with a broken wheel.

"I thought you were the same old Celia."

The carriage skidded sideways on a slight side slope, straightened, and kept on. Celia grabbed her hat to keep it from blowing away. "What's that have to do with anything?"

"You used to enjoy a fast ride, I thought! Remember?"

The carriage lurched from side to side. The slower conveyances spreading across the meadow blurred as they raced past. Cheers and cries of exhortation erupted along with instantaneous wagers as Rafe and Phillip's carriages swept across the verdant landscape toward the jagged line of split rail fence that marked their goal. The bouncing threw Celia's hat askew: she tore it off and tucked it carefully between her legs. Rafe's hair and hers, contrasting jet black and light honey blond, streamed behind them in the wind. Beyond screaming, Gaillee's face was white and drawn as Phillip's carriage slowly drew abreast of Rafe's. Phillip himself, half standing, arms raised, hands gripping the reins had the grim look of an ancient Roman charioteer.

Faster and faster still. Excited—it had been years since she'd ridden like that—Celia held her face to the wind and, left arm holding onto Rafe, beat the seat beside her with her right hand and urged the valiant little mare to greater speed. Gouts of rich black soil dug by the horse's hooves splattered them. The right wheels hit a small hummock, and for a few breathtaking seconds they careened along on the two left wheels. All the time, the fence came closer, and between it and the carriages, a low spot shined with surface water left from a rain two days earlier. Both men saw the puddle, each knew he must take a drenching at full speed if he wanted to win. Phillip chanced a look at Rafe, another at Gaillee, and decided. Foot nudging the brake, hands hauling on the reins, he slowed and turned aside just as Rafe's carriage exploded into the depression.

The mare stumbled, caught her balance, and plunged forward. Water thrown by her hooves drenched Rafe and Celia from the front, more carried by the wheels rained on them from the rear. Celia yelled and ducked against Rafe as the carriage slewed to the left, then hit solid ground and bounced up and out. The fence loomed ahead and the mare balked. Rafe turned her violently, whipped her back to speed. The carriage skidded sickeningly, almost hit the fence, and then straightened out behind the frightened mare while fence rails skittered by like a train of bones. Laughing, Celia mopped her face with her kerchief. "You should have come home sooner," she yelled. "My God, what a ride!"

"You liked it?" Rafe asked, pleased with himself and slowing the carriage.

"Liked it?" She'd spent two years driving at the sedately boring pace her father and Nathaniel preferred. The race had stirred her blood, reminded her of the daredevil extravagances of more joyful times when, at sixteen and seventeen, she had ridden in forbidden, impromptu races run by Vicksburg's young men. Exhilarated, all restraint forgotten, Celia threw her arms around his neck and kissed him. "I loved it!"

"Whoa. Whoa!" The mare slowed, stood quivering, sides heaving. Rafe's hair was wet and matted with mud. Beads of water dripped down the dark planes of his face. "I'd do it again in a second," he said, touching her face. "For another kiss like that. Well?"

Celia smoothed the hair away from his eyes and, surprising herself almost as much as him, kissed him slowly and languorously. "You won't have to," she said as their lips parted. "You never had to run races to get a kiss from me, Rafe Lattimore."

"Madness!"

Rafe twisted to his left. Celia dropped her kerchief.

"You're mad!" Phillip snapped, driving up beside them.

"Because I won?" Rafe asked. "Not in the slightest. Winning—"

"Meant nothing, for all the good you garnered." Phillip adjusted his curled brim hat adorned with a black feather. "Not a coin was wagered. Not a cent. He raced for nothing."

"On the contrary, Captain," Rafe said flatly. "I raced to win. The stakes were priceless."

"Oh? Tell me then. What was worth possibly ruining a good horse and endangering your own lives as well?"

The back of Rafe's hand brushed lightly against Celia's breast as he shrugged out of his wet coat. "Why, honor, my timid friend," he explained, the reference to Phillip's long ago failure well understood by Phillip. He twisted to throw the coat across the rear seat. "Honor was worth it."

Phillip stiffened, unsure whether Rafe's divestiture of his coat in public hinted at a challenge, or whether it simply meant the coat was uncomfortably wet. "Honor?" he finally asked, an implied sneer tainting the word. "Just exactly whose hon—"

"You silly men," Gaillee trilled, instinctively interrupting in order to defuse what was rapidly becoming a ticklish situation. Rafe's damp shirt clung to his chest, and she demurely averted her eyes. "And just look at poor Celia. She's positively drenched!"

Celia was as aware as Gaillee of the unvoiced antagonism between Phillip and Rafe. "Just hang me out to dry," she quipped, following Gaillee's lead. Neither wanted to see the day marred by an altercation.

"Your pardon then, Celia," Phillip said stiffly, bowing in place and sweeping his hat in a gallant arc. "I must take blame for instigating such foolishness and, judging from your escort's response and conduct, must also apologize for both of us."

"Why, my goodness, Phillip, but aren't you generous to a fault," Celia cooed with exaggerated sweetness. And just as sweetly turned the knife. "But unnecessarily so, I'm afraid. After all, as Rafe explained, we did win."

Phillip's expression soured and he glanced at Gaillee as if scolding her for her choice of friends. "Perhaps," he said very formally, "we'd better head back, my dear. Celia? Rafe?" He bowed curtly. "If you'll excuse us, please?"

The picnic was getting well underway. Conveyances were emptying, and tables were being loaded to the groaning point with food. Blankets were spread and some families were erecting canvas flies. Children ran about in games, and men in raven black frock coats strolled arm in arm with women in pastel silk gowns, in gaily printed gingham sun dresses, and multicolored bonnets. "Shall we ride until the breeze dries us?" Rafe asked as Phillip and Gaillee drove off.

"It might be best. If your father sees me soaked like this, he's liable to be upset."

"More than liable," Rafe agreed.

"I know. More often than not, these days, he thinks of me as a daughter."

Rafe popped the reins. The mare started forward at a slow walk along the fence. "Just as long as he doesn't expect me to think of you as a sister."

Celia dug through the picnic basket loaded not only with Immelda's delicious viands but some of life's necessities as well. She found a hairbrush. "Did you mean what you said?" she asked, brushing her hair so it would dry faster. "About honor?"

"Of course."

Celia listened to the fiddles and the strumming of a distant banjo. She thought about her past, the painful and unshared secret she carried. "A funny thing, honor," she mused aloud.

Curious, Rafe shot her a sidelong glance, then looked quickly away toward the sound of muted explosions. Three ridges away, beyond thick stands of trees, the artillery that commanded the Mississippi was emplaced. Beyond them, soldiers manned the trenches that protected the city. Further off to the east, perhaps at that precise moment, Grant and Pemberton were clashing. "No, it isn't," he said.

"I didn't mean—"

"Honor is one of the least funny things I can think of," he went on, stopping the mare at an open gate. "Well? Shall we go on?"

A lane led into the woods and the deep forest hiding secluded glades and glens where lovers could hide from prying eyes. "I think we'd better join the others," Celia whispered, focusing on the hairbrush that she turned and twisted in her hands.

"You think . . ." Rafe asked slowly, placing one hand over hers.

Celia sat motionless. Going with him, letting one thing lead to another as she had dreamed so many times would be easy. He would wonder, though. Why wasn't she a virgin? Why did she give in so quickly? But that didn't matter, did it, she asked herself. And as quickly answered. That was one touch of his she could not take with her. Better always, for each of them, if they never knew that final intimacy, for that memory could only sour and perplex as the years passed. "Your shirt is dry," she said, meeting his eyes. "I want to go back."

Rafe sighed, turned the mare, and drove silently. They had ventured midway across the grounds searching for a clear space to call their own when a man loomed out of the crowd and caught the mare by the bridle to halt the carriage. "Well, little brother! Fancy seeing you here."

Rafe stared blankly at his brother, almost as if he'd never seen him before. Each time he had mentioned Micah to Nathaniel the night before, the answers were evasive and limited to the repetitious scrap of information that Micah was gone and would remain gone. Except there he stood.

He touched his hat and winked lewdly at Celia. "And the lovely Celia Bartlett. Together again with her sweetheart, just like in the good old days."

Celia's fingers dug into Rafe's arm and felt the tension there. If someone had asked her, she wouldn't have been able to say which frightened her more: Micah's presence itself, or the possibility that he would allude to the rape in such an obvious manner that Rafe would know, and a fight would ensue.

"Best take it easy, Micah," Rafe warned, ready to drop the reins if Micah started anything.

Micah noted the slight movement of Rafe's hands and decided that he didn't care to learn right then if Rafe still carried his snickersnee. Or, for that matter, if their father had told Rafe about the rape. "No offense, little brother." He stepped back from the mare's head, kept his hands in view. "Quite a coincidence, eh?" he asked, putting on cordiality like a shirt. "Imagine that, both of us coming back at the same time."

The tension eased slightly. "I suppose so," Rafe agreed. His father had refused to be specific, and Micah wasn't volunteering any information. That there was no love lost between the two brothers was no secret. "Father said you hadn't been around for a while," he said, probing a little.

"You know the old saying." Micah wasn't going to be taken in. "Black sheep, just like bad pennies, have a habit of cropping up. I'm sure everyone is tickled pink to see me. Isn't that right, Celia, honey?"

"Of course, Micah," Celia said faintly.

An unappealing smile spread like a white gash across Micah's clean-shaven face. "See? Even Celia says so." The smile was replaced by a concerned frown. "But wait a minute! I heard down in New Orleans that you were dead, and then damned if just five minutes ago someone didn't tell me you were here parading around as if you'd never left." Micah shook his head in mock despair. "Such a shame, Rafe. Seems like your only brother should've been the first to know, not the last."

"You would have if you'd been home," Rafe said, meeting his brother's stare.

"Ah, yes. Home. Home *sweet* home. Seems I remember something about that."

"You spent enough time there."

"Not that I was particularly wanted."

"You walked out, Micah. No one forced you."

"The devil!" Micah flared angrily. "That's what he told you, eh?" His eyes narrowed to obsidian slits, shifted from Rafe to Celia and back to Rafe. For a moment, one single fleeting moment, the words were on the tip of his tongue and he almost said them. It would be interesting to see them both crumble at the disclosure. It would also be dangerous as hell, for madmen were hard to kill. And in that moment, Micah read his own vulnerability in Rafe's eyes. If Rafe ever did learn what had happened that afternoon in the warehouse, no power on earth would keep him from killing Micah.

An unseen shiver passed through Micah. Someone stepping on his grave. To cover his discomfort, he shrugged as if to say that what Nathaniel had said was of no importance to him. "Just goes to prove," he said with a brief, barking laugh, "a man can't be sure of what's going on under his nose, right?"

Celia blushed violently and cringed as if slapped. Rafe wondered about, but could find no good reason for, the sudden change in tone. "Are you calling Father a liar?" he asked, intent on Micah and not noticing Celia's reaction.

"A liar? Me?" Micah asked with a disingenuous shrug. "Now why would I do that?" His laugh was light and easy as his eyes left Celia

"At any rate, I've no time for this. Old man McGivern's brought in some dockworkers and put up a forty-dollar purse for a free-for-all wrestling match with the last man standing to take the pot. Thought I'd see if they'd let me play along. Don't guess you'd like to join in the fun, eh? Seeing as your coat is already off?"

"Fight with dockworkers? That should be quite a spectacle, Micah. You're really determined to embarrass Father, aren't you? Why don't you just—"

"Why don't you just step down and we'll have a little go-round all our own?" Micah taunted. "For old time's sake?"

Without warning, Rafe snapped the reins. The mare, already spooked, reared and bolted forward past Micah, who stepped lightly aside and saluted sardonically as the carriage passed him.

"Some timing. Sorry you had to be subjected to that," Rafe apologized as he pulled the mare to a halt on a sparsely occupied rise. He nodded toward a large open tent nearby where the Lattimore servants were arranging a square of tables around which the inner circle of Vicksburg's elite would congregate. "A Lattimore against a bunch of dockyard bums," he snorted derisively. "McGivern'll let him, too, just to get Father's goat. Which is all Father needs. I just hope Micah stays away from him."

"Why is he like that?" Celia asked in an anguished tone. "So angry and threatening? It's hard to believe he's your brother."

"Well, he is. He's ridden to a wild wind as long as I can remember. But then," he added, jumping down and circling the mare, "we might be more alike than I care to admit."

"No, you're not," Celia blurted. "I could never lo . . ."

His hand raised to help her from the carriage, Rafe paused and stared at her.

Celia caught her breath. "I could never *like* him," she amended quickly, and before Rafe could respond, took his hand and climbed down.

"That's not what you started to say," Rafe said, holding her wrist when she tried to turn away from him.

Celia's heart raced. A slip of the tongue, an accident. A word not to be repeated. Not to Rafe, who was the only one she had ever . . . "You're hurting my wrist," she said evenly.

Rafe's eyes bored into her but his grip relaxed. A quick surge of anger washed through him, then faded almost immediately as he realized how unrealistic he was being. They'd been separated for two and a half years, back together for less than two hours, and he expected her to fall all over him? Pretty silly, really, Rafe, old boy, he told himself. "Sorry," he said aloud, smiling and backing off. Routines and rituals. That's what was required. The emptiness of social nicety to ease the way. Love was a flower, not a keg of explosives. Flowers needed time and nurturing. Give her time. Give yourself time. We have plenty. "Shall we?" he asked, offering her his arm.

And when they stepped into the tent and greeted their friends, everyone remarked on what a handsome couple they made.

The air dripped with silence. The admission galled him, but the colonel's palms were sweating. Damn! Just to wait! To stand and wait! What was Grant up to? Why wasn't he doing something? It was out of character for him or his corps commanders, Sherman, McPherson, and McClernand not to do *any*thing. Damn Yankees, anyways.

And Pemberton. The Confederate general had set up his headquarters somewhere far west of the horseshoe in the Big Black where his army had dug in to face the enemy. Why wasn't Pemberton where he was needed, though? Any damned fool knew he should be close enough to direct the defense and ensuing counterattack that would, at long last, break Grant's back and send him bruised and reeling right into Johnston's grasp to be chewed up and mauled beyond effectiveness once and for all.

Quiet. Ominously quiet. Those woods, there on the Union right. Packed with infantry. Those on the left, too, no doubt. And the artillery? In the center, of course, along the railroad. And there to the far right, too, backed up to the river behind a stand of cane. Maybe.

But all quiet. Too quiet.

The colonel wiped his hands on the side flaps of his uniform coat and wished they wouldn't sweat so.

Pale chocolate icing clung to the corner of Solange's mouth. Conscious of Warren Hibber's scrutiny, she flicked out her tongue to lick away the sugary tidbits. Solange enjoyed being the object of scrutiny. It somewhat ameliorated her anger at Tom for having left her to fend for herself at the picnic. She turned languorous eyes on Warren and leaned forward, the better to tantalize him with a glimpse of the whiteness of her breasts. "I'm so glad you came by," she said in her sultriest manner. "A single woman driving alone?" She frowned ever so slightly. "This war is horrible, *n'est-ce pas?* But then, if there were no danger"—she brightened, and her eyes were songs sung to Warren alone—"we would not have ridden together."

"It was . . . *is* my . . . that is, *our* pleasure," Warren stammered

unsure of how to handle this surprising assault, and yet daring to hope
that perhaps . . .

Brassy laughter to his side momentarily brought him up short.
Guiltily, yet covering it well, he thought, he checked on Mildred. His
wife was majestically reclining on a nearby blanket and chattering
away rapidly, exchanging the gossip of the day with two of her
friends. He might as well have been a hundred miles away for all the
attention she paid him.

"I'm sorry Tom had to work," Warren said, boldly letting his eyes
drop to her breasts. Solange's flesh was pale, the tops of her breasts
where they swelled above the delicately laced bodice faintly traced
with the light blue of veins. When she moved her shoulders, the flesh
rubbed together, producing in him an insane desire to reach out and
touch her, the consequences be damned.

Solange tilted her parasol and slowly turned the handle. The
shadow moving on the tops of her breasts made them appear alive.
She could sense Warren's pulse quickening. "I find the company most
invigorating," she purred, adding to his turmoil. Men were prey to
compliments. All men. She had learned this lesson early in life. How,
if ever, she expected to use Warren Hibber she hadn't the foggiest notion, but one never knew. Solange had been left high and dry before,
and the way things had been going with Tom lately, she couldn't
afford not to have at least a few possibilities on which she could fall
back in an emergency.

A cheer went up from a crowd of people gathering some fifty yards
behind Warren. "Whatever is that?" Solange asked, craning to see
over the banker's shoulder.

Warren twisted around on the blanket to follow her line of sight.
"The wrestling match, I imagine." He sneaked a quick look at his wife
and judged her adequately distracted. She would never notice his absence. Solange had been giving him signals ever since they had arrived at the meadow, and it was now or never. An innocent stroll
wouldn't be remarked upon by anyone and would give them the privacy they needed to discuss a . . . what? A more intimate future relationship, he thought, would strike the right tone. "There is, I suspect,
a marvelous view from Indian Mound," he said, turning back to Solange. "I don't suppose . . ."

She was gone. The space across the blanket from him was empty.
The only sign of her was a glimpse of her hat, moving in the direction
of the ring McGivern had had erected. "Well!" Warren sniffed. "If
she prefers a bunch of sweaty louts to the vice-president of the Vicksburg Mercantile Bank, so be it."

As fate had taken her to the balcony that morning, fate and a prickling in her fingertips led her to the ring of spectators surrounding the free-for-all. Other women watching were escorted, but the prickling sensation was too strong for Solange to ignore. A touch here, a nudge there, gentle pressure always toward the center. The men in front of her nodded or touched their hat brims and made way for her until, suddenly, she was in the front row. A faint shimmering of dust, just enough to tickle the nose or bring moisture to an eye, drifted over her. And not two yards away, separated from the spectators by a hemp line strung three feet off the ground, a knot of grunting, straining men stripped to the waist fought for the entertainment of Vicksburg's finest.

Her pulse began an insane hammering. He was there. Somewhere in that milling mob, the man she . . . Her eyes narrowed and the wind whistled through her clenched teeth as she inhaled sharply. A giant of a man, black hair on his head matted, more on his chest glistening with sweat, staggered backward out of the center of the ring, and lifting another man, threw him out of the boundaries. Not waiting for an invitation, he reached into the center of the struggling knot, grabbed another man by his belt, and spun him free of the others.

"Two to one on Micah," a voice called from across the ring. "In a dozen blows or less."

"Taken," came an answer, followed by a spate of conditions and odds Solange couldn't follow.

What followed was short and brutal. Micah's opponent, a chunky block of a man three inches shorter than Micah charged. Micah stepped aside and stunned him with a blow to the head as he passed.

"One!" someone shouted.

The man squared away, threw a left, a right, and another left.

"Two, three, four!" another man yelled, laughing as all three blows missed.

The dockworker caught Micah low with a right and connected with a left jab to the face. Micah grunted and backed off momentarily, then shook his head like a bull and waded in.

"Seven, eight, nine, ten!" came the shout from a half dozen voices in unison.

Blood poured from the dockworker's nose and left eye. Only seconds ago he had seemed well in command of the situation; now he stood like a teetering, unsupported pole. Micah took his time. Suddenly, his left hand dug deep into the dockworker's midriff. The half-unconscious man doubled forward, only to be straightened, lifted off his feet with a short, vicious uppercut.

"Eleven, twelve!" the original bettor shouted ecstatically as the dockworker hung poised in the air for a half second and then, totally unconscious, fell backwards onto the rope and the outstretched arms of two of the spectators, who dragged him out of the way.

Only four of the original ten dockworkers were left. Micah watched them at work, flexed his right hand, and took his time before committing himself. One of the four fell and, spitting blood, crawled out of the ring, finished. His opponent turned and, surprising the other two, caught them in neck locks and bashed their heads together. Dropping them, he straightened to catch his breath and found himself looking at Micah.

A hush fell over the crowd. Two men left. Micah, over six feet tall, dark, muscles long and smooth, looked indomitable. The dockworker, short and almost pasty white, nearly hairless, looked harmless but had proved he wasn't. Slowly, the two men circled and took stock of each other. The dockworker stepped over one body, leaned down without taking his eyes off Micah, caught the man's ankle, and dragged him out of the way. Micah did the same with the remaining defeated contestant and then, looking past the dockworker, grinned as he recognized Solange.

"Any bets before we start?" he asked the crowd, focusing again on the dockworker.

"Two hundred on Luke," a voice called from the rear.

"Covered!" Micah snapped, wanting to hear bets placed on him.

"Fifty on Lattimore!"

"You're crazy," someone behind Micah called back. "I've seen Luke hold a six-hundred-pound bale of cotton over his head. He'll break Lattimore in two and throw him from here to the river."

More bets were called and accepted. Luke hadn't moved and stood still as a stump, his chest slowly rising and falling. Flexing his shoulders and hands, Micah forced his mind off Solange. Looks were deceiving. The man they'd called Luke looked flabby, but Micah had seen such men before. Built low to the ground, they were as tenacious as bulldogs and often as strong as bulls. They were also frequently underestimated, a mistake Micah wasn't about to make.

When at last the fight started, it looked more like a dance. Slowly, each man crouched slightly and took slow, shuffling steps forward. Slowly, their arms raised until their hands touched and then, with fingers interlaced, locked palm to palm. The silence was eerie. The muscles in their forearms and shoulders bulged as each tried to bend the other to his will. Ten seconds, thirty, a minute: neither gained headway. And then, suddenly, as if each had decided on precisely the same tactic at precisely the same instant, their hands parted, and they stepped forward into a mutual bear hug. Micah grunted and locked his fingers behind the shorter man's back. Luke leaned forward slightly, then back, pulling Micah off balance for a fraction of a second. By the time his feet were planted again, Luke's arms were locked around him.

No one made a sound. Micah and Luke's muscles stood out as they fought in the brutal silence. The salt smell of humanity, the heady musk of primeval man hung heavily in the air. One woman swooned and had to be carried from the press of spectators. Solange winced and sucked in her breath. The sight and smells excited her and, feeling giddy, she opened the fan at her wrist and fanned her neck and suddenly perspiring forehead. Music was playing and children were shouting elsewhere in the meadow, but no one took notice. The crowd had eyes and ears only for the two fighting men.

No crowd, no sunshine, no grass, no sky. The soft popping of an overstressed joint. Air whistling through clenched teeth, in and out of tortured lungs. Sweat mingling unnoticed where the side of their heads touched like lovers, where their chins dug into each other's shoulder, sweat mingling and pouring down their naked chests. Strength ebbing—a man can take only so much. Eyes closed—looking consumes energy and every ounce is required for the task . . .

A sudden whoosh of air, and Luke jerked spasmodically. The pressure on Micah's ribs was gone. Only slowly, by willing his muscles to relax, could Micah let go. His hands finally separated, the unconscious dockworker silently slid down his chest and crumpled in a rag doll heap at his feet. Panting, his chest on fire, Micah stepped over his downed opponent and stood alone in the center of the ring.

Some cheered. Others, Nathaniel's friends and wanting to see Micah get his comeuppance, grumbled and wandered off before McGivern could award the forty-dollar prize. The money no real objective, Micah collected the two hundred dollars he'd won on himself and looked around for Solange, who was nowhere to be seen. He could feel her, though, he was sure. Every sense alert, he drank deeply from the water bucket McGivern provided, pulled on his shirt, and started for the buckboard he'd taken earlier from his father's house, ignoring a startled servant's protests.

Solange, meanwhile, was halfway to Indian Mound. Disturbed, confused, and excited since their brief, silent, and distant encounter that morning when she stood on the balcony and he watched her from the road, she had known the moment she saw him half naked in the ring that she had to escape before they met in person or be lost forever.

And however angry and frustrated she was with Tom, she had no immediate desire either to leave or harm him. As a consequence, she had slipped from the crowd the second the dockworker slumped in Micah's arms and, discreetly deciding to remove herself from temptation's way, moved as unobtrusively as possible toward the lane that led to the main road back to town. If on the way she met Tom, she would tell him that the sun had given her a blinding headache and that she wanted to go home. He would think that strange, of course, but less so than finding her in the arms of Micah Lattimore.

No one paid her the slightest bit of attention. Her stomach churning —she wanted Micah, yet she was terrified at the very thought of him— she hurried past Indian Mound and stopped to catch her breath. Ahead, the lane was empty. Only after she had started walking again did she hear the sound of a horse and the creak of wheels.

Never had she felt more aware of herself or her surroundings. The sun glowed through the translucent fabric of her parasol. She could see and smell the little puffs of dust kicked up by her feet. Each breath was an effort: she could feel the air rush through her nose, feel her chest expanding and contracting. Her skin tingled almost painfully where her thighs brushed together with each step. Her nipples rubbed against the bodice of her gown. And Micah Lattimore was nearing.

Her step firm, her head straight, she saw the horse out of the corner of her eye. Muzzle, head, neck, withers, croup, tail. Then the reins, the footboard, a pair of boots, a leg.

"The only reason I came to this picnic was because I figured you'd be here."

His voice was low and harsh, not a lover's voice. "Oh?" Solange heard herself say. "There must have been better reasons than that."

"Not that I can think of. I certainly wasn't invited." The wagon stopped and Micah moved over on the seat. "Get in."

"Somebody might—"

"We're alone and you know it."

Solange looked at him for the first time. A trickle of dried blood ran down from the corner of his mouth where his lip had been cut. His hair was wet and matted to his head. His shirt was soaked with perspiration. His right hand, holding the reins, was swelling grotesquely. Her mouth was dry and she had to lick her lips before she could talk. "I don't want—"

"You do want. So do I. You left because you want, I followed you because I want." His left hand reached out for her. "Get in."

The world had become a quiet place. Micah's gelding stamped its foot, a squirrel chattered, the wind soughed through the trees—but

Solange didn't hear those sounds. Mesmerized, she felt her hand rise, watched her fingers slip into his. A second later she was at his side and they were driving down the lane. His left arm touched her right. His left thigh pressed against her right. She was filled with the aroma of dirt, of perspiration, of man smell. She felt alternately numb and sensitized to the slightest stimulus. Her stomach convulsed. She was hot, she was cold. And then, suddenly, she was terrified, for Micah was turning into a narrow bylane from which, no matter where it led, there would be no turning back.

The lane dipped into a small muddy slough, climbed a short sloping knoll, detoured around a fallen tree, and ended in a shallow depression in the center of which was a secluded glade carpeted with grass and wild flowers. The horse stopped. Unassisted, her heart pounding, Solange climbed out of the carriage and walked toward the treeline where a dogwood bloomed in the shade of a mammoth old moss hung oak. "I have done many things in my life," she said, as much to herself as to Micah, "but never have I cheated on my husband."

"There's always a first time," Micah said from behind her.

"Yes," she whispered, hating herself for what she could not stop herself from doing. If only Tom were there. But he wasn't, of course, and hadn't been. He had turned on her, left her alone and lonely with no one to whom she might turn. Except the man whose aura enveloped her, whose body heat she could feel behind her, whose scent, like rutting musk, pervaded her nostrils and made her head swim. "Yes," she repeated, turning. "There's always a first . . ."

His shirt off, naked to the torso as she had seen him in the ring, he stood no more than an arm's length from her. Solange's knees turned to water, and she swayed forward into his arms. Micah caught her in a savage embrace, crushed her to him, and bruised her lips with a demonic kiss that left her defenseless. "You'll ruin my gown," she whispered hoarsely with what vestige of sanity remained in her.

"Who cares?"

"I do."

"Then take the damned thing off."

Tom was forgotten. All sense of shame and propriety lay crumbled with her own self-imposed standards. Slowly, she reached behind her, began releasing the hooks that held her gown together. When the last one fell open, she shrugged and the gown dropped from her shoulders leaving her, too, naked to the waist.

Micah's eyes narrowed as he inhaled and then, matching her sudden frenzy, shed the rest of his clothes. Slippers and boots kicked off. Trousers ripped open and cast aside, next to the heap of pink silk and linen petticoats. Naked and aroused, they faced each other in the sunlight, and then met to fulfill the promise of the morning, sank to the ground, and coupled like wild animals which, impelled by nature, can no more stop themselves than can the falling tree split by lightning.

Animal sounds and smells, lusty, carnal, primitive. He was in her, driving, painful, forcing her apart, tearing her in two, thrusting, burning . . .

Solange gasped while his weight crushed her, took her life, and filled her with life. No longer caring about the pain, beyond the fear of discovery, bathed in sensations so exquisite she was forced to fight for breath, and demanding, demanding as much as he.

More than he. "More, damn you!" she hissed, the animal sounds deep in her throat. "Damn, damn, God damn you! Yes, yes, yes . . ."

Burning . . .

In her, around him. All of her, all of him. Joined, coupled, the beast faces itself and has two backs, connected pulses with animal fury fed by hatred and hunger, twin energies that melt the bones and . . .

"Now . . ."

. . . Paralyze the body with unbearable spasms . . .

"Now . . ."

. . . And sear the soul with . . .

"Nooowwww!"

"Take Natchez, for example," Miles Bishop thundered, enjoying an argument in which he could shout. His forehead was red with excitement and his beard bounced on his chest.

"Natchez?" Nathaniel roared. "Natchez was betrayed, given to the Northern scum through the perfidy of men more interested in profit than ideals!"

"It would have fallen in any case," Miles answered. "It is quixotic to think—"

"Quixotic, by God!" Nathaniel pounded on the table. "Don Quixote was a dreamer, sir. I say our cause is no dream, and that the cream, sir, the cream of the South shall prevail. The darker the hour, to the greater glory shall our sons and daughters' glory be revealed. We taught them, nay, raised them for just such an hour as this!"

"Which hour fast approaches! Do you imagine . . ."

"The cream of the South," Rafe said with a laugh to Celia. "That's me. I'm one of Father's favorite sayings."

"He and Miles can go on like that for hours," Celia said, laughing. "It all gets terribly repetitive, but they seem to enjoy themselves."

A soldier wandered past, wearing his gray coat like a shield of honor. His buttons were polished and his tunic crisply laundered. He tilted on his crutches and dangled a pinned up, empty trouser leg. His face was that of a boy, fair and round-cheeked, but his neatly parted hair was streaked with silver and the flesh around his eyes—empty, hollow eyes—was crinkled like burned paper. "My God!" Rafe whispered. "Is that Billy Clark?"

"Yes," Celia replied. "Ever since Shiloh. His brother's a colonel I hear."

"Billy Clark." The list Nathaniel had given him the night before had been incomplete, but woefully long. The cream was thinning. First families were toppling like tenpins, bled dry of youth and vigor and succeeding generations. War was culling them, leaving none unscathed. Where were Miles Bishop's four sons? Where were the McPherson twins? Now poor Billy. "Some cream," Rafe muttered sarcastically and closed his eyes against the sight.

When he opened them, the soldier was gone. "Sorry," he said, pouring himself a fresh glass of wine. "Too much news too fast. That and Micah, I guess. He always brings out the worst in me."

"I understand."

"Do you?" Rafe asked, watching her over his glass.

More than you know, Celia thought, careful not to let the bitter hatred show. "I think so. Is that so strange?"

"No. Perhaps not." Rafe folded his hands and leaned on his elbows. He was close enough to smell the sweet clean fragrance of her. "If anything's strange, it's me."

"Now you're being silly."

"Not silly. Very, very serious. Two years—" He stopped as a shadow fell across them, looked up to see a young officer standing just behind him. "Yes?"

"Your pardon, ma'am. Captain Lattimore? There's to be a shooting match, and Phillip Laughton asked me to tell you you could use his gun if you wanted to join in. Everyone's put up ten dollars apiece. The winner takes a hundred and the rest goes to buy medical supplies."

"How many are shooting?" Rafe asked, not particularly interested, far more content to spend his time with Celia.

The officer shrugged. "I don't know. Sixty, maybe? Lots of boys no one has heard of. Major Crawford will be the judge. Well? Will you raise a rifle with us?"

"Seems a shame to take that kind of money from you," Rafe

drawled. "If you don't mind, I'll just sit this one out and give the rest of you a chance."

"Just as Phillip predicted," the officer said. "That you feared losing your reputation and wouldn't compete against your betters."

"He said that?" Rafe asked, coloring.

"Yes, indeed. Well, I'll tell them—"

"That I'll shoot. And cover all side wagers anyone cares to make."

The man grinned. "Done. Fifteen minutes. We'll be at the north end of the meadow," the officer said, turning and leaving immediately.

"He did that very smoothly," Celia observed, stifling a laugh. "Clay in the hands of a master potter."

"Just whose side are you on?" Rafe asked, bridling and then quickly realizing she was teasing. "That's all right. Clay can turn to rock. And then doesn't give an inch. Anyway, shooting beats listening to Father and his diehard generals discuss the storming of Chapultepec. Or another discourse on the nature of my miraculous return. C'mon. Let's go."

Shooting matches were as popular in Vicksburg as they were elsewhere in the South and Southwest. Boys who had been brought up with a gun in their hand and who at an early age had been responsible for providing the family table with meat were common. With a good Kentucky rifle, many of them could take the head off a squirrel at well over a hundred paces nine times out of ten. The war and the influx of strangers to Vicksburg had increased the normal population of these marksmen and more importantly, brought new blood to town. Everyone knew what to expect of a Rafe Lattimore or a Phillip Laughton or a Johnny McArthur, who, the best shot of all, bless his heart, had been decapitated by a cannonball at Bull Run, but no one had the slightest inkling of the capabilities of some of the dark-eyed, close-mouthed, unobtrusive boys from up and down river.

Six shooting stations had been set up at the north end of the meadow. Seventy-five yards away from each station stood a target post. Beyond each post, four more had been sunk at twenty-five-yard intervals. In front of the center two stations, two extra posts had been added. Just inside the tree line at the edge of the meadow, they took the range up to two hundred and fifty yards. If more than one man hit targets at that distance, each would continue shooting until he missed, and the last man to hit his target, then, was declared the winner.

Well over three hundred spectators sat and stood on the slight rise behind the shooters' stands. While Rafe left to enter, draw the number that would determine his order of shooting, and fire a few practice rounds with Phillip's rifle, Celia wandered through the crowd. Gaillee was there holding court. Celia worked her way behind Gaillee and then turned when she heard her name called. "Why, it's Lynna O'Grady!" she cried out, hurrying to greet a woman her own age, but pregnant and obviously much poorer. "Just look at you! Married and soon to have a family?"

"Lynna Hays, now," the woman said, awkwardly returning Celia's embrace. "Don't I look just awful?"

"You look radiant!" Celia said, stepping back and fondly inspecting her. Bright copper-red hair spilled in soft waves down her back and a sprinkling of freckles gave her an almost tomboyish appearance offset by a full and lush figure that a poorly cut gingham gown couldn't hide. "And make me feel positively spinsterish. Where have you been? I haven't seen you since . . . Lord, your father's funeral. Who's the lucky man?"

"His name is Jonathan and he's from Natchez. We moved back here last summer after Mama died, and took over the old place."

"Oh, dear." Celia took Lynna's hand and squeezed it sympathetically. "I didn't know. I'm so sorry."

"It's all right. I . . . I heard about your father. I was going to come by, but it seems there's always so much to do . . ." She trailed off awkwardly.

"Lynna O' . . . I mean, Hays!" Celia warned.

"Well, it *is* a little awkward . . ."

"Nonsense!" Celia embraced her warmly for the second time and held her at arm's length. "I can't *believe* you still have this silly thing about money. Dear Lord, we all wear linsey these days anyway. Well, except for today. There's no reason—"

"Ladies and gentlemen!" a voice boomed, interrupting her. "We've changed the rules slightly due to the shortage of powder and shot. In today's match, each man will shoot once at the seventy-five-yard target. Those not eliminated will fire at the hundred-yard target, and so on. Will the first six gentlemen take their places, please."

"Is your Jonathan shooting?" Celia asked, spotting Rafe standing behind the third stand. "Which one is he? What does he do?"

Lynna searched through the crowd, and finally spotted him. "There at the fifth post," she said, pointing. "The short one with light hair and the blue shirt. He's a schoolteacher."

"A schoolteacher?" Celia asked, surprised.

Lynna's face reddened. "He doesn't believe in violence," she said defensively. "That men should kill men. Is that so terrible?"

"I didn't mean that the way . . ." The beginning shots and the cheers or groans from the crowd gave Celia the excuse she needed to let her apology die. A schoolteacher and a pacifist! Only an uncommonly strong man could walk that particular course in times like these, Celia thought. Leave it to Lynna. Of all her friends, Lynna had been considered the most practical and logical, yet Celia had known how deep and pure her emotions had run. Whoever this Jonathan Hays was, Celia was sure there was more to him than the unconventionality of pacifism.

Five of the six clay target discs shattered in the first volley, and the next six shooters took their places. Celia and Lynna found a place to sit and watch, and as shooter followed shooter, they reminisced over the days of their youth and caught each other up on what had happened to them during the past few years.

They had first met fifteen years earlier when Hal Bartlett hired Lynna's father, Nick, who was an experienced riverboat pilot. The two girls, both of an age, needed no time to become fast friends, and by the time they were ten they were virtually inseparable. Nick's purchase of the farm south of town forced a wedge of distance between the girls, for two miles separated them. Still, they played together frequently until, when they were thirteen, Nick and Hal came to a parting of the ways when Nick refused to pilot a boat he considered unsafe in a race. This break was more serious, for neither father wanted his daughter to spend time in the company of the other. The girls drifted apart slowly. Celia was from a well-to-do family from the good part of town, Lynna was poor and lived in what amounted to the country, so they met only on rare occasions. The picnic marked the first time they had seen each other since Nick's funeral, five years earlier after a boat he considered safe blew up under him and burned to the waterline.

A thousand mutual memories, and as many details of the past five years of not seeing each other. By the time their initial enthusiasm had worn down, the contestants had been winnowed to a final nine, and the discs were being placed on the two-hundred-yard targets. The crowd was still and attentive now as the first in line took his place, tested the wind, fired, and was rewarded with seeing the tiny white spot atop the post disappear. The second shooter, a local boy from south of town, wasn't so lucky, and the crowd groaned in disappointment. By the end of the round, six had missed. Only three, Rafe, Jonathan, and a young man with a club foot were left.

"Tell 'em your name, young fella," Major Crawford instructed while the Negro boys moved to the two-hundred-and-twenty-five-yard marker and set the first targets.

The young man ducked his head and mumbled something.

"He says his name's Matthew Broussard, and that he's from Lake Charles, and would rather be fighting than shooting at clay targets. The second man"—he pointed to Jonathan, and a tone of curt disapproval colored his voice—"is Jonathan Hays. The third, most of you know, is Rafe Lattimore, who could use a ship if any of you have a spare one. The distance is two hundred twenty-five yards."

Broussard was to shoot first. Rafe stood back and watched the young man. Hardly taller than his rifle was long, he couldn't have been a day over seventeen. Peach fuzz whiskers sprouted from his chin and cheeks. His hair was long and stringy, and his feet—one horribly deformed and giving him an awkward limp—were bare and calloused from a lifetime of going without shoes. A wad of tobacco swelled his left cheek. Carefully, he spat toward the target, then double-checked the wind with a wet finger, and at last raised his rifle, inhaled, held his breath, and squeezed off what seemed like an abnormally fast shot for the distance. A second later, the white clay disc disappeared, and the crowd cheered.

"Pretty nice shot," Rafe said as the boy stepped back to make room for Jonathan.

"Luck," came the laconic reply. "At this distance, pure luck."

"I'm not sure about that."

"Sure as gators'll bite your hand off, you dangle a pinkie in the water," the boy said, not disrespectfully. "You, him, an' me. We're shootin' fer a lucky hundred dollars."

Jonathan raised his rifle and sighted. Two hundred twenty-five yards. A slight breeze blowing from right to left. The ball would drop . . . how far? Three and a half inches? Four? The patch of white drifted into sight below the barrel to the right. He steadied, breathed deeply, and willed himself steady. The left edge of the disc appeared on the right, below the barrel, just as the rifle bucked against his shoulder and blew black smoke and a flash of flame from the barrel. A second later, the sound of the report still strong in his ears, the disc exploded.

"He'll take the money, I reckon, even if he won't fire at no Bluecoat," a voice said from behind Lynna as she alone cheered her husband's feat.

Lynna colored and started to turn, then thought better and sat in subdued silence.

"Henry David Thoreau said that some men walk to the sound of a different drummer," Celia said, taking Lynna's hand. "He didn't say anything about other men agreeing."

"I know," Lynna said, grateful for Celia's understanding. "That was one of the milder comments. How he puts up with them, I don't know. Sometimes I think he must be the strongest man in the whole—"

"Shhh!" Celia hissed abruptly, intent on Rafe. She let go Lynna's hand and crossed her fingers just in time to hear the report of his rifle, see the target disintegrate, and join in the boisterous cheers and applause.

"You and Rafe Lattimore?" Lynna asked, unbelieving, when the racket diminished.

"Well . . ." Celia almost denied any affection between her and Rafe, yet found she couldn't. Being with him had rejuvenated her, and given her soul a lift. Just watching him made her feel good—warm and soft and needed and loved in a way she hadn't felt for far, far too long. "Yes," she said simply. And edging carefully around the pain—live for the moment, for this one second—added, "Rafe and I."

A new target waited for the Broussard boy. Limping to the line, he went through the ritual of testing the wind again, only to fire at the same instant a gust of wind bent the grass near the target and pushed the ball far enough to the left to miss. "Up to ya'll, I reckon," he said with a shrug, stepping aside.

"Two marksmen left," Major Crawford bawled needlessly.

The wind gusted, died, and gusted again. Jonathan Hays waited patiently, picked his time, and fired. A sigh went through the crowd as, at first, nothing happened, and then the top half of the target toppled and fell. "Nicked it enough to crack it, I guess," he said as he and Rafe exchanged places. "Break yours and you win."

Luck, the Broussard boy had said. The same wind that had pushed his bullet aside had toppled Hays's nicked target. Luck. And skill, too, he thought grimly, pushing the crowd and the other shooters out of his mind. Not an easy shot, but one he'd made many times before. A steady hand, a steady eye. Feet firmly planted, back and neck relaxed. Slow breath, hold, squeeze smoothly, always surprised but never flinching when . . .

There! A good shot and true, he thought, motionless until he should see the disc disintegrate and then not believing when the crowd groaned and he realized he'd missed completely.

Completely! Emptied, he lowered the rifle and turned as a hand clapped him on the shoulder. "Nice try," Phillip Laughton said, barely concealing a smirk.

"The sights are off," Rafe growled, handing Phillip his rifle and stalking off to find Celia.

"Like I said." The Broussard boy stood leaning on his rifle, blocking Rafe's path. "That's a lucky hundred dollars." He made a clicking sound with his mouth, spat a stream of tobacco juice. "Sure coulda used it. Hundred dollars is a lotta money. For some," he added, his eyes lingering on the cut of Rafe's clothes and the gold watch fob he wore.

Rafe opened his mouth to curse but held his tongue. A hundred dollars. The clothes he wore cost well over that, and he had a half a dozen suits just like them at home, not to speak of the Lattimore wealth at his fingertips. The boy who stood in front of him, club foot turned and calloused on the side, trousers and shirt tattered, had probably never owned a hundred dollars in his whole life. "You're a good shot," he said, the anger draining from him. He stuck out his hand, wasn't at all surprised to find Broussard's grip firm and sincere. Rafe grinned. "I was proud to face off with you. And better luck next time."

"Good shooting," Celia said, coming up to him as Broussard hobbled off.

Rafe shrugged. "Everyone misses sometime. Just my turn, I guess."

"I'm glad it was," Celia said, somewhat cryptically. "Do you remember Lynna O'Grady?"

"Of course," Rafe lifted his hat, bowed slightly. "It's been some years, but you're as beautiful as I remember."

"She's Lynna Hays, now," Celia said. At the same time Lynna said, "And you're as gallant as I remember you."

"What?" Rafe asked, not sure he had heard correctly. "Lynna who?"

"Hays," a male voice answered. Jonathan stepped to Lynna's side, put his left arm around her waist, and stuck out his right for Rafe to shake. "You're a fine shot. The boy was right. Two hundred yards is skill, two twenty-five is luck."

Rafe's immediate reaction was anger, for he did not suffer losing lightly, especially to what appeared at first glance to be a farmer. His shoulders stiffened then relaxed again as he studied the man in front of him. Jonathan Hays was well under six feet tall with wide shoulders out of proportion to his height. Curly, sandy-colored hair and full beard gave him somewhat the look of a compact, diminutive lion, except for his eyes which were startlingly blue and almost as soft as a woman's. How much he weighed would be a guess, for though he was short, he looked formidably dense and compact. Most striking were his hands, large and rawboned—hands that had worked and worked hard—but clean and evenly manicured, a tantalizingly mysterious contrast to the almost painfully simple and inexpensive clothes he wore. What and whoever he was, Rafe decided quickly, he was not a man with whom one easily could be angry. "Rafe Lattimore," he said, accepting Jonathan's hand. "A skilled man makes his own luck. The pleasure's all mine, sir."

A bell ringing followed by a burst of music floating across the meadow signaled it was time for the dancing. "Well . . ." Rafe said awkwardly. He took Celia's arm and glanced over his shoulder. "I suppose we'd better find Father. If you'll excuse us?"

"Of course. And I think Lynna has had quite enough excitement for one day," Jonathan said in obvious reference to her advanced pregnancy.

"An Irish lass never has enough excitement," Lynna said, laughing gaily but firmly disagreeing with her husband. "Come and I'll show you while there's still room to dance." She started to pull Jonathan away, but paused to reach out and take Celia's hand. "Our school's at the corner of Walnut and Veto. Come see us, won't you? Please?"

"I should like that," Celia replied without hesitation. "And you," she admonished, "come see me. And none of this you-know-what talk. I mean that, Lynna."

Lynna smiled shyly, brushed Celia on the cheek with a light kiss, and hurried off with her husband, the two of them buoyant with their prize money.

"They are a fortunate couple," Rafe said, his voice soft.

Celia gave a start. He had spoken her very thoughts. The two of them looked so happy. And she . . . She was happy, too. Determinedly so, stealing an afternoon and tucking it away to be pulled out and savored at some unknown time and place when . . .

"Why, they're playing 'The Rose of Alabam'," she said, silently repeating her vow not to be morose. "Mr. Lattimore?" she asked, with a deep curtsey. "Would you be so gallant as to invite me to dance?"

"Miss Bartlett," Rafe answered, bowing and offering her his arm, "my heart has not stopped dancing since I first set eyes upon you this morning."

"Why, Mr. Lattimore! What a perfectly delightful thing to say. And now, if you can only dance better than you shoot . . ."

Protected. That was the key word. The sweetest word in military science, the colonel decided. Marsh and impenetrable—another lovely word under the circumstances—woods to the north and south. Nothing for Billy Yank to do but come straight on, headlong across three hundred yards of open ground right smackety, by God, dab into the leveled rifles, into the cannon muzzles, into the prettily gleaming bayonets of the Confederate defense. It was the kind of battle the men in gray had been waiting for since Grant successfully ferried his bluebellies across the Mississippi and landed them south of Vicksburg eight weeks ago.

The colonel tugged at his mustache and raised his glass to study the lay of the land and the Union lines. The Confederate breastworks were nearly a solid mile of cotton bales reinforced and topped with dirt, behind which lay thirty thousand men, almost six men to each foot of line. The ground in front of them was level and devoid of cover except for one insignificant zigzagging gully that only a fool would use because it was more a trap than anything else. There was still little movement, but the Union artillery had started firing almost an hour ago, which indicated the attack would come soon. When it did, the bluebellies would meet the Gray Reaper point-blank.

"Let the party begin," the colonel said to himself. Whip Billy Yank and send him packing, and then return to Vicksburg wreathed in glory. There was a young lady there he planned . . .

Firing. Definitely rifle fire, and heavy at that. The colonel stiffened to the sound of bugles blaring and men yelling. One hell of a commotion. He focused his glass on the far line of trees, from which the Union forces would have to come, and saw nothing. And yet more firing, shouts, and screams.

"What the devil?"

Only then did he lower his glass to sweep the ground along the Confederate left, and there saw, pouring out of the gully and over the breastworks, wave after wave of soldiers in blue. The party had indeed begun.

"Now this is what I call a party," Rafe said, expertly swinging Celia in his arms and then taking the lead in a series of quick three steps that moved them into the flow of the dancers. There were fiddles and banjos and hands clapping and a slightly out-of-tune piano.

"They don't know anything slow," Celia said, laughing, catching her breath as the tempo increased.

"Hold tight!" Rafe shouted.

"Are you kidding? For dear life!" Celia squealed as they whirled and spun. The board dance floor laid by slaves was a sea of motion, constant, sudden, surging, and flowing. Gaily colored gowns caught the air and floated, daringly, ankle high. Gentlemen unbuttoned their coats and spun and leaped to the happy notes concocted by the musicians. Older couples stood around the edge, cheering and clapping hands and remembering when they had stepped so lively and danced so daringly.

The music spun away Celia's cares. There was no room in her for worry. For the moment she was filled with a happiness, with a lightness that she had not known for too long. Dancing and music and frivolity and flirting and sweet breathlessness and laughter—oh, God, dear God, such laughter—enough to ease any burden.

"Let them play," she whispered. "Don't let them stop. For these moments, let the world tilt and spin to music. And never, never end . . ."

Never ending. The colonel had imagined his life to be without end. Though demonstrably untrue—he had seen too many soldiers fall and never rise—the belief was not without practical value, for it did, through instilling confidence, enhance his ability to survive. That ability was now being sorely tested.

The initial surprise onslaught of the breastworks had been so cleverly and well executed that the defenders had had time for little more than one volley before they were overrun. Already tired and hungry, their demoralization was complete, and they fled. The colonel and other officers all along the line had threatened and shouted to no avail. As more and more bluebellies poured over the fortifications, the rout became complete. No more than fifteen minutes had passed since the original contact, and the mile-long line no longer existed. In its place, masses of men sprinted for the railroad bridge crossing the Big Black River at their backs. The psychological crutch that command had counted on to give the men an added measure of backbone had crumbled and left them all helpless cripples.

The colonel was not so young that he could not appreciate tragedy. Minié balls whizzed around him. Flames from the burning trestle licked at the frayed and torn edges of his uniform. He wept, he shouted, he roared. Sword flaying the air, he exhorted and pleaded. "Turn and fight, you fools!" he screamed, grabbing the nearest soldier and trying to stem the tide. "Cowards. You sons of Mississippi . . . Men . . . We can hold the bridge! Stand with me!"

Some of them tried. Some but not enough. There on the west bank, the Vicksburg side of the Big Black, the few rallied futilely, turned bayonet and saber to face the Union onslaught.

Smoke—in his eyes, eating his lungs, and driving him mad with thirst! If he could only kill a man and find a full canteen! The river flowed beneath him, wide, wet, and unreachable. He tore his eyes from the water and shouted the order to fire as blue-clad figures emerged through the smoke and flames and spattering muzzle bursts. He lifted his revolver and fired all six shots one after another. The Yankee targets were impossible to miss, and impossible to stop. The ones who fell were replaced by two and three, and if these fell, were replaced by four and five and six. The colonel's revolver clicked empty, and someone struck him in the chest. Puzzled—there was no one close enough—he stared at the front of his coat and, with a detached and puzzled expression wiping blank his features, watched blood spurt from a hole there. Little plumes of red, one to each pump of his heart. The streamers were impressive at first, then gradually lessened to a pink froth.

The colonel hit the riverbank shoulder first. Sliding, sliding easily down the black muck, he felt no pain. Just thirst. Incredible thirst, only the water was just beyond his fingertips. Looking up, he could see the last of the Rebels fling their empty weapons at the onrushing Union army and run for their lives. Hot on their heels, rank after rank, Billy Yank by the thousands began the final, triumphant march on Vicksburg.

"The marsh, the ravine . . . ," the colonel mumbled. "How the hell did they?"

And wondering, died.

Like the wrestlers in the ring of men, like the soldiers at the Big Black, the boys were fighting. Four of them had ganged on one, and with no promise of any prize beyond a swollen lip or bloody nose. The outnumbered youth was crying. His eyes were swollen and bruised, but he was meting out as much punishment as he was taking, mostly because there were enough targets for even his wildest swings to connect. Until, that is, the largest of his attackers dove head first into his stomach and knocked the wind out of him. He landed hard on his back and, the breath rasping in his throat, tried futilely to raise his arms to block the kicks that were sure to come. Only one landed before he heard the lad who had downed him give a holler, not of triumph but of surprise. When he dared to open his eyes, three had run off. The fourth dangled from the outstretched arm of Jonathan Hays.

"Bert Wilder! Tommy Fraser! You boys are friends."

"Not now we ain't," Tommy gasped, gradually getting his wind back. He came off the ground and slammed a tight little fist into Bert Wilder's ear. Bert howled in pain and, as Jonathan tried to subdue Tommy, twisted free and scampered into the crowd of townspeople. Tommy tried to give chase, but was caught from behind and held in place.

"Lemme go," he screeched, in a rage. "Lemme go!"

"What in heaven?" Lynna asked, a little out of breath herself as she joined them. She and Jonathan had seen the fight from their blanket and had run to break it up. Tommy Fraser, a favorite of them both, was an intelligent and earnest student, one of ten children and, at eleven years of age, the youngest member of a farm family.

"Lemme go!" Tommy shouted, his face contorted in a caricature of adult fury.

"Not as long as you keep up this outlandish behavior," Jonathan said.

"They deserve it," Tommy insisted. "C'mon, Mr. Hays. You ain't my pa. Lemme go."

"Just look at you!" Lynna sighed, kneeling in front of him and dabbing at his bruised and bleeding face.

Tommy winced, let her hands calm him. "Awww. I ain't hurt. Leave me be."

"Sure," Jonathan said, half carrying the lad to his and Lynna's blanket. "Now sit down until you calm down."

Lynna produced a leg of fried chicken from a wicker basket crammed with chicken, syrup-sweet preserves, and fresh bread. "Here. Eat this before you ride off to smite the Philistines," she ordered.

Anger was one thing, appetite another, and never the twain should meet. His anger fading fast, Tommy attacked the drumstick.

"I'm disappointed, Tommy," Jonathan said, resting a hand on the boy's shoulder. "I thought we once had a long talk about violence. Didn't we reach the conclusion that fighting never decided much of anything?"

"Yessir," Tommy said and sniffed. "But this was different." He looked sullenly at the ground, squirmed his toes against the mud that had worked its way into his shoes. "Had to."

"When we begin to make exceptions for actions we know to be wrong, then we are truly lost," Jonathan explained gently.

"This was different," Tommy repeated.

"Oh? What did Bert and the others do this time? Kid you for winning the spelling bee last week?"

"Wasn't what they said about me, Mr. Hays. I wouldn't'a fought if they was talkin' about me," Tommy protested around a mouthful of preserves and bread. "Honest. They was sayin' things about . . . about someone else. Mean things an' all."

Jonathan shook his head. "Why didn't you let this someone else decide if he wanted to fight or not, Tommy? Seems to me that was his decision to make."

"He wouldn't'a. I know. So I sorta had to stick up for him."

"This other fellow sounds like an admirable person," Hays said with a smile. "Just who is he?"

Tommy reddened, kept his attention focused on the bread and preserves so he wouldn't have to look Jonathan in the eye. "You, sir," he finally said in little more than a whisper.

"Oh."

"Just what were they saying?" Lynna asked, ignoring a disapproving glance from Jonathan. "I think we ought to know, but you don't have to say if you don't want to."

"Well . . ." Tommy struggled with himself, finally made up his mind and looked up with a stricken expression on his face. "About how everybody else is soldierin' an' how all of them are ready to shoulder a gun if need be 'ceptin' for Mr. Hays, who ain't about to fight 'cause he's . . . he's afraid an' ain't got the stomach for puttin' himself on the line an' all." Once started, the words poured out of him. "Bert said you were yella, too. I couldn't let him get away with sayin' a thing like that 'cause I know it ain't—isn't—true. I just couldn't. It ain't right."

"Oh, Tommy." Jonathan hitched himself over so he was facing the boy. Not too far away, the fiddlers were playing. Close by, an aged, rheumy-eyed black musician wandered through the picnickers and strummed his banjo in search of praise and pennies. Jonathan took Tommy by the shoulders and looked directly into his eyes. His voice was low, but cut through the din of activity. "I guess I have to say I appreciate you standing up for me, but at the same time I have to tell you I think you were wrong."

Tommy's head dropped and tears came to his eyes.

Jonathan tipped the boy's head up and looked directly into his eyes. "Hurting another person's feelings is a terrible thing to do, and I'm sorry if I hurt yours, but I'll tell you why I did. Because it's important, is why. I want you to remember something, okay? Listen to me, now." He leaned forward for emphasis. "No matter what you do in this world, there's always going to be folks who think you should do the opposite, do something else. You have to go on with what you think is right, and to hell with what other people say or think."

Tommy nodded gravely. He had never heard Mr. Hays curse. It was as if the two of them were speaking man to man, and that made what was said all the more important. "I was right, wasn't I, Mr. Hays? You ain't—aren't—yella, are you?"

"There are times when a man needs more courage not to pull a trigger than to pull one," Jonathan said.

Unsure he had been answered, Tommy quizzically tipped his head to one side.

"You think about that," Jonathan said, standing and ruffling Tommy's hair. "But remember what I said. Now run along. I'll bet your folks're wondering where you are. And I'll see you in school tomorrow, right?"

"Yessir!" Tommy got to his feet and looked questioningly at a piece of bread piled high with pear marmalade.

Lynna laughed warmly and handed him the bread. "You'd better take this with you," she said. "I'd hate to think I'd let a growing boy starve."

"Thank you, Miz Hays," Tommy said, and darted off.

Jonathan watched him leave, then sat heavily. "How do you explain to them that after the last man has died and the last city has burned, after the rifles are empty and the last cannon has fired, that the teachers are the ones who return to begin the rebuilding? How do you explain?"

"You don't," Lynna said. She set his hand flat on her thigh and smoothed the work worn skin, touching each finger in turn. "Not really, not completely. You just . . . try."

"Yeah."

The fiddlers played, the dancers cheered. A baby cried, and five small boys howling like Indians ran past in a file.

"Try. I just try."

The afternoon sun slanted through the trees.

Bits of grass clung to Solange's hair, needled the skin on her bottom, and were lost in the bunched folds of her dress. She worked a hair from inside her mouth and plucked it off her tongue. Held up to the sunlight, the hair was black and shiny and curled. She tasted of salt, smelled of salt and sweat and lovemaking. When his thigh stirred, she shuddered and squeezed her own legs tight around him. His hand slid along her side and left her skin tingling from its calloused sweep. He cupped her hip, nibbled at the underside of her breast, and teased her nipple with his tongue.

"We have . . . to leave," Solange whispered.

"So leave," Micah replied. His hand slid down her back and found the moistness between her legs.

"Why don't you ever do what I ask?"

"I am," he answered, rolling her onto her back.

"Damn you!" she whispered.

Laughter rumbled deep in Micah's throat. "Tell me to stop," he said, his arousal complete as he rose to his knees. He took her hands and placed them around himself. "Tell me."

"Damn you," she answered and, guiding him, damned herself.

The hours slipped away. Sunlight slanted from the west, balanced on a swooping flock of kites grudgingly being reeled in, muted the bright colors, and tinted the laughter and music with the melancholy realization that all good things come to an end. Families were rounded up and gathered in wagons and buckboards and carriages. Tables were dismantled and loaded aboard drays and caissons borrowed from the military. Reverend Lundquist and Father Razzoni had turned the collected donations over to a military adjutant standing in for General Pemberton who was away whipping the Yankees at the Big Black River. The picnic had been fun: the celebration that night when the news came would be even more so. There would be dancing in the streets.

Now there were too many people trying to leave at the same time. Rafe held the mare to the edge of a clot of conveyances funneling into the lane leading back to Vicksburg from Kileen's Meadow, at last decided the hell with following the crowd and popped the whip. The mare pulled out of line and headed across the south edge of the meadow, then onto a narrow trail that would pass Indian Mound and appeared to lead to the bluffs overlooking the river. "Where are we going?" Celia asked, gripping his arm in surprise.

"To watch a sunset," Rafe replied. "Do you mind?"

Celia felt a tinge of alarm, but against her better judgment made no protest for she had no wish to trail the procession back to town. The carriage skidded, fought loose of ruts, and rocked forward as the mare dutifully maneuvered onto firmer clay.

"Used to come squirrel hunting here," Rafe said as the trees closed over them. "There's a small hollow a little further on. Got my first one there. It was a Saturday morning." He chuckled, warm with the memory. "Old Uncle William, Father's first slave, was with me. I was so proud of myself! We cooked that squirrel right there and ate it for lunch. Never tasted one better."

The trail narrowed, turned onto another wider one that led east and at last opened into the hollow Rafe had been talking about. At the same time, just leaving the hollow, another carriage, driven by Micah rolled past them. Celia sensed Rafe tense at the unexpected encounter, and then tensed herself when she realized that the woman riding beside him was Solange Stewart. Solange sat back beneath the carriage shade in a futile attempt to hide herself. Micah's face was fixed in a display of wry amusement. He didn't care in the slightest what people thought of him or Solange. As the carriage drew abreast and passed, Micah touched the handle of his whip to the brim of his hat in a facetious salute. Celia felt her cheeks redden for the second time that day as he scrutinized the two of them with a knowing glance that cast an air of tawdriness over what until then had been the most innocent of intentions.

Rafe pretended to ignore his older brother, but sighed in relief the second Micah was out of sight.

"I'm sorry," Celia said lamely.

"For what? Blood ties?" Rafe snapped, immediately regretting his tone. "Now I'm sorry."

Celia was quick to forgive him. "I feel like letting out my claws now and then, too. I suppose our being here has all the appearance of a clandestine meeting."

"There's a difference, damn it," Rafe growled, still angry. "You're not a married woman and my intentions are entirely honorable." He sawed on the reins and guided the mare to a narrow trail that led out of the hollow. "Well, hell!" he said, the anger dissipating as fast as it had risen. He looked at Celia out of the corner of his eye and winked. "Pretty near honorable, anyway."

"Mr. Lattimore!" Celia exclaimed, affecting shocked surprise. "Have I unwittingly chosen the company of a lothario?"

"Have no fear, lady. You're in the presence of the cream of the South. Safe as in the lap of heaven. Curse it all."

Their laughter took them through the trees and to the bare edge of the bluffs. Alone, they stopped parallel to the edge and set the brakes. Below, the ground sank in sickening plunges to flat bottom land that flooded every spring when the Mississippi swelled above its banks. Further out, the Great Muddy itself rolled and heaved past the De Soto Peninsula. Beyond that the low bayou land stretched to the west. And above it all the sun lay red on the horizon, half hidden by banks of salmon-colored clouds. Gray water, green trees, pink sky. The mellow sunlight melting around them. A southwest breeze pushed the dank, fetid smell of swamp and forest up the bluffs and filled the air with the spring perfume of fecundity.

A pause in the world, Celia thought to herself, letting herself lean against Rafe as his arm went around her shoulders. A pause during which all things were possible if only she would let them be possible. Why not let go? she asked herself for the umpteenth time since that morning. How wondrous to feel just once in time of war the innocence of yesterday's peace, before the world again became a kaleidoscope of conflicting, colliding elements.

Here and now, she thought. Only here and now was the music of silence, the fire of passion. *Oh Lord,* she mused. *I journey still, nestled in Rafe's unassuming warmth, feeling his heartbeat against my breast. Or is it mine?* she wondered. *Or both? Mingling, wanting to be more. We are less only when we dare not to be more.*

He was waiting and she knew it. The impulse to give way to desire was as clear to her as the sunset burning blood red above the tree-flattened horizon. His hand was beneath her breast and pressed against her. If he stirred, if her breast were free of silk and cotton and ribbons, if she moved ever so slightly and placed her hand upon his leg . . .

Desire coursed through her like molten jewels, sparkling, searing, precious, painful.

"You dare not," Hawkmoon scolded silently.

"Dare," Celia Bartlett cried in unheard response. "Dare, you fool." Forsaking the sunset for his eyes, she brought her face around to his for the first of many kisses, and in those eyes saw too much love, his pride unbounded: two strengths that created their own weakness—the inability to accept any less from anyone, much less the woman he loved. Allow herself to be raped? She hadn't, of course, but she knew that was the way men perceived these things. Willingly become a traitor to her own people and homeland and then, even though under duress, continue on that course? Two such explosive secrets could not be kept forever. Micah was in town, Anthony was in town. The truth was no further away than a slip of a tongue—her own included—or a deliberately planted rumor. And then how fast would love turn to hate and soured pride turn to shame! Dare? An easy word to bandy about. Her dare, his consequences, and only nightmares left. The only thing she dared do was keep a strict distance between herself and him, and leave as soon as possible.

"Celia?" Rafe asked. He had seen a glimpse of something totally and inexplicably guarded. An awful secret. "Celia? Is there something you want to tell me?"

Never, never, never. The twisted dream, the dare turned in on itself. Her heart tolled that single word, a mournful, deep-sounding bell whose vibrations shook her to the core. Never, never, never.

"Take me home," she said, her voice little more than a croak.

"Celia?"

"Please, Rafe. Now. This moment. Take me home, please."

Rafe ran a hand through his hair as she moved away from him, tried to think of a way to persuade her to stay, and realized he was too much the gentleman to insist, to force himself on her no matter how much he was aroused. Cursing silently, he grabbed the whip, released the brake, and turned the mare away from the bluff and back into the tree-shaded lane. One moment so close, the next so distant. Women were by nature mercurial, but Celia was more so than most. He chanced a look at her. Light gold hair streaming long and silky down her shoulders, her skin glowing in the dying light. She looked so strong and was, yet, so secretly vulnerable. Something was bothering her, perhaps frightening her, certainly threatening her. All he could do was wait until she wanted to tell him what it was. Wait and protect her and be with her when she needed help, no matter what the reason or time. As for the war, he could only hope the Navy took its own sweet time finding a ship for him. Or perhaps they'd just let him work out of Vicksburg. Given his knowledge of the river and a small, fast boat, he could function like the proverbial hornet. Move in fast, disrupt, provoke, wreak tiny havocs that, added together, might significantly weaken the whole of the Union campaign on the Mississippi.

They paused where the trail met the Yazoo City Road to wait for a straggler from the picnic to pass. The lights of Vicksburg loomed ahead. "Look!" Rafe said, pointing excitedly at the bonfires. "Celebration, by God! We won! God damn! Grant beaten at last!"

Celia closed her eyes and swayed, almost fainting with relief. She was free! The information she had given had been useless. "Thank God," she whispered, clinging to Rafe's arm for support. "Oh, thank God!"

Rafe wielded the whip, pushed the tired little mare to her limits, tore past the stragglers who had been ahead of him. The carriage rumbled over Glass Bayou and up Cherry Street where, eyes widening with incredulity, they slowed. Something was awry, was terribly wrong. This was no celebration. Bathed in the lurid firelight, the streets were choked with humanity. Soldiers stumbled drunkenly along the streets, slumped wearily on walks, porches, and storefronts. Rafe's face froze into a mask of disbelief. Celia felt an icy chill creep up her limbs. The world around them was suddenly and horribly transformed to wailing, weeping, groaning madness. They crossed Main, Jackson, Grove, and China streets with no surcease. The mare fought her reins and shied skittishly as soldiers wove in front of her and shuffled out of the way.

"What's happened?" Rafe shouted to a private with a bloodstained bandage around his head.

The private winced and stared at them. "We never had a chance," he croaked, barely able to stand. "They was on us before we could spit. Never no chance."

"My God," Rafe said, his spirits sinking. He took Celia's hand. "Pemberton's army. That's what this is. The whole by heaven army!"

The mare was forced to slow to a walk. The farther they went, the more the confusion. Stunned and frightened citizens stood silently, watching helplessly as the horde of defeated soldiers filled their city. A child cried. Men called out the names of their units, sought friends and comrades. The fallen wounded cried for help or water. The air reeked of blood and grim filth and burned powder and the sweat smell of fear.

"They ran," Rafe said, unable to believe what he was seeing and hearing. "I've seen that look before. They ran." He looked to the hills and the darkness beyond to the east. "And Grant will be right behind them. Right God damn behind them!"

Celia said nothing, sat stiffly and watched dully until they pulled up before her house. Here, too, the streets were full of soldiers and spectators, but when Rafe started to climb down from the carriage, Celia alighted without his help.

"I can manage," she said, stopping him. "See to your father. No telling what has happened to him. Don't worry. I'll be fine."

Rafe nodded. "I'll try to learn how bad it really is," he said, voice rising above the din and confusion. "Listen. You stay put. I'll be back . . ."

"I can't hear you," Celia interrupted, reaching out to touch his arm. "I'll be fine once I'm inside. Don't worry," she added, repeating herself as she whirled from the road and, leaving Rafe to drive off alone, hurried through the gate.

"Lawd, Miss Bartlett," Tobias exclaimed, opening the door seconds after her knock. "Immelda and me done worried ourselves plumb sick. You get in this house 'fore somethin' terr'ble happens. She back, Immelda," he called. "She back safe and sound!"

"Praise the Lord an' all the saints!" Immelda cried, running in from the kitchen and enfolding Celia in a hug. Her coffee-colored features were haggard with worry. "Them soldiers started coming in 'bout an hour, two hours ago, an' the whole town is fit to be tied. Folks sayin' we all gonna be slaughtered by them Yankees. We wasn't sure jus' where you was, child."

"I'm here now," Celia replied reassuringly. "And never was in any danger. Is the house all right? Did anyone come in?"

"Yes'm. No'm. We kep' everything locked tight. Word is them soldiers that ain't kept 'round the city is supposed to camp down by the river."

"Good. Keep lights burning in front so they won't think the place is deserted." Celia smiled and hugged Immelda. "Stay up here, Immelda. You, too, Tobias. I'll be out back. I need . . ." If she had to say another word, she thought, she'd break down. Vicksburg lost, and she—". . . need to be alone," she explained, blinking back the tears.

Immelda patted her arm, took her hat and gloves. "Sure thing, honey. You go on. We'll keep watch here, an' you call out loud if . . . Well, you heard what she said," she snapped at Tobias as Celia disappeared out the hall door. "Get them lights lit an' . . ."

The voice faded and Celia was alone. Breathless, frightened, she hurried along the hall and into the sun parlor, shaded now and illuminated by a single lamp that did little to dispel the gloom. The side door was unlatched. Quickly, she exited to the garden where the glare and noise spilled over the vine-draped wall but was hidden from sight. Morbid curiosity pulled her to the black wrought-iron gate that opened onto Monroe Street. There, hidden by vines and the thick wall, she watched the desperate figures filing by.

"Pleased?" a voice asked from the shadows.

Startled, Celia jumped and cried out.

Anthony Rutledge edged into view along the outer wall, flattened himself against the wrought iron, and pretended to slump in weariness. "You did well."

The hour was late, defeated men trudged the streets. "I take no enjoyment in any of this," Celia replied brittlely.

"You did what had to be done," Anthony said, stabbing a thumb toward the street.

Celia was sick with the realization that the responsibility for the debacle was very likely largely hers. "What I was forced to do," she corrected.

"As was Powell. And the rest of us."

"Powell's a bastard," Celia replied contemptuously. "And so are the rest of you, whoever you are."

Anthony laughed. "My pretty cousin swears like a sailor. An unseen facet. But take cheer. It's been a good day for the Union, for the country. Grant will invest the city. These Rebels are caught. And if they think today was bad, why then hell itself is on the way. The jaws of the trap are snapping shut."

"Oh, that's nice, Anthony," Celia replied, filled with loathing. Had not the gate separated them, she thought for one second, she would have attacked him. Slowly, she regained control of the bitterness that welled in her, choked it back to save it for another time and place. "That's very nice. But in your gloating you've overlooked one small thing."

"Have I?" Anthony asked, smirking. "What?"

The last hour, the last minute, the final fragment of the day.

"The trap," Celia answered, her voice ominously susurrant on the night as she walked away. "We're trapped, too, Anthony. We are in it, too."

PART III

CHAPTER 11

Vicksburg was a city under siege. When drawn on a map, the lines of the Union army that surrounded Vicksburg, looked like a gigantic ear whose lobe connected to the Mississippi about two miles south of the center of town. Those same lines actually seen from the top of Sky Parlor Hill, which afforded the Confederate command a view of the battlefield, appeared as an impenetrable ring of trenches, redoubts, laboriously constructed earthen works, artillery emplacements, and rifle pits.

Vicksburg woke the morning after the demoralizing defeat at the Big Black River to find itself cut off from the rest of the Confederacy. The citizens tasted a palpable fear as they wondered when the inexorable pressure from without would implode the thin lines of defense that protected them. But there simply wasn't time for panic. Defensive positions on the periphery had to be solidified, and all able-bodied men were assigned tasks. Supplies of every imaginable sort had to be apportioned, and lines from hurriedly established depots within the city to the trenches were established. Barns and warehouses were turned into hospitals. Drinking water supplies were placed under the control and protection of the army. Equally important, regulations governing the disposal of the waste of thirty thousand extra men and half that many animals were promulgated. A thousand logistical problems, both simplified and complicated by the closely restricted area in which the Confederates were forced to operate, had to be solved.

Work had barely begun when, at two o'clock on the afternoon of May 19, the Union army struck. The battle raged until dark when the bluebellies retired after suffering grave losses. Again on May 22, after a four-hour bombardment, Grant attacked in a bid to end the siege quickly. The blistering offense lasted throughout the day and left attackers and defenders alike exhausted. By the time the sun set, Grant and his generals, stymied for the second time, no longer expected surrender while Pemberton and his generals, buoyed by a victory of sorts, had become adamant in their determination to hold out. Both armies dug in deeper and sat down to wait each other out.

One week passed and a second week began.

The rumble of cannon fire became commonplace. Women made

bandages, worked in hospitals, and cooked. Men carried supplies to the lines, cast bullets, and repaired wagons. Merchants protected and doled out dwindling supplies. Farmers dreamed of the day they could go back to their crops and animals, drummers of their freedom to roam the countryside, and preachers of marriages and christenings in place of funerals. Children chafed under restrictions placed on them by worried parents, and mothers grew hollow-eyed and snapped at fathers who, tired and hungry, grunted noncommittal replies and fell into bed for a few hours of sleep before they had to rise and rush off to whatever tasks had been assigned them now that the storms of war raged about their homes.

A desultory pattern of life was established in defense of sanity. Nathaniel rose in the morning, breakfasted, spent the day talking with old friends or staring out over the fields behind his house, the nights reading and, the better to sleep, sipping bourbon. Rafe became involved in the City Guard, assuming temporary command of all the city except the docks, which remained under direct army control. Tom Stewart worked himself to the bone, a cynically acidic pun he himself used as he stood helplessly by and watched a helper pull a blanket over the face on an amputee he had just lost.

The siege effectively spoiled Celia's planned escape. Trapped, she spent hours during the day at the church helping Reverend Lundquist arrange food and beds for those whose homes had been destroyed, and during the night found herself forced to attend clandestine meetings with Anthony. The strain of these two disparate and conflicting activities was almost unbearable. During these first two weeks, with both of them so busy, she and Rafe saw each other only occasionally.

One and all, they and five thousand others lived through the initial shock and gradually became inured to the new life imposed upon them by two warring armies. One and all, they . . . adjusted.

A mist in moonlight hid the wounds, cloaked the dead, obscured the ravaged hills, and muffled the sound of the occasional artillery or mortar shell in its shrill descent. Far removed from the action, the Confederate private stared at the river, finished relieving himself, and decided there was no sense in hastening back to his post when his commanding officer and comrades at arms didn't expect him until morning. It had been a stroke of luck that things had gone so well back at the commissary. The medical attendant on duty had handed over rations of salts for the men in his company who were suffering from the runs. The private had taken his and was feeling much better. The corporal at the commissary had issued a whole box of tinned dried apples. At forty-eight to the box, that was eight more than the forty men in his company, so he had traded two for a plug of tobacco and five for a half pint of rum. None too anxious to share his booty—a half pint of rum and a plug of tobacco wouldn't go far among forty men—the private was only too happy to dally.

The atmosphere down by the river was peaceful. The private bit a chew off the plug, rolled the gummy leaves around in his mouth, and stared at the river and the log floating toward him. When a twig cracked behind him, he swung his head around and scrutinized the black wall of brush and trees that grew down almost to the river's edge. An army of hobgoblins might be standing in those spiny shadows, though, so he wasn't about to go exploring. Besides, they might be but weren't. The simplest fool knew that there were nothing but shadows there, and shadows never hurt anybody. Relaxed, warmed by the rum, the private turned to spit into the river and did not see one of the shadows detach itself from the line of vegetation and cautiously advance across the narrow strip of sand.

The river was pretty under the full moon, especially for a river-bred boy who'd been too long inland. The private leaned on his musket and watched the logs—he now saw there were two of them—slowly working their way upstream.

Upstream?

The private lifted his musket and started to cock the hammer just as a tree limb whistled through the air and exploded against his head. His cap flipped off and landed at the edge of the water. The private collapsed soundlessly across his musket. The woman dressed in black shrugged her midnight cloak out of the way and turned the unconscious man over to keep him from smothering in the moist sand, then threw his musket far out into the water.

"Good work," a voice from the water said. The logs paused and swung back downstream. In their place, a limber, river-drenched figure emerged from the water. Anthony Rutledge shook the water from his hair, untied the boots from around his neck, and pulled them on. He stood and slipped a dagger from his belt.

"Don't," Celia said as he approached the unconscious Rebel youth. "He saw."

"He saw nothing," Celia corrected, and tossed the limb down in front of Anthony's feet. "Leave him alone."

"Look," Anthony growled. "Celia, for heaven's sake—"

"No. You look. We can stand here gabbing and wind up on the gallows, or we can return to town before someone else comes along."

Anthony glowered, but to no avail. He knew his cousin, knew her secrets and what had been done to her. The fall of Vicksburg meant the turning point of the war, for the South would be cut in half. Didn't she realize the importance of the role she played in that drama? Where was the animosity she had once harbored? Mellowed, obviously, but why? Because of Rafe Lattimore? Oh, he remembered Rafe from the old days, remembered him and his family well and knew that Celia had been seeing him during the last week. If there were some way he could rekindle the old hatred . . . "It goes against my grain," he muttered, staring at the unconscious soldier, but fitting the knife back into its sheath.

"And killing him needlessly goes against my grain," Celia said, turning away from the water's edge. "Come on."

Anthony followed Celia through the gloomy, vine-covered cypress. "You're sure he was the only one?" he asked, catching up to her.

"Very sure. You found Powell?"

"Right where we'd agreed. Only problem was the sentries, but he'd coached them well. He said to say hello."

"How nice of him," Celia replied, her voice dripping with sarcasm.

"You don't have to be that way. He's just doing his job."

"So do hangmen."

"Touchy, touchy. In any case, he wants to be kept posted on everything you learn about the possibility that Johnston will try to relieve the city."

"He ought to know more about that than anyone here."

"Maybe, maybe not," Anthony said, not revealing any more than he had to. "Also anything concerning supplies being run past the blockade, especially ammunition. An estimate of how much ammunition is available and the condition it's in would be helpful, too."

Celia whistled softly and clucked to the horses as she approached them. "I can't do that, Anthony." Her knees felt weak, but she continued to say the words she had planned earlier that night. "I've fulfilled my obligation to him. Gathered my last bit of information. Tonight is the end."

"What's that?" Anthony hissed, grabbing her arm.

"You heard me. I'm stopping. Powell needn't know. He has you and God knows how many others and doesn't need me. Tell him I'm doing the best I can, but—"

"You can't quit now," Anthony interrupted, his voice harsh and unyielding. "You're in too deep, and I'm damned if I'll lie for you. The rules are still the same as they were that night at the old Silverhaus Plantation, and Powell wouldn't hesitate for one second to—"

"You'd tell him?" Celia asked, her stomach sinking. "You'd let him? . . . We're *family*, Anthony."

"Tell him and more." Anthony realized he was squeezing her arm, let it drop. "It's Rafe, isn't it? He's the one who's turning your head. And him the brother of—"

"Rafe has nothing to do with my decision."

"The hell, you say! This is Anthony, Celia, not some stranger. You're still in love with him, aren't you? Him and his house on the hill and his land holdings and his slaves. The first family of Vicksburg. Lots of talk about him since I've been here. It's plain to see he has his eye set on you. On my pretty little cousin, the spy. What would *he* think if he learned just what you've been up to these many months."

"I haven't—"

"The Big Black River?"

"I didn't mean . . . that was the first time anything I said or reported mattered. You had me confused. You . . . I mean Powell . . ." Celia leaned her forehead against the mare's neck, tried to collect her thoughts, and fought back the tears. "I don't know what I mean, Anthony, except that I can't continue. I just can't."

Anthony sighed, leaned across his saddle, and stared at her. "All right. All right. Maybe Rafe is bighearted enough to accept your indiscretion even if it borders on treason. But what do you think he'll say when he learns his true love is soiled property? That she let herself be had by his own brother? 'Think nothing of it, dear? These things happen? Let's just forget—'"

No longer listening, Celia stared at Anthony as if seeing him for the first time. The hair on the back of her neck prickled and the foul taste of revulsion stole her breath. Anthony, the loyal friend, the confidant, the comforter. He had won her over, fueled her hatred, and introduced her to Powell. He had placed her in a position where she was nothing but a tool to be exploited. She was being blackmailed. Anthony held a trump card. Gossip in the right place to the wrong ear would spread through town like wildfire until, at last, the vile stories reached Rafe. It would no longer matter that Micah had taken her against her will, or that she had initially agreed to spy out of pain and a burning need for revenge and then had been unable to extricate herself. For even if Rafe understood that neither had been her fault, the certain knowledge that everyone in Vicksburg knew would destroy him as utterly as it destroyed her.

"—And if I am brutal," Anthony concluded, "I'm sorry. War is brutal."

"You distort truth to your own ends," Celia said, suddenly so tired she would have fallen had she not been holding on to the horse. "War exists—is brutal—because men are brutal."

Anthony ducked under his horse's neck and went to her side. "Powell needs information," he said. "I'm committed to seeing that he gets information. And soon. Is that plain enough?"

Celia drew back as if from a viper. "Plain enough, *dear* cousin," she whispered. "More than plain enough. Now, do you mind?" she asked, starting to mount.

"Yes. I do." Anthony grabbed the stirrup and lifted it beyond the reach of her foot. "When and where?"

"Next Sunday night, June seventh, sometime after midnight. I'm entertaining officers, and I imagine there'll be some talk that might be useful to you. I'll meet you by the garden gate and have written down anything that might be of value. You can arrange a delivery with or without my help. Check the house and give me time after the last guest leaves."

"Excellent," Anthony beamed. "I'll be there. Why they even bother I don't know, but I've been conscripted into making repairs on the docks. I'll sneak off somehow. Just don't keep me waiting. If I'm caught out in that part of town so late, I'll be hard pressed to fabricate an excuse."

"I'm sure you'll manage," Celia said, ignoring Anthony's offer to help her mount.

"I'm sorry, Celia. Sorry I had to lay the cards on the table like that. But you left me no other choice."

Celia jerked on the reins and the mare reared in alarm. "My dear cousin, my friend," she said, spitting out the words. "You can go to hell!"

"Sunday night," Anthony called hoarsely as Celia disappeared into the deeper shadows of the meandering trail that led back to the center of town. There was no answer, and the soft thump of the horse's hooves on the soggy ground quickly faded. Alone, wearily, Anthony swung aboard his own horse and took a different course toward Vicksburg. Hours had passed since sundown when he slipped into the river for the short trip downstream to the rendezvous with Powell. Cautiously, he slipped past the sentry posts and rode into the seedy collection of shell-pocked storefronts and yawning cave mouths that marked the saloons and bordellos of Vicksburg Under the Hill, then left the horse to wander in search of grain and shelter, and its rightful owner. Fifteen minutes later, his wet clothes hung to dry on a peg, he rolled up in the dirty blanket he'd stolen from a dead soldier, and fell into the calm deep sleep that only the righteous enjoy.

No trains echoed down the long hill of night. No more did the distant, painful wail of steam whistles hover on the air like fleeting wisps of memory, like recollections too fragile and too dear to subject to morning light. The Seth Thomas tolled once at the half hour. Eleven thirty. The dregs of yet another day. In the parlor Nathaniel Lattimore stopped thinking of trains and once more pondered his options. The red checkers outnumbered the black by three. Black could not afford a trade. Black needed to even the score without suffering a loss, yet black's resources were limited.

Like Vicksburg and the Confederacy itself, Nathaniel reflected. Defeat was the remotest of possibilities with God on the side of the South. God and Bedford Forrest and Robert E. Lee and Joe Johnston. No, not even with Grant himself knocking at the gates of Vicksburg was defeat anything more than a niggling worry. Minutes crept by slow as winter molasses. Nathaniel moved and swiveled the checkerboard to take up the cause of the red. What a relief to be the attacker. He tried to be objective and play without prejudice, but the Yankees were red and the move was not really the best. Quickly, before he fell prey to pangs of conscience, he turned the board again and, resting one forearm on the table, considered his choices but a moment before jumping three red pieces and removing them from the board.

"Even, by God," he cackled, turning the board again. "And a superior position to boot!" A celebration was in order. Nathaniel poured a whiskey and favored himself with a sip, then another.

The clock chimed midnight. "Now look at that," Rafe chided, standing in the open door. "The servants are all in bed, the old day's gone and a new one's come, and my father, with the blood of owls in his veins, is still up."

"What?" Nathaniel asked, drawing back in mock surprise. "What? Don't tell me! Sunday night and my son is here when he could be standing beneath the Bartlett balcony, spoon-eyed and whispering poetry?"

Rafe shrugged and sauntered in. He was dressed in a loose shirt and trousers and his feet were bare, the latter a nasty habit that Nathaniel had decided his son had acquired while marooned. Rafe crossed the room, stood in the open door to the veranda, and looked out over the garden and, in the distance, over the newly plowed fields and the tracks and engine house where no trains came. Not one train since Grant had severed the line to Jackson. He saw only the mist and heard from far off the cough of a mortar and a smattering of rifle fire as opposing sentries exchanged lethal cordialities. When he walked back inside, Rafe saw his father pour another drink, and wondered how many that made for the evening.

"Why aren't you in her parlor instead of standing here all but naked and with that disapproving stare."

"The hour is late and you just got over a malarial attack. You need sleep. And I'm barefoot, not naked," Rafe pointed out as he sat and studied the board. "And I probably would be there if Celia hadn't suffered a headache and went to bed early."

"*Tsk, tsk*," Nathaniel clucked softly.

Rafe moved, closing off a double jump for Nathaniel. "What's that supposed to mean?" he asked.

"Humph!" Nathaniel snorted, beginning a sequence that guaranteed him a two-for-one exchange and an unbeatable board position. "You must be mistreating her."

"What makes you think that?"

"You've upset her."

"I have not," Rafe protested, defensive now.

"When a woman says she has a headache, let a man beware."

"When a woman has a headache, it might just mean she has a headache," Rafe shot back. "It's been a nerve-wracking week for everyone. I'm tired myself."

"Red's move. You going to play or not?"

Rafe pulled at his chin and studied the board. "If you insist," he finally said, his hand hovering over one checker, then moving quickly to another and descending to force his father to jump and lose two to one.

"You are a . . . spiteful boy!" Nathaniel grumbled, looking for a way out and finding none.

"I thought that was an epithet you reserved for me," Micah said from the veranda.

Nathaniel's head jerked up as if pulled by a string. Rafe tensed and slowly looked over his shoulder in time to see Micah loom in the doorway, then head for the liquor cabinet.

"Marvelous reception," Micah slurred, opening the milk glass doors and removing a crystal snifter and an amber, tear-shaped bottle. "Wonderful. I can tell you're glad to see me." He poured two inches of Nathaniel's private stock of peach brandy into the snifter. "Nonetheless, cheers!" He sipped and rolled his eyes in exaggerated pleasure. "Now that makes Fancy's finest taste like mule piss."

"You're drunk," Nathaniel snapped in disgust.

"Does he do this often?" Rafe asked.

Micah belched, aimed himself toward his father and brother.

"What? Get drunk?" he asked, his voice thick. He smelled of cheap liquor and cheaper women. His coat was missing and the sleeves of his ruffled shirt were rolled up. His knee-high boots were sticky with mud and his black trousers were indecently tight. "Of course. Every chance I get. I'm drunk and you"—he gestured with the snifter—"are losing, Father."

"Not for the first time, unfortunately," Nathaniel said between clenched teeth.

"Oh, oh. Metaphor—or is it allegory, I can never remember which—rears its ugly head."

"What do you want, Micah?" Rafe asked, pushing his brother's hand away from the table.

The brandy sloshed in the snifter and a drop fell on the board. Micah steadied himself against the table and pointed a finger beneath Rafe's chin. "Little brother, the war hero. Little brother, the gentleman. Watch yourself, little brother, or big brother will take your head off at your God-damned neck."

Rafe was halfway out of his seat when he caught a sign from Nathaniel and slumped back down. "Okay, Micah," he said. "Have it your own way. This time."

"Why, thank you, little brother. That's nice of you. Real nice," he added, leaving the table and flopping down into a broad-backed cane chair. "Don't you agree, Father?"

"I thought I made myself plain. You aren't welcome here," Nathaniel said, making no effort to hide his anger.

"Plain enough. But did you really expect me to keep away? You ought to know better, Father. I go and come where I please." He yawned hugely and blinked his eyes against the light. "Of course, I try not to make a nuisance of myself," he added with a short, barking laugh.

"Trying not to be a nuisance, for you, sounds like a Herculean task," Rafe observed dryly. "Father, why don't you go on to bed. I can handle things down here."

"Sounds like a good idea," Micah said, rousing himself. "Then little brother and I can visit properly."

"What would you know about propriety?" Nathaniel asked, rising and crossing to his son. "You are a lecher and whoremonger. You have sought and taken every opportunity to disgrace me, your mother's memory, and the Lattimore name itself."

"Whereas little brother simpered and pleaded and plotted and waited his chance to take over my position as your firstborn?" Micah snarled. "Hell, yes, he did, and you know it. Came crying to you whenever I chanced to stray from the narrow, cheerless path you in your boundless wisdom decreed that I and every other God-damned Lattimore in the world should walk. Well, Father"—he raised the snifter in sarcastic salute—"here's to your path, and here's to where it leads."

Nathaniel's hand lashed out just as Micah started to drink. The snifter glittered in the lamplight as it sailed through the air and shattered against a teak bookshelf. Brandy sprayed over leather-bound books. The tinkle of falling glass filled the silence. Nathaniel shuddered and, appearing to shrink as the anger drained from him, turned on his heel and left without another word.

Micah laughed mirthlessly, walked a determinedly straight line across the room, and took another snifter from the cabinet.

"You've had enough," Rafe said quietly, still seated at the checkerboard.

"Stow it," Micah said, and poured another drink. "I'm just getting started."

"How long has this been going on?"

"What?"

"You torturing him?"

"Balls!" Micah snorted, circling Rafe to examine the room he had seen hundreds of times. "No matter how badly you want me gone, I am the eldest and have a right to be here. And when he dies this house will be mine one way or the other."

"You are so wrong," Rafe said. He followed Micah onto the veranda where the larger man leaned on the railing and stared past the low garden walls to the freshly turned fields. There would be a good orchard this year. The trees were bound to bear heavily. "Why, I don't know, but you're the one who poisoned him against you. We both raised our share of perdition, but you had a cruel streak. Which you still carry."

"That's the way you see me, eh?" Micah asked, drunkenly turning to half sit and half lean against the rail. "Well, I guess you would, and maybe with some reason. But not with Hal Bartlett. That was you, little brother. You turned Bartlett against me. Celia, too. She was mine, but you got to her and turned her head." He shook his head to clear the cobwebs from his brain. "Then lost her, of course. I wonder why, little brother?"

Rafe shrugged. "I've taught myself not to worry about why's, but that's not the point. I never turned either her or her father against you."

"I suppose she was influenced by your natural charm," Micah

growled. "Well, Hal is dead and his estate is in shambles, or so I hear."
Micah knew he was playing with fire but was just drunk enough to
stretch his luck. "And maybe Miss Celia isn't such a high-and-mighty
find after all. Maybe I could tell you things."

"Maybe you could drop the subject. Celia is a lady."

"A lady? My, my, and all the talk I've heard!" Micah knew he'd
struck a nerve and grinned besottedly. "I think I saw that lady tonight, little brother. Dressed mighty mysterious in black and riding
hell for leather. Of course, it was a brief glimpse, and me coming up
from the river with a few under my belt. My horse threw a shoe and
when I dismounted to check, this rider came right through the alley
and damn near ran me down. Don't know why I think it was her, but
I do."

"I think—"

"Yup. Mighty strange behavior for a lady. But then, maybe she was
trying out some of the boys that Fancy Darren can't service. Sort of to
break herself in for you."

Rafe's fist caught Micah flush on the mouth. Micah staggered a few
steps sideways. The snifter shattered on the floor. Lantern light revealed a streak of blood at the corner of Micah's mouth.

"If I stay here too much longer, there won't be any crystal left for
me to inherit," Micah said, wiping the back of his hand across his rapidly swelling lip.

"You're a liar and a reprobate," Rafe said evenly. "Never speak of
Celia that way again, or by God, I will call you out and kill you."

"A cheap shot, little brother," Micah said, advancing. His fists were
clenched, his arms cocked for battle. "Want to try again?"

Micah swung. Rafe ducked and his brother's fist crashed into the
porch post, a solid, six-inch-thick tree trunk.

"*Yeeeooowwww!*" Micah howled.

His face grim, Rafe moved in quickly, pushed Micah on the chest
with the flat of his hand. Micah flipped over the railing and landed on
his shoulder. Shaken, he rolled to his feet, wagged his head to clear
his senses, and spit mud and blood from his mouth. He shook his hand
and gingerly worked his fingers until feeling returned. Above him on
the porch, two images of Rafe coalesced into one and split apart
again. One of him or two, there was no doubt he was ready to continue the contest. "We'll finish this some other time," Micah finally
said, almost falling. "When I'm sober."

"That'll be a cold day in hell, *big* brother," Rafe said and then, sad
of spirit, watched Micah stagger off through the darkness.

The gate squeaked closed. A mockingbird woke and complained

about being disturbed. Small arms fire pattered like rain in the distance. Rafe gingerly scraped the broken snifter into a small pile under the railing for the servants to get in the morning. Things were bad enough with the Yankees at the gates without them fighting among themselves, but Micah shouldn't have talked like that about Celia. "I could have taken just about anything else from him," Rafe muttered, sucking at the broken skin over his bruised knuckles. "Anything else except that." Suddenly tired, infected with Micah's nagging bitterness, he turned and saw Nathaniel in the parlor. "Sorry you had to see that," Rafe said, entering and sliding the latch into place. "I should've closed the door behind me."

"I leave it open all the time. I don't know why." Nathaniel ran a hand through his hair. "I keep hoping he might change, that a different person will walk through that door and still be my son. When a man feels himself dying, it's important that what and who he leaves behind is good."

"You're tired and exaggerating," Rafe said gently. "Come on. Bedtime for both of us."

Nathaniel let himself be led into the hall.

"You needin' somethin', Mistuh Lattimore?" a servant asked, poking his head through the dining room door.

"We're doing fine, thank you, Robert."

"I'm Andrew, Mistuh Rafe."

"Sorry."

"Thas' all right. Good night, suh."

They reached the stairs, where Nathaniel resisted for a moment. "A man wants to know. Doesn't want to leave things up in the air. All neat and tidy. Everything worked out right."

"You can't play checkers to save your soul, Father, but I daresay you needn't worry about leaving anything yet. You're too mean and cantankerous to die."

Nathaniel felt terribly light-headed, but wasn't about to admit it. "Not a mean bone in my body," he replied indignantly, leaning on Rafe's arm as he let himself be propelled up the stairs.

"Right. In you go," Rafe said.

"Never been cantankerous a day in my life." Nathaniel let go Rafe's arm and walked alone through the door to his bedroom. "Celia's a good girl. Marry her, boy. Carry her off."

Rafe laughed. "Pretty hard to do, surrounded by Yankees." He steered Nathaniel toward his bed, and helped him sit. "I will, though, one of these days. Just as soon as I get a minute."

"If you try to undress me, you'll get worse than you gave Micah," Nathaniel threatened glassily.

"Okay," Rafe said, stepping back and holding up his hands.

Nathaniel yawned, serious now, fighting sleep, and lay back with his head on the pillow. "I must admit I was surprised to see you get the best of him," he admitted around a second yawn.

"Times change," Rafe answered. "And he was drunk." He started to leave, but paused to glance up at the portrait of his mother over the fireplace. A woman of reposed beauty, her soft brown hair was highlighted in a way that made it appear hard and flat instead of soft as down, as Rafe remembered. Her patrician face and neck, her sensitive hands and fingers, were gently, almost lovingly, rendered.

"I loved her," Nathaniel said, half asleep already. "Nights like this, though, I'm glad she doesn't have to be here."

"I know, Father."

"See her in you sometimes." He was struggling to speak. "She was a kind and sensitive woman, but could lose her temper with the best of them. And I love her. You listen to me, boy. Hear me now and remember what I say no matter how I change it come sunup. If you love somebody, then you, by God, love 'em first. First, you hear? Anything else . . ."

Nathaniel began to snore. Rafe tiptoed to his father's bedside and pulled a light blanket over him, then leaned over and blew out the lantern. "Good night, Father," he whispered, and then stopped halfway to the door and looked back. Only a little moonlight crept into the room, but it was enough. The blanket rose and fell to the accompaniment of Nathaniel's snores. Rafe sighed, remembered the whispered good nights that had seen him to sleep when he was a child. The world turned, the seasons changed with the slow clockwork of passing time. Nathaniel wasn't old, but old enough. Malaria and two rifle balls that still lodged in his body had seen to that. And so the roles reversed and the son whispered good night to the father.

And gently closed the door behind him.

CHAPTER 12

On Tuesday morning, June 2, a tiny black dot appeared against the pale blue midmorning sky. Growing quickly and trailing a spiral wake of smoke, the dot grew, diminished again, and disappeared in the east. Seconds later there came a dull thumping sound not unlike that of a sledge striking the earth. Another Yankee shell from one of the gun-boats on the river had fallen in the general vicinity of the Confederate trenches.

Two weeks to the day after the first abortive Yankee attempt to storm the hastily contrived defensive ring around Vicksburg, Celia Bartlett watched from the broad, spacious rear window in the sun parlor as the breeze from the river nipped at the corkscrew arc of smoke left by the fuse and gradually tore it apart completely just in time for another to take its place. The shelling was constant, varying only in the number of projectiles in the air at any given time. Most sailed over the city, as intended, but some few invariably fell short and plummeted into residential or business areas. At first the missiles had aroused a feeling of terror, but as the citizens had suffered few injuries to date, and as there was nothing to be done about the bombardment, the populace had learned to go about their lives more or less as usual.

A wheezing, impossible chord from an accordian, followed by the introduction to "Lord of All Hopefulness," distracted Celia. Turning from the window, she watched Gaillee Calder struggle through the hymn one more time. Gaillee had worked long and hard to learn the notes, but was cursed with a poor sense of timing that had made the song flow as smoothly as a child's first steps, a punished progression at best. A little flat, but on cue, a half-dozen voices launched into the first verse. The full-throated women's voices quivered with the emotion of their tender message. The young ladies were all in their late teens or twenties, and each was determined in her own way to support the gallant resistance that protected them from the depradations of the devil Yankees. To that end, Gaillee had arranged, with Celia's coaxing, for several groups of young ladies to visit the trenches two miles out from town and there offer moral and emotional support to the soldiers. The elderly ladies of Vicksburg, at the same time, were preparing baked goods for the choir to distribute after they had performed.

Gaillee hesitated, tried to catch up, and became hopelessly confused. "Miss Bartlett," she snapped peevishly over a broken, sour chord, "you might join us, since this was your idea." The instrument hung like a millstone around her neck. "Oh, maybe this is a terrible idea."

"You didn't sound all that bad," Margery said. The oldest of the group, Margie was a handsome woman nearly thirty with a warm smile and gentle, understanding manner.

"She didn't sound all that good, either," Rosemary, the youngest of the women, added mischievously.

Mary, a tall, thin, stern-looking girl of twenty-three, nodded sagely in support of Rosemary's criticism.

"We can't sing the right notes if she can't play them," Claudia chimed in. Mary and Claudia were sisters, but Claudia, unlike the spinsterish Mary, was a voluptuary and was enjoying her third husband at the age of twenty-eight.

"I could be a virtuoso, and you still wouldn't sing the right notes, Claudia Warwick."

"Is that so?" Claudia huffed, rising to her own defense. "I will have you know that just the other day Father Razzoni told me how much he loved my solo last Sunday, so what do you think of that?"

"Father Razzoni is tone deaf," Rosemary interjected in a flat, Gregorian chant, feeding the flames of a good quarrel.

Gaillee laughed aloud and Claudia turned red. Celia groaned inwardly.

"I can play the accordian," a soft voice spoke up. All eyes turned to Lynna Hays who was present through Celia's personal invitation and insistence, and only in part accepted by the others. "I think Gaillee's only having trouble because the song is new to her. But we sing it in school, and I'm familiar with both the melody and the tenor harmony."

"She's right. I just need practice," Gaillee explained, grateful for a face-saving excuse to be rid of the instrument which was giving her talents such a poor showcase.

"Of course," Lynna said. "The squeeze piano looks simple, but isn't at all. If you don't think you'll be ready by Saturday, then I'll be happy to try to play in your stead."

"Well, I *will* be preoccupied—"

"With Phillip Laughton, no doubt," Rosemary finished, an impish glint lighting her young face.

"I'll not deny something of which you are so profoundly jealous," Gaillee sniffed, handing the accordian to Lynna.

"Are you sure you can manage that?" Celia asked, helping Lynna with the straps.

Lynna settled the instrument against her abdomen. "Of course. Did you know that an old black lady once told me that fetuses were aware of music?" She sent her fingers trilling over the keyboard. "Now where were we?" she asked, turning to the group.

The ladies looked impressed. Even Gaillee, who might normally have been oversensitive, appeared to appreciate Lynna's expertise. And the ensuing rendition of "Lord of All Hopefulness" filled the room with a ray of hope.

Having finished singing and gossiping, the happy group called a halt to practice at noon when Immelda served cakes and tea in the sun parlor at the rear of the house. Margery left with Mary and Claudia. Rosemary lingered to visit for half an hour until Tobias notified her that a young gentleman had arrived to escort her home. Seconds after she had left, Gaillee, unable to suppress her mirth, ran into the sun parlor from the front of the house. "Oh, my, my. Ollie Johnston! Just about the homeliest boy in all of Vicksburg," she chortled, delighted with the results of her snoopery. "Wait until I see that girl again. Oh, hurry Saturday!"

"Now, Gaillee," Celia chided, wanting no more conflicts that might interrupt her plans. "Poor Ollie may not be the most attractive of young men, but he *is* General Johnston's nephew."

"I merely think it's more than a little silly for a sixteen year old to be throwing herself at the first man who comes along, is all," Gaillee explained patiently.

Celia glanced up as a shell whistled overhead. "Sound advice for all of us, perhaps, under the circumstances," she commented dryly.

"Sound but tardy, as far as I'm concerned." Lynna smiled and patted her abdomen. "But then, pursuit has its compensations."

"Agreed," Gaillee said, a dreamy look in her eye. "My Phillip compensates me whenever he can." She winked and, a movement in the garden catching her eye, grinned lasciviously. "Celia, of course, will claim not to know what we're talking about, but I suspect—"

Celia blushed and, following Gaillee's gaze, saw Rafe Lattimore standing by the azaleas. He wore a uniform of gray coat and trousers and shiny black boots. The soft, smoke-colored cape around his shoulders and the unruly curls of his hair black as rich soil made him look gallant in the extreme.

"Miss Celia?" Immelda called from the kitchen.

"She sees him," Gaillee answered in Celia's stead. "And so do I," she added with hungry emphasis.

"And I really must get back home to spell Jonathan," Lynna said quickly. "He was up nearly all night guarding the garden and barn."

"I'll take you back," Celia offered, feeling weak in her stomach. She had plotted to avoid Rafe, to give herself some kind of breathing room, and to allow her emotions to resolve their sense of disarray.

"Don't be silly. I'll take her," Gaillee said, already putting on her hat.

"I hate to trouble either of you," Lynna protested awkwardly.

Gaillee patted her hair in place, picked up hers and Lynna's purses. "Nonsense," she insisted. "I could use an excursion. I've little else but time on my hands these days."

"You don't have to leave," Celia protested.

"Of course we don't, dear," Gaillee replied facetiously. She preceded Lynna into the hall. "Tobias can show us out. I'm certain you have more urgent matters with which to concern yourself." Gaillee's fluttering laugh filled the hall and drowned out any attempt by Celia to protest her innocence. "Urgent compensations and the like?"

Lynna and Celia embraced quickly. "Thank you. I enjoyed myself," Lynna whispered. "More than you imagine, perhaps."

"Just as long as you come back," Celia said and smiled, truly grateful that she and Lynna had become reacquainted. "Often."

"I will."

Celia waved as Lynna hurried away to catch up with Gaillee and, alone in the sun parlor, turned pensively toward the French doors. The stories Gaillee would spread! But wasn't that what she wanted? Certainly anyone romantically involved with Rafe Lattimore would have to be unquestionably loyal to the cause. So what was the problem?

The problem was Rafe Lattimore, Celia admitted, disquieted by the thought. And the quickening dangerous pulse of her desire that, in spite of the danger, she found increasingly difficult to ignore.

"Letting things like this go isn't like you, Tobias."

"Yes, sir, Mr. Rafe," Tobias winced as he looked mournfully at the dead vines that grew around the gazebo. "I'm pained to see plants in such a state. I tried to keep them vines alive so that gazebo would be cool an' shady inside, but Miss Celia likes 'em just the way they are, sort of sad. No, sir." He shook his head, let his hands drop helplessly to his sides. "This garden ain't no laughin' place like other folks have. But what Miss Celia wants, well, that's what I gonna give her."

"Then we'll just have to find a way to cheer her up, I suppose," Rafe said, snapping off a piece of the brittle wisteria for emphasis.

"Cheer up who?" Celia asked, approaching from the rear of the house.

"You," Rafe grinned, turning to her and taking her hand. "My carriage is in front and I was on my way to the Widow Prentiss's to see if she could duplicate my uniform before driving out to the Hays's."

Celia glanced up in time to see Gaillee's carriage turn onto Monroe Street. "You just now missed Lynna. Gaillee's taking her home."

"No matter," Rafe shrugged. "It's Jonathan I need to talk to. Like to come along, since you're free?"

"Free?" Celia extricated her hand from Rafe's. "I'll have you know, Mr. Lattimore, that I've been busy the entire morning. My word, but you take liberty with a girl. I do have other ambitions in life but to be at your beck and call." She popped open a blue parasol as pale in hue as her summer gown. The shade hardly dimmed the golden glory of her artfully braided and coiffed hair. "I happen to have a life of my own," she added with coy finality.

"Really?" Rafe asked, trying not to sound too piqued. Micah's drunken accusation that he had seen Celia late Sunday night had preyed on him ever since, and now he had to know. "And I must admit to jealousy," he said carefully keeping his tone light, almost jocular. "Why, just the other night a little bird whispered to me that you were out riding after midnight. If I have a rival, announce him. Let me meet him face to face."

Celia felt a blush creep up her naked throat. Her mind reeled with astonishment, as quickly strove to retain some degree of control. She had to remain calm. Had to. But who had seen her? Rafe? No. He would have said so earlier. Then who? "If your desire was to impugn my honor and good name, sir," she said with rigid dignity, "you needn't have bothered to call on me. Good day."

Rafe caught her arm as she whirled on her heels and started for the house. "I spoke in jest, for heaven's sake, Celia. Good Lord!"

A dozen roles, a dozen facades came to mind. Willing composure where there was none, Celia turned to him with a smile that at the same time masked her inner turmoil and announced her outburst as a sham. "You are the silliest person, Rafe Lattimore. Of course, I know you're teasing. Another suitor, indeed! I have but a single admirer. And a single, dearest friend, though he can be such a terrible pest at times." It was her turn to take his hand. "I think you know him. He is a handsome naval captain, brave and daring and terribly gullible."

His hand in hers, Rafe relaxed. "There's that terrible word again. Friend."

"So terrible? Then what would you have me call you?"

Lover, husband, dearest—any one of a hundred endearments would have been preferable, but Rafe wisely held his tongue. "For now," he quipped, "what about your escort to the party Sunday?"

Celia's laughter tinkled brightly, a dazzling contrast to the dry wisteria vines in the background. "I'd intended that task for you from the onset," she said, brushing him lightly on the cheek. "Sunday I shall dance every dance with you. Unless, of course, since this awful General Grant has made soldiers of us all by camping outside our gates, some unconscionable general levies explicit orders that I dance with him."

"In which case," Rafe said with a chuckle, taking her arm as they started for the house, "rank insubordination will be the only course. I shall expect you to be a traitor and disregard his orders."

And so can lies become a truth of sorts, Celia thought, watching Rafe out of the corner of her eye as she stood at the mirror to put on her hat. Expected to be a traitor! What rich irony! And an irony not to be dwelled on too long. Practicalities intervened. A brief consultation with Immelda about dinner. A quick trip upstairs to fetch a gown that she wanted the Widow Prentiss to repair. At last they were in the carriage and turning onto Monroe Street for the short trip toward the center of town and Betsy Prentiss's shop.

"You *do* stay busy," Rafe commented, gently working the brake as the carriage started down a steep slope.

"And so many of my projects amount to absolutely useless activity," Celia said, letting the sun bathe her face a moment before opening her parasol again. She glanced over at Rafe and rested one hand on his arm. "Has anyone today told you that you are really quite handsome? In your new uniform, that is?"

Rafe couldn't suppress a pleased smile. "Only you, I'm afraid."

"Pity. But why ever do you need two? Oh!" A twinge of alarm, quickly hidden. "You heard? It's official?"

"The final order signed by Pemberton himself." Pride was tempered with a sense of responsibility and the enormity of the job he faced. "Commander, Home Guard. Signed, sealed, and delivered."

"But I thought Colonel—"

"They amputated his leg last night."

"Amputated?" Celia asked, shocked.

"Gangrene. The job is mine by default." A frown clouded his face.

"Close to an impossible task. I'll have a few soldiers. The rest will be mostly boys and old men. Able-bodied men are at a premium, but any I find I can keep. That's the purpose of this trip. See if I can convince Jonathan to help out."

"You'll need a tongue of gold, I'm afraid. Lynna says he's adamant about not bearing arms."

"How can he refuse?" Rafe asked. "Police the town against the very people who threaten his livestock. Apprehend looters, enforce the law, protect"—his eyes twinkled merrily and he let his hand touch her leg—"you innocent ladies."

"I see," Celia replied, pointedly removing his hand. "And who is to protect us from you?"

Rafe laughed out loud. "Not me," he admitted at last. "At least where you're concerned. But don't worry. I'll be too busy keeping track of my so-called militia. That and trying to ferret out spies."

Celia's stomach flip-flopped. "Oh, dear! Spies? Here?"

"There's some concern in that direction. A soldier stumbled into one of the camp circles yesterday morning. Quite early, before sunup, I'm told. He'd suffered a stout blow to the skull about the time he spotted someone coming up out of the river. That implies at least one accomplice, which gives us a total of two. The whole thing may mean absolutely nothing, but I intend to act on the assumption that we have mischief afoot in the city."

"But only two?" Celia asked in a hushed voice. "What harm—?"

"You ever see what happens when a couple of hornets get into a church full of people? No. If we've spies among us, we need to find them." His face was grim and unyielding. "And when I do, I'll lead them to the gallows personally."

Celia could no longer bear to watch him. She was too afraid her expression would give her away. Her heart pounding, she stared at the gravel lane and the shrapnel-riddled buildings and the pedestrian traffic that moved from shop to shop as if nothing out of the ordinary was happening.

"Celia?" Rafe looked concerned as he tilted her chin toward him.

The sun through the blue silk parasol gave her cheeks the cool pale blue and white tone of alabaster. To avoid his scrutiny, Celia turned toward him and rested her head lightly against his shoulder. "Oh Rafe," she whispered, miserably. "It's so sad. Everyone is out. Look at them. All so brave, as if the world isn't falling apart. As if the Yankees were a thousand miles away and not at our doorsteps."

"Not really," Rafe said, too happy to have her touching him to worry about Yankees. "We just won't be terrorized, is all. Anyway, owe them a debt of gratitude. You're closer to me than you've been in days, even if out of concern and not undying rapture."

"Rafe Lattimore, you are terrible," Celia scolded, drawing away momentarily and playfully slapping his arm.

"Terrible? I'm merely honest."

"Honestly feeling sorry for yourself, you mean." She slipped her arm through his and squeezed gently. "You wouldn't know undying rapture if it kicked you in the shin."

She had kept a cool distance between them for the two weeks since the broken embrace after they left the picnic. Oh, he had seen her, talked and walked with her, but always, as it were, at arm's length. "You could try me," he said, the soft pressure of her breast a fire against his arm.

"Perhaps I will," Celia said languidly, hoping he would not notice how hollow her smile was. Only two weeks. Barely time, with all that had transpired, to sort out her thoughts. She had loved him so, once, given him up as lost, and then found him as alive in reality as he had been in her dreams. So much, so much! Powell's summons, Anthony's arrival on the scene. Rafe's return, soured by Micah's, too. The siege, wrapping the city in a cocoon of fire and blue-uniformed soldiers, thwarting her escape and leaving her wrecked with tension and torn by fears both real and illusory. And now, to make everything infinitely worse, there was all this talk of spying—from the very man who had aroused in her such powerful desires. Desires she thought that years and trauma had buried, desires that, as Lazarus had risen from the cave of death, were rising from the ashes of her heart.

CHAPTER 13

Jonathan swam groggily out of sleep, realized he was sweating profusely, and rolled onto Lynna's side of the bed where the sheets were dry and cool. In the same instant he remembered that Lynna wasn't home, that she had insisted on going alone to Celia Bartlett's. A brief moment of panic brought him bolt upright, but then reason forced him to lie back down again and try to relax. Nothing was going to happen to her. He couldn't protect her completely. She was as capable of taking care of herself as the next person was.

The pillow was cool under his head. Jonathan twisted his head until it was comfortable and let himself drift. He'd been awake all night guarding the livestock and garden, for while not many people visited this far out of town, the relative isolation made their small farm an obvious target for foragers. It was a lazy time of day.

Through the open window he could see that the sun had crept inside the hayloft in the barn, which meant that one o'clock had come and gone. Sleepy afternoon sounds seeped into his consciousness. The soft cluck of chickens, the muted rustle of magnolia leaves on the shading tree outside the window, the soft low of the cow. Peaceful sounds, quiet sounds. Sounds that, here on the far southern edge of the city, the siege had yet to affect.

Strange, the war seemed so remote. Other than the foragers and the occasional faraway rumble of artillery fire, one could almost forget the current predicament. Their quiet lane was rarely traveled. They were almost three miles from the heaviest concentration of troops north of the city, a mile and a half from Square Fort and Railroad Redoubt, about which the action to the east revolved. Two miles to the south the troops thinned out to little more than picket lines, for the swamps and bayous and low-lying marshes made anything like real warfare impossible. Most importantly, few Union artillery rounds passed over their heads, so far fewer fell by mistake in their vicinity.

A noise intruded. Jonathan sat up, peered out the window to see a carriage rolling to the garden gate, and sighed in relief as Lynna stepped out. Home safely after all, he thought, pulling on his trousers, followed by a worn work shirt. He followed her from his window vantage point as she quickly made her way around the house without checking inside. Perhaps she thought he was still angry with her for being so determined to accept Celia Bartlett's invitation. Not that he could blame her for seeking a change in pace, he was forced to admit. Their school had been closed and, requisitioned by the army, turned into a magazine packed to the ceiling with powder and shot. And as theirs was a small farm geared for supplying the necessities and in no way a producer of cash crops, the only work left for them was to tend the garden and animals.

Lynna was among the chickens by the time Jonathan reached the back porch. Crooning softly, she scattered spare handfuls of rationed grain to the farm's feathered beggars who, clucking and flapping their wings, swarmed about her feet and ate greedily. A determined congregation, they took no notice of the baby chicks scurrying between and under their feet, and parted only for the vain rooster strutting forward to eat his fill.

Lynna set down the nearly empty sack, straightened and, poking out her abdomen, began to rub her back and massage the muscles above her hips. Jonathan watched her fondly. Some fathers demanded a son and nothing else would do, but Jonathan didn't care. Health was all he asked for. A boy or a girl or both, if it came to that, was fine with him. Just as long as they and Lynna were healthy. Jonathan was a man ready to give love, to see the extension of his life and behold the future gurgling contentedly in his arms, and to be able to say, this is a part of me, the part of me I leave behind to carry on.

The grain was gone, the chickens leaving. Only four tiny chicks, the color of freshly churned butter, remained to peck at the toes of Lynna's slippers. Theirs were simpler desires: the food had stopped, and they had yet to eat. Lynna's laugh was warm and throaty as she reached into the sack and sprinkled a few grains of dried crushed corn right on top of the chicks, who peeped excitedly and fell to with a vengeance. She started to turn back to the house but stopped when a dull thud from the east pulsed through the afternoon heat. A second later, eyes shaded, she watched the squiggly smoky line of a fused shell pass overhead toward the river.

"There they go again," Jonathan said, his shadow meshing with hers as his arm slipped around her waist.

Lynna pointed to the thin strip of river visible through the trees just as a plume of spray erupted behind a ship made toylike by distance. "Not even close," she said, liking the feel of his arm around her.

A pair of shells flew overhead and landed even further from the craft before the firing stopped. "And not worth wasting powder on at that distance," Jonathan said. "They'd best save their shot for the troops in front of them. Unless, of course," he added with a wry smile, "the war's over. That would be a pleasant surprise. Except someone would have to get the Yankees to agree."

"As soon teach pigs to sing 'Dixie,'" Lynna said and sighed. She turned her face, lightly complected and sprinkled with freckles, framed by bright auburn red hair, toward her husband.

Jonathan well knew the signal and responded with a kiss. "Speaking of pigs," he said, his broad, frank face creased with a smile as his wife pressed against him with far more ardor than their brief kiss warranted, "we'll have to keep Samantha in the barn during the day as well. For the duration, I suppose. Jessie, too," he added, prompted by the low of the milk cow they'd brought from Natchez with them when Lynna's mother died, and they moved to the old O'Grady farm. "Those three I chased off last night looked like they'd be back."

"Really?" Lynna asked, not really caring. She pulled the top of his shirt open and kissed his chest. "You taste salty." Swollen with child, she pressed against him and looked up into his eyes. "Did you feel him kick?"

"I wasn't paying attention."

Lynna's eyes twinkled happily as she reached up and kissed his chin. "You should have been." Her eyelids dropped and her voice became husky. "You know that, don't you?" she asked, tugging him toward the house.

"I know that Tom Stewart said—"

"Tom Stewart talks too much," Lynna said, shushing him. "And so do you, sometimes." She rubbed her nose and forehead across his chest, drank in the smell of him, and reveled in the feel of his arms around her. "Oh, Jonathan. You smell so good, you feel so good. Is it any wonder I love you so much?"

"Because I smell good?" Jonathan asked wryly.

He was hard from physical labor, and had the calloused hands of a farmer. She was glad he was something more, a man of some education concerned with more than too much rain or too little. "Good enough to eat," Lynna said, playfully biting his nipple.

"Yeow!" Jonathan grabbed her wrists, pulled her free of him. "Now look here, woman. You're over seven months along and—"

"Seven, seven," Lynna mocked. "Listen to the man! He can count! Which is what I get for marrying an educated man!"

"Well, it's true . . ."

"My mother, though she liked you well enough, Johnnie Hays, warned me of the consequences. Marry not an educated man, she said, for they are fond of excuses and will ever be finding one at the most awkward times."

"And my father warned me of Irish girls." Jonathan laughed.

"He did no such thing." Lynna huffed, hands on hips. "What a liar you are!"

"Am not," Jonathan insisted, tracing a cross over his heart. "Told me how there's no satisfying Irish ladies. He was more graphic, of course, but such talk isn't fit for mixed company."

"Oh!" was all Lynna managed to say, and swung the sack of grain. Jonathan ducked, tripped over a piece of wood, fell, and rolled away from her. The chickens scattered in a profusion of feathers and raucous squawks. "Now wait just a—"

The bag whistled past his head. "How dare you!"

Jonathan jumped to his feet and stumbled for the safety of the barn. Lynna followed him into the cool interior and swung again, catching him on the rump. Jonathan fell into a pile of hay. Off balance, Lynna tripped over his legs and landed sprawling next to him. She tried to crawl away, but he caught her by the waist and pulled her backside to him. "Oh, no, you don't!" he exclaimed, one hand grabbing her skirt to pull it up around her waist.

"Let me go." Lynna gasped, trying to catch her breath and not laugh at the same time. She felt him unbuckle his belt and slide his pants down over his hips, then the warmth of his erection against her back. "Johnnie . . ." She felt hot, and yet shivered, pushed upward until his hardness slipped between her legs.

"Not too deep, Johnnie. Gently. Gently," she instructed, guiding him into her, tilting her hips to accept and hold him. "Gently, Johnnie my love, my Johnnie, my love . . ."

And then only the long slow strokes and the rustle of straw and the quickening of breaths and the utter silence of that moment when there is nothing else in the whole wide world but two made one, and the oneness speaks in a tongue that God and humans alike know as the language of love.

Two stalls down, forlorn and wanting company, Jessie bawled loudly. Her noisy complaint woke Jonathan and Lynna on their bed of straw where they had dozed off in the afternoon heat. Jonathan yawned widely, stretched, and squeezed Lynna to him. "Oh, my! Imagine! Sleep all morning and make love in the afternoon."

"All afternoon?" Lynna asked drowsily.

"Tempting, tempting. Beats hell out of teaching school."

Lynna turned toward him and rubbed her leg across his. "Or anything else I can think of." A quizzical look crossed her face, and she propped herself up on one elbow. "Wait a minute! Did your father really say that? About Irish girls? Me?"

"Yup." Jonathan tried not to grin, but gave up when Lynna leaned over until her nose was almost touching his.

"Look me in the eye and say that again," she demanded. "If your pupils dilate, you're lying."

"Pupils dilate?" Jonathan protested. "That's the silliest—"

"It's true. Go on. Your father said?"

"Well . . ."

"See? See?"

"He *did* tell me to be wary, or you'd always get your way."

Her nose touched his. "So you are extra cautious?" she asked, covering his mouth with tiny kisses.

"Yup."

More kisses, trailing off to his ear. "And cannot be tricked?" she murmured. Jonathan repaid the kisses and nibbled on Lynna's earlobe. "Nope," he said between clenched teeth. "I'm wise to you, Evlynna O'Grady Hays."

Lynna's laughter was music. "It appears, Mr. Hays," she said triumphantly, "that I just got my way."

"Yup," Jonathan conceded. "You sure did. Just had your way with me."

"So what do you say to that, Mr. Know-it-all?"

"Woe is me," Jonathan said dolefully. The grin, irrepressible now, stretched across his face. "It's a terrible thing when a man's wife is smarter than he is." He cocked one eyebrow and moved his leg between hers. "Sure you don't want to try to outsmart me again?"

"You!" Lynna snuggled closer, nestled against him. "Am I wrong to be this happy?" she asked. "If I am, I don't care. Tell me you don't either, Johnnie. Tell me you love me."

"I don't," Jonathan promised. "And I do. More than . . ." Suddenly he sat upright. "Oh-ohhh!"

"What?" Lynna asked, and then heard the approaching carriage, too. "Oh, Lord!" she exclaimed. "And look at us!"

They rose as one and hastily straightened, fastened, buckled, and brushed off their clothes. Jonathan peeped through a knothole. Squinting against the brightness, he made out a carriage, then a man helping a woman down. The man was in uniform. "Damn," he cursed under his breath. "More soldiers."

Lynna angled toward the open door. Standing invisible in the deep shadow, she had a clearer view. "Why, it's Celia Bartlett and Rafe Lattimore."

"In a uniform, right?"

"Don't be such an old grouch."

"I'll try. But if he's come like some of the others . . ."

"Celia!" Lynna called, already out the door and walking toward the carriage.

Celia waved in return, looked around to see a humble but tidy house skirted about with a dust-covered fence. Calico curtains flapped in the windows. A hen worked her way through the neatly spaced pickets of the fence to forage for insects under the front porch. An open shed to one side held a few modest implements evidently used in the large garden well greened with young beans and carrots and turnips and peas poking through the earth's black blanket. How beautiful, Celia mused wistfully. Here on the outskirts, the city seemed far away. Here one could live in peace and privacy, demand little from life, and in turn be left free from scrutiny and responsibility and protocol. Of course, she knew she was painting a far rosier picture than reality warranted. Still, the foundation was true. Lynna herself was proof of the possibility that a woman *could* live at peace with the man she loved, and build not financial empires but a family. "Forgive us for intruding," she said aloud as the teacher approached.

"Nonsense." Lynna embraced Celia warmly and the two friends exchanged kisses. "Jonathan and I were just working in the barn. We're always ready for an excuse to avoid making repairs."

"What's the trouble now?" Jonathan said, nodding to Celia as he approached but directing his question toward the man in uniform.

"Now, Jonathan," Lynna chided. "Please excuse his tone," she went on to Rafe. "You see, every time men in uniform show up we lose livestock."

"They got all our shoats and a half a dozen chickens so far," Jonathan added, barely civil. "Conscripted, the soldiers said. Thievery, I say."

"These are times of trial, Mr. Hays," Rafe pointed out stiffly. "The hospitals are always running out of fresh meat. Surely you wouldn't begrudge wounded and dying men a decent meal? Perhaps a final meal before entering judgment?"

Jonathan's eyes dropped, and he stared at the ground at his feet. "Now you shame me, sir," he said at last.

"I didn't mean to, I assure you."

The rooster chased a young cockerel across the yard. Ill at ease with the bad beginning, the two couples watched, then listened as the rooster crowed in triumph and reassertion of his dominance in the yard.

"Just look at me!" Lynna said, sounding too loud in the awkward silence that followed. "As hospitable as a rock! Won't you come in and have some coffee?"

"In a moment perhaps," Rafe said, the formal iciness just barely thawing. "After Jonathan and I talk. You don't mind, do you?"

"Of course not," Celia said, jumping in adroitly and taking Lynna's arm. "I haven't been out here in ages."

Lynna glanced once at Jonathan and, seeing his anger had subsided, led the way toward the house.

Rafe and Jonathan strolled slowly away from the carriage and stopped at the gate that opened onto the lane. Looking to his left, Rafe could see the thick profusion of willows that, except for one gap created by a path, masked the view of the river. Ahead and slightly to his right, the city was a multileveled panorama of spires and peaked roofs, dominated by the grand copper-sheathed tower of the courthouse gleaming like a beacon in the afternoon sun. At his side, Jonathan waited for Rafe to speak. Rafe looked over his shoulder, carefully chose his words while he waited for the women to go inside. "It's a good thing for a man to know he has a child on the way," he finally said.

"A better thing if he were brought into a world of peace."

"He?"

"A suspicion," Jonathan chuckled. "Either way, I'm a lucky man."

"You are indeed," Rafe concurred.

The fence gave slightly as Jonathan leaned on the top rail. "But you didn't come out here to tell me that of which I'm already aware."

"No."

"Well then," Jonathan asked point-blank, "are you paying this call as Rafe Lattimore or as that uniform?"

"I note a curious tone of disrespect."

"Wariness would be a more appropriate word. With due cause, I believe. Soldiers have come not only for my livestock, but for me. My school has been emptied of books and made into a powder magazine. I have been robbed of my livelihood and my students are being deprived of their education."

Rafe shrugged. "All very well and good," Rafe said, "except that books make poor weapons against seventy thousand Yankees."

"Books and education are vastly more important than guns, and the sooner you and the rest of the world understand that, the better."

Many men, under the circumstances, would have considered such talk tantamount to treason. Rafe liked to think he was capable of greater depths. "In the long run, yes," he agreed. "But we're not allowed the luxury of the long run. No one likes this war, but it's been thrust upon us by a tyrranical government that wouldn't let us depart in peace. Right or wrong, guns and powder are immediately necessary. And right or wrong, each of us must do his part."

"Which brings you to your point," Jonathan said dryly.

Rafe studied the teacher for a moment. A solid chunk of a man in dirt-stained overalls and homespun shirt with rolled up sleeves, his appearance disguised a man of sharp intelligence and keen wit. "Which brings me to my point," he conceded.

"I won't fight," Jonathan repeated doggedly for perhaps the hundredth time in the past month. "Which is the same answer I've given all the others who've asked. The last batch wanted me to infiltrate the Yankee lines at night and get into the woods somewhere near Grant's headquarters. They said anyone who could shoot as well as I ought to be able to pick off a general or two. I told them what I'll tell you. The Good Lord made life sacred. Shooting at clay targets is one thing and killing men is another. I'll not take a human life."

"I'm not asking you to kill anyone," Rafe said, not yet willing to take no for an answer. "I'm asking you to join the Home Guard, which is really just a glorified police force."

"Six of one, half a doz—"

"For Christ's sake, man!" Rafe exploded. "Take your head out of the sand! Already some of the riffraff from the waterfront have attempted to loot and disrupt the orderly progression of life."

Jonathan's laugh was a cynical bray. "Orderly?" he asked. One arm swept in a circle that encompassed the whole city. "You call this an orderly progression?"

"I call it damned close, considering the circumstances. Most people are digging in and making the best of an impossible situation. Some few aren't, and someone has to keep them under control. Now I'm stuck with a bunch of old men, boys, misfits, and walking wounded. I need you, damn it. You're healthy. You're physically capable. Like it or not you've acquired a reputation as a marksman. I can't do this job alone, Hays. I need a few good men to help me if I'm to demonstrate to the lawless element from Under the Hill even a semblance of control."

Jonathan exhaled loudly and rubbed a hand across his stubbled beard. "I don't know . . ."

"I'm not asking you to shoot anyone," Rafe repeated insistently. "Not even asking you to do anything you haven't done before, from the looks of that nose. Right or wrong? You've cleared a house or two in your day, haven't you?"

"Well . . ." Jonathan fingered his nose, then self-consciously shoved his hands in his pockets to hide the scar tissue on his knuckles, the legacy of a boisterous past. He seemed to struggle for a moment, then finally asked, "Is there any pay?"

"Next to nothing, but it beats being conscripted and sent to the trenches despite your convictions."

"They wouldn't—"

"They damned well would, as you well know. Within the week, too." His mind raced. He didn't want—couldn't afford—to let this one get away. "The Home Guard's your last chance, man! Come with me!"

He couldn't hide his knuckles forever. Jonathan leaned on the fence, inspected his fingers, and considered. They couldn't make him shoot to kill, but Rafe was right: they could conscript him and send him to the trenches as they had others, there to be used as cannonfodder if nothing else. Once in the trenches, they'd see that he never got out alive, and what would happen to Lynna then? And the child? The choices were as limited as they were hopeless. "What about this place?" he asked abruptly. "What happens while I'm watching everybody else's house?"

Relief washed over Rafe. The main issue was settled, and now they were discussing terms. "I'll see that you're mostly at this end of town," he promised. "Little will change. You'll be near your wife and neighbors. And can sleep here," he went on, not giving Jonathan a chance to ask, "during the day."

"And a horse?"

"Horses are hard to come by," Rafe said. His face creased in a grin. "Would you settle for a healthy mule?"

"Mules ride kind of hard, but—" Jonathan glanced around, saw Rafe's grin and stuck out his hand. "I guess I'm your man, Mr. Lattimore."

Two hands, one calloused and creased with dirt, the other longfingered and patrician but equally strong, met and clasped. A mischievous glint in his eye, Jonathan began to squeeze. His fingers, short and stubby, dug into the back of Rafe's hand. Realizing what was happening, Rafe began applying pressure in return.

"Will I need a uniform?" Jonathan asked, his teeth clenched.

Rafe moved his right foot back a few inches to gain a bit of leverage. "I'll see that you get a coat," he said with a grunt. "There'll be a badge, too, of course. You can come by tomorrow morning and pick them up."

"That's . . . nice . . ." Jonathan groaned.

"Yes. Isn't . . . it . . ."

Beads of sweat popped out on Rafe's forehead. The veins in Jonathan's neck stood out like ropes. Their hands were pale and bloodless from effort. Each man straining to the utmost, the tableau held for a long moment. At last, as if some signal passed between them, they quit at the same moment to end the contest in a draw.

"You are full of surprises, Mr. Hays," Rafe said, pretending his hand didn't feel as if it had been stepped on by a mule.

"And you can shake hands—for a hilltop man, Mr. Lattimore," Jonathan conceded, wriggling the feeling back into his tortured fingers. "And now, how about that coffee?"

"Fine." Rafe laughed. "If someone will help me lift the cup to my lips."

At ease, the animosity and distrust between them laid to rest, the two men walked together toward the house. And neither noticed the incongruity of a handsomely shined mahogany-and-brass carriage drawn by a fine Tennessee mare tethered before the plain, pine board, three-room farmhouse with calico curtains in the windows. And with hardly a view of the river.

A carriage rolling to a stop in front of the Hays farm brought Jonathan to the window. "Haven't had this many visitors in a month of Sundays," he said, recognizing Tom Stewart as the doctor stepped down from his carriage and tied his mare next to Rafe's.

"Who is it?" Lynna asked from the table.

"Tom Stewart. But I thought he was doctoring for the army like all the others."

"He said he'd try to come out once a month to check on me." Lynna rose and looked about nervously. "I told him there was no need . . ."

"Well, he's here."

Celia nudged Rafe with her knee. "Perhaps we'd better be getting on," she said, rising from her place at the table and going to Lynna's side. "We've had a lovely visit."

Rafe stood, offered a parting handshake to Jonathan. "You'll report to the office on Washington, then?"

The two men shook hands gingerly. "I'll tend to the animals and be there shortly after eight," Jonathan promised.

"Good. I'll issue you a revolver. Just for show," Rafe added quickly.

"I suppose," Jonathan replied. He turned to Celia. "I ought to tell you. I'm going to try to dissuade Lynna from accompanying you and the others on this fool mission to the trenches. In her condition—"

"In my condition a woman can do anything she pleases," Lynna interjected.

A knock saved Jonathan from the necessity to answer. Fists clenched, he held the door open for the physician.

"Jonathan," Tom said. "Good to see you."

"Surprised to see *you* out this way," Jonathan said, shaking hands. "Thought the army'd be taking up all your time."

"I told them I needed at least one morning a week to see to some of my civilian patients. They didn't have much choice, really."

"It's afternoon, Tom," Rafe said, stepping forward to greet the man who was also his father's physician.

Tom appeared surprised to see Rafe, even more so when he noticed Celia.

"Is something the matter?" Celia asked, self-conscious under his intent gaze.

"Uh . . . no! Pardon me, I just . . ." His mouth worked silently for a moment, and he looked around as if he was lost. "I thought you were rehearsing for a visit to the trenches or something. Solange told me—"

"Oh dear, I forgot," Celia interrupted. "Gaillee mentioned that she had invited her. I hope she isn't ill."

"She wasn't there?"

"Well . . ." Celia glanced at Lynna for help, but Lynna appeared as helpless as she. The troubled expression on Tom's face made her wish she'd been more circumspect. "I'm afraid not," she said gently.

"Odd," Tom reflected. "We left together. She insisted on taking her own sulky."

"Why, then she must have changed her mind," Celia said much too brightly. She could have bit her tongue off. "No doubt she's home. I wouldn't blame her. Traveling alone is dangerous these days."

"Of course," Tom agreed lamely.

Rafe remembered seeing Solange and Micah together and guessed immediately where Solange had been. "Well! It looks as if we're in the way here," he said with forced good cheer and pretending ignorance. He crossed to Celia and took her arm. "With conditions as they are, we ought not to delay Dr. Stewart any longer than necessary."

Suddenly being addressed by his title seemed to break the spell. Tom looked up at Rafe, then to Lynna. "Time is important these days. More precious than ever, I'm afraid. Especially since time is running out." No one knew quite how to answer such pessimism. Luckily, Tom seemed to realize the extent of the pall of gloom he was casting. Abruptly, he switched to the brusque, no-nonsense, professionally optimistic bedside manner he reserved for the hospital. "Speaking of which—" He wagged an accusing finger at Lynna. "I'd better take a look at you, young lady. I can tell already your diet is less than adequate. I suggested an early garden, didn't I?" He gestured toward the open front door. "If you don't mind?"

Jonathan, his foul mood returning, walked outside with Celia and Rafe. "Early garden," he growled. "And every night for a week it's been pilfered and robbed. Eat better. What does he expect?"

"Doctors are forever suspecting the worse," Rafe said, clapping the teacher on the shoulder. "Pessimism's their duty. They paint a bleak picture, and when things turn out fine, we're relieved and consider them miracle workers."

"I wish I could believe you."

"Lynna is fit as a fiddle and you know it," Celia scolded gently.

"I suppose so . . ."

"But if you're that worried, I'll contrive to leave Lynna behind and Caillee can just make do on the accordian."

"Leave Lynna? Lord, no!" Jonathan laughed. "She'd blame such a conspiracy on me and flay me alive. No, ma'am. If Tom has no objections, then neither do I." Levity couldn't hide his very real concern. "But take care where you ladies step."

Celia took his hand and squeezed her assent. "From what we're told, the most trying enemy is boredom. Beyond that, I don't intend to let us get involved in anything even remotely resembling the precarious."

Rafe helped Celia into the carriage and turned to shake Jonathan's hand. "Tomorrow, then?"

"Creeps in this petty pace from day to day," Jonathan replied.

"Until the last syllable of recorded time, right?" Rafe went on, to the other man's surprise. "You see? We're not such ignorant dolts as you'd think us, for all our hilltop houses and numerous conceits."

"It's been a day of surprises." Jonathan grinned. He tipped his hat to Celia and stepped back as Rafe climbed in the carriage, touched his whip to his mare's flank, and drove off back toward Vicksburg, leaving a plume of dust to waver and then vanish on the wind.

Pea Grove Cemetery was on the east side of town, off Clay Street just past Second North Street. Bordered on two sides by flowing creeks, this plot of manicured land offered a shady and peaceful haven in which to await eternity. Vicksburg's finest lay interred here, among them Celia's uncle, Phillip, and her Grandfather and Grandmother Bartlett. Here, too, lay her father and mother, Hal and Chloë, deep under a double white marble stone shaded by magnolias and close by the white picket fence over which, in her youth, Celia had scrambled in her haste to the creek.

Celia and Rafe had dined early. Now, as dusk fell and the spring greens grew vibrant in the waning light, Celia stood with her hands folded and the toes of her slippers at the edge of the still mounded rectangle of earth that marked, more starkly than stone, Halliburton Manson Bartlett's final resting place. Her father was as vivid in her mind as if he stood at her side, and his presence dredged up old wounds. His gradually deteriorating health. The destruction of his warehouses and his painful ostracization by his old friends. The conscription of his ships both in Vicksburg and New Orleans as the ship-hungry Confederate Navy purchased, at derelict prices, every one of his freighters and effectively put the Bartlett Lines out of business. The onslaught of war, and the death and destruction on a scale unheard of in the country he loved so well. The bitter disillusionment in his voice as he told her of the gold that lay buried in the basement—the gold he had foreseen Celia would need to live comfortably, but had not foreseen would weigh her down and actually threaten her life.

"Oh, Papa," Celia whispered.

A breeze stirred the white blossoms overhead and made all the air redolent with their almost cloying perfume. Celia skirted the rectangular border of stones that delineated the family plot and opened the gate that led to a narrow meadow that sloped down to the creek. Dragonflies greeted her, darted away in sharp angles to pursue mosquitoes rising from the jasmine-covered ground. The creek itself danced darkly in the deep shade, showing only the whites of its eyes where rounded rocks broke the surface. Across the creek, separated from the water by a thin strip of clover, plowed furrows stretched in parallel lines over the top of the gentle slope. Alone, utterly so, Celia stood silently in a world removed until she heard soft footfalls approaching. A moment later, his hands gently encircling her waist, Rafe joined her. "I thought it best not to let you out of my sight. Do you mind?"

She could feel his chin brush against her hair, his chest touch her back. "No," she whispered, resting her hands on his.

"Do you remember playing here? Once we even climbed this old willow and watched a funeral. I can't remember whose."

"We were terribly irreverent, I'm afraid."

"Children aren't supposed to understand death," Rafe said. "Irreverent, yes, but innocently so. Not maliciously."

"And innocence ends soon enough," Celia said with a sigh.

Rafe shrugged. "I suppose. So?"

"Too soon. Sometimes I wish I could just go to sleep and never awaken."

"You'd miss a beautiful morning or two," Rafe said, his lips close to her ear.

"Perhaps. But pain, too. And loss."

Rafe kissed her shoulder and lightly traced a path to the nape of her neck. "And love. Don't forget love."

Celia yearned to yield to him, to turn and surrender, to lie back on the grass and give herself to him. To give herself and take from him enough of passion and desire and love to slake the most famished appetite. To unburden herself of the secret fears, to dispel the choking loneliness, to shatter the binding cocoon of lies that imprisoned her. If only the truth were not so awesome! How, after all, would it sound? "Your brother took me, Rafe, but I know you can live with the ghost of that obscene coupling. I have committed treason, Rafe, am one of those you have sworn to send to the gallows, but I trust you will forgive this little lapse of judgment on my part. Now love me, Rafe!" Love, indeed. Now there was a laugh.

But how badly she wanted him! His hands were warm on her stomach. His breath stirred the hairs on the top of her head with excruciating lightness. His sex was a firm pressure that burned her buttock through the layers of clothing which mercifully protected her. The front of his thigh pressed the back of hers, and she thought she would weep with frustration. For one maddening second she saw him naked against her, entering her, possessing her, saw his eyes widen, heard his low moan and her own tortured cry. In that second, that brief, flaring second . . . his hands would cradle her head. She would hang from him—oh, God!—her ankles locked behind his back. She would consume and enfold him, revel in him. She would torture herself with him, satiate herself with him, lie fulfilled and faint under his damp weight. And never . . . never . . . dare . . .

He could not hide his disappointment. "Still so reluctant?" he asked when she tore his hands free and stepped away, barely in control of herself. "Why, Celia? For the love of God, open up to me. Why?"

Hands to face, fingers pressing eyes, breath labored. "No reason, every reason." The words lacerated her throat, and she shrugged helplessly. "Up there, perhaps," she said, manufacturing an excuse and gesturing toward the cemetery. "I don't know."

"Please, Celia?" He sounded tired. "Can't we let the dead bury the dead?"

"Aren't you ever at a loss for words?" Celia snapped, indulging in anger as an antidote for pain.

Rafe caught her by the arm, turned her toward him. "I could ask the opposite of you. Never an answer. Never once—"

"Let me go."

"No! Not until you talk to me and let me inside your silence. Damn it, Celia, you know how I feel."

"It's getting dark. Late . . ."

"Celia . . ."

"Try to be patient with me." The truth was too awful. The tension too great. She would split like a tree struck by lightning if he went on much longer. "I need time, Rafe. Please?"

"You've had two and a half years!" he shouted, his own anger spilling out of him at last. "What more do you want? Isn't that enough?"

"No!" She choked back a sob. "Yes!" She wanted to force him away, to save herself, to save him, yet she could not say the words. "Try to understand."

"What? Try to understand what?" He was ranting but didn't care. "You don't even understand yourself. Yes. No. I don't know. I want you, Celia. Don't you understand that? I've never stopped wanting you."

"Stop it! Just . . . stop . . . it . . . please!" Unheard by the dead, her scream echoed from the hills, soaked into the churned earth, ran with the water. Her fingernails bit into the palms of her hands, and her fists bruised her thighs. "I can't take this any longer, do you hear?"

Startled, Rafe backed away from her, held his hands palm out in a placating gesture. "All right. Okay. I'm sorry. I'm—"

"Please take me home," Celia interrupted stiffly, her temper under fragile control.

"Celia—"

"Please?" she pleaded, suddenly exhausted. "Please?"

Rafe threw his hands into the air and started back toward the carriage. Celia followed through the cemetery, closed the side, and then the front gate behind her. By the time she reached the carriage, Rafe had gained enough control to help her in without speaking. Celia waited for him to untether the mare and climb into the seat beside her for the silent ride back into the city. "Are you still angry?" she asked when he reined in the mare in front of her house.

He, too, looked exhausted, and spoke without looking at her. "No. Not angry. I wasn't angry. Just . . ." He searched his brain for a better word, but couldn't find one. "Just angry, I guess."

Celia nodded and touched his arm. "I'm sorry."

"No need," he answered tersely. "I'll live."

"Until Sunday?" Celia asked, trying for a lighter tone. "I should hate to be the only unescorted lady at my own party."

Rafe sighed and slowly turned to face her. His eyes said everything, and nothing. At last, he raised her hand and kissed her fingertips. "I'll live until Sunday," he said.

CHAPTER 14

War heightens lust. Where men are fighting and dying, so too will men be drinking and carousing and fornicating. War is the great stimulator, for the senses are sharpened in the presence of death. Life moved at a frantic pace in Vicksburg Under the Hill at night. The outward signs were few, but if one listened, the proof was behind a hundred drawn curtains and buried in as many excavated caves. There, safe from the wayward shells, men danced and drank and wrangled and fought and paid for women with wildly varying amounts of gold or silver or whiskey or meat or even salt. Anything went. The constraints were few and imposed with fists or guns.

Outside, the noise was muted, the light subdued. Only the occasional straggler moved about on the darkened docks, for it was there the most shells fell, and only fools dared that kind of luck. Away from the waterfront, a small but steady flow of men scurried along the streets on their way from one saloon or bordello to another. None lingered outside longer than necessary, for there was comfort in light and the press of bodies and the sound of voices.

Anthony blended well. Unassuming but not withdrawn, he visited one establishment after another, drank sparingly, and judiciously allowing for the power of rumor, kept his ears open for possible meaningful information. That he had heard nothing startling during the two weeks he had been so occupied didn't deter him in the slightest. Information was like gold, rarely found, and then, unless one was extremely lucky, only after a long and diligent search. He had visited four bars so far this evening, lingering longest in those frequented by soldiers, moving on quickly the moment he determined there was nothing to be learned outside of the usual bragging and boasting and complaining. Now, on his way to the fifth, he lurched in feigned drunkenness along the street to blend with his surroundings and paused to take stock of the night. Skylarking, a half-dozen dockworkers roared out of one saloon, stumbled across the street to another. A dray full of coffins passed. A trio of gray-clad marksmen sauntered down the sidewalk in the direction of Fancy Darren or Mollie Bunch's or any of the lesser sporting houses hollowed out of the bluffs. The men were laughing and exchanging ideas of how best

cross the siege line and, as they put it, "have some easy pickin's on
e Federals."

"I'll have some pickings of my own," Anthony muttered to himself,
nd stepped out on the street. A mist clung to the air and the distant
emors of a far-off storm charged the air with an aura of latent en-
rgy. A carriage clattered down the street, swerved to miss an
nfilled shell hole by inches, and in the process also missed Anthony
s he leaped out of the way. A second later, when a powerfully built
gure emerged from a nearby door and stood silhouetted against
e faintly lit sky, he abandoned his strategy of open anonymity and
ucked quickly around a corner.

There were few men in Vicksburg Anthony feared. Micah Latti-
ore, who he knew well from his earlier summertime visits, was one of
em. He had seen Micah at Fancy Darren's and escaped without
eing recognized and having to explain his presence in Vicksburg, but
asn't willing to take the chance his luck would hold. His breath tight
his chest, he squatted behind a rain barrel as Micah stretched and,
ithout seeing him, walked down the wooden sidewalk and around a
rner out of sight. Anthony heaved a sigh of relief, stepped out of
ding, and paused before the door Micah had exited. Strange. No
hts, no sound. Something about the building, though . . . Of
urse! Bartlett Shipping. One of his uncle's warehouses! One of those
rned? If so, what was Micah Lattimore doing there?

Interesting, interesting. Anthony looked about, saw no one, and
ed the door which creaked open at his touch. The ineradicable odor
burned wood struck him immediately. The door closed easily bend him. Anthony chanced a match, discovered that he was in an
ice that, though empty, had escaped destruction. A further look
vealed a feather mattress covered with a soiled sheet against the
ll to his right. Anthony grinned. Micah might have been disin-
rited and deprived of his father's wealth, but he was certainly mak-
g do.

The match burned his finger. Anthony felt his way across the room,
und a door in the brief seconds of light, and opened it. The odor
elled. Soot-blackened timbers rose in irregular and jagged relief
ainst the starlit sky. Gutted. Yet enough remained for Micah to use
a lair. Frequently, too, from the newer smell of liquor and sex that
errode the old smell of the fire. Anthony wondered who Micah was
aring the room with and if Celia knew about it, and filed away his
wfound knowledge. After checking the street, he slipped out and
sed the door behind him.

Nine o'clock or thereabouts. The fire stuck in his mind as he ambled off down the street on his way to check out a few more saloons. Fire. Not a bad idea at all. He wasn't in Vicksburg as a saboteur, of course, but the thought appealed to him. His job was to collect and evaluate information, and to pass on anything important to Powell. Still, carefully contrived damage could speed up the secesh capitulation, and what Powell didn't know wouldn't hurt him. A fire, then. But where? What would make a real difference?

Another man might have rushed off to the nearest powder storage depot and, trying to fire it, get killed in the process. But Anthony took his time and correlated cause and effect. Powder would be too closely guarded. Minié and cannonballs didn't burn. A hospital was out of the question even for Anthony. Houses were meaningless and a waste of time. There were too many stores to make the destruction of one important. Only . . . That was it! Only that day he and a hundred others had moved tons of grain and hay for mules to one of two warehouses. If only one of those warehouses burned, the available feed would be cut virtually in half. How many mules could be fed for how long under those circumstances was incalculable, but the effects had to be significant. No food for the mules, no mules. No mules, and men, already tired and hungry and weak, would have to carry ammunition and shot and food, would have to carry the wounded and reposition the batteries of heavy cannon.

Anthony ticked off the steps he would have to take and laid his plans with infinite care. Johnny Reb didn't know it, but there was going to be an accident in a few hours in and next to the shed where the hay and grain for the mules was stored. A dead sentry or two. A kicked-over lantern, a thrown torch, a hasty escape back to the security and anonymity of Vicksburg Under the Hill. By the time anyone discovered what happened, the damage would be done. He adjusted the pocket revolver hidden beneath his worn and soiled vest. He double-checked to make sure the knife he carried in his boot slipped freely in the sheath, then honed the blade on the side of his boot. He spun at a noise. A cat-sized rat scurried out of the alley behind him and disappeared into the shadows beneath the wooden walk. Anthony sighed and resheathed the knife. Then he too melted into the darkness and padded soundlessly toward his destination.

Tom Stewart recognized the man from the slash of white that diagonally divided his beard. An artilleryman, he had been wounded by a minié ball that found its way through an embrasure, ricocheted off his cannon, and lodged in his foot. Wedged between the smashed bones, the ball had been impossible to extract, and since the foot was

ıseless, it had been removed. Now gangrene had set in and the leg
had to go, as usual in these cases, above the knee.

There were so many "as usuals." As usual the man was a poor surgi-
cal risk due to malnourishment and infection. As usual Tom was so
ired he could hardly stand. As usual there wasn't enough light to see
by. As usual his knives were dull, and he could only hope that an orderly would sharpen them properly before morning, when the whole
sickening routine would begin again. The man's leg had been washed,
and Tom had painted a line around it. The line bulged downward in
the front of the thigh to mark the skin flap that would cover the
stump. The anesthetist, a corporal from Meridian, was dripping chloroform onto the mask held tightly over the man's face. When the man
stopped struggling and lay peacefully still, Tom picked up his knife
and began.

Cutting through healthy tissue and bone always bothered Tom. It
was necessary of course, because it was impossible to remove only
that which was infected. Working swiftly, he cut through the skin,
stripped the flap of unneeded tissue, and staunched the bleeding.
"Ready?" he asked.

His assistant, a student learning his trade much too quickly, laid a
thin hank of ligatures on the table and separated one, ready for use.
"Yes, sir."

"Good. Here we go."

The blood always spurted. Tom cut neatly through muscle, found
the femoral artery, and isolated and clamped it before double-tying it.
The femoral was the worst, for it could bleed a man dry in less than
two minutes. Once done, though, the rest of the operation proceeded
smoothly. Exposed, the femur lay white and glistening, waiting for the
saw. Within minutes, the severed leg with the green and black infection lay in the pile of legs in the corner of the room. Sometime during
the night, they would be carted away and buried. Tom was working
automatically now. A few scrapes of the file to blunt the sharp edges
of the bone, a half-dozen small bleeders cauterized, and last, with a
drain in place, the skin flap sewed over the raw stump. There was
nothing else to do. Except hope. With luck, the ex-artilleryman would
have to learn to walk on a wooden peg. There were worse things that
could happen to a man.

So that was that for the night. Tired, Tom shrugged out of his long
white surgeon's smock and left it for the orderlies to wash, as if mere
boiling in lye would remove the bloodstains that dyed the fabric. Five
minutes later he was out of the hospital and heading home, only to
stop suddenly a block away and, afraid that Solange would still be

out, turn down Grove Street and pull to a stop in front of the Washington Hotel. Inside, the lights were dim, the room bathed in the soft murmur of men's voices and the pungent odor of cigar smoke. Tom found a seat, ordered a brandy, and tried to relax. His hands smelled of alcohol and chloroform and turpentine, which he used in compresses to treat malaria. His shoes, trousers, and coat cuffs were stained the dull rust color of dried blood. Bloodier than a Shakespearean tragedy, he thought, sipping the brandy and wondering again if Solange was home yet. If only he hadn't met Celia that afternoon and learned . . . No. He refused to think about it. The time would come soon enough when he would have to make his way back up Grove Street and learn exactly where she had been.

"Thought I spied you!" A familiar face bent forward into the dim light, and Nathaniel Lattimore reached out to shake hands. "Cursed light. So dim a body stands a good chance of tripping over a table. Lucky a physician is present, eh?"

"Good evening, sir." Tom stood and offered Nathaniel the chair opposite him.

"Thanks, but no. I just stopped by for a word. Don't get to see you often these days."

Tom smiled apologetically. "I know. I've been busy."

"My point, young man. Precisely my point. You doctors've been working 'round the clock, it seems. Thought somebody who doesn't need immediate attention ought to thank you, is all." Nathaniel shook his head in admiration. "Your father would've been proud of you, Tom. Damned proud."

All the times Nathaniel had huffed and puffed and made his displeasure known! Tom found himself touched deeply by the older man's gesture, and all the more so because it was for no specific service rendered. "I appreciate that, sir," Tom said. His eyes watered, and he blamed exhaustion and a haze of cigar smoke. And, he admitted analytically, feeling a little sorry for himself. "Aren't many who take the time, these days—"

"Time?" Nathaniel boomed. "What else do I have but time? Hell's bells, boy, I have time to burn." He waved a hand toward a table across the room, around which his friends were sitting. "Old soldiers with the fire of battle in our veins and time to keep a hundred damned clocks ticking from now to Kingdom Come. We're plotting how to get into the Home Guard. My son, Rafe, is heading it up, you know, but keeps denying us the right to serve. As if a man in his fifties was too old!"

Tom recognized A. A. Payne and Tyrone Crowell, both men in their seventies. "Fifties?" he asked gently.

"Well, I am," Nathaniel blustered, "even if they aren't. Plenty of room for a half dozen other fifty year olds I can think of, damn it."

"But not with malaria and a bad hip and knee. I have men healthier than you in a half-dozen hospitals around town. Perhaps Rafe's afraid he couldn't attend to his duties for worrying about your well-being," Tom suggested.

Nathaniel snorted indignantly. "Well-being? I was looking after my well-being long before my son came on the scene, and consider myself an expert." He winked, patted Tom on the shoulder. "You get a spare minute, come by the house. I'll save a cigar and some brandy for you."

Tom watched Nathaniel cross the room through the packed tables and chairs. Rafe was a lucky man, he thought, to have a father still. Sometimes a man needed a father to turn to for advice or even just to talk out his own thoughts and hear how they sounded. "So here I sit, a grown man needing advice," he mumbled into his snifter. He swirled the brandy and sipped. "I'm a man, aren't I? And isn't a man a fool?" The range of possible answers was limited. Tom finished off the drink and stared into the empty glass. "Well, then, I'll be a manly fool!"

He dropped a coin on the table, slid back his chair and, with gradually quickening steps, grabbed his walking stick and hat from a Negro by the door and hurried out into the night. Another servant brought his carriage around after a brief moment's wait. And with the taste of the Washington Hotel brandy still warm in his mouth, he drove pell-mell up the climbing, descending undulations of Grove Street. His breath came fast, as if he were running. He whipped his horse around the corner onto Locust. The carriage tilted onto two wheels, almost tipping and spilling him onto the cobblestones. The idea of being maimed and broken, of having to submit to the same obscene pryings and cuttings he perpetrated so often on so many others, tempered his haste, and it was a far slower pace at which he arrived at his own front gate.

A hooded lantern cast a feeble glow on the front porch, and Harmon opened the door as Tom bounded up the steps. "Have the boy take care of my horse," he snapped. "Is Mrs. Stewart home?"

"Uh . . . yes, suh . . ."

Tom didn't like the hesitation in the old man's voice. "Why do I get the feeling you're not going to tell me something unless I ask specifically?" he demanded, dropping his cane in the holder and handing his hat to Harmon.

Harmon stared blankly at a corner of the wall over Tom's shoulder. "Suh?"

Twenty years didn't mean a damned thing. You still couldn't trust them, Tom thought sourly. "When did she arrive home today from her music practice?" he asked, furious at being made to voice his curiosity in so many words.

"Well, Doctuh Tom, that ain't something I exactly recollect. 'Bout an hour ago, maybe."

"An hour!" Tom paled. It was ten o'clock. She'd been gone for over ten hours. And not at Celia Bartlett's, by any means. Suddenly, he was terribly tired and wanted nothing more than to drink himself into oblivion. "But not yet," he mumbled. "Not yet."

"Suh?"

"Nothing." He shook his head and fought off a yawn. "Nothing, Harmon. Make sure the boy sees to the horse, and then go on to bed."

"Yes, suh." For how many years, the venerable servant wondered, had he been thus caught in the middle, and at fault whichever way he turned? Poor Doctuh Tom working so hard, just like his daddy had, an' their women running around on them. Work so hard to help folks, even black folks, and get nothing but grief in return. Weren't no black man's place to feel pity, though. White folks' troubles was white folks' troubles, an' that was that. Still, couldn't help feel a little sorry. "I done tol' Lucy to keep the coffee hot, should you want some, Doctuh Tom."

"Set it on the side of the stove. If I want some, I'll fend for myself," Tom said sharply, brushing past the old servant only to pause at midway up the stairs. "Harmon?"

The venerable black face, lined from years of work, turned toward his master. "Yes, suh?"

"I'm sorry I yelled at you."

"That's all right, Doctuh Tom. Your daddy used to yell, too. Sometimes it helps."

Tom nodded and hurried up the stairs, stopped to get his breath outside the master bedroom. The door opened soundlessly at his touch. He stepped inside and made his way to the bed. Solange' breath was the faintest of whispers, barely audible over the sudden ringing in his ears. His hands shaking, Tom lit the lantern and re placed the shade. Solange's eyes squinched at the sudden light, bu she did not wake. "Dear?" Tom asked, sitting on the edge of the bed

She stirred and rolled onto her back. "Tom? Is that you?"

"Who else?"

"Don't be silly." Solange yawned, opened her eyes, and shade them from the light. "We don't have to go into the cave, do we? You know I hate sleeping in that dank horrid place unless we have to."

"No." She was so . . . normal. Innocence personified. "The river batteries and mortar boats aren't firing tonight."

"Mmm. Thank heavens. You had a long day. Coming to bed?"

"Not quite yet." Solicitous, too. It was now or never. "Harmon tells me you came in late."

The hand that shaded her eyes from the light shifted slightly to shade her eyes from Tom as well. "He would," came the surly reply.

"I asked him specifically," Tom said in the old servant's defense.

"You would," Solange retorted, her voice strained. "May I sleep now?"

"You said you were going to Celia Bartlett's, but you didn't. Where were you?"

The silence that filled the room seemed imbued with a sentient life that swelled and pressed against flesh and walls.

Guilty, Solange's only course was to attack. "Are you my husband or my interrogator?" she asked stridently.

The sound of her voice startled him. The ringing in his ears became a high-pitched whine. "I just want to know where you were."

"I decided I didn't want to sing, so I went for a ride," Solange hissed. She sat up in bed. The covers fell from her chest to reveal soft, full breasts. "You're never with me and I get lonely. The day was beautiful, and I didn't want to spend even part of it trying to sing, which I do badly. So what did I do? I went to Mademoiselle Cognaisse to be fitted for a dress. Then I went to Giselle's, where I bought bread and wine at an exorbitant price. Then I drove to Stonebridge Park and lay on the grass and ate and listened to the birds sing. And *then*"—consumed by the role she played, her voice became flatter, shriller, and uglier with each word—"I pretended I had never come to this horrid country, and that I wasn't a prisoner in this dreadful place with bombs bursting and soldiers in the streets at all hours of the day and night!"

Panting, she lay back. Her porcelain features were no more than a vaguely discernible assemblage of soft contours in the white folds of the pillow. That afternoon Micah had brought her to the depths of unabashed lust. He had humiliated her, violated her senses, and forced her to perform acts unimaginable by any proper lady. Yet the passion he had aroused in her was like a drug. A dangerous and deadly addiction that consumed her very being. "I fell asleep," she concluded sullenly. "When I woke the sun was down and I hurried home. Are you satisfied?"

His ears had stopped ringing. Or had they? He could hear his heart. Or was it hers? Reality was a many-headed hydra: which head told the truth was an impossibly complicated conundrum. Tom stared down at his wife. He wanted desperately to believe her, for Solange alone kept the madness at bay. Without her . . .

He had to believe her. She had gone to Mademoiselle Cognaisse. Had to. She had bought bread and wine. Had to. She had driven to the park, and she had slept. *Had to!* Blinded, he bent forward and kissed her on the mouth, the chin, the neck, the breasts . . .

And saw in the dim light, dark spots, new bruises. And saw the toothmarks, red against the porcelain white. And saw, and saw those breasts with a clarity he could not accept. The moan he heard didn't come from Solange. Rather it issued from inside his skull. Better the suffering he witnessed day in and day out than the tainted flesh that screamed of infidelity. Better the gunshot wounds, the malaria, the severed limbs, the piled arms and legs of his nightmare. These were reality, and he clutched them to him. Easier to contemplate man lying in their own ordure, men dying in their own vomit. But not breasts, bruised and swollen and bloodied, speaking reams of love sullied and desecrated.

The moans grew to a roar. Devastated, Tom shoved himself from the bed and stumbled across the room to stare out the window at the night-shrouded city. She had been fitted for a dress, had driven to a park, had eaten and slept. Nothing had happened, as any fool could tell. Nothing!

"Are you coming to bed?"

"Yes."

Dully, his brain anesthetized by the chloroform of wishful thinking, he undressed, blew out the light, and lay at Solange's side. He would teach her of his love, he swore, and rekindle hers. But when he reached for her, she did not respond. It hardly mattered, he realized, for no matter how badly he wanted her, passion for him was as dead as the corpses stacked like cordwood behind the hospitals, stacked for the burying crews who every day made their distasteful but necessary rounds.

Solange lay motionless, an object he poked and pawed and stroked to no avail, until at last he admitted defeat and rolled away from her.

Nothing. Only the silence.

Solange rolled onto her side and put her back to him. "You smell of blood," she said matter-of-factly.

"I know," Tom said. "Oh, God, I know."

CHAPTER 15

Graveyard Road ran northeast from the city, passed City Cemetery, and entered a wasted, ravaged countryside. That the road should be named Graveyard Road was a quirk of fate that engendered macabre jokes. The biblical Valley of Death was no myth. Blasted wagons, shattered wheels, and bloated dead mules sprawled obscenely in the shredded, rotting vegetation. A cannon, breach blown, lay tipped and abandoned. Denuded trees, trunks, and remaining few limbs, black, mute, deformed fingers, pointed to an uncaring sky. A stone chimney, leaning awkwardly, waited to topple. And down this narrow, mud-holed corridor lined with the detritus of war, straggling columns of walking wounded bearing the less fortunate trudged in a gray procession toward the city and relief from the duty of the front-line trenches.

Celia, Gaillee, and the other women riding in the mule-drawn ambulance studied the shell-plowed landscape and the blank, dulled faces of the men with morbid fascination. Each had read of Roland and Arthur, but the glorious tales of knighthood and chivalry and glorious battles in no way prepared them for the vista that lay before them. The ground swelled upward. The surrounding profusion of gray-clad soldiers thickened. The creak of the swaying ambulance in which they rode faded, displaced by a jumble of new and frightening sounds. A moan, a cry. A command, a curse. The dull thud of an ax. Sporadic small-arms' fire, sharp and staccato. The scene was one of unimaginable turmoil. The ground, stripped for a hundred yards, looked like a vast sandbox in which giant boys had played. Shell holes, ditches, trenches, many filled with ground water. Great piles of dirt thrown up to cover small log buildings in which officers sat and issued orders. A myriad tiny caves, large enough to shelter a single man from everything but a direct hit. Further away, a long, recently constructed ridge studded with angled and sharpened tree trunks and broken by sandbagged ports for cannon ran from left to right. As they neared the ridge, they became aware of an intricate network of trenches buttressed with boards and logs and sandbags that zigzagged off to either side before disappearing in the distant perimeter of defenses guarding Vicksburg. It was here the ambulance rolled to a stop.

"Good morning, ladies!" A spare, clean-shaven officer of average height and with a sober face emerged from one of the sheltered command posts and approached the ambulance. "I am Major General Martin Luther Smith. Welcome to"—he gestured behind him to an outward bulge in the defenses—"Stockade Redan. Should you press any further forward, but half a hundred feet or so, you would find yourselves in the company of the enemy."

Mary Warwick tittered nervously, clamped a hand over her mouth at a scathing glance from her sister, Claudia.

Major General Smith looked sympathetic. "An understandable reaction, I assure you. However, this is a Saturday, they are as tired as we are, and even soldiers must rest. If I felt there were any real danger, you wouldn't be here. I ask only that you listen closely to the men assigned to be your escorts, and heed their advice in all ways. Are there any questions?"

No one spoke.

"Very well. And now, if you'll forgive me, I have a staff meeting I have to attend. Captain?"

Phillip Laughton stepped forward and saluted smartly.

"I understand at least one of you knows Captain Laughton"—the general allowed himself a smile—"who will be your escort. Ladies." He touched the rim of his gray, braid-trimmed hat. "My compliments."

A private leading a bay stallion stepped forward. The general mounted and, with a salute, rode off in the company of his aides. No sooner had he left than Phillip gestured behind him. Immediately, six sergeants, each of whom wore a clean uniform in contrast to the mud-encrusted garb of virtually every other soldier in view, strode forward. "These men have been instructed to remain at your sides at all times," Phillip said, claiming his own place at Gaillee's side. "As the general asked, please obey their wishes. And now, ladies? . . ."

The scene that followed was one of grinding contrasts. Surrounded by mud and grime, by men as gaunt as ghosts, a veritable rainbow of gowns descended from the ambulance, each with the help of a parade-polished sergeant. A bone thin lad of perhaps nineteen, his face beet red, introduced himself to an equally embarrassed Mary Warwick. A grizzled veteran with a foreign accent clicked his heels and bowed to Rosemary. Lynna, in a blue-and-red-flowered gingham greeted a red-headed man who, though as it turned out was no relation, was named O'Grady.

"I know I said I'd help," Phillip whispered to Gaillee, handing her down, "but I want you to know that I still personally disapprove of this whole venture."

"Oh, Phillip, don't be an old worrywart," Gaillee scolded, handing him the basket she carried and showing a bit of ankle for the assembled infantrymen.

"We'll need some help with the baskets, I'm afraid," Celia said to her escort, a gangling, raw-boned lad. "Would you mind terribly, Sergeant—"

"Fullbright, ma'am." The young man gestured and a half-dozen men came running. "Some of the boys would be glad to help."

The reception was awkward but well managed under the circumstances. Their escorts at their heels and loaded down with baskets, the ladies circulated among the thousand or so men assembled, and passed out cookies and small cakes of bread made with real flour, an ambrosial treat after an enforced diet of pea-meal bread on which the troops subsisted. Lynna was treated with special deference and courtesy, but not a one was accorded anything but the deepest respect, and many a war-worn, beard-stubbled face showed signs of tears before the ladies finished their brief visit and stopped again at the ambulance for Lynna to retrieve her accordian.

A hush fell over the men as the ladies arranged themselves on a small platform the general had ordered constructed. Gaillee stepped forward and cleared her throat. "I guess y'all wonder why we called y'all here," she began nervously. "Well, I wonder, too. Y'see, the General said that y'all'd be washed up and in your dress uniforms." She grinned and took heart as someone guffawed. "I mean, the General, he was all washed up. I mean, just the *teensiest* speck of mud on one boot—"

The laughter was infectious and spread rapidly in spite of Phillip's frown.

Gaillee was enjoying herself enormously and departed from the simple script she had rehearsed in front of the mirror at home. "Whatever are those Yankee boys gonna think when all these *muddy* men march over there?"

"Gonna think they been whupped!" a voice called out, followed by a rousing cheer.

Tom Stewart and all the other doctors in the Confederate Army couldn't have prescribed a better antidote for the boredom and low spirits that pervaded the trenches. A dram of silliness, an ounce of cheer, mixed with the heady spirits of seven beautiful women equaled or surpassed a whole pharmacopoeia of remedies. And to top it off, Lynna stepped forward and after a few chords launched into a rousing "Dixie." At first only the ladies sang, but within moments a thousand male voices, cracked and off tune but swelling with pride and emotion, joined in.

They sang "Lord of All Hopefulness," and "Lorena." They sang "Rose of Alabama" and "Shenandoah." And when they returned to "Dixie," Celia and Sergeant Fullbright led them from the improvised platform toward the trenches. The men on the lines had heard bits and snatches of the music, and were waiting. One by one, grimy scarecrows in tattered butternut and gray, they rose as the rainbow procession neared and, the boredom of the siege forgotten for however short a time, stood in awe of the sweet voices and the tender graciousness of Southern womanhood.

A sergeant boiling water and chicory in a shot canister rose, his mouth slack. An exhausted drummer boy woke, rubbed his eyes, thought he was dreaming, and slumped down in sleep again. Claudia placed a cookie in his outstretched hand, and no man touched it. A youth of no discernible rank save a bloodstained bandage wrapped around his head in place of a cap struggled to his feet and walked toward the women. He halted in front of Celia and stood like a statue. Flies buzzed around his head. His rifle rested in the crook of his arm, his chest was crisscrossed with cartridge and canteen straps. He looked more like a waif, more like a vagrant, than a soldier. Fullbright started to order the soldier to move, but Celia stopped him with an outstretched hand and stood, silently, at arm's length from the youth. It was a holy moment. Two people, different in sex, in station, so far removed from one another, touched across the empty space between them. And in that moment, Celia realized that, revealed in dignity, here was the true spirit of the Confederacy, the driving force that was as vital to survival as sunlight to spring blossoms.

She was a spy. She had divulged information that could help the enemy. And yet, she felt a deep sense of pride and a kinship for this young soldier who stared so reverently at her. A bitter conflict tore her heart: She owed allegiance to this youth and to that for which he stood, and in the same moment she feared for her own life if she dared to refuse to cooperate with Anthony and Powell. And if she had understood the dilemma in an intellectual sense earlier, she understood it now in the pit of her stomach and in her heart.

The youth stared. The song came to an end.

"Something the matter, Private?" Phillip said, making his way forward. "Clear the way there. Are you deaf? Clear the way."

"Ma'am?" the youth said. "Would ye favor us with 'Amazing Grace'?"

"Certainly, Private . . ."

"Bufkin, ma'am. Private Emory Bufkin of the Glen Allen Rifles. We've took Sherman's worst twice now, and will hold 'til Judgment Day or 'til hell freezes over, whichever comes first."

"We would be honored to sing for you and all these gallant men, Private Bufkin," Celia said, touched to tears. "Lynna? Do you know 'Amazing Grace'?"

Incapable of speech, her cheeks streaked with tears, Lynna nodded and began the introduction. One by one, the ladies began singing,

> "Amazing grace, how sweet the sound
> That saved a-a wretch like meeee."

Private Bufkin retired to his place along the fortification and, softly and reverently, joined in.

> "I once was lost, but now am found
> Was blind but now can see."

Inspired, officers and enlisted men alike took up the tune. Hands reached out to touch a hem or accept a piece of bread, a cookie, or a morsel of cake. Others passed boards or coats to lay a hasty footpath through the blood-drenched mud. Wistful, fervent voices rose to echo over the contested battlements and, beyond, the amazed besieging Federal host. Once Celia stepped onto a carton in order to attempt to peer over the top of the cross timber and sandbag wall. A nearby soldier, his dark sunburned face lending him a sinister look, caught her by the wrist and pulled her down. "Them bluebellies don't know the difference 'tween soldiers an' ladies, ma'am," he said, wagging his head. "Be a shame to have that pretty bonnet of yours parted"—he ran a finger across his neck—"down to here. Beggin' your pardon, ma'am."

"Uh . . . yes. Thank you," Celia stammered, feeling suddenly very foolish. She handed the man a basket she was carrying. "Would you see these are distributed among the men?"

The soldier took the basket, held it away from his body so the bread it held wouldn't get dirty. "Be a pleasure, ma'am, an' an honor." He touched his cap. "Me an' the boys, ma'am? Well, we just wanted to say it's ladies like you who make this all worthwhile."

The sun overhead beat down. The air was thick with dust. Hands reached out. Faces blasted of emotion suddenly melted into sensitivity and gratitude. And at last, when it was time to leave, one of the soldiers stood on a cannon and called for three cheers for the ladies of Vicksburg. The clamor was deafening, and followed them back to the ambulance, continued as Celia and Gaillee and the others were helped aboard. A mere two hours, and all of the women were exhausted.

The sergeants saluted their ladies, and Phillip kissed Gaillee's hand. A whip cracked, and the mules leaned into the traces. And as the ambulance turned from the trenchline, the soldiers erupted into "Dixie" once more and waved their hats in salute. The voices echoed after the departing ladies, after the blasted trenches had faded into the dust.

The women listened and chatted with tired excitement about all they had seen and experienced. Only Celia was withdrawn and aloof, lost in her own turbulent thoughts. Gaillee, Lynna, and the others guessed only that she was exhausted, but they guessed wrong.

Saturday afternoon late, the sixth of June. The nineteenth day of the siege. Rafe stared out the window of his office, a converted bookstore on Washington Street, wondered if Celia and the women had gotten back safely from their visit to the trenches, and watched the night watch of the Home Guard assemble for inspection. Thirty men. Five were one-armed veterans. Nineteen were men over fifty. Four were boys of thirteen. One, Matt Broussard, was a cripple—at least he could shoot, Rafe thought gratefully. And one was a pacifist teacher who probably wouldn't fire his weapon even in self-defense. Some Home Guard. At least the night group was better than the day group.

A hell of a tune to pipe. The poor of Vicksburg resented the more affluent for their ability to afford the almost hourly rising prices for food and clothing. The more quarrelsome elements, mainly the denizens of Vicksburg Under the Hill, took what they pleased. The law-abiding majority pitched in with a will when they were called. The riffraff made themselves generally obnoxious while managing to elude impressment when the orders went out for men to aid in all manner of civil and military chores. Rafe, in the meantime, found himself in the middle. He was charged with keeping a semblance of order and easing the multitude of tensions that had developed between all parties, rich and poor, law-abiding and lawbreakers, civilian and military. He was responsible for the equitable distribution of staples and water. He reported, ultimately, to General Pemberton and his Chief of Staff, and to the citizens of Vicksburg, who had placed their faith in him. The task was well-nigh impossible, he thought, folding his hands on his desk and wishing he had something simple like a ship to run.

"You going to tell us what you want done?"

Rafe looked up, saw Jonathan in the doorway. "What?"

"We're waiting. Any orders?"

He had long since given up expecting even a modicum of military protocol. "No. Same as every day."

"Right," Jonathan said, withdrawing.

"Wait!" Rafe called. "Come here a minute."

Jonathan reappeared, entered. "Yeah?" he asked, tugging at the ill-fitting gray coat that he wore over his homespun breeches and loose cotton shirt.

Rafe winced. Even in the civilian Home Guard one did not address a commander in such a way. "Where's your revolver?"

"I gave it to Felker. He can't load and fire a rifle very well with one arm. I brought my own rifle."

"Is it loaded?"

"Certainly," Jonathan replied, then grinned self-consciously. "With a powder charge."

Which figured, Rafe thought, drumming one thumb on the tabletop. "I suppose I'll have to accept that."

"I suppose. We haven't had too much trouble on the south end, though, and the average perpetrator is pretty easily spooked."

"Right," Rafe agreed, opening a drawer and taking out a letter, which he tossed on the desk for Jonathan to read. "Except we have a few above average on the loose. That arrived from Colonel Lampman this morning."

Jonathan read quickly and learned that the fire that had destroyed one of the feed barns had been no accident. Unless a soldier named Private Daniel Joad had torched the hay, spread coal oil around the inside of the building, lit it, and then stabbed himself in the back with his own bayonet. "And we just now hear about this?" Jonathan asked, handing the letter back to Rafe.

Rafe ticked off the days on his fingers. "The fire was Tuesday night. They found what was left of Joad Wednesday morning. One of the doctors finally got around to looking at him late that afternoon. Lampman got the report Thursday and sent me a letter yesterday. Who knows why it takes a day for a note to go a mile?"

"A saboteur, then."

"Who isn't afraid to kill. And now, just two hours ago, the guard at Andrew's well was found killed. There were two dead and putrefying dogs in the water. No one will dare use the water for a week, which will hurt."

"In broad daylight," Jonathan said, whistling through his teeth. He sat in the chair. "This is getting serious, I guess."

"Really? I'm glad you think so," he said with scathing sarcasm.

Rather than insulted, Jonathan seemed quietly amused. "And so I'm to shoot the first suspicious-looking person I run across?" he asked. "I'll tell you what. *You* do that. I'll keep an eye peeled, and guarantee to keep the lid on my end of town until Johnston comes. That sounds like a deal?"

"Like the only deal I'll get," Rafe said. "I can't keep an eye on you every minute. But do you want to know what I think?"

"You're going to tell me anyway."

"That's right." Rafe stood at the window and watched the night watch lounging about the walkway. Matt Broussard, the boy sharpshooter from the picnic, noticed him at the window, grinned and saluted. Soldiering at last, the lad was happy as a bear cub who'd found a bee tree on the ground. Rafe returned the salute, crossed back to his desk, and perched on the edge. One leg was braced stiffly against the floor and the other dangled freely.

"I think . . ." He glanced at the window and saw the faint reflection of himself hunched forward like a conspirator. He'd been gone from the military too long. Here he was, prepared to confide in a man to whom a month ago he would have spoken only briefly if at all.

"I think you'd better load your damn gun," he said shortly, rising and heading out the door. "But you do what you want."

Jonathan followed, formed up the men for what they jokingly called the daily inspection, and then waited in his own version of attention.

"Very well, men," Rafe began. He outlined the new threat to Vicksburg, warned everyone to be especially wary around anything which, destroyed, would weaken the city's staying power. "Otherwise, no change," he finished. "Hays and his men on the south side, Felker and his the north, Jones and his the east, Kerby and his downtown. Any questions?"

There were none. The men broke up into their squads and, discussing the new developments, ambled off to their respective parts of town. Alone, Rafe watched them leave before retiring back to his office. "Oh, Lord," he said with a sigh, leaning on the bookshelf where he kept a pitcher of water, a china cup, a worn Bible, and a copy of Gibbon's *Decline and Fall of the Roman Empire*. He took a sip of water, leaned against the bookshelf, and pressed his forehead against his arm. "Thirty men," he said. "Thirty men to stem a tide . . ."

But that wasn't the real problem. The real problem was one he hardly dared say, even to himself. For deep inside, he had a nagging premonition that General Johnston, the hope of Vicksburg, wasn't coming. Help wasn't on the way. Vicksburg would have to prevail alone.

CHAPTER 16

Tobias held a smoked oyster between his thumb and forefinger, and shook the rubbery, dark gray glob of smoked flesh. "*Uhhhhnnn-uhhh.* No way this poor child gonna eat the likes of this. No, sirree."

"Well, they ain't for you. An' they cost a pretty penny, so they must be good. Fact is, they was the last in Mr. Schweicker's market. Now get your hands off. An' leave that cake be, too."

"Woman, you ain't got a heart," Tobias grumbled, replacing the oyster and glancing hungrily at the spice cake. He sneaked a finger toward a drop of maple-colored frosting on the edge of the plate.

"An' you be missin' a finger as well," Immelda warned, brandishing a butcher knife.

The hand disappeared behind Tobias's back. "Lawdie! All right, woman. You made your point. You are plumb on the poor side of good times these days."

"Miss Celia has got to impress these folks. Which means I can't be lettin' you—" Immelda cocked an ear as a military orchestra consisting of two violins, a guitar, and a piano struck up a cotillion. She had prepared custards, pies, cakes, four roasted geese, fresh vegetables, a sweet potato casserole, and a half dozen other snacks from whatever was available. Tobias had worked himself to the bone for the last three days. He had trimmed away the dead wisteria, transplanted blooming flowers, cleaned and whitewashed the gazebo and, under Celia's direction, festooned the garden with ribbons and colored paper garlands. A great deal of effort had gone into this party, and Immelda was as anxious as Celia that everyone be duly impressed.

"Well, you just keep them fingers where they belongs. As for me, I'd best get this here food out on the table. They'll be workin' up a hunger before long, with all that dancin'."

"Dancin', hah! Them white folks give 'emselves too much to remember. Put your foot this way, sashay left an' sashay right. Sort of takes all the fun out, all that thinkin' 'bout where to put your foots an' are you gonna hit up alongside some other folk." He eased around the table, gave his wife an affectionate slap on the rump. "Now you take you an' me, Immelda, honey. We'd know how to have ourselves some real fun."

"Yeah," the black woman snapped, busying herself arranging trays. "We'd know how to have fun, right 'nough. Sweatin' in the fields an' toilin' at the docks. Master this an' master that."

"Lawd, 'Melda," Tobias hissed, shocked. "You watch your tongue, gal. Gen'r'l Pemberton hisself an' half the other gen'r'ls in town out in that garden. An' there's them that's just lookin' for some poor soul to pin the cause of their hard times on. Anyway," he asked, having checked to make sure no one was listening outside the door, "you feel like that, how come you work for Mistuh Bartlett all these years? How come you stay on with Miss Celia? We free. We could've skedaddled. There's others that done run to Can-ayda."

"'Cause Miss Celia done need me, that's why," Immelda replied. She was tired and her mood was deteriorating rapidly. "An' I'll say whatever I please."

Tobias's head wagged emphatically. "Stubborn as a mule, an' about as much sense. You take my 'vice, girl, an' watch you flappin' them lips. The wrong folks hear talk like that an' they'll hang you an' me just to liven up the party."

"Ain't nobody hangin' nobody, old man, so just quit that foolishness," Immelda retorted.

Stung by her vehemence, Tobias turned away. "I was just . . ."

"Oh, forget it," Immelda said with a sigh. "I be snappin' 'stead of workin'." She left the trays, walked across the kitchen and brought back the bowl in which she had mixed the icing for the cake. The residue of milk, eggs, and cane syrup had hardened into a sugary paste. "Here. I saved this for you."

Tobias brightened and took the bowl.

"Sometimes can't seem to stop my tongue from waggin'. But I'm worried for Miss Celia." The black woman sagged against the table. "I worried, Tobias. This trouble she done got herself into is too much for that little gal. Like a man tryin' to break up a dogfight. There ain't no way out without gettin' bit."

"She find one," Tobias said confidently, chipping away at the icing. "You wait an' see. Mark my words."

"An' how come you so sure, nigger?" Immelda asked, hands on hips.

"'Cause," Tobias answered, smacking his lips, "anybody fool enough to eat them smoked oysters ain't got sense enough to latch on to what she about."

Immelda shook her head in despair, but went back to work on the trays. And in spite of herself, she was smiling.

Moths fluttered and mosquitoes buzzed around the lanterns gently swaying in the breeze. The guests appeared not to notice. They were more interested in the freely flowing wine and the surprising abundance of food. The music formed a pleasant background to genteel conversation and the lilting laughter of Southern belles whose grace and loveliness were complimented by the courtly ministrations of dapper, well-groomed young officers. The sprightly strains of the last cotillion only just fading, the gentlemen and ladies made way for the departing guest of honor and his staff.

General John C. Pemberton, commander of Vicksburg's defense, crossed the garden and, declining a final glass of wine, bowed before Celia and kissed her hand. "My dear Miss Bartlett." His voice was deep and courteous, his manners impeccable. "You're a most gracious hostess," he said formally, "but my time, alas, isn't my own, and I dare not remain too long from my duties. I hope you'll forgive me."

Celia curtseyed. "Forgive, General?" she demurred. "On the contrary. I'm flattered that you accepted my invitation, and honored to be permitted to show, in some small way, my deep gratitude for your efforts in our behalf."

"Yes." The general cleared his throat. "Well . . ." References however oblique to his army's predicament, were embarrassing in the extreme, the young lady's intentions notwithstanding.

Her faux pas immediately evident, Celia rushed in to repair the breach. "And I trust you'll not think me forward, sir, when I say that I think you're one of the South's ablest generals." She modestly lowered her eyelids. "If we only had more like you . . ."

"Now, now. Enough of that, my dear!" The general stroked his full, black beard, an indication of his pleasure. "A beautiful young lady like you . . . Turn my head . . . vanity most unbecoming an officer." His eyes twinkled. "But I shan't be tempted."

"I do hope," Celia said with a gesture around the assembled company, "that your officers won't have to follow your own strict regimen. The night is young, and—"

"By heavens, no," Pemberton chuckled. "Order that and I'll risk mass insubordination. These brave young men deserve a reward for their great efforts and responsibilities. What richer one than the company of these lovely ladies, the epitome of whom stands before me?"

"You are generous, sir." Celia's eyelashes fluttered alluringly. "Overly so, I fear."

"I am, I assure you, most conservative," Pemberton replied, spying Rafe approaching with two glasses of wine. "Wouldn't you agree, sir?"

"I beg your pardon?" Rafe asked. "Agree with what?"

"That Miss Bartlett's the fairest flower in any garden?"

Just as soon as ask Rafe if he liked the morning breeze or the feel of a ship under his feet. "Without reservation, sir," he said, handing Celia one of the glasses. "But that is, you see, a fact I've known for some time."

"So your father tells me."

Rafe's eyebrows rose in surprise. Nathaniel had seen Pemberton? Knew him, even?

Pemberton enjoyed the effect of this news and laughed heartily. "Mexico, young man. We served together in the late war there. My dear?" His demeanor changing abruptly, and he bowed shortly to Celia. "I really must go. No! No need to see me out. Good night. Good night."

"I'll be damned," Rafe swore under his breath as the general strode up the rear steps and disappeared into the house. "Pemberton and Father! Who would've guessed?"

Arm in arm, Phillip Laughton and Gaillee Calder approached from the side of the garden, where they had been conferring with the orchestra. "Hurry up, Celia, honey," Gaillee called, "and bring Rafe with you. They're going to play a waltz."

"I'm afraid my maneuvers are best carried out from a ship's deck," Rafe said and laughed, holding back.

"Nonsense," Celia replied, patting his hand. "You can't refuse. You're my escort."

"But not so far as the jaws of doom."

"Doom, sir?" Celia laughed. "Indeed!"

Rafe shrugged apologetically. "Too many years've passed since I attended Mrs. Robinson's dancing school for young gentlemen. And few chances to practice since then."

"Old talents are oft rediscovered in the attempt." Celia winked coyly at him over her wine glass. "There's no chance I could persuade you?"

Two could play that game. "You could persuade me to go off somewhere alone with you."

"And *that*," Celia said, placing her glass on a table and taking Gaillee's arm, "is precisely why we are going to dance." She linked her free arm with Rafe's. "You're my witness, Gaillee. Our actions are above suspicion."

"Not above everyone else's amusement, though," Rafe added, suspiciously eyeing the musicians as they began to play.

Laughing, the foursome hurried to the dance floor at the center of the garden. Bare miles away, bare thousands of yards, men lay i grime and feared for their lives. Here, in rarely worn gowns pulled from cedar chests, beautiful women danced to the strains of the waltz from Vincente Martin's famous opera, *Una Cosa Rara*. In the garden, tables groaned with food that, if not equal to the usual standards of Vicksburg's gentry, was a king's feast in comparison to the hunger and privation in the trenches. The contrasts did not end there: crisply tailored and freshly cleaned uniforms in the garden; the torn and rotting clothes barely able to cover insect-bitten limbs in the trenches. The delicate aroma of cologne, toilet water, and perfume in the garden; the stench of unwashed flesh, of ordure, of death itself in the trenches. The elegant movement of the waltz or the studied, nonchalant pose in the garden; the grotesque attitudes of exhaustion and pain and death in the trenches.

Celia had no time for contrasts, though. Keenly aware of Anthony's scheduled arrival after midnight and her role as an impressed collector of information, she was too busy. Two artillery officers, a major and a lieutenant, conferred to one side. She tried and failed to hear what they were saying as she danced by. Major General Martin Luther Smith was chatting with Major General John S. Bowen: she would have given half the coffee left in the house to be privy to their conversation. Margery had been escorted by one of Pemberton's aides, who had left with the general. Now she had cornered a frock-coated, well-dressed merchant's son and was steering him toward the gazebo. Perhaps, with a little luck, Margery could be pumped for information later. Lord knew she'd need *something* to tell Anthony, and she hadn't heard anything at all of note.

The piano dominating, the tempo becoming more languorous, Fréderic Chopin replaced Vincente Martin. The floor filled with swirling couples. Rafe glanced down at Celia, resplendent in a heather blue silk gown with a daring décolletage of lighter blue silk. The sight of her smooth skin and the coiled golden tresses spilling down her neck and shoulders left his mouth dry. The touch of her hand, lightly perspiring in his, sent waves of desire surging through his body. The delicate fragrance of her perfume weakened his knees. Lost in a dream, he tripped, apologized, and made himself concentrate. The spell was broken. The enchantment, however, was unending. For long ago, Celia had captured his heart and made a prisoner of his soul.

"Lovely party, Celia," Rosemary said. The orchestra was resting. Rafe had steered Celia to the tables and what little remained of the food. He helped himself to a slice of mince meat pie while a half dozen others closed round to find what they could.

"Thank you," Celia replied, standing aside to allow the younger girl and her escort, Oliver Johnston, access to the table. As Gaillee had noted, the newly arrived Oliver, nephew to General Joseph Johnston, was one of the homeliest men in Vicksburg. He was short, very round, and scraggly red whiskers sprouted unevenly from his pink cheeks. His nose was flat and formless, his hairline receding though he couldn't be a day over twenty-five. He nodded to Celia and took the last two hard-boiled eggs, which he added to four of the remaining six pieces of cheese and the next to the last piece of mince pie. Celia winced, and wondered if he was privy to his famous uncle's plans, for any information regarding Johnston's impending moves would be of inestimable value.

"I'm glad he left something for us," Phillip said at Celia's elbow as Rosemary and her escort wandered off.

"Now, Phillip," Celia said, turning to him. "I couldn't very well slap General Johnston's nephew's wrist and tell him he was a naughty boy. You'll just have to make do with what you find."

"He's eaten twice already," Gaillee said, her tone accusatory.

"And been hungry four times," Phillip said, snagging the last piece of mince meat pie but leaving the cheese. "Thank God for Immelda's pies. At least there's some reward for those who've given so unstintingly of themselves."

"Reward?" Gaillee asked.

Phillip helped himself to a glass of wine. "For allowing you to tramp all over my feet," he said with droll dry humor.

"Oh, you're awful! Isn't he awful?" Gaillee squealed, slapping Phillip's arm.

The two couples wended their way through the thinning crowd and found a spot to sit on one of the benches inside the gazebo. "Remarkable party, Ceel," Phillip said around a mouthful of pie. "Can't imagine how you managed it."

"I wouldn't have, without Immelda," Celia admitted.

"Any time you want to sell her, I'm in the market."

The thought of selling Immelda turned Celia's stomach, but she forwent comment.

"Any rate," Phillip went on to Gaillee. "This is incredibly good." He held up his fork before popping a bite of the pie into his mouth. "You should have tried a piece."

"I couldn't. You took the last," Gaillee reminded him. "Besides, just barely struggled into this gown. So get thee hence, Satan."

"You won't have to worry about *what* you eat much longer," Rafe broke in dryly, "but when."

"There you go. Father Gloom and his dreary forecasts again," Gaillee chattered, refusing as always to take anything seriously.

"Perhaps we could talk about something else?" Celia asked, sensing Rafe wasn't jesting.

"Believe me," Rafe said, refusing to be deterred. "We're lucky. We have food in our cellars. Our families have savings. We can afford the already exorbitant prices charged by anyone who has anything edible to sell. There are many who can't, though. Many who have already begun to tighten their belts and are going without. Soon we all will be. Yes," he insisted, ignoring Celia's silent plea to stop, "even the Calders, Miss Gaillee. Your family and mine, Celia and Phillip's."

"Bosh!" Phillip snorted. "If Grant thinks he can starve us into submission, he has another think coming. And if everything else fails, we'll eat mules before allowing the damn Federals in our streets."

Gaillee's nose crinkled in disbelief. "Mules? How disgusting! Really, gentlemen. If you persist, Celia and I will find new company to keep."

"And when the mules are gone?" Rafe continued.

Phillip stiffened angrily. "Then Johnston's army will arrive, and we'll dine on the delicacies the Yankees leave behind in the wake of their retreat. You puzzle me, Lattimore. Here you are assigned to protect the city against threats from within, and you sound like some Federal pamphleteer delivering messages of defeat to poison our minds and weaken our resolve."

"I think I'd retract that statement if I were you," Rafe cautioned, glowering at Phillip. "And before too much longer passed."

The silence between them was charged with animosity.

"Really a lovely party, Celia, honey," Gaillee blurted desperately, jumping to her feet and resorting to a non sequitur. "The first for any of us in such a long time! Do you know what I think?" she asked, digging an elbow into Phillip's ribs. "I think we should have one more often. No matter what's happening."

"Hear, hear!" Phillip chimed in half-heartedly.

Gaillee didn't give up easily. "And do you know when?" she asked, the image of optimism. "On the day General Johnston arrives!"

Rafe looked dubious.

"But we don't *know* he will, do we?" Celia asked, feigning innocence. "Do we really?"

"Realistically, . . ." Rafe began.

"Of course he will," Phillip interrupted, refusing to be a defeatist.

"We heard just this morning that he crossed the Pearl above Jackson with more than fifteen thousand effectives."

Which was little more than wishful thinking, Celia was virtually certain. One more of the dozens of rumors that swept through the isolated, news-starved city every day.

"But is that enough?" she asked, just in case there was some truth to the matter.

"Of course! Grant thinks he has us trapped, but we'll turn the tables on him yet. We'll smite him front *and* rear."

"Well, I certainly *hope* so," Celia said, giving the impression she had grave doubts.

"And what's that supposed to mean?"

"Well, I'm no expert, but Gaillee and I have been to the trenches ourselves and conditions were dreadful. Absolutely pitiful. I know the men are trying, but without food and ammunition . . ."

"Not ammunition, Celia," Phillip explained, enjoying the role of military tutor. "Caps. Detonation caps, without which the military musket won't fire. But we dare hope not for long. One shipment! One man who knows the swamps—"

"I thought military matters were a subject not to be touched upon during the course of our recreation," Rafe interrupted, obviously irritated by Phillip's breach of protocol.

"Well I for one find them fascinating," Gaillee exclaimed, her eyes alight with excitement.

Relieved, Celia let her exuberant friend do her work for her.

"After all, here we are surrounded by Yankee soldiers, and not a mouse, to hear tell, able to get in or out. How on earth?"

"Not really all that difficult, dear," Phillip explained with just a touch of condescension. "Daring, yes, but wars are decided by daring ventures. One or two men who know the terrain, each loaded with, say, a case of hundred thousand caps strapped to his back, might make it through the Southern lines. The way is mostly cypress swamps and vine-choked marshes, quicksand, and what have you. Billy Yank is thinly spread and won't be expecting anything. A moonless night, a little luck, and *voilà!* If even one is successful, we'll have what we need to give Lincoln's lackeys a first-class surprise." He paused and stared pointedly at Gaillee and Celia. "Of course, we wouldn't want news of this sort spread around."

"No, we wouldn't," Rafe added pointedly.

Phillip sniffed defensively. "Which is not to suggest," he went on quickly, "that anyone here would be foolish enough to commit even

he slightest indiscretion. I include, ladies," he warned, wagging a
nger, "gossip at tomorrow's sewing circle get-together."

"We shan't tell a soul," Gaillee promised in a conspiratorial whis-
er, her eyes large and round. "Not a soul, shall we, Celia?"

Celia's expression was frozen and her lips were set in a firm line.
Of course not. I . . ." A blush stole up her throat. She sipped her
'ine and avoided Rafe's gaze. The way he was watching her, as if he
ispected . . . "I shouldn't have been so curious. But you can trust
ie."

"I didn't mean to imply—" Rafe began, chagrined.

"But you did, and I shan't forgive you. Unless"—a sly, mischievous
nile replaced what she hoped Rafe would think had been a genu-
iely angry frown—"you waltz with me this minute, Rafe Lattimore."

It worked. Whatever Rafe had been thinking, his train of thought
ad been interrupted. "I will waltz you, Miss Bartlett," he promised in
is most villainous manner, "right out of your slippers. Gaillee? Phil-
p? You'll excuse us?"

Alone in the gazebo, Gaillee slipped an arm around Phillip. "My,
y," she said as soon as Celia and Rafe were out of earshot. "Celia is
rtainly the audacious one. Positively audacious, and high time, too.
hrowing herself at Rafe like that?" She clucked approvingly. "I cer-
inly can tell what's on *her* mind."

"Oh?" Phillip asked, amused. He bent to kiss her neck, let his hand
ide up to touch her breast. "The voice of experience?"

"Mmmm." Gaillee moved so her skirt covered her hand where it
sted on his thigh. "I can read her like a book. There's no mystery to
elia Bartlett. No mystery at all."

Dance with your loved one. Dance with your beau. Move in magic
the music of bygone days when Dixie evenings were lived with the
irm breezes of romance that washed over the eternal river and the
orning sun rose over the verdant eastern hills and blessed the heart
th a new day. The generals had retired either to bed or to head-
uarters, and with only young folks remaining, the pace of the music
celerated. Warfare is a drab affair. Requiring great concentration, it
io permits excessive release. Drab clothes, a drab diet, and dull
ork with needle and thread had filled the ladies' days for the past
'o weeks. Long stretches of boredom punctuated by brief moments
heart-thudding action or narrow escapes from extinction had
etched the men's nerves taut as bow strings. Once released and lu-
icated by free flowing wine, pent-up emotions exploded in a frenzy
activity.

No dervish ever danced more exuberantly. Spinning, whirling, slid
ing to the side, coattails flapped and full gowns swayed like multi
colored blossoms in a great wind. Laughing and out of breath, Celi
begged Rafe to stop. Rafe whooped, rent the air with a high-pitchec
Rebel yell, and spun her even harder. The garden became a blur o
color and streaks. Celia locked eyes with her partner. Rafe wa
defined, a resolute, steadying force that anchored her in the mael
strom.

Forget the gunboats in the river. Once there had been steamboa
races. Once the wharves had been stacked with exotic goods, spice
and silks from the East, fashions from Europe. Once the walkway
had thronged with gamblers and troubadors and pioneers headed fo
the West.

Forget the besieging Union host. Once there had been picnics an
moonlight rides and trysts and time for lovers. Once there had bee
fields choked with cotton dotting the world white, like snow in sun
mer. Once there had been the aroma of fine cuisine, the muted clin
of elegant crystal, and the soft hum of civilized conversation.

Forget the war! Once life had been gay and ordered and each mir
ute was a ripe berry to be plucked and savored on the tongue. Onc
death had been only for the old and, rarely, the unfortunate and acc
dental few.

Even Celia forgot. Safe in Rafe's arms, she whirled through th
crowded dancers and became one with the wild motion and emotio
until reality faded and became lost in all the yesterdays, and ther
was no tomorrow.

The Union lieutenant on the lead mortar boat didn't know a par
was in progress. Now and again, if he had listened, he might ha
heard the faint stirrings of a song, but he was not listening. He had
job to do, and his job required his undivided attention.

The lieutenant was a husband, a father, a Christian, and a huma
man. The lieutenant was also an officer in the Union Navy of th
West, and carried in his breast pocket an order that, promulgated l
the highest echelons of command in the western theater of the w
had been signed by Captain Sirls, his commanding officer. The ord
signaled a marked change in tactics. No longer would the Confedera
trenches and gun emplacements be the mortar boats' prime targe
The city itself was henceforth the enemy. If Vicksburg could not
taken frontally, by storm, the mortars would drive it to its knees fro
without. This night began the death of Vicksburg. This night and su
ceeding nights, the mortar crews would adjust the elevation of th

weapons to focus not on the belligerents but on civilians, who were innocent. Acting according to the stern dictates of war, Union command had deemed that herein lay the key to capitulation.

The lieutenant watched through his glass, saw the first flash, and decided his guns were registered correctly. "And so we turn the key," he muttered, pleased with the results of the aiming round.

"Sir?" his gunner's mate asked.

"Well-aimed, guns," the lieutenant said. "Pass the word. Ten more rounds each at approximately one-minute intervals."

"Aye, sir."

"You may begin."

The first shell exploded.

Poised, suspended, the music stopped, the last notes shattered by the reverberations of the registering shell. Merriment faded from faces turning to the sky. A mistake? A fluke? Why then, at midnight? On a Sunday night when all was normally calm? A nervous titter, a gruff reassural. No damage. Nothing to worry about. What's a war without a shell or two? Now what happened to that wine?

"Another one!" Rosemary screamed, pointing.

Mouths open, eyes wide with disbelief, the party-goers raised their heads as one to stare at the arching meteors of destruction streaking downward into the city.

A scream. Another and another, drowned out by a drum roll of explosions. The ground erupted outside the garden wall, sent rocks toppling through the shrubbery and the colored paper garlands. Mortar shells, spheres of hollowed iron packed with gunpowder, rained indiscriminately on streets and houses. The calculations had been precise. Fast-burning fuses precisely cut to detonate the shells a fraction of a second prior to striking the ground or, if the mortar boat bobbed a rifle, upon or shortly after impact.

The house across the alley flew apart. A servant's cabin at the rear of the Cutters' house vanished in a great upheaval of fire and earth. Boards and bricks and pieces of pottery and flesh were flung into the darkness that was soon brightened by the fierce illumination of half a dozen more buildings transformed into pyres. The party reduced to bedlam, Celia's guests scattered. Ladies in finery ran aimlessly or cowered in the open. Gentlemen striving to remain calm in the face of unbridled destruction hurried their dates or wives through the Bartlett house or made for the garden gate, crowding through as more and more explosions rocked the night. Celia tried to speak, tried to think, and dazed, clung to Rafe. What seconds before had been an ordered party had disintegrated into panic and mindless flight.

A shell landed inside the garden itself and the ground shook as if struck by a great maul. Celia fell. Rafe covered her with his body as dust choked the air and dirt rained down on them. When Celia opened her eyes, she spied Rosemary sitting against the wall, her brown hair undone and dishevelled, a gorgon's knot of sorry ringlets and unkempt curls. Her white dress was covered with wet crimson and clung to her thin legs. She held out her hands, pointing. The sound she made, more like the mewling of an animal in pain, made the flesh on Celia's arms prickle. Only then did she see the crater.

The shell had landed between Celia and Rosemary and, throwing up a ragged circle of dirt, had devoured part of the gazebo and all of a banquet table. Smoldering splinters and chunks of wood stuck out of the ground. Fat, homely Ollie was crying as he crawled to Rosemary's side and cradled her in his arms. Blood streamed from her ears from the concussion. She rolled her eyes back and fainted. And then, her gorge rising, her stomach churning, Celia realized what else she was looking at. Mingled with the fragments of the table and gazebo were charred hunks of human flesh, the remains of one of the musicians.

Rafe dragged Celia to her feet and shoved her toward the house. "The basement!" he shouted into her ear.

Phillip Laughton staggered out of the house toward them. His coat was torn, his face black with soot. "Jesus . . ." he said. "Jesus . . ."

"What?" Celia yelled, torn between obeying Rafe and going back to help Rosemary.

"I said, get to the basement!" Rafe repeated.

His voice seemed unnaturally loud in the sudden calm. A piece of the gazebo fell. Someone was screaming in the street. A dog barked. Incredibly, the bombardment had ended. The mortars had abruptly ceased fire. "That was no over shooting," Rafe yelled. "They purposefully shelled the city. The Yankee bastards purposefully shelled the city!"

"I sent Gaillee and a couple of the others home!" Phillip shook his head.

Celia knew how he felt. Her ears were ringing, too.

"I'm going to need more than a Home Guard to help put out these fires and protect against looting," Rafe shouted, perspiration beading his begrimed face. "Can you help round up some people? Stray soldiers will do. Anybody. Will you come with me?"

Phillip nodded and rubbed the back of his neck. Behind them, string of lanterns crashed to the ground. Rafe gripped Celia's arms. "You heard me? I want you in that basement!"

"You go on," Celia gasped, her senses slowly returning. "Rosemary needs help."

"Better yet, take her home and stay in her folks' cave. I don't want you spending the night in the house."

"I won't be driven out," Celia retorted angrily.

"And if they start firing again?"

"I'll worry about that when it happens. If worse comes to worst, I'll go downstairs. There's room in the cellar for all of us."

Immelda appeared on the side porch. At the same time, Tobias hurried into the garden carrying a shovel, with which he began to throw dirt on the coal oil fires started by the broken lanterns. "Lawd, Lawd, Lawd," Immelda moaned. "What on earth them folks tryin' to do? I just heard. Cassius Rawlins, Miz Cutter's stableboy, got hisself blowed up. Him an' his three young'uns. Right over yonder." She pointed toward the ruined cabin visible through the gap in the broken fence. "This here's a white folks' war. Why they wants to kill po' Cassius an' his chillen?"

"I'll be fine," Celia tried to assure Rafe. He patted her arm and embraced her a moment, his lips searching for hers. Caught off guard, frightened and confused, her defenses down, Celia responded to the kiss with an ardor she'd not allowed herself before.

When the kiss ended, Rafe stared at her in complete surprise. A slow smile wreathed his face in spite of the carnage that surrounded them. "Come on, Phillip. Let's go," he shouted, turning and taking the back steps in two leaps.

Laughton coughed in embarrassment. "Uh, nice party, Celia," he said lamely. And then realizing how foolish he sounded, in the midst of the wrecked garden with Tobias putting out fires and the remains of mortal flesh drying in the ruined earth, jammed his cap on his head, and left.

Celia made a wide circle around the crater on her way to help Rosemary. "That's got the fires," Tobias said as she passed. "You reckon I, uh . . ." He gestured with his head toward what was left of the musician and, closing his eyes, managed to keep his stomach where it belonged.

"Someone has to," Celia said, touching him gently on the arm. "I'll have Immelda bring a bag. We can take him to the cemetery tomorrow."

"Yas'm," Tobias said, shuddering, and reluctantly began this new and grisly chore.

"Come on, Rosemary. We'll get you home now," Celia crooned. "You'll be safe there, honey. Ollie, help me get her to her feet—"

And alone on the porch, watching and weeping, Immelda swayed slowly back and forth. "Why'd they kill them chillens?" she asked, wiping her eyes. "Why, Lawd? Why they kill them po' little chillens?"

The homes and businesses in a twelve-block area whose center was at China and Walnut were the hardest hit. Within minutes after the shelling had stopped, scores of citizens emerged from caves and basements and rushed to help put out the fires and care for the wounded. Bucket brigades formed rapidly to assist the fire crews, but by the time they brought one blaze under control, another next door or down the block would be burning out of control. In one block alone, a haberdashery shop, a barbershop, a restaurant, and Dunn's coffin warehouse, complete with the remains of two of Vicksburg's recently deceased, were lost. The funeral parlor alone was saved, and although gravedigger Dunn wrung his hands and wept bitter tears, he did not complain too strenuously. As long as the siege continued, business promised to be exceptional, and he would recoup his losses.

Rafe had little time for the fires. The effects of the wine wearing off rapidly, he sat in his office and, as fast as they reported to him from Phillip and other officers on loan from the army, assigned men to each block of the ravaged section of the city. By midnight, the fires had died down or had been brought under control, the wounded or killed had all been sent to hospitals or mortuaries. Knots of exhausted men clustered about the mouths of caves, kept wary eyes on the sky, and discussed the events of the last few hours. Little else remained to be done until morning. Exhausted himself, Rafe finally turned the office over to a young lieutenant sent to him from the docks and went out for his first real look at the damage.

Downtown was quiet and, save for the soldiers on guard duty against looters, virtually empty. Pensive, Rafe turned his horse onto Washington Street and rode slowly to the end, then turned right on First East Street. The silence here on the northern edge of the city was almost complete, for most of the residents, once assured their homes were safe, had sought the safety of the caves in case the mortars began firing again.

A dog in a fenced yard barked at him and sulked back to the porch when he passed without stopping. A single light glimmered faintly inside another house. Rafe slowed, wondered who had the temerity to face the fierce fire, and rode on. He stopped at the corner of Cherry Street, pondered idly which way he wanted to go, and rubbed a hand across his eyes when he saw what he had taken to be a post straighten itself, bend, and straighten again. A second later, another "post" emerged from a window of the house.

Looters. Thieves. He and the others had concentrated so much on those areas where destruction was greatest that they'd overlooked the obvious. With the whole focus of the town toward the center, thieves could operate with impunity around the fringes, and by the time Rafe could get help, they'd be long gone. The only alternative was to pretend he had the whole Home Guard at his back, go in fast and loud, and hope to hell that surprise would do the trick.

Two revolvers, four extra cylinders. Quickly, he checked his weapons and then, with a whoop and a yell, kicked his horse in the ribs. The startled gelding leaped forward in an instantaneous gallop. Rafe fired into the air and gave a piercing Rebel yell to add to the effect. It worked. The first "post" dived headlong off the porch, rolled through a hedge, and lit out running. The second paused to hurl an ax handle at Rafe, who dodged and leveled a shot at the departing ruffian.

The gelding shied and pulled up of its own accord at the iron picket fence. Rafe jumped down and crouched, took a moment to fit new cylinders in his revolver, six fresh charges each, and then darted through the open gate. Four carpetbags loaded with what appeared at first glance to be silverware, candlesticks, and other valuables lay abandoned on the porch. Rafe flattened himself against the wall and waited silently for a few moments. Lord only knew how many other houses were being broken into at that very moment. He'd have to close up as best he could here, then head back for town and arrange patrols for the whole city. Where, of course, he'd find enough manpower was another matter entirely. Discouraged, he reached for the first carpetbag to put it back in the house and then, hearing a faint scraping sound inside, froze. A third man was inside and evidently heading for an escape through the back door.

Stealth made more sense against one man. Treading softly, Rafe worked his way along the side porch, jumped down and, taking advantage of an outside summer kitchen, circled to face the back door. Bare seconds later, he was rewarded by the creak of a door and, as he edged forward in the shadow of a woodpile, a glimpse of feet and the gleam of silver.

"Hold it right there!" he shouted.

"Ga—" Startled, the thief tripped over something on the porch and fell down the back steps.

Silver glinted in the moonlight. A baptismal flew through the air and landed closer to Rafe than the thief. "I said hold it," Rafe repeated, aiming.

"Well, shit!"

Rafe shook his head in disbelief, almost lowered his gun but then, at the last second, gritted his teeth and held his aim.

"Bet you think you're pretty smart, huh, Little Brother?" Slowly, painfully, Micah stood and faced his brother in the wan moonlight. "If you're gonna shoot, you'd better shoot now."

Micah! His own brother! Rafe's mouth opened, but his tongue wouldn't work until Micah was halfway to the corner of the house. "I will, Micah. Don't make me do it. So help me, I will!"

What better target than that broad back? Contemptuously, Micah turned and faced Rafe full front. "Sure," he said. "Sure you will, Little Brother," and turned and loped off into the night.

Rafe sagged against the woodpile, at last stuck one revolver in his belt and holstered the other. Mindlessly, he picked up the silver font and set it inside the back door, then went around to the side and shoved the carpetbags in the window. His head ached; a hammer pounded inside his skull. His shoulders were stiff with tension. Worn, he leaned against the side of the house and shut his eyes. What was he supposed to do? Kill his own brother?

"Mr. Lattimore?"

Rafe jerked at the sound of his name and heard the unmistakable limp of Matt Broussard. "What are you doing here?"

"The army has everything taken care of downtown, so I decided to sort of ride around and check things out. Heard the ruckus and came a runnin'. What happened?"

"Looters, thieves, whatever you want to call them. Hard cases from Under the Hill, from the looks of 'em." Rafe shrugged, walked out to the street and his horse. "No one I know, far as I could tell."

Except Micah. His own brother. Had it come to this? Suddenly, Rafe was so tired he didn't think he could mount his horse. So disillusioned and despondent that for the first time since he'd been a child he thought he wanted to cry. "Do me a favor, Matt?"

"Sure," Matt said, adding a hasty, "sir."

"Go tell that lieutenant, I don't remember his name, down at the office about this. Tell him I want mounted patrols of two or three men each to range around here, in the east, and down south to help out Hays. Until morning, anyway. I'll work out a plan for tomorrow night when I get in."

"Yes, sir!" Matt limped to his horse and mounted. "Can I tell him where to find you if he needs you?"

"No." Rafe's hands shook with the effort as he mounted, "Just tell him . . . No."

The new page lay blank before her. She had filled two pages with generalities; observations from the trenches and comments on the morale of the city. Useless information, really. And now came the hard part. The part that made the difference, in much the same way as that single kernel of information about the gully had made a difference at the Battle of the Big Black.

Her hand didn't want to move and found excuses not to touch nib to paper. But she wasn't the poet laboring by nightingale and candlelight. She was only a spy, a betrayer of her people. She needed write only the cold, simple, bald facts. A shipment of caps . . . through the southern swamps . . . on a moonless night . . . probably Thursday, Friday, or Saturday. . . .

A year, two years earlier, she would have written gladly. Rushed the words onto paper, even, for then she hated. Now she no longer hated but was trapped. Now her life balanced on a line stretched taut between North and South, and at each end zealots waited to shake the line and send her spinning to destruction. The paper was as wan in the faint light as the flesh of her hand. And empty, the nagging thought returned. Empty and waiting for the words.

But wait! What kind of a fool had she become? Had they so unnerved her? Was she a puppet to dangle on Powell and Anthony's strings? *They* depended on *her* for information. Not the other way around. And they presumed to threaten her with disclosure if she didn't tell them something they didn't know? The whole proposition was absurd! Absurd! And infuriating. How dared they treat her so? Trick her, play so foully with her emotions? Who did they think—

"Oh, Lord," she said aloud, stunned by the equal enormity of a further discovery. "I let them, didn't I? Celia Rose!"

It was ludicrous. One by one the veiling shrouds of fear fell away. They had no hold over her! None at all unless they caught her in a blatant lie, but she wouldn't give them that chance. Turning quickly, flush with the inventiveness that accompanies a new idea, she wrote quickly, filling two more pages with innocuous blather that every fool and his uncle already knew, and threw in for good measure the latest rumor about General Johnston's crossing of the Pearl. And if they believed that, she thought, pleased with herself as she scrawled "Hawkmoon" across the bottom of the page, they deserved to lose.

There. She'd said enough. Relief flooded through her as she tore out the pages, folded them, and placed them in an envelope. The Seth

Thomas clock on the bookcase ticked away the passing seconds. Preferring the moonlight, she turned down the lamp and placed a smoked shade over the chimney. She could feel the tension draining from her neck and back, feel a pleasant drowsiness stealing over her. Everything was so simple, really. But if that were so, why were the obvious simplicities so hard to come by? Life was full of examples. Bemused, she rose and, her silk night gown whispering softly as she crossed the room, went to the window to look down at the city of a hundred hills.

Vicksburg lay sleeping, renewing itself for the ordeal that would surely continue. Once a beautiful jewel, it now lay scarred like a virgin brutally taken. Like herself, Celia thought, for the first time able to accept her own total innocence on that horrible day over two years earlier. Another example of the unseen obvious. The world was full of Micah Lattimores. Some wore blue and some wore gray, but other than that there was little difference between them. One and all they were rapists and pillagers, murderers and thieves. Shivering, she realized how close they had come—how close she had let all the Micahs of the world come—to robbing her of not only her home but herself. Thank God, they hadn't, for she loved this place. Here was her youth: the praise and love of parents, the first rainstorm, the first autumn with the world a festival of color. Here was the first horseback ride, the first tree climb, the first skinned knee. Yes, the first tears, too, were Vicksburg memories, and she loved them as much as the laughter. More, more, more. Never-ending memories. The first snowfall, watching enraptured in the parlor window as the downy flakes fluttered through the gray air. The first song sung. The first Christmas tree, bright with candles and silk balls and strings of popcorn. Here, too, were memories of first love, of only love, of lost love, and of love regained, she dared to hope. She had never *meant* to forget, but then neither had she been wise enough to remember. She had thought only of her pain, and the need for revenge. Tragically, she had gained not one iota of satisfaction and had lost almost everything.

"Celia?"

Yes, that voice, too, she thought sadly as another verity burst in her mind. Had she truly not known how lonely she was? Lonely. A word, a time, a place. A way of being that burns and burns until all that's left of the heart is a remnant of cobwebbed dreams and unlived futures, a universe of unfulfilled moments and lost moments and moments that never were, stillborn in time. Lonely. A way of life—no. Not life. Not *real* life . . .

"Celia."

She heard the door close, knew that he stood behind her. A slow, warm flush crept down her body and her knees grew weak.

Did he speak her name again? Her name was a mystery, a beloved, impassioned mystery spoken so softly and gently. She heard muffled footsteps on the rug and turned to wait for him in the moonlight. She didn't speak. Protest never entered her mind, because suddenly she knew he was supposed to be in this room, in any room, with her.

Him. Rafe. Not any man. Rafe. Face grimed with soot and clothes in disarray, he didn't look the gentleman now. His eyes were not gentle—not threatening—but set and determined. He was not a gentleman, but she did not fear him. Not now. Not this man whose hand rose like a dream to loosen the silk bows of her gown and, brushing the straps from her shoulders, watch it catch, just momentarily, on her breasts and then slip soft as moonbeams to the floor.

And was she now naked? Yes, she thought. Naked before the man I love. She was intensely aware of the cool air on her legs and back, of the warmth that spread from her groin. She could barely keep her eyes open, swayed unconsciously as his hands brushed lightly against her hardening nipples. He smelled of ashes and fire and horses and sweat and a deeper, more profound maleness that seemed to emanate from him in powerful waves as he removed his coat and shirt and then, slowly, with his eyes on hers, his boots and trousers.

All things were possible. Together, not yet touching, they stood waiting in moonlight and truth. Her breasts were taut, her breath quick in her throat. Rising, his sex brushed the abundance of dark amber, honey-colored ringlets adorning Celia and then, slender but full, arching gently, pointed his way to her. A deep, vast tremor shook her, left her too weak to stand. Rafe caught her in his arms and carried her to the bed and sheets cool against her fevered back.

Shadows and highlights, the soft play of moonlight and lantern on taut lines of muscles and sheathing skin. Rafe kneeled at her side. A single warm drop from him touched Celia's hip and, moaning, she guided him to her and opened to him as a blossom opens to the life-sustaining tears from heaven. And when he bent to her, she was moist for him, warmed to his hardness, and gasped at the sudden joining.

She did not close her eyes. Not once. But watched him, rather, as he watched her, and understood, for the first time, nature at her fiercest, most wondrous and awesome moments of grandeur. Together they mirrored the first storm stirrings at sea. Placid, the water ripples in the freshening wind. The sky darkens and the waves rise and crown themselves with foamy jewels. All turbulence, the air spits fire that arcs down. The sea, not to be outdone, rises to meet the fire until sea and sky are inseparable. One's storm is the other's storm, one's fire the other's fire. Rising, consuming, melding, blending. An ancient, primordial shriek in which pain and ecstasy are inseparable and two, at last, become totally one.

Unity. A cry, a tear, a name implored. The essence of life and death shared in one long instant that stretches to infinity and replaces, in its intensity, all time.

The storm subsides, but does not withdraw. The ensuing calm is more like the center of a hurricane, more like a calm fulcrum about which the holocaust of sea and sky whirls and whirls.

Rafe kisses her throat, her eyes, kisses away the tear that lies on her cheek. Celia cannot hold him tightly enough. His tongue touching hers, she drinks of his soul even as, below, she drinks. Joined one and still, the sweat of their bodies is a common pool. The sea is calm, the sky above blue and cloudless. Lassitude replaces turmoil, and a sense of well-being swells the chest, and she nods to his unspoken question.

There are no metaphors this time, no stirring fantasies of storm and sky. Only the truth and reality of two real people in a real bed. Now there is time to take and give, to know and enjoy, to share love. This hand just so. These kisses circling one breast and then another. This finger trailing down hip and thigh and knee and calf. This tongue, tentatively at first for new lovers never dare too much, touching and tasting.

"I didn't know you felt like that."

"Touch me here, and here."

"Like this?"

"Again."

True lovers know they are in love as well when they can smile and do not have to finish sentences or pretend. True lovers are not rushed, not impatient, do not seek to end too soon their dalliance. True lovers understand that the road to ecstasy is paved with delights that are an end unto themselves, and are the milestones of their love.

Rafe and Celia, Celia and Rafe. They need no storms, no earthquakes, no rushing tides. Together they are more than storms or earthquakes or tides, as a sun is more than a candle. And when she settles down on him, when he pierces and fills her, when her hair encloses his face in a tent just large enough for the two of them, they know . . . they know . . .

Their names mingle in that shuddering moment when the searing burst of energy calls life out of darkness. They share that most sacred of possessions, oneself. And they are not alone, which is wholeness.

Spent, they slump together and in each other's arms, with the innocent purity of children, drift into sleep.

This ultimate verity is love.

Dreams, like embers, die, wink out as wakefulness returns.

Tat. Tat. Tat.

Celia's eyes opened grudgingly, searched the darkness where the
Seth Thomas ticked out the passing seconds.

Tat. Tat.

Pebbles on the windowpane? What in heaven's name? Curious, she
rolled away from Rafe's warmth, slid her feet over the side of the bed,
and froze. Anthony! He had expected a note, and she had left nothing
for him!

Tat. Tat.

More pebbles to attract her attention. The faint patter sounded for
all the world like a drumbeat loud enough to wake the dead. Celia
started to stand, only to feel Rafe's fingers tighten around her wrist. "I
hear it, too," he said.

"I didn't want to wake you," Celia whispered.

"I know." Rafe patted her thigh. "Someone outside, and I can just
imagine who."

Celia's blood turned cold and sluggish. An icy claw of fear squeezed
the breath from her. "You can?" she asked, scarcely able to disguise
her alarm.

"The city's crawling with ruffians of every sort." He rose and began
to pull on his trousers. "They're out prowling the wreckage and looking for empty houses. Wait here." Rafe checked the load in his revolver by the dim light of the lamp and started for the door. "I'll give
him a surprise."

The door closed and she was alone. Celia grabbed her gown and
slipped it over her head to cover her nakedness, then hurried to the
window. Below, Anthony stood in the open halfway between the
wrecked gazebo and the house. If Rafe saw him . . .

Frantic, she struggled with the window latch, at the same time saw
Anthony step forward. My God, he had seen her and obviously was
mistaking her actions for a signal to approach! Calmly. She had to
remain calm. Push down. Turn, lift . . . Down and to her left she saw
a shadow slip around the corner from the house and begin to stalk Anthony. If Anthony were caught, and if he talked . . . The window
swung open.

"Rafe!" Celia shouted. "Behind you!"

Anthony and Rafe both jumped, Anthony for the cover of the

ruined gazebo, Rafe from a clump of bushes at the side of the house.

"What the hell!" Anthony shouted.

Rafe rolled to his feet and dashed toward the gazebo. "Hold it!"

Anthony dodged the wreckage of the gazebo and table, raced for the garden gate, and darted through and loped down the street. Rafe took the long way around the gazebo and, remembering he had bare feet, halted just outside the gate. Whoever it had been was long gone. But at least gone, he added mentally, grateful that no harm had been done. He turned and looked up at Celia as he walked back to the house and entered the back door.

"Who up there?" Immelda called, her voice drifting up from the cellar. "Miss Celia?"

"Celia's fine," Rafe called down to her.

"That you Mr. Lattimore?"

"Yes. Go back to sleep, Immelda. There's nothing to worry about."

"Oh, my, oh, my! At this hour! Whatever you—"

"I said, go back to sleep, damn it!"

"Yes, suh!"

Seething, Rafe took the steps two at a time. "Thanks for the warning," he snapped sarcastically, entering and confronting Celia. "I could've had him."

"I'm sorry," Celia answered, almost sick with relief—and with having to continue the lie. "I thought he had a gun. His right hand . . . I . . ." She sagged despondently. "I'm sorry, Rafe. He frightened me."

Rafe studied her a moment, finally sighed as the anger melted from him. "All right," he said. "All right. I guess that's understandable."

"Did you recognize him?"

"I thought so for a moment. Something about him. Doesn't matter now. He won't stop running 'til he reaches the river. You've seen the last of him. The last of Immelda, too, if I don't quit scaring her," he added with a chuckle. Rafe crossed to the desk, placed his revolver on the blotter, and in the dim light picked out a single word at the bottom of a page. "Who's Hawkmoon?"

"What?" Celia asked, her heart leaping into her throat.

"Hawkmoon. You've written it here."

She remained calm and under control only with the greatest of effort. "Oh, that." She rose and walked toward him. "A fantasy. A will o' the wisp. A daydream. You're responsible, really."

"I?" Rafe asked, distracted from the damning letter.

"We are the hawks of night," Celia recited. "Have you forgotten?"

"Wings across the moon. As swift, my thoughts return to you . . . Of course not. But—"

"A letter that will be never sent or read," Celia explained. She touched his chest and felt his heart beat with the palm of her hand. "There is no need. After tonight," she whispered. "Everything I wanted to say"—she came into his arms, rested her head on his chest—"has been said."

"Everything?" Rafe asked hoarsely.

Celia stepped back, looked up at him. "Almost everything?" she amended.

Mesmerized, Rafe undid his trousers and stepped out of them. "There might be . . . one or two . . . more words. . . ."

His muscle-ridged body was almost ghostly white in the pale light. Now rising, his aroused sex jutted from the wiry black ringlets covering his groin. But not frightening, Celia thought, pushing the earlier encounter with Micah from her mind. Not frightening at all, but more beautiful than she had imagined possible. Sensual, and seeking her. Encumbered, eyes glued on his, she crossed her arms, slowly raised the gown over her head and let it drop to one side. "Rafe?" she said. "We . . ."

". . . Are? . . ." he prompted.

"The only thing left . . ."

". . . To be said."

His length, the skin stretched taut and the tip bright with moisture, pressed against her belly. His lips met and parted hers, and their tongues met. Groaning, Celia tipped her pelvis forward to touch as much of him as she could. Somehow, they were walking backward. Rafe kissed her chin, her eyelids, her nose, her ears, her neck. When Celia's legs hit the bed, they stopped. Rafe's hands cupped her breasts, raised her nipples to his tongue and his kisses.

"What?"

"Shhh. Relax. This, too, should be said, but you must relax."

He laid her back, lifted her legs onto the bed. He raised one of her feet, kissed the instep, then her ankle and, with a dozen more kisses, worked his way to the tender back of her knee. He wasn't going to stop! Confused and a little frightened, Celia covered herself with her hands. He couldn't . . . wouldn't . . . She had never even looked at herself, much less let a man . . . let a man look . . . or kiss! . . .

"No." Halfway up her inner thigh, the kisses stopped. His hand took hers, firmly moved them away. "Don't be afraid. I won't hurt you."

Celia clutched the sheets on either side of her. Her arms and shoulders and back stiffened as his lips came closer to and then actually brushed against her. Her eyes closed and her teeth clenched, she twisted her head back and forth on the pillow. Suddenly, he was touching her. His fingers parted her, slid through the moistness, opened her . . .

"Rafe? Please? Please?" She tried to close her legs, but he wouldn't let her. Wide-eyed with disbelief, she watched him, realized that the soft heat she felt against herself was his tongue. His tongue! . . .

Hard but soft, his tongue probed and pressed. A spasm rocked her. Unable to stop herself, she felt her back arch, felt herself pressing against him even as his lips caught her and held her while the tip of his tongue stroked and stroked and brought her, moaning, twisting violently, hips heaving . . .

"Oh, my God! My God!"

A slow explosion erupted in her groin and spread like liquid fire through her. Her hands held the back of his head, held him to her as the bone-wracking climax shook her like a reed in the wind. An animal cry started deep in her throat, emerged as a rasping wail. And still his lips . . . his tongue . . . No! They had become part of her, indistinguishable from the tortured nerve endings that, at last, could stand no more. Slowly, a great lassitude stole over her and the tension drained from her until she felt limp and languid.

"Oh, Rafe. Oh, Rafe . . ."

"Shhhh." Rising, he lay next to her, kissed the tears from her face.

Eyes swimming with tears, she looked at him as if she'd never seen him before, ran her fingers over his face as if mere seeing wasn't enough. She wanted to laugh, and she wanted to cry, and she wanted to sing and dance and touch and hold . . . "I'll bet you think I liked that, don't you?" she asked, unable to stop touching him.

"Well—"

"I didn't, you know. Well, maybe"—she held her thumb and forefinger a scant quarter inch apart—"this much. Oh, Rafe!" She was laughing uncontrollably, so full of joy she thought she would burst. "Do you have any idea of how much I love you?"

"Yes." He held her head and, totally serious, stared, one after another, into her eyes. "I do." His lips touched hers fleetingly, softly. "I think . . . you love me . . . as much as I love you. Which is, my sweet Celia, very . . . very much."

No further words were needed. Caresses served to fuel the fire that consumed them then. He entered her slowly, completely. Celia tasted the musk of herself in his kisses. She felt her strength in him. She wrapped around him, held him deep inside her, reveled in the precious agony that contorted his face and left him shuddering against her, and at last subsided.

She loved him. She loved him with her whole life. Always had loved him, always would love him as he did and had and would love her.

Would always love him . . .

He loved her . . .

Slowly, melting, satiated. Her whole body . . . drifting . . . sailing into sleep . . .

And on the mantel, the clock relentlessly ticked, ticked, ticked, toward morning.

CHAPTER 17

Tuesday morning, the ninth of June, dawned bright and clear after a shelling that had been even more brutal than Sunday night's. Pleasantly tired—Rafe had come to see her sometime around two and hadn't left until after four—Celia had decided to spend part of the day with Lynna, away from the chaos of the town. The idea had been inspired. Dressed in the horrid gray homespun everyone was wearing those days and carrying a precious handful of coffee beans and a half-dozen cookies salvaged from the Sunday night party, she arrived just as Lynna was beginning to mix and stuff a huge tub of beef sausage. "What happened?" Celia asked, noticing the smoke house was going full blast.

"We had to slaughter Jessie, our cow," Lynna explained. "Looters hit us Sunday night when Jonathan was helping out with the fires. They got into the root cellar and took most of what he had stored. Poor Jessie got frightened and ran. We found her with a broken leg in the morning. We spent all yesterday butchering her." Lynna looked haggard and tired, almost asleep on her feet. She pulled out a chair and dusted the seat. "I'm glad you came. I could use someone to talk to."

"Talk?" Celia asked indignantly. "Lynna Hays, you do take the cake. Lord in heaven above, but do you think I don't know how to make sausage?"

"Well . . ."

They finished at ten, ground the coffee and drank some, saving the rest for Jonathan, who was still asleep after a night patrolling the south end of town. "That tastes so good," Lynna said at last, draining her cup and setting it down. "Strange, how we take things like coffee for granted—until there isn't any left, and none to be bought even for a fortune."

"The siege won't last forever," Celia pointed out, sounding a good deal more optimistic than she felt.

"I know." Lynna sighed heavily, rested her head on her hands, "Lord, but I'm tired. I think I could sleep for a month."

"You could for an hour or two anyway," Celia said. "I'll watch things if you want."

Lynna looked tempted, but finally shook her head no. "I'd better not. Jonathan might wake up and—"

"Be absolutely delighted, if he has a brain in his head. Go on. Shoo! Nothin's going to happen."

She hadn't needed much more prompting. Ten minutes later, the house was quiet except for Jonathan's soft snores, and Celia slipped out onto the porch. She couldn't have asked for a nicer day. Other than one or two smudges of smoke rising from the city beyond the hills, and the occasional muted sound of gunfire, there was little to suggest that they were under siege. Pensive, but enjoying the quiet and the fresh air, Celia strolled the barnyard and ended up at the south fence. The view was beautiful, bucolic. Green fields broken by tree lines that hid the river sloped to the marshes that protected the southern end of town. A hawk circled far overhead. Just being there felt good, Celia thought, thankful that she'd decided to come. Could it be possible that Sunday night, a bare day and half earlier, she had still been obsessed with leaving? What an incredible difference a day and half made. No. What an incredible difference Rafe made.

I love him, she thought, mouthing the words to the sky. Her head thrown back, she let the sun bathe her face. Never had she felt so alive, so vibrant, so complete. She felt as light and fluffy as thistle-down, giddy with joy . . .

"*Pssst. Pssst.*"

"What?" She looked around, spotted a gray hat waving over the fence where it turned north at the corner, then a glimpse of red hair. Immediately apprehensive, she glanced around to make sure she was alone, then strolled to the corner of the fence. "Anthony?"

"Who do you think?" came the grumbled answer from behind a low hedge. "Abe Lincoln?"

"What're you doing here? Are you mad?"

"Nobody saw me. I followed you this morning, then fell asleep. Jesus! What the hell you been doing all this time?"

"Just helping out." Celia bent to see behind the hedge. "There's nobody around. We're safe. Do you mind if I talk to you instead of a hedge?"

The bushes swayed, then parted. Groaning, pulling himself on his elbows, Anthony wriggled through, then rolled onto his back. "Oh, Lord, that hurts!" he grunted, holding onto his right knee.

Celia looked down, stepped back in shock. Anthony was hardly recognizable as the handsome young Bostonian she'd known before the war. The last few days had taken a tremendous toll. His hair was filthy and matted to his head. He'd been wet, covered with dirt, and wet again. His eyes were bloodshot, his face haggard, his beard dark and frizzy where it had been singed. "You look . . . terrible," she gasped.

"Nothing compared to how I feel. This thing stiffens up when I sleep." Holding his left knee, he twisted so he could see her better.

"Your knee?"

"Isn't as bad as it looks." He removed his hands, showed her the torn trousers and a ragged, rust-colored wound that started in the front and went to the back of his knee. "Would've been all right if the bastards hadn't caught me last night and put me to work fighting fires. Hurts like the devil when I walk, and worse when I run. Dancing," he added with a dry laugh, "is out of the question."

"But how—"

"I fell in the damned street Sunday night. Or Monday morning, to be accurate. That was a nasty little trick you played on me, Cousin Celia."

"Trick?" Celia didn't have to pretend to be angry. "I saved your life! He was armed, you know."

"If you'd left a letter for me as we'd arranged, the occasion wouldn't have arisen."

There was no way he could make her feel guilty. "And if you had arrived earlier," Celia said, trading accusations, "perhaps—"

"How? I was busy putting out fires, along with everyone else."

"Then you could have come back the next night. Or waited."

"Waited!" Anthony sputtered. "Waiting's all I've been doing. Counting the days before these fool Johnny Rebs surrender, and I can become Anthony Rutledge, civilized man again. Hell. I thought I'd be on my way home by now."

He'd tricked her and used her. He'd betrayed her worse than she had Vicksburg or the South because he was family, of her own blood. Under the circumstances, she found herself unable to summon even a whit of sympathy. "You mean we surprised you?" she asked with malicious delight. "You didn't expect tenacity and bravery from shop-keepers and farmers?"

"Blind foolish stubbornness, I call it."

"Yes. You would."

Surprised, Anthony let go his knee and stared up at her. "What the hell, Celia? You sound damned near proud of them."

"I am. This is my home. These are my people."

"Was your home, were your people," Anthony corrected. He glared at her, was about to go on, but then seemed satisfied with making a point. Lying back, he fished a battered stub of a cigar out of his pocket, lit up, and exhaled an oily blue white cloud of smoke. "So what *did* you learn?" he asked at last. "Anything?"

Celia shrugged, concentrated on a far line of trees. "Nothing."

"Nothing! All those generals and not a—"

"A new rumor about Johnston crossing the Pearl. But if Powell doesn't know more about that than anyone in Vicksburg, I'd be surprised."

Anthony grunted his agreement. For a long moment he lay thinking and then, evidently reaching a decision, rolled onto his side and propped himself up on one elbow. "I've done better than that," he announced, speaking rapidly. "Stumbled onto something important. A clerk from the quartermaster's office got drunk last night in Liz Ford's place and did some curious bragging. When I bought him a drink, he bragged some more." He paused and a grim smile crossed his face. "The secesh are expecting a shipment of percussion caps."

He knew anyway! "Oh?" Celia asked, careful not to betray any emotion other than a normal curiosity.

"One man," Anthony continued. He pointed over his shoulder to the south with his thumb. "Right through there. And with a damned good chance of success. Unless Powell's alerted, of course, in which case he could put a picket line so thick around those swamps that a fly couldn't get through. But he has to be told." Anthony watched Celia's face closely. "And you'll have to be the one to tell him."

"Me?" Celia blurted, alarmed. She'd been so sure her solution would work, and now she felt the trap tightening around her again. "I was only supposed to—"

"I know. But I don't stand a ghost of a chance with this knee."

She was frantic and fought to keep the panic out of her voice. "You'll be better in a day or two. If the knee isn't broken—"

"We don't have a day or two. The moon's almost empty. They'll try any night now. The next three or four days is my guess."

A germ of an idea sprouted in Celia's mind and grew quickly. It would work, she was certain, but only if she protested—just enough. "I thought there were others," she said, now letting a hint of panic tinge her voice. "You and Powell both said you had other agents in Vicksburg. Why can't one of them go?"

Anthony contemplated his cigar. "I'm afraid," he finally admitted, "that was a . . . well, a . . ."

"You were lying!" Celia hissed. "Lying! Just to make me think—"

"Damn it, Celia, it isn't as if you haven't gone out before."

"That was north." He was biting, she gloated. Falling for her lie. And Powell wouldn't know the difference until it was too late.

In some small way she could redress at least in part the grievous harm she had caused at the Big Black. "I know that part of the country better. There are roads. I can't do it, Anthony. I *won't.*"

"Can't?" Anthony's eyes narrowed. "Won't?" Slowly, viciously, he ground out his cigar on a small stone. "I thought we'd had this conversation before? Do you want me to refresh your memory?"

Inexplicably, Celia began to laugh and then, with a touch of hysteria, to giggle.

Anthony sat bolt upright in alarm. "What's so funny?" he asked, peering past her toward the house, afraid someone would see her and become curious enough to investigate. "What's wrong? Damn it, Celia! What's so damned funny?"

"You," Celia finally managed.

"What about me?"

"You're funny. Look at yourself! Dirty, beat up, filthy clothes. Do you really think you're in disguise? Why, you're in your own true colors, Anthony." If asked, she wouldn't have been able to say whether she was sadder or angrier. "You're a schemer and a man of deceit. You no more hesitate to kill than to subject a defenseless woman to blackmail. You're no better than any of those you hate and deride!"

A slow flush crept up Anthony's neck and face. His breathing labored, he twisted awkwardly and pushed himself to his feet. "If I thought for one minute you were right, I . . . I . . ." Words failed him and he sputtered helplessly before he could control his temper long enough to issue a final, peremptory command. "You leave tonight. And remember, dear cousin, what's in store if you fail."

Celia let him go, called out only when he was a good twenty paces away. "Oh, Anthony?" Her voice was sweet as honey. "Aren't you going to tell me where to go?"

Damn her, Anthony cursed silently, hobbling painfully back to the corner of the fence. She'd done that on purpose, just to make him angry. "You know the Warrenton Road?" he asked, refusing to give her the satisfaction of seeing him lose his temper again.

"Yes, of course."

"And can find it in the dark?"

"I . . . I think so. Unless I'm captured."

"That's the chance we take. Won't matter if you are, so long as it's the Federals who do the capturing. They'll take you to Powell if you ask. Just tell them he's this side of Warrenton, the second house on the right after you cross the Big Bayou Bridge. Once you're with him there'll be no problems. Any questions?"

"Absolutely none," Celia said without a trace of pleasantness. "Hawkmoon will ride a little after ten tonight and deliver your message. And give Powell your regards."

Anthony almost returned her sarcasm, then decided not to, and limped off again, keeping the hedge between himself and the house.

Success! So sure of his power over her, so immersed in deceit, Anthony had been pitifully easy to deceive. The rest would be simple, Celia thought, starting back to the house to wake Lynna. All she had to do was ride seven miles through two armies, convince a man who was skeptical by nature that a bald-faced lie was the truth, and return home safely.

Simple, indeed.

The sun was so bright it hurt his eyes. The summer heat had driven Rafe out onto the porch of his office. Up half the night with the bombardment, then from two until after four with Celia, he had less than three hours sleep before rolling out of bed and reporting to the office that morning. After twenty-two days of being cut off from the rest of the world, a myriad of details had cried for decisions and solutions. His presence was required at a brief meeting of what was left of the town council. Another meeting with representatives of the army concerning water supplies, food distribution, medical care for civilians, and authority over the army personnel assigned to the Home Guard consumed a full hour. By the time all the details had been sorted out to everyone's approximate satisfaction, it was after one and he felt as if someone had tipped him over and let everything run out of him.

"You had anything to eat today?"

Rafe blinked, turned to see Matt Broussard climbing off a tired horse. "Come to think of it, I don't think so," he admitted, glad to see the young man who'd taken on more and more responsibility during the last two days. "Any ideas?"

"I got some fried meat and pea bread and a canteen of water, if you can sit a spell."

"What kind of meat?" It was the standard question to ask.

Matt shrugged and limped over to join Rafe. "Didn't ask," came the standard reply. "Smells fresh, though, and ain't green."

"Sounds better than salt pork, then." Rafe said, laughing, remembering the dull fare of his shipboard days.

Two barrels were their chairs, a broken wagon their table. The two men, more and more like brothers with each passing day, ate silently and quickly. "Didn't know how hungry I was," Rafe finally said, passing the last of the water to Matt. "Gonna take a look around. Things got kind of rough last night, and I've been stuck inside all day. Want to go with me?"

They talked as they walked, Matt filling Rafe in on the street talk he'd missed. "That one there," the young man pointed out, after they'd gone a few blocks.

"Doesn't look like shell damage," Rafe said, heading for the flame gutted remains of Schweicker's grocery.

"Wasn't. Word is a gang from Under the Hill fired it. Most everyone was at the north end of town at the time."

"Jesus!" Rafe cursed, checking the ceiling before walking in. His boots stirred up small clouds of dismal ash. The stench of burned flesh hung heavily in the air. "Under the Hill, eh?"

"Just a rumor. Probably true, though. You think they was the same men you caught the other night?"

"The same . . . different?" *My brother,* Rafe thought, fighting the sinking feeling in the pit of his stomach. "Does it matter? The result is . . . this."

"I reckon there's a craziness comes over some folks," Matt allowed, groping for an explanation. "I seen a sow kill all her young'uns once. Weren't natural. Just a craziness."

"Men aren't pigs," Rafe snapped. "Some rally to protect and serve, others are outcasts concerned with no more than their own gain. They aren't crazy. They're greedy, selfish, lazy, treasonous cowards."

Matt thought that over. "I reckon that's true, too," he finally said, nodding in agreement. "You think—"

Rafe didn't want to hear anymore. Cutting Matt off with a curt wave, he walked through the debris to the counter, a soot-streaked and charred coffinlike structure whose shelves had been emptied long before the blaze. Behind the counter, approached by footprints in the accumulated soot and dust and smoke, the shadow of a man lay outlined on the floor where Schweicker's corpse had been found. Dark rust-colored bloodstains blotched the clean wood where the body had lain. Poor old man. Bludgeoned to death in retaliation for not having any food to give the looters, his death had been a needless act of malicious spite.

Micah. Micah's hand. If it had been Micah, he'd . . . what? A new rage filled Rafe, and without warning, he whirled and dipped and caught the counter low down and lifted.

"Now, wait a minute! What'cha?" Alarmed, Matt stepped back out of the way. "Look here, Mr. Lattimore. You oughtn't'a—"

A roar of anger and rage and frustration. Rafe's muscles bulged and his face turned red with effort. Suddenly, the massive counter gave

vay and tipped onto its side. Panels popped loose as it crashed to the
loor in a shower of splinters and broken glass. The front of Rafe's uni-
orm was covered with soot. Sweat streamed down his face, and head
ack, he breathed heavily as the tension drained out of him.

"Feel any better?" Matt asked hesitantly, looking at the shattered
ounter.

"Old man didn't deserve to die like that," Rafe said dully. "Go
omewhere and get some sleep, Broussard." His mind made up, he
tepped over the wreckage and started for the door. "Be another hard
ight. Get some sleep while you can." There was only one way to find
ut, and that was to ask. "Go on, now, and don't be following me. Get
ome sleep."

The streets were quiet, almost empty. Rafe headed directly for
evee, turned, and made his solitary way through the war-torn streets.
Details caught his eye, but he paid them little mind. A cannon, evi-
ently thrown high in the air by an explosion, stuck in the planking
ke a thick iron thumb. A uniform coat hung from a nail on the side
f a warehouse. A wagon, all four wheels splayed out in perfect order,
ngletree and reins leading to imaginary horses or mules, lay upside
own on its bed. A door hung loose and creaking on one hinge. At the
nd of Levee and up from the water a little he came to Vicksburg
nder the Hill, a puzzle of interlocking narrow streets and alleys that
ead-ended into the hills and sharp bluffs separating this collection of
loons, brothels, and cheap hotels from the rest of the city. The
acks and false shop fronts were like the faces of the dead. Windows
lank, glass shattered, so many sightless eyes. Doorways dark as gap-
g mouths.

Like human moles, the denizens of Vicksburg Under the Hill were
uly under the hill now, for the hillsides behind the broken buildings
ere dotted with the dark openings of caves. Rafe chose an alley at
ndom and turned into it. At the first corner, a soldier in tattered
ay sat propped against the ravaged wall of what used to be, a bro-
n sign said, Hostetter's Emporium. The afternoon sun sent a slash-
g wedge of bright light across the soldier's legs.

Rafe stopped and took stock. He was surrounded by dull grays,
owns, and blacks. A dog barked somewhere in the distance, but he
uld hear nothing but the buzz of flies close at hand. The soldier
dn't moved and didn't even seem to be looking at him. Still, Rafe
came aware he was being watched and realized that he was wholly
t of place, and that his tailored uniform was more an invitation to
uble than the object of authority. Just to be on the safe side, he un-
ttoned his coat and checked the derringer secreted in a hand-sewn

pocket, then loosened the more conventional navy revolver holstered at his side.

A name out of the past and linked to Micah came to mind. Rafe moved toward the soldier and stopped in front of him. "Where'll I find Fancy Darren's place, soldier?" he asked.

Nothing. The soldier stared straight ahead.

"I said—"

"He's blind," a woman's voice interrupted.

Rafe turned, saw a woman dressed in purple velvet fitted snugly to a solid waist, robust hips, and bosom. A white lace collar circled her throat and a purple parasol decorated with black stitching shaded her from the sun. Her hair was dull brown, her cheeks heavily powdered and rouged, and slightly moist from sweat. "I beg your pardon?" he asked.

"He's blind in the head. Doubt he even dreams. There's plenty more like him too, more's the pity." The woman stepped past Rafe and kneeling, put a chunk of pea bread in the soldier's outstretched hand. "Well?" she asked, standing. Her eyebrows arched as if daring Rafe to accuse her of a kind and generous act. "You mind?"

"Ah . . . no," Rafe answered, taken aback and not sure of how to respond. "Of course not."

"Good. And now, sonny boy, I'll do you a favor, too. By tellin' you to take that pretty uniform back to where you belong before you cause us all trouble." The woman's eyes flashed angrily and she turned her back on him. "Get, sonny, while the gettin's good."

"I'm looking for Fancy Darren's," Rafe said, not so easily dismissed.

The woman stopped and appraised Rafe sharply. "I should think a fine gent as yourself would keep better company than the likes of her," she sneered.

"*Cooo,*" the soldier said.

Rafe started, glanced at the soldier and back to the woman. "Be that as it may, I'm looking for her." He gestured toward the pocket hills. "There's not much to distinguish one cave from another, I'm afraid."

"Distinguish, eh?" The woman's laughter was derisive, mocking. "Well, don't worry, dearie. Fancy isn't one to let herself be forgotten. Had one of her niggers paint a sign for the front, she did, just so soldier boys could find their way to her."

"Ah, yes," Rafe said, uncomfortable with her evaluation of his intentions. "You, ah . . . Can you show me the way?"

The woman tipped her parasol back toward Levee Street. "Go back the way you came and head toward South Street. Before you ge there, you'll find an alley, and that is Tinker's Alley. Up Tinker's Alley you'll see her sign. Painted right fancy it is, but then that's her name, ain't it?"

Frankly curious, Rafe watched the woman hide herself behind her parasol and move off up the alley. When she disappeared, he retraced his own steps toward the river and Levee Street. The woman in velvet, the mute soldier, the ruined buildings, and the ominous presence of unseen others staring at him from the surrounding caves left him uneasy and anxious to finish his business quickly and be away from Vicksburg Under the Hill.

Tinker's Alley was an uneven winding cobblestone aisle between brooding shop fronts that threatened to cave in and crush passersby at the slightest provocation. Rafe wrinkled his nose at the stench as he passed a burned-out house that reeked of carrion. He steered clear of a gaping, half-collapsed wall. Around one curve, just as the woman had described, he found a cave closed with a handsome oak panel door that had been fitted into the hollowed-out hillside with expert care. Next to the door where it had fallen from a beam that jutted out from the dirt, an expertly painted and highly explicit sign announced that this was, indeed, Fancy Darren's establishment.

Apprehension faded, was replaced by cold resolve. Rafe lifted the brass knocker and dropped it against the strike.

The door opened immediately. "You got a long stride," the woman in velvet said. "I took the short cut and just got here myself. Come in, Rafe Lattimore. You've found your Fancy Darren."

Rafe managed to conceal his surprise and stepped inside. The interior of the cave was refreshingly cool, which accounted for the heavy dress the madame wore. Heavy coral-colored drapes concealed the earthen walls. The room smelled of cinnamon and a lighter yet forceful aroma from an incense Rafe couldn't place. Painted oil lamps added to the lush colors of the parlor and emphasized the rich fabrics that covered the furniture. Fancy gestured toward a plush easy chair and chose a nearby couch for herself.

"You know me then?" Rafe asked, sitting.

"I know everyone. Some more . . . intimately than others. You look little enough like your brother, but the resemblance is there." She sat in the corner of the couch, her back against the armrest, tucked her feet up under her long velvet skirt, and clapped her hands. Immediately, a side door opened and a young mulatto no more than fifteen years old entered carrying a long-necked wine bottle and two glasses on a silver tray.

Rafe wondered if the silver tray had been stolen from someone's house, watched while the girl poured the wine and then departed. "I'm looking for Micah," he said stiffly when the door closed and he and Fancy were alone again.

Fancy leaned forward to pick up one of the glasses. "This is an excellent wine," she said, shifting slightly to better display her breasts.

"I think you know where I might be able to find him."

"The bouquet reminds me of my youth. Did you have a youth, Mr. Lattimore, or were you always an insufferable ass?"

Rafe colored, held his temper, and then his tongue when a Negro servant emerged from one of the back rooms, nodded to Rafe and half bowed to Fancy. "Afternoon, Miss Fancy," he said, and walked over to a piano in the far corner of the room.

The black man began polishing the piano and Rafe turned his attention back to Fancy. "Maybe I am a bit of an ass," he admitted with a straight face. "But to know me is to love me."

Fancy almost choked on her wine. When she finished coughing, she took a silk kerchief from her bosom and dabbed at her lips. His hands folded over his stomach, Rafe remained impassive. The black man looked up at the sound of so much mirth and then returned to his labors.

"Fair enough," Fancy said with one last cough. She stood, walked to Rafe and, smelling of sweat and powder and spilled wine, leaned over him. "Fair enough. I'm a whore and you don't care much for me or my wine, but I'm going to help you. And do you know why I'm going to help you, Mr. Lattimore? Not because you're an ass, but because your brother is an asshole."

Imperious, Fancy stalked across the parlor and flicked the latch on the door directly behind Rafe. "Well? she asked as the door slowly creaked open.

Rafe joined her, followed her into an opulently appointed bedroom. There, stretched across the bed, snoring loudly, his chest rising and falling with each broad, rasping breath, was Micah. He was fully dressed. His slouch hat dangled from one of the bedposts. A dark purple quilt and a small snowdrift of down pillows almost buried him. Rafe took a water pitcher from its china basin on the bedside table, swirled the contents for a second, and then poured a stream of water on the back of Micah's neck.

The bedding muffled the awakened man's cry of outrage. Micah erupted from the bed but, groggy and off balance, fell back again when Rafe pushed him. "What the hell!" he sputtered, unable to understand what Rafe was doing there. "You?"

"That's right, big brother. Me."

"Well, shii-it! Doesn't that take the cake." Micah started to sit up, then quickly lay back down when Rafe's revolver suddenly appeared just inches in front of his face. "What the hell?"

"Stealing's one thing, Micah, but murder is quite another."

"You're crazy, you know that?" Micah asked, "Crazy as a God-damn loon."

"Am I? Schweicker was an old man who lived a long life well enough to deserve dying in bed. I don't have any proof you killed him, Micah, but I wish to hell I did."

"I don't know what the devil you're talking about," Micah protested, the very picture of outraged innocence. "Hell, I was here all night, wasn't I, Fancy?"

Her face paling beneath the layers of powder, Fancy solemnly nodded.

Rafe sighed, stepped away from the bed, and holstered his revolver. "Brother or no," he said, stabbing a finger at Micah, "you remember one thing. The next time I see you out at night, I *will* shoot. And order my men to do the same. So if I were you, Micah, I'd spend the rest of my nights in bed, too. And tell your friends to crawl under a rock and not come out until they're damned sure the sun is high in the sky, be-cause otherwise they'll get shot, too. You understand that?"

"I understand you better not miss, little brother," Micah said, ready to kill at the moment but remembering how fast Rafe's revolver had appeared. "Just . . . don't . . . miss."

Rafe whirled and brushed past Fancy, who managed to avoid a col-lision by inches. "Your pardon, Miss Darren," he said, touching the brim of his hat.

"Any time, darlin'," Fancy replied, following him into the parlor.

"And a free piece of advice," Rafe added, pausing at the door. "If I were you, I'd watch the company I keep."

"Blood and business. There isn't much a lady can do about either of 'em," Fancy said and chuckled.

Micah loomed in the doorway to the bedroom. His wet shirt was plastered to his shoulders. His face was all angles and glowering lines. Knotted brows and burning eyes and taut skin stretched over trem-bling muscles. The Negro began to play a gentle little tune on the piano. "Shut the hell up!" Micah roared.

The black man quit playing. Rafe opened the front door and stepped into the alley.

"Wha' cha doin' under the hill, bub?" a voice asked.

Rafe squinted against the bright sunlight, stepped to one side so the open door wouldn't be behind him. A hard-looking lot of unkempt, ragged men blocked his way. They were nine in number and armed with an assortment of knives and lengths of wood tucked in their belts.

"Ast'cha a question, fancy pants." The man nearest Rafe stepped forward. Of indeterminate age, he was thin and wiry with rotted teeth in a hatchet-shaped face split by a sneer. He wore only a pair of ragged pants. A tattoo of a dagger pierced his left breast where a long scar descended from his right collarbone and disappeared behind his back. Evidently just awakened, his eyes were bloodshot. Obviously no stranger to fighting, the man might have been locked up at another time. But there was neither room nor men enough to guard the likes of this sort, and no soldier on the line would have tolerated him in the trenches.

"Been to see Micah, I'll warrant," someone else offered.

"Best you ask him that, Cairo," a third voice suggested.

"Don't need to ask'm," Cairo said, stepping close enough for Rafe to smell his breath. "Reckon he'll tell us of his own accord."

Rafe sensed a presence behind him. He glanced to the side and rear, saw Micah standing in the doorway and obviously enjoying his brother's predicament. His right leg moving back slightly, Rafe turned back to Cairo. "You're right," he said with a smile, and reached up to tap his teeth, a gesture that distracted attention from his right foot and leg. "I'll tell you. You ought to clean your teeth more often."

The sentence ended with a sickening crunch as Rafe's leg swung forward and the tip of his boot struck the end of Cairo's toes. A bone snapped. The nail on his big toe split and blood squirted. Cairo paled and his mouth formed a soundless O as the breath whistled through his nose. Paralyzed, powerless to stop Rafe as he shoved past him Cairo sank to the ground and lay writhing on the cobblestones Whether Rafe had made his point or if the other men had glimpsed how close his hand was to the revolver holstered at his side, no one moved to stop him as he walked down the alley and quickly disap peared from view.

"Son of a bitch!" Micah cursed, loathe to watch Rafe leave un punished, but at a loss to decide exactly what to do.

"You did kill that old man, didn't you?" Fancy said from the door way behind him.

Micah shrugged and watched Cairo's friends carry him off. "The stiff bastard wouldn't tell us where he'd cached his money. Cairo tried to make him talk and got carried away. Didn't make me happy, but Schweicker brought it on himself."

"Ah, Micah." Fancy wagged her head, backed into the parlor. "I guess that means we split the blanket."

"What's that?" Micah asked, following her inside.

Fancy backed toward the piano. "You and your friends aren't welcome here anymore, Micah, so you can clear on out. Right now. Pack up your kit an' sashay. Take your business elsewhere. I don't ever want to see you again."

"The hell you say!"

"Really?" Fancy stopped by the Negro on the piano stool. "You were a fine boy, Micah, and fun for a ride. Made me feel important 'cause one of the Lattimores was sharin' my bed. But I guess a bastard can come from the hilltop as well as the alley."

"I'll leave when I get good an' God-damn ready," Micah snarled, advancing on her.

"Suit yourself," Fancy said, reaching behind her and taking something from the Negro.

A stick, Micah thought, taking another two steps before he realized Fancy was holding a shotgun whose barrel had been sawed off to little more than the length of a pistol. "Now, Fancy . . ."

"But if you stay here, you stay as a gelding."

His bowels tightening, Micah froze in his tracks. He wanted to wring Fancy's neck, but both barrels were aimed right below his belt and her finger was tight on the double trigger. Slowly, his hands came up and he backed away. "Okay. Okay, I'm going. Don't you do something you'll regret now, Fancy."

"I won't." The ugly double barrels didn't so much as waver. "Not for one second, Micah."

If she were going to shoot, she would have already. Micah made himself relax and shrugged nonchalantly. There was always the warehouse and Solange, both of which would do, especially since Fancy had begun to be a pain. Without another word, he turned around and left.

Before he was through the door, the Negro piano player had begun to play.

CHAPTER 18

Four o'clock, a little after. Celia had spent the last three hours helping Lynna, now rode down Crawford on the way home. A cool bath and a nap awaited her, after which she'd eat and prepare for the night's ride, which she had so far refused to think about in detail. Daydreaming, she didn't notice Rafe's carriage parked in front of her house until she was almost around the corner. For one brief second she was glad he was there, and then as quickly knew she couldn't face him. Fighting the mare, who was anxious to get home, she turned left down Monroe, made the block, and then turned into the circular drive in front of the Hampsteads' shuttered estate.

Carson and Felicity Hampstead had vacated their property almost a year earlier and shipped out of New Orleans aboard a Dutch freighter bound for France. The gaping holes in the front of their house and an enormous crater in the side yard attested to the wisdom of their decision to leave. In the year that had passed, the front gardens had grown wild and the lattice-work tunnel covering the center of the drive provided ample concealment from where she could watch for Rafe's departure.

Slow minutes passed, and then suddenly there was movement in front of her house, and she saw Rafe walking with brisk, even strides to his own carriage. Resolve melted: The impulse to see him face to face was impossible to deny. She had to talk to him once more just in case anything went wrong later, even if she had to lie to him. Hadn't she been lying to him all along? Terrified that she'd miss him, Celia laid the whip to her mare and guided the animal back onto Crawford, then proceeded straight ahead as if she were just coming back from Lynna's.

"Just in time," Rafe said as she pulled to a stop beside his carriage. "I was afraid I wouldn't see you until much later, so I took a chance on dropping in. Immelda said you'd gone to the Hays's?"

He trusted her so completely! If only she could tell him. Tell him everything. But then he'd never let her go, and she'd never get the chance to redeem herself in her own, even if in no one else's eyes. "What a day. We made sausage and washed every sheet and curtain in the house. I think I'm bushed. Were you here long?"

"Half an hour, maybe." Rafe helped her down from her carriage and yelled for Tobias to come get the mare. "Is something wrong?"

"I . . . I . . ." Celia's stomach was filled with butterflies and she felt dizzy. Not sure what was happening, she leaned on Rafe's arm for support. "I guess I did more than I thought. Or too much sun." She felt her cheeks flush and the inside of her skull seemed light and airy, awhirl and unsettled.

"Come on, let's get you into the house."

"If I could just drink something, maybe. Lie down for a minute . . ."

Rafe helped her up the steps. Immelda opened the door at the first knock. "Tobias on his way . . . Lan' sakes, girl, what's the matter with you?"

"Nothing." Celia gulped, then swallowed. "Just a bit giddy in the stomach."

"Get some brandy," Rafe ordered Immelda, helping Celia inside. "Something cool, too. Tea, sugar water, whatever. I'll get her up to her room."

Immelda hurried off to the rear of the house. Rafe scooped Celia into his arms and started up the stairs. "Good Lord," Celia protested. "I'm not that sick."

"Maybe, maybe not," Rafe said, not stopping. "Doesn't matter."

"Do you know how silly this makes me feel?"

"Sorry, but I've always wanted to carry you upstairs. Helpless maiden, strong and stalwart gentleman, right?" he quipped, joking to cover his very real concern.

The hall was shadowed and cool in contrast to the bedroom. Rafe deposited Celia on her bed and pulled the drapes, then went back to sit by her. "Better?" he asked gently, smoothing a wisp of hair from her forehead.

"Rafe?"

"Yes."

Her eyes swam. Anything might happen. Quicksand, a snake, a trigger-happy soldier who shot first and asked questions later. The idea of not seeing him again was more than she could bear. "Will you kiss me?" she asked in a tiny voice.

The bed creaked . . .

Much as it had the night before and the night before that, Celia thought, the memory of his body so strong she could almost feel him in her.

. . . And he leaned toward her. Slowly, her arms rose to circle his neck and pull him to her in an ardent, furious kiss. The taste of him!

The man smell! His touch kindled a warmth that spread from his hand to the pit of her stomach, to the emptiness between her legs, to her heart where the fear lodged . . .

So be it, my love, Celia cried silently. *So be it.* This kiss to last, to remember you by, for you to remember me by . . . just in case. "I . . . I want to tell you," she stammered as their lips parted, "I want you to know . . ."

"What?" he asked. He smoothed the hair at her temple. His thumb brushed the corner of his mouth. "Tell me what?"

Courage failed her. She couldn't tell him the truth. "I love you, Rafe," she whispered, substituting that truth for the more dangerous one. "I'm glad you came to me Sunday night and last night."

Rafe bent, kissed one breast, then the other, kissed her neck and, lightly, her lips. "Tonight, too, Celia," he promised, "as soon as I can."

"No," Celia said, a touch too quickly.

"No?"

A reason! Her brain whirled, grasped at the single most plausible excuse she could think of. "It's—" How many women had used this excuse over how many years for how many reasons? And how many men had unquestioningly accepted? It was a lame substitute for the truth, but all she could think of. "—My time," she explained. "Maybe if I just . . . slept. . . ."

Incredibly, he laughed. "Ah, Celia! Christ, but I love you. And you were embarrassed to tell me?" The laughter faded and his face grew serious. "Listen to me. You don't have to be embarrassed to tell me anything, do you hear? Anything, because I love you, remember?"

"Yes." She took his hand, kissed his fingertips. "I remember." She was so frightened. If she failed, if she was killed or found out . . . "You'll remember, too?"

"Of course," Rafe said, surprised that she should ask. He kissed her fingertips in return. "You'll be all right?"

Celia nodded, but couldn't meet his gaze.

"Tomorrow, then. Sometime after noon. You'll be here?"

Her eyes closed, and she could feel the tears welling behind the lids. "Yes," she whispered, praying this too would not be a lie, the final lie. "I'll be here."

Rafe's lips brushed her forehead. The bed creaked as he rose. His boots thudded softly in the rug, clicked on the bare wood, then on the stairs.

Alone, Celia sat on the edge of the bed and brushed the tears from her eyes. Immelda entered a moment later with a tall glass of tea garnished with fresh mint and a china plate holding three cookies.

Celia waved the refreshments aside and bowed forward, cupping her face in her hands.

"Honey?" Immelda whispered, her round wide eyes reflecting worry. "Miss Celia?"

"Oh, Immelda!" Celia shuddered, fought back the tears, swallowed, and exhaled slowly. Under control, she reached out and took one of the cookies, nibbled, and made a wry face. "That is the worst thing I have ever tasted!"

"Ain't it, though?" Immelda chuckled, relieved at her mistress's change in mood. "It's amazin' what a body can't do with pea meal an' molasses."

"Ummm." A faraway look came into Celia's eyes for a moment.

"You sure you ain't right 'nuff sick, honey?" Immelda asked, now thoroughly confused.

"Yes. Very sure." The look faded and was replaced by one of determination. "There's no other way, no other choice if I want to live with myself."

"Honey, you—"

"I'm going to take a bath and then a nap. Whatever's for supper, I want it at nine. Tell Tobias to have the bay mare ready for a hard ride at ten." Her mind made up, she began to strip. "And, oh yes. I'll be wearing my special suit. See that it's ready, Immelda."

Horrified, the black woman stared at her mistress. "You can't," she whispered, shocked. "Them Yankees'll . . . That's crazy, Miss Celia honey. You *crazy!*"

"Crazy?" Celia asked, considering the thought. A slow smile crossed her face and she inspected herself in the mirror, as if seeing herself for the first time. "Maybe I am," she conceded, "but then again, maybe I'm finally sane, only nobody can tell the difference."

"Tell me you love me," Solange cooed, rubbing her naked leg along Micah's thigh.

"Would you believe me?"

"Don't be cruel to me, Micah," she pouted. "I love you."

Micah twisted his fingers in her hair. "Prove it," he said, jerking her head back.

"You're hurting me."

He could see the pulse beat in her throat. Micah thought of wild beasts, of wolves that tear the throats of their prey, and pictured doing that to Solange. Hot, insatiable Solange. He ran his hand down her arm, down her side, along her thigh. Ten blocks away at the Corinth Street Surgery, Tom Stewart was cauterizing a leg stump, his boots slipping in the blood, his ears ringing to the bedlam of groans and shrieks and the rasp of a bone saw at the next table.

Solange lifted her leg, placed her foot next to Micah's. He raised onto his elbow and traced a line up the inside of her thigh to part the tight brown curls and find the pink flesh, the moist, engorged lips of love. His fingers stroked, probed, and teased. Solange's mouth stretched tight over her bared teeth. Her hair still held tight, her legs forced apart, she writhed like a demon chained. Micah lowered his mouth to her breast. In his mind he saw the contemptuous Fancy forcing him from her place at gunpoint. Damn Fancy, he thought. Damn Miss High-Handed Celia Bartlett. And Solange? . . . Damn her as well.

Now I'm going to hurt you, he thought, and bit down hard.

No one heard Solange's scream. Nor, moments later, her whimpered pleas for more as he drove into her with increasing ferocity. Never had her need been so great. Never had she been so driven. Not until an hour later as, dressing, she noticed the teeth marks on her breasts, did she realize that he had hurt her this time more than pleased her. Carefully, she wrapped a bit of cloth torn from her petticoat around her breast so the blood wouldn't stain her dress, and told herself that every man had his moments of brutality. That was, quite simply, one of the things that made him a man.

"We have to get away," Micah said in that deep throated, fuzzy voice that meant he was satiated.

"We?" Solange brightened. She ran to him, wrapped her arms around his waist and buried her face against his spine. "We! *Mon amour!*"

"But need money first."

"We will have each other!"

"That will pale, Solange." Absentmindedly, he patted her hands. "For both of us."

"But how can you be so cruel?"

"I'm not cruel. I'm practical."

Solange pulled her gown up over her breasts. "Money would be nice," she mused.

Micah laughed, turned around, and lifted her chin with one finger. Her mouth was as red as smeared cherries. "Your husband?" he asked, leaning to kiss her.

"Wouldn't part with one cent," Solange answered, returning his kiss and then going on. "Not that he has much to begin with. Too often he accepts something foolish—a chicken, produce, even hardware for payment. But what about your father?"

"Father?" Micah dropped to the bed, lay with his hands behind his head. "You must be joking."

"He has money," Solange said with a typically gallic shrug. "Everyone knows that. But not everyone knows where he keeps all this money. Perhaps only his son?"

"Yeah," Micah said, his voice turning ugly. "His son." The notion was inconceivable. Almost. He knew the wall safe was hidden behind a portrait in the study, that the combination, if Nathaniel had changed the old one, could be found in a secret drawer in the desk. But even if he were to commit such a brazen act, where could he go with an army of besieging Federal soldiers encircling the city? Unless, of course, the city were to surrender. A man might make a break in the ensuing confusion. A diversion might be helpful, of course. Cairo and the others . . .

"A penny for your thoughts," Solange said, kneeling at his side and running her hand across his chest.

"A penny? Ha! I was thinking of real money," Micah replied.

But not just yet. Patience. There was the rub. Micah had never mastered the art of patience. Perhaps, though, it was time to learn.

Nine thirty. Dark. Most people retiring to caves for a few hours' sleep before what had become the nightly shelling. Too early for the looters. Not expecting anything, Rafe's Home Guard still relaxed. The perfect time.

Celia pulled on her boots, stood, and let Immelda help her into the specially made uniform coat. "I still say this is powerful dangerous," the black woman chided, not yet willing to accept the fact that Celia was going out.

"And staying in Vicksburg is safe?"

"We stays in the cellar like every other night, it sure is."

Further argument was a waste of time. Celia buttoned her coat, gray side out, and checked herself in the mirror. "Which is why that's where I intend to be in a few hours. You worry too much, Immelda." She pulled on her hat and made sure it covered her hair. "Look natural?"

"'Pears like, yes." Immelda grumped. "An' if they starts shootin' early tonight?"

"I'll take my chances like anyone else. Speaking of which—" She crossed to her desk, took out a packet and an envelope. "The envelope," she explained, tucking it under her pillow, "is for Rafe in case I don't get back. And this," she handed the packet to Immelda, "is for you and Tobias."

"Now, honey . . ." Immelda protested.

"No. It's yours."

Immelda stared uncomprehendingly at the packet.

"There's a thousand dollars in Confederate money and—"

"A thousand!" Immelda whispered, shocked.

"And another thousand, half in bills and half in gold, of U.S. money. I know Papa gave you your freedom papers a long time ago, so money is all I can give you. If I'm not back by morning, use it, do you hear?"

"But Miss Celia!"

"I don't have time for this, Immelda. Neither do you. Now, listen to me. The letter to Rafe explains everything. He's a good man and so's his father. You and Tobias can stay at their house until Vicksburg's back to normal and the war's over. When it is, use the money to build with. Here or in the North is up to you."

"Oh, lawd, lawd!" Immelda looked totally stricken. "Ain't there nothin' I can do or say? Ain't there nothin'?"

"Yes," Celia said, pulling on her cape. "You and Tobias can leave right now on those errands, and," she smiled, putting on a brave face and hugging the weeping black woman, "just in case, you can say good-bye."

CHAPTER 19

Strange how things worked out. One minute you were a well-dressed, well-to-do young man with a glowing future, the next little more than a wharf rat with no more future than a penny cigar. Well, not exactly a minute, Anthony thought, adding up the months since the beginning of the war, even if it sometimes seemed that way. Funny, too, how a man changed inside. Would he have guessed, even two years ago, that he was capable of killing a man? With a gun, perhaps, and at a distance, but with a knife, close enough to hear the last sigh as life fled and feel the warm blood run over his hands? Not likely, and yet he had. More than once.

Anthony seldom thought about these things because it was easier not to think. It was enough to know he was playing an important part in maintaining the integrity of the Union, and in ridding the world of the scourge of slavery. Never again would he or anyone else have to witness the castration and lynching of another human being.

So it was that Anthony Rutledge lay in wait and watched to make sure that nothing went awry. The shell-ravaged Cutter mansion was a perfect vantage point. Half destroyed—the roof was gone and the interior had been fire gutted—no one was likely to venture inside at night for the simple reason that it might collapse at any moment. Best of all, the view of the Bartlett grounds from any of three upstairs windows was virtually unobstructed. High overhead, visible through the naked rafters, he watched the stars brighten. Nearly ten, he thought, checking the watch his father had given him on his eighteenth birthday. Any minute, now, if dear cousin meant what she had said that afternoon.

A faint, out-of-place noise, startled him. Anthony rolled onto his side with his back against the wall and drew his revolver. The noise stopped, started again. Favoring his leg and being careful not to silhouette himself against the gaping hole that had once been a window, Anthony stood and limped quietly toward the door. A rustle of paper, a soft scratching sound, a boot inadvertently brushing against a board? Anthony inhaled and held his breath. Revolver ready, he stepped into the hall just in time to see a rat dive for and disappear down the stairs.

A false alarm. Anthony exhaled slowly, hurried back to the window, and squinted through his spyglass, sweeping slowly along the side of Celia's house all the way to the rear gate where the horse was still tethered. Damn. Not gone yet, at five minutes after ten. He flexed his knee and winced. It didn't hurt as much as it had that morning. He might even have been tempted to chance the trip himself in another day or two. God knew he didn't relish sending Celia, but the information was too damned important not to be transmitted immediately.

Which was why he couldn't stop worrying. Celia had been acting strangely. Moody and sarcastic, he felt she was wavering dangerously close to the brink of rebellion. But what could he do except watch and wait and hope to hell she rode and found Powell and delivered the warning about the cap shipment? Not a damned thing, he thought sourly. Not one single, God-damned thing. Silent as the night sky, Anthony limped to the next window and, mindful of glass splinters, rested his elbows on the sill and returned to the task at hand, oblivious to the fact that he was not alone in his vigil.

Celia examined the image in the mirror. Gray cap and cloak, smoke gray tunic and trousers. "Hawkmoon," she said, her voice barely a whisper.

Downstairs, she heard the front door close. Immelda and Tobias were gone. She was alone. Quickly, she set to work. Her mother's jewels went in the long thin pouch she'd sewed in the lower hem of the cloak. Her father's money belt, the one he'd used years earlier when he was a young man, went around her waist under the tunic. Packed with fifty one-ounce gold coins, some bills, and drafts on a bank in New York, the belt weighed well over five pounds. She bore the weight gladly: no one she knew of other than Anthony had gotten out of or into Vicksburg for the last month, and while she had few doubts about escaping, she had to be realistic about her chances of returning. For the same reason, she carried spare clothing and a two-day supply of pea bread and jerked mule meat in a lightweight saddlebag. Just in case.

"Good-bye," Celia whispered to the walls of her youth. "I'll return. Somehow . . ."

Her black leather high-topped riding boots beat a swift tattoo down the hall and backstairs of the unanswering house. Everything was accounted for. Immelda and Tobias would be seen abroad and therefore unimplicated should their mistress be caught or disappear forever. The letter to Rafe, leaving out Micah's involvement but bluntly explaining her life as a spy, lay on her pillow. The money belt was a welcome pressure around her waist. Candles cut short to burn out before midnight glowed through the cracks in the closed shutters: passersby would think nothing out of the ordinary.

The garden was quiet until she stopped to think, and then the broken, vine-covered walls could barely contain the tumult of happier days. Grimly determined, Celia shut out the sounds and hurried to the rear gate where Tobias had tied the bay mare, her best night-riding horse. Nothing stirred. She tied on the saddlebags and made sure the rope and machete hanging from the front of the saddle were easily accessible. She checked the street and found it empty. The time for nostalgia had ended. The time to ride had come. Swiftly, Celia led the mare into the street, mounted, and rode away. The sound of her passing had only just faded when a figure detached itself from the broken side wall and hurried off into the night, unnoticed by Celia or by Anthony Rutledge.

Nathaniel Lattimore sat in *his* chair in *his* parlor and would not budge for the devil himself.

"Why?" Rafe demanded. "Why? I know it takes effort, but why for once in your life can't you be reasonable?"

"Pity," Nathaniel said, sipping the strong black coffee one of his servants had just brought from the kitchen. He made a wry face. "Work hard all my life, build an estate to be reckoned with, and still can't get decent coffee. Chicory! Cajun brew!"

Rafe's face was turning red. "Coffee is not the issue here."

"I know. Chicory is."

"You can't stay here again, damn it!"

"This is my home. If you think for one minute I'll let some infernal Yankee gunboat drive me underground, you're wrong." Nathaniel set down his cup, picked up and opened his Bible to the center section where the family lineage for seven generations was penned. "To my son, Nathaniel," said the inscription at the top of the first page. Son. Nathaniel didn't think of himself as a son anymore. Hadn't for years. Thought of himself as a father. Should have been thinking of himself as a grandfather, damn it, if Rafe would get busy the way a son . . . That word again. Nathaniel looked up at Rafe, his little boy become a man, but still a son. Where had the years gone? It wasn't fair, damn it. What bitter amusement must God derive from watching humanity creep relentlessly from crib to grave?

"You're not even listening to me, are you?"

"Of course I am. But you tend to repeat yourself, and the message pales in the repetition."

"Father," Rafe said. He spoke slowly and clearly in the hope that, somehow, the words might bear more weight. "We've been bombarded for two nights in a row. There's no reason to expect we won't be bombarded again tonight. The shells fall where they will—here, there, everywhere. Sunday night the center of town took the brunt. Last night the north end. That leaves the south end and the east side. Either way, there's a damned good chance that—"

"Then what are they waiting for?"

"What?" Rafe asked, exasperated.

"What are they waiting for? It's after ten. Why haven't they begun?"

"Jesus, but you're stubborn! How the hell do I know why they haven't begun? Maybe they're taking time over brandy and cigars. Maybe they're dawdling over coffee. Maybe they're swabbing down the damned decks, and maybe, just maybe—"

"This is my house."

"—They're trying to give stubborn old mules like yourself time to seek shelter!"

"I stay here."

Rafe threw up his hands. "And if a ten-pound explosive shot falls through the roof?"

"I'll die in bed. *My* bed. Because that's where I intend to be." Nathaniel stood and patted Rafe on the shoulder. "Good night."

"I won't give up," Rafe warned.

"And I won't give in. That's the way it is with us Lattimores."

A black girl in her early teens appeared in the doorway. "Mistuh Rafe?"

"What is it, uh?"

"Lucy, suh. A man to see you, suh. Says it's powerful 'portant."

Rafe sighed in resignation. "Okay. Tell him I'll be right there. And as for you," he bristled, "we'll talk about this later."

"You'll talk alone, then," Nathaniel replied, starting for the side door. "I'll be asleep."

Cantankerous, single-minded, mule-brained old man, Rafe thought, trying to think of a new tactic as he walked down the hall. Might as well try to talk to a— He drew up sharply, then hurried the last steps to the door where Matt Broussard waited. "What the hell are you doing here?" he asked, irritated at finding his orders being disobeyed.

"I watched as long as there was something to watch," Matt answered quickly. "And then I seen something I figure you oughta know about."

"What?"

Matt took off his cap and twisted it in his hands.

"Well? Speak up. Someone tried to sneak in?"

"No, sir. Someone snuck out."

Rafe frowned. "You've lost me, Matt."

"Sorry, sir. I was watchin' like you told me, makin' sure none of them looters could hit Miss Bartlett's house. Nary a cat could of slipped past me. I been huntin' since I was six and know how to keep a watch. Ain't no one went in that house, but someone did come out. Them old niggers first, an' then, a half hour later, a soldier, looked like, I thought at first. Yessir. A Rebel soldier ridin' a bay mare."

A bay mare. The first tinge of alarm. "What do you mean, looked like? A soldier or not?"

Matt took a deep breath. "I think it was Miss Bartlett," he blurted. "Kind of dressed up."

"You're mad," Rafe said, not letting himself believe. "Or blind."

"I'm tellin' you what I seen," Matt huffed with youthful indignation. "Not much I can do about it if'n you think I'm a liar."

"Now wait a min . . . No. I didn't mean that. I don't think you're a liar." Rafe's mind whirled and tried to make sense of what he'd just heard. Matt had a keen eye and sense to spare. Still . . . "It's just that I . . . find it a little hard to believe . . ." A bay mare. Looked like a soldier? "You must've seen someone else. Hardly Miss Bartlett . . ."

"You want me to go back an' check? There was lights burnin'. Somebody ought to be there."

"No!" Rafe pulled his watch and checked the time, pasted a false smile on his face. "Tell you what," he said, a little too heartily. "It's well after ten and I need to get down to headquarters. You go on ahead, and I'll stop by there on my way. Probably just a horse thief after some fresh meat. Or a friend. After all, you didn't hear any sort of commotion, did you?"

"No, sir, but I could've sworn—" Matt scratched his head and replaced his cap. "You sure you don't want me to come along?"

"Yes. I'd rather you get on down to headquarters and tell that lieutenant that I'll be along in a half hour or so."

"Yes, sir!" Matt saluted and retrieved his rifle from where it leaned against the porch rail. "The garden gate, Mr. Lattimore. That's where he left by."

"Thanks," Rafe said, and "Thanks" again, more to himself, as Matt's distinctive footsteps faded into the night.

A bay mare. Looked like a soldier. "My time of month," she had said, which was a perfect excuse if he had ever heard one. One thing more, he remembered. Micah had also claimed, once in drunkenness, to have seen Celia riding alone at night. And if Micah's accusation could be taken as just another aspect of his jealousy, no such motive applied to Matt.

Still, he refused to believe. Coincidence, he decided, casting doubt aside. Coincidence and nothing more. Two nights in a row they had made love. Two nights in a row they had sworn their love. And then she should ride off to someone else? That Celia could be guilty of such treachery was inconceivable. She was home, he told himself, his footsteps quickening as he walked to his horse. In bed asleep, he assured himself as he tightened the cinch and mounted. Home, alone, asleep, and safe. Home, alone, asleep, and safe.

The gelding's shoes struck sparks as it hit the cobblestone street at a gallop and headed toward an empty house.

Lynna and Jonathan Hays's house was marked by a faint glimmer of light. Celia paused for one last fleeting moment to stare at the warm distant gleam that meant home and hearth and love, and then rode down the long hill that led to the bottoms. She had known there were soldiers in abundance here, but was totally unprepared for the hundreds of civilians who, recognizing uncontested and safe ground, had chosen to encamp on the fringes of Vicksburg rather than live in caves and endure the nightly bombardments.

Stealth would have aroused suspicion. Riding slowly but boldly, playing the part of one of the multitude of boy messengers, Celia stopped frequently to ask the whereabouts of a nonexistent captain who, she said, she had been ordered to find. Not one person stopped her. The civilians had learned not to question the military, and the military couldn't conceive of anyone wanting to brave the Union lines.

Only when the fires thinned did she begin to avoid encounters. The ground became soggy. Her pace slowed as the trees thinned and the safe paths became more tortuous. Tall stands of cane in clumps broke the open, marshy land across which she had to ride wholly unconcealed. Celia dismounted at the edge of one stand of cane and disrobed, then turned her clothes blue side out and dressed again. When she had buttoned the last button and replaced the gray cap with a black cap, she was to all appearances a Federal horse soldier.

"Who goes there?" a voice called.

Celia paused, caught her breath, and waited until her breathing was even. The accent was Southern. Whoever had called was probably a picket on advance, lonely and frightened of the dark. She nudged the mare's flanks.

"Hold up!"

She ignored the voice this time. If she couldn't see him, she doubted he could see her. When the next sentry called, he was too far away to understand and she dared to hope the Confederate lines were behind her.

Night and night sounds. The gurgle, thump, and sounds of the unseen, the soughing breeze in the dark tree line ahead, causes the hair to stand rigidly on the back of the neck and prickles the flesh. Dank odors, old as the earth, stir long dormant fears. Shadows hide mythical beasts that gnash their teeth and wait for the unwary. Celia stopped the bay mare at the edge of the swamp, then edged the animal on. Twenty yards later, already deep in the vast lostness, she stopped again, this time to picture in her mind the long ago days of exploration when her father, lacking a son, had led his daughter into the emerald gloom. There he had taught her the look and feel of solid land, the winding variations in natural paths, and the way of the wetlands. There, too, she had learned that the safe negotiation of swamps and sinuous, sluggish bayous is as much an ingrained sense as a skill. And that all the skill in the world brings only trouble without the accompanying sense.

"Come along, Celia. There's nothing in the dark that wasn't there in the daylight." Her father's words. And, "Don't try to see. A horse's eyes are better than yours in the dark. You must have that faith."

The darkness deepened as the cypress blocked the faint starlight that had earlier lit her way. No more wanting to blunder into bog or quicksand than her rider, the mare's ears pricked forward, and she slowed to a cautious walk. They entered a cloud of mosquitoes. Tiny silken wings assailed Celia's face, tickled her nostrils, sang a maddening single note in her ears. Celia draped a gauze mosquito bar over her hat and slapped at the few insects trapped inside. More attacked her hands and wrists, found their way inside her tunic. Her only defense against them was to wrap her cloak completely around her. The mosquito bar hindered her breathing and the cloak became unbearably warm. There was nothing to be done but grit her teeth and continue in the blind and fervent prayer that all things came to an end.

The mare stumbled and surged onto a hummock. Vines plucked at Celia's cloak, which she was forced to open so she could wield her machete.

The rush of nightwings, the screech of an owl. A splash nearby in the turgid water, followed by a careful descent and the slosh of hooves in swamp mud. And then the long, eerie passage in a tunnel of blackness.

A slight breeze drifted down through the cypress cover. Celia looked up, saw her first star in fifteen minutes and, against the faintly lit night sky, the ghostly sway of Spanish moss high in the trees. The mare paused, tried to turn back to the high ground, and skid away from something in the water. Frightened and skittish, she reared and almost fell over backward. Celia shifted her weight forward and pulled back sharply on the reins until the pain of the bit was a worse threat than the unseen danger.

The mare calmed and, after a moment's urging and a swift kick, relented and moved forward. The water deepened, and Celia lifted her feet. A spider web tugged at the veil over her face. Then she knew the worst was past, for she could sense the ground slowly sloping upward. Within minutes, the mare had found dry land again, and shortly thereafter, the cypress growth ended and the sky opened up overhead.

Celia reined to a halt, tried to figure out where she was. Big Bayou ran from the northeast to the southwest, and emptied sluggishly into the Mississippi. The Warrenton Road ran roughly parallel to Celia's path, which was almost due south, and lay to her right. If her calculations were correct, the Big Bayou bridge should have been somewhere between a half mile and a mile to her right.

A less cautious rider might have struck out for the road right then, but Celia decided the danger of being discovered by the wrong people was too great. A hundred trails led across the bayou, any one of which would branch to the right sooner or later and eventually lead her to the Warrenton Road south of the bayou. Nudging the mare in the ribs, she descended into the vegetation-choked bed and searched for the first trail.

Nothing there in the dark that wasn't there in the daylight. They found a trail, took it. Hal Bartlett had loved the bayou for its silence, for its age-old solitude. A bayou was the wisdom of the world, virgin for the most part, untainted by the mark of humanity. A bayou was holy, and in spring it was paradise. Bayous teemed with life. Crayfish, frogs, raccoons, opossums. A hundred species of birds. Carnivores, wolves and large cats, bears, it was said, in the old days. A veritable jungle of plant life exploded from every square inch of exposed ground. Grasses beyond number, mosses, and fungi. Flowers with petals like jewels opened opal and roseate, amethyst, sapphire, and pale emerald. The air was heavy with the perfume of dank earth, the musk of animals, the sweet aroma of flowers, the cloying weight of fecundity and death, hand in hand.

The trail ended at water's edge. Celia dismounted, inspected the broad, shallow central stream whose sluggish flow could not be discerned, and at last led the mare forward. Thick mud underfoot sucked at her boots. The water crept up to her knees, then her thighs, then her hips. The mare snorted in alarm and fought the bit. Celia tripped on a submerged branch, almost screamed when she thought it was a snake, but then recovered quickly when she realized her fear was feeding the mare's.

Another fifty yards. At no other time during her brief journey had she been so totally vulnerable. There was no moon, true, but the starlight was bright enough to silhouette her clearly against the water. At last she felt the water falling past her thighs and knees, and then she was on dry ground once again. All business, she dumped her boots and jammed them back on her feet, then stood stock still to listen.

Insect noise. The flat splash of a jumping fish. The rustle of an animal pushing through the underbrush. The whisper of wings passing overhead. We are the hawks of night . . . The struggle never ceased.

But enough of that, she chided herself, remounting. Only a few more miles, less than an hour. She turned the mare to her right and followed a trail paralleling the bayou. As she had guessed, she had to go no more than a half mile or so before the vegetation thinned and light streaks of cleared dirt marked the road. She stopped the mare and reconnoitered. No one. That was it, then. She had escaped from Vicksburg. Now all that remained was to convince Powell of a lie and, daring the virtually impossible, retrace her steps. Buoyed, she edged the mare onto the road and turned her head south.

"You can stay put, or you can get your head blowed off."

The voice had a Yankee accent and came out of the darkness. It belonged to a shadow she had mistaken for a clump of marsh briar. And the click of a rifle being cocked proved that it meant what it said.

CHAPTER 20

Colonel Powell took his time. He rolled the cigar against his upper lip, the better to enjoy the bouquet. He meticulously clipped the tapered tip. He wetted the outer leaves with his tongue. Finally, he held the cigar over the lantern chimney until the tobacco was hot enough to catch. Only then did he put it to his mouth and puff slowly until the whole end glowed evenly and then faded under a cover of gray velvet ash.

The aroma of tobacco blended maddeningly with that of real coffee, an untouched cup of which sat on the table in front of Celia. "You might as well drink it," Powell said, the cigar going to his head.

"You're sure you have enough to spare?" Celia asked sarcastically.

"Enough," Powell answered.

"Fresh coffee's nice after a meal."

Powell regarded her through a haze of cigar smoke.

"You do eat well, I hope."

"Well enough."

The coffee was tempting, but Celia was damned if she'd touch so much as a drop. "Beef?" she asked.

"Yes."

"Chicken?"

Powell nodded. "And pork, occasionally."

"Fresh vegetables?"

Another nod. "I can read the resentment on your face, my dear," Powell said tiredly. "You've made your point."

"Living off the land, they call it. General Grant appears determined to live up to Richmond's assessment of him. A man given to barbarity and ruthlessness."

"A man who moves relentlessly toward victory," the colonel amended.

"A man not overly concerned with committing atrocities. Does he enjoy plundering innocent farmers?"

"Not at all." Powell saw no reason to let his coffee get cold, and took a sip. "Neither is he willing to starve his own army."

Damn the coffee! Celia's mouth watered, but she shoved the cup away from her. "Those poor people—"

"Now, look here, my dear," Powell interrupted, beginning to get irritated. "There are no innocents in war. Especially here. Innocent
farmers, indeed! War has only victors and victims, and these particular victims brought this particular misery on themselves."

"Really? History may argue that."

"No doubt it will, and I might even agree. Then. But we are here
and now, and reality tells me I'd rather be dining on fresh beef, drinking real coffee, smoking a fine Kentucky cigar, and anticipating the
glass of sherry I shall drink before retiring than eating mule meat and
pea bread and enduring a nightly bombardment. I prefer to be a
victor."

Celia looked out the window. As far as the eye could see, the night
was alive with campfires, around which a well-fed army of siege lay
and took its ease. Count the fires, she thought. Add them, one plus one
plus one. The sum equals victory. "I didn't slog through four miles of
marsh and swamp and risk having, as the man who surprised me so
quaintly put it, my 'head blowed off,' just for the pleasure of your company or to hear your theory of victors and victims, Colonel," she said,
suddenly sick of the whole affair. "Do you mind if we finish our business?"

"My, my. Such a vitriolic nature ill fits one so young."

"War has no more sympathy for youth than it has for victims. Do
you mind?"

Powell's cigar glowed a baleful red. "Corporal!" he called.

A middle-aged man who looked more like a clerk than a soldier hurried into the room.

"Take this down, please." Powell rose, walked to a large map that
hung on an otherwise bare wall. "Well?"

"Within a week, a shipment of either one or two hundred thousand
percussion caps will be smuggled through the Union lines."

"What the . . . Damn!"

"Anthony learned about the shipment from a clerk in the quartermaster corps. I verified it Sunday night at a party that was attended
by some of the highest officers in Vicksburg." Celia's mouth was dry
and her heart beat wildly. The trip through the lines had been easy
compared to what would follow. "Command expects the shipment either on Saturday or Sunday night. Both nights should be relatively
quiet, and there will be no moon. If there are clouds Saturday night,
the shipment will be sent Saturday. If not, they will certainly try Sunday."

"Where?" Powell asked. "The same way you came out, right?"

"No. From the north."

Powell looked at the map, at Celia, and back to the map. "North? That's impossible! A rat couldn't sneak through there. The southern lines—"

"Are the obvious choice, except for two reasons."

"I find the north hard to conceive."

"Which is the first reason," Celia said, warming to her task and her tale. "Nobody in his right mind would try the north. Men with packs wouldn't stand a chance. But if they avoided the masses and went by water, and if even one of them got through?"

The clerk wrote furiously, paused and waited. "I see, I see . . ." Powell said. The clerk's pen scratched briefly. "And reason number two?"

"That's where they are, and no one wants to risk carrying them all the way around the city through country held by enemy forces."

"Which makes sense," Powell agreed. He tapped the map and handed a pointer to Celia. "Where and how?"

"You know about the *Cincinnati?*" Celia asked, moving to the map.

"Of course. An ironclad, the Confederates' last in this area. Docked up the Yazoo and destroyed on the nineteenth."

"Yes, a week ago tomorrow night. Before Grant's men destroyed the Confederate yards on the Yazoo, a picked group managed to spirit away certain supplies. Some were too heavy or bulky to be smuggled into town. Others, like the caps, aren't. They needed only to establish contact with the city before attempting delivery."

"You mean—?"

"One man, in once, out once, and back in. Who or when or how I don't know."

"Damn, damn, damn," Powell cursed. He puffed furiously on his cigar and at last jabbed a finger toward the map. "Where are they now? Maybe we can catch them before they get started. Lock the barn door before they get in, so to speak."

The pointer traced a heart-shaped outline on the map. "What we call the Delta," Celia explained. "The Yazoo River here, the Missis sippi here. Your map doesn't show it, but here is what they call the Old Bed or the False River, which is where the Yazoo used to be Over here, Flat Lake, here Channel Cat Lake."

Powell looked worried. "We don't have a better map of this area Corporal?"

"That's the best one, sir."

"Hell of a way to run an army." Powell snorted. "Well, go on."

He looked so worried, Celia thought jubilantly. One or two more "facts," and he'd be totally convinced. "I think—I more or less gath ered—that they've been holed up somewhere south of Flat Lake and within easy reach of Hart's Bayou. The caps are in large waterproofed boxes designed to float just under the surface of the water. I heard something about canteens. Anthony thinks they're either inside the boxes or lashed to the outside."

"Of course," Powell grumbled. "For buoyancy. And?"

"And so they swim for it. Go in at Hart's Bayou—" The pointer tapped the map once again. "Swim to the Mississippi and let the current carry them downstream. Earlier in the evening, men will row out from Vicksburg and place anchored lines in the river for the smugglers to catch and pull themselves to shore. An hour later . . ." Celia shrugged, handed the pointer back to Powell, and let him finish the thought.

"Hmmm." Powell stared at the map, ran a slow hand over a two day stubble of beard. "Anything else?" he finally asked abruptly.

"No," Celia answered. "That's all."

"I see. Very well, Corporal. If you'll write that up in triplicate, please."

"Yes, sir."

The corporal slipped quietly out of the room. Powell regarded the map a moment later, then poured fresh coffee for himself and Celia. "We went through this the last time we met," he said, handing her the cup. "You might as well drink it. I have no surprises for you this time."

Celia added honey to the coffee, sat back, and wished her clothes were dry.

Powell sat and propped his boots on the table. North, not south. A very bold idea, and probably as easy to execute as any other, especially if the material were already north of the city. If, of course, was the important word in that particular sentence. A conjectural word. One to raise doubts. If Celia had heard correctly in the first place, and if she wasn't lying in the second. He stole a glance at her as he sipped his coffee. She'd told her story well and without hesitation or the excessive confidence of a seasoned liar. The last information she'd given him, regarding the gully at the Big Black River, had been accurate and timely. Had she been a soldier, he would have recommended her for a commendation.

What else? It was true the *Cincinnati* had been destroyed six days ago, true that the makeshift Confederate yards on the Yazoo had been razed, and entirely possible that a small group had escaped into the wild and unmapped area dubbed the Delta. It was likewise true that delivery by water would be far easier than by land, even given the total control of the Mississippi by the Union Navy. One man camouflaged by a branch was a far different cry from a ship that could easily be spotted and blown out of the water.

The moments dragged. Celia finished her coffee and replaced her cup on the table. The ash on Powell's cigar drooped and fell to the floor. Curse Rutledge's knee, Powell thought, staring at his boot tip. Curse the complications brought on by a bunch of beaten Rebel riffraff who refused to admit defeat. If they'd just lay down their arms . . .

"Very well," he said abruptly. His boots hit the floor and he strode to a cabinet across the room. "I believe you." He took out a bottle of sherry and returned to the table. "And if we catch them, you'll have earned the undying gratitude of the men whose lives you've saved tonight. Will you celebrate with me?" he asked, bringing two glasses from a side table.

Success! Celia wanted to shout or laugh, but carefully maintained her poise and turned a tired face to her—yes, she thought—victim. "Celebrate what?"

"A job well done, of course. A difficult task completed." He poured two glasses and handed her one. "Not many men would have dared try what you did tonight, much less succeed."

"I suppose so," Celia said, suddenly drained. "Unfortunately, getting here was only half the game."

"Not necessarily," Powell disagreed, raising his glass. "Cheers. And congratulations, my dear."

Celia frowned and sipped her sherry. "I don't understand. Why not necessarily."

Powell drained his glass and poured himself some more. "Because you don't have to go back."

"Why ever not?"

"Because Vicksburg will fall within days, and I can't imagine what further information you could bring out that would make any difference." Powell puffed contentedly on his cigar. "If you want, I'll arrange for a gunboat to run past the city tomorrow, and passage up river to Saint Louis and eventually to Boston and your aunt's house, where this all began."

"And Anthony?" Celia asked, wondering how to decline this unforeseen offer.

Powell shrugged. "He's a resourceful young man. I imagine he'll either slip through the lines in a few days or just wait until the city falls. Either way, he's capable of taking care of himself."

The sherry was too sweet and contended with the coffee. Celia's stomach churned. All she wanted was fresh air and a chance to be away. She had made amends, had at least partially counteracted the harm done at the Big Black River. A little dizzy, she pushed the sherry aside and stood. "No," she said, unbuttoning her tunic.

"No?" Powell asked, incredulous. "No what?"

"No, I'm not going to Boston. I'm going back to Vicksburg."

"But that's—"

"May I borrow your office for a moment, Colonel? I need to change the color of this uniform back to gray."

"I don't understand."

"That I can't enter the city wearing Yankee blue?" Celia asked, obviously more distressed with each passing second. "Would you—"

"You can't be serious!"

The tears came unbidden and were real.

"There's an officer, a young officer, a captain, who I love. I stood at his side with my arm in his, and heard . . . and heard the information I brought you." The truth at last! How ineffably sweet to tell the simple, unvarnished . . . truth. She closed her eyes, swayed, and steadied herself against the table. "My father is dead, and life, as he and many who went before him have said, goes on. I believed and still believe that slavery is wrong, but I'm not at all sure that becoming a spy has helped free one black man or woman." She caught her breath and looked Powell directly in the eye. "I'm afraid I've played a fool, Colonel. A fool and a traitor. But I won't be a traitor to . . . this man. I want to go back. I want to be with him, no matter what happens next."

The cigar stank, the sherry was too damned sweet. Powell was sick of them both and of himself. "I can't allow it," he said so softly he was forced to repeat himself. "I can't allow it. I could do all the rest, but I can't send you back to what might be your death."

"How suddenly and touchingly thoughtful," Celia flared. Anger wiped her tears away and settled her stomach. "Well, I'll tell you what, Colonel Powell. I'm going to change clothes whether you leave the room or not." She fought her arms out of the tunic and threw it on her chair, then began unbuttoning her trousers. "And when I'm finished, I'll depart and hope we never meet again. When I do, you can leave me on my own, help me with an escort through your lines to the bayou, or have me shot!"

"Now, wait!" Powell held his ground while she pulled off her boots, then circled the table and backed toward the door when she started on her trousers. "Damn it, girl!"

Her pants unbuttoned, fully prepared to pull them down, Celia paused and faced him. "I'd like to get back before one. That's when the night's delightful bombardment starts, isn't it?"

Powell's face reddened.

"Well?"

"Okay! Okay!" Powell said, stalking out and slamming the cabin door behind him. "Corporal! Sergeant!" he shouted. "Where the hell is everybody, damn it?"

Celia turned her trousers gray side out, slipped into her boots. Footsteps and voices seeped through the door while she shrugged into and buttoned her tunic. By the time she reached the door, her cape was buttoned to her shoulders and her hat was firmly in place.

"Now look here, Hawkmoon . . . uh, Miss Bartlett," Powell began. He stepped aside as Celia bore down on him. "Damn it, girl! Stop, I say!"

Celia swept by and headed for her horse. Powell threw down his cigar and ground it into the dirt with his heel. "Damned impertinent female! Well, Sergeant?"

"Well, what, sir?" the sergeant asked, unsure of what was expected of him.

"Well follow her and catch up to her, you damned fool!" Powell roared.

"Yes, sir!" The sergeant started off, then stopped. "And then what?" he asked again, suddenly realizing he knew no more than he had before.

"Then . . . Well, shit!" Powell rubbed his chin and sighed heavily. His eyes felt gritty. He hadn't slept well for the past two nights and was tired as hell and would be up until damned near dawn making sure all the right people knew about the shipment of caps. It was a hell of a note. One hell of a note, and no damned way to run an army.

"Then do as she says, Sergeant," he finally said, turning and stalking back to his combined cabin and office. "Just do as she says."

CHAPTER 21

The Confederate sentry thought he heard something and cocked his rifle. The breeze had died. To his right somewhere in the dark stillness was a patch of relative silence where the insects had momentarily stopped their sawing, rasping tintinnabulation. The sentry's pores oozed sweat. He could taste salt on his upper lip. He heard his own heart thudding.

Bobcat? Wolf? Man? The insect noises increased to a more normal level. Whatever had been out there was gone. The sentry wiped his hands on his shirt, took his rifle off cock, and relaxed. Nothing important ever happened along this desolate stretch of swamp anyway. Getting nervous was a waste of time. Better to worry that some damned fool general would move him north or east, where the real action was.

Fifty yards past the Confederate picket, Celia sighed with relief but didn't allow herself the luxury of relaxation yet. That she hadn't spotted the sentry until he moved to cock his rifle worried her, for she was afraid she wouldn't see the next one until too late. Soothingly, she patted the mare's neck, stroked the soft pink velvet muzzle, and led the animal around a canebrake before mounting. Time had become very much of the essence, for not much remained before the nightly shelling began. *Silly*, Celia thought, riding low to minimize her silhouette: *this ride and all it entails, and I'm afraid of a random shell? Doesn't matter. Anything that gets me back to Rafe alive . . .*

Functioning came almost automatically. She was seeing the ride out in reverse. A steady, measured calm through the hovel encampments and families lost in hungered sleep, past the lines of patched tents where soldiers dreamed of food, and at last breaking into a tired gallop that the mare could barely sustain, past the Hays's farm, and into the outskirts of town. She had ridden fifteen miles and delivered her message in a little less than three hours, which wasn't bad considering the terrain she'd covered. Now she was tired and wanted only to go home.

The bay mare's pace picked up as they turned onto Clay Street, for the horse too was tired and smelled home. The first shell landed a half-dozen blocks away just as horse and rider turned into the garden gate on Clay Street. One o'clock, Celia thought, hurrying the mare to the stable. Quickly, she unsaddled, rubbed down, and turned loose the mare into a stall, gave her fresh water and an armful of hay. "I wish there were grain for you, baby," she crooned. "God knows you earned real food tonight."

Most of the candles had burned out, as she had planned. A dim glow, barely discernible, came from her room, but other than that the house was dark. Hurrying across the lawn, Celia took off the Rebel cap and shook out her hair. An explosion sounded nearer as she darted up the rear steps. She stopped in the kitchen for a fresh candle, lit it, and started down the hall. She'd sleep in the cellar, she decided, after changing her clothes and burning the ones she wore. And the letter to Rafe, of course. Before the clothes, before anything else, she'd feed the letter to the flames.

"Well, well. Nice trip?"

Celia stopped at the bottom of the stairs and whirled to see Anthony standing in the doorway to the sun parlor. "What are you doing here?" she hissed.

"I saw you leave, knew the black folks were gone, so came on in and helped myself to some food and a bed." He gestured to the sun parlor. "Nice couch, cousin. I slept like a babe until . . . Boom, boom," he said comically mimicking the explosions that came from the center of town. Hobbling, his knee stiff and swollen, Anthony advanced on Celia and circled menacingly behind her. "Silly of you to come back to this, of course. You . . . ah . . . did go, didn't you, cousin? Not just for a little ride around town? Sewing circle, maybe?"

"Of course, I went. Interestingly enough, the trip isn't nearly as difficult as I thought it would be."

"And you found Powell and told him about the caps?"

"Of course! What is this, Anthony? I'm not sure I appreciate . . ."

"In the second house on the right on the road to Warrenton after you crossed Big Bayou Bridge, right?"

"On the *left*. That almost got me in trouble. Luckily, I could pretend I was confused, and . . ."

A wolflike grin on his face, Anthony was looking right through Celia as if she didn't exist.

"Why, you bastard!" Celia swore. "You didn't trust me, did you? You had to trick me to make sure I . . ." She heard a slight noise behind her at the top of the stairs at the same time Anthony's head jerked upward. Celia whirled. "What are you—" *Oh, no,* she thought. *Oh, my God, no!* "—Looking at?"

A form at the top of the stairs loomed tall and terrible, the face indiscernible in the dim light. The form moved, descended. The stairs creaked at each silent footstep. One hand he held extended, and that hand held a piece of paper that Celia knew . . .

"Rafe?"

"No." His voice was somber. "Don't say anything."

"I—"

"This letter speaks for you." He held the paper above his head and crumpled it with one hand. "Eloquently and informatively. Quite . . . self-explanatory." He dropped the balled paper, which bounced down two steps and hung neatly balanced on the edge of a third. Rafe continued down the stairs, paused midway as Celia moved to intercept him.

"You have to understand," Celia said, her voice a desperate whisper. "You can't leave without hearing me out."

"I do hear you, Celia. Lies. I hear lies."

"I love you!"

"Why did you come back? If you hate us enough to spy on us, why in God's name, once you were out, did you return?"

"I love you!" was all Celia could think of to say. "I love you, Rafe."

"You lie!" Rafe stopped abruptly, looked beyond Celia to Anthony. "And who is—"

"Who I am doesn't matter," Anthony interrupted, pulling a revolver from inside his coat. "This gun's all the identification I need."

Rafe ignored the gun, rather studied the man and mentally erased the dirt and foul clothes and a handful of years. "Tony. Of course. Anthony Rutledge!"

"One and the same, my friend. Come to visit my fair cousin and your beautiful city." The revolver steadied on a spot between Rafe and Celia, ready to move instantly to either. "A most productive and enjoyable visit, I might add. One that, unfortunately, seems to have come to a sudden end. For us both, Celia," he finished, taking his cousin's arm.

"I'm not leaving, Anthony."

"Of course you are. Don't be a fool."

"A spy," Rafe said, as if he'd just then come upon the word for the first time. "Spy. So that's what you've come to."

"I prefer patriot," Anthony snapped. "You and your kind are bloody insurrectionists, Lattimore. You're rebels and deserve everything you get. No," he warned when Rafe descended a step. "Don't try any heroics, because Celia will verify that I won't hesitate to shoot. And with that racket going on outside, no one will be the wiser."

The bombardment had swollen to the same earth-shaking magnitude as on the preceding two nights. "Well if you're leaving, then leave!" Celia shouted above the din, "So the rest of us can go somewhere safe."

"Not so easily, cousin." Anthony waved the gun at Rafe. "He knows who I am now. And if we can't get out of town somehow, he has to die. You see how it is."

The house sounded like it was rattling itself to pieces.

"No!" Celia stood between Rafe and Anthony. "You kill him and you'll have to kill me, too."

"You think he won't?" Rafe yelled to Celia over the roar of an explosion.

"He does and he'll have to stay or else find his own way out."

Caught in an untenable position, Anthony wavered. Celia had been hovering on the brink of revolt ever since the meeting with Powell. If he killed Rafe, she would certainly inform on him if he didn't kill her as well. And yet how could he? His own cousin? Had he come that far? Of course, if it came down to her or him . . .

Rafe saw Anthony's dilemma and thought he knew how the question would be resolved if he didn't intervene. His main concern, no matter what crime she had committed, was Celia's life. "Look, Rutledge," he improvised, his brain racing. "She'll take you through the lines. She did it once and she can do it again. I'll go with you as far as I can without actually leaving myself, so you'll know I can't compromise you."

"Oh, no," Celia shouted above the incessant roar. "I'm not going out again."

"You damned well are!" Rafe disagreed. "Either that or he'll kill both of us, and I'm not about to have your life or death on my soul. Well, Tony? What'd'ya say? We have a deal?"

"You have a horse that'll carry me?" Anthony asked, aware that the mare Celia had ridden would be tired.

"You can ride mine. He's rested, and he's bigger and stronger than any of Celia's. Dangerous out there now, though. Sure you don't want to wait awhile?"

Celia looked up at Rafe, and was frightened by what she saw. The man she loved had undergone a complete transformation. His face was empty of emotion, and he stared at her and Anthony as if they were complete strangers and he was a puppet made of wood with button eyes.

"We go now," Anthony decided. "Where's your horse?"

Rafe pointed to the front of the house.

"Okay," Anthony yelled above the din. "Out the front door, then around the side to the stable. Celia, you walk with me, with Rafe in front of us."

Anthony searched Rafe, found the derringer and the Navy revolver, then gestured for Rafe to lead the way. The door opened to a blast of hot air from a nearby fire. Rafe's horse was trembling with fear but, soon calmed by Rafe's hand and voice, allowed himself to be led around the corner of the house and toward the stables.

The night was aglow with lurid firelight as the Union mortar fire rained down on the city. Rafe tried to figure out how much longer the bombardment would last. Fifteen minutes had been the time of firing the last two nights. How many minutes had elapsed since the first shell had fallen this night was a matter of conjecture, for he had lost all sense of time. If he could stall until the shelling ended, though, there would be men aplenty in the streets, and possibly a chance to turn the tables on Anthony after all.

An opportunity materialized sooner than expected when, just as they reached the stables, Rafe saw a figure dart in through the back gate and hurry toward them.

"Damn!" Anthony hissed, not sure of what to make of the peculiar lope. "Tell him to get out of here, whoever he is!" he told Rafe.

"Cap'n Lattimore? That you?"

Anthony raised his gun and took aim.

Jeopardizing the deal they had struck, as well as Celia's and his lives, Rafe reacted automatically.

"Matt!" he shouted, at the same time diving sideways to strike Anthony's arm. "Duck! Get help!"

Anthony fired high into the air and brought his revolver down to clip Rafe alongside the skull and stun him. Matt hit the ground rolling. By the time Anthony could aim again, Matt had disappeared behind Rafe's horse. Anthony saw legs, tried to crouch to fire under the horse but couldn't because his knee wouldn't bend. One to either side of him, Celia next to him. Anthony had no idea how badly off Rafe was, no idea of even who the one called Matt was.

"Cap'n?" Matt called, somewhere off to the side of the stable.

"He has two guns!" Rafe called, still in a daze but aware enough to roll into the shadows as he spoke. Sure enough, a pair of bullets dug into the dirt where he'd been lying. "Take your time. Wait for a good shot."

"I'll kill her!" Anthony shouted, grabbing Celia again. "Help me to the horse," he ordered her. "Now! I mean it!"

"No!" Celia said, and dropped like a stone, almost taking Anthony down with her.

At the same time, a shot roared out from the vicinity of the stables, and the gun Anthony had taken from Rafe flew out of his hand. The pain in his knee forgotten, Anthony cursed and took off running. Matt tried to grab the horse, but the animal, now thoroughly spooked, reared and ran away, simultaneously blocking Matthew's second shot.

"Who the hell was *he?*" Matt asked, as Anthony disappeared through the rear gate.

Rafe accepted Matt's helping hand, shook his head to clear the cobwebs from his brain. "Stay with her," he ordered, not bothering to answer, and raced off in pursuit.

Clay Street was deserted for the duration of the bombardment. Rafe burst through the gate just in time to see Anthony illuminated by an exploding shell. The spy's pace had slowed due to his bad knee, and it appeared he was heading straight down Clay toward the waterfront. Weaponless, Rafe followed him.

The ground shook. A building to the left took a direct hit, seemed to swell out, then slowly sag inward. Desperate, Anthony cut down Walnut to the heavily beamed shed at the corner, one of many such shelters throughout the city where men and animals could seek safety when necessary. Never more necessary than during the nightly bombardment, the shed was packed with mule-drawn caissons that had been delivering supplies to units all over the city when the bombardment started. Anthony ducked in the door around a half-dozen mules, and stopped in front of a team just under the edge of the roof.

"Hey!" the driver said, standing. "Wha'd'ya' think you're . . ."

Firing from point-blank range, Anthony shot him. The force of the bullet at such close range plucked the man straight out of his seat and sent him flying across the next wagon.

"What the hell!" the driver of the next wagon shouted as the body of his friend collided with him.

Anthony fought the mules, realized someone was firing at him, and fired back blindly. A mule screamed. A man cursed. Somehow, Anthony got the team into the street, but that was a mixed blessing because now he was clearly visible. Slugs whined around his legs and head. The reins had fallen, and he couldn't find them . . .

Rafe hit the shed about the same time Anthony was leading his stolen team from the other end. He could hear firing and cursing above the general tumult of the shelling, but little made sense until he reached the wagon next to the one Anthony had stolen. "What's going on?" he screamed at the driver.

"I don't know. Son of a bitch shot Harry an' took his team an' caisson. Now the damn fool's out *there* with a God-damn load a' powder!

One a' them mortar shells hits anywhere near to him, the crazy bastard's gonna go sky . . . Hey!"

There wasn't time to explain. Rafe grabbed the driver of the second caisson and pulled him from his seat just as Anthony finally got his team under control and started them down Walnut Street. The race was on. Neither man thought beyond the atavistic urges that drive men in battle. Anthony was fleeing blindly. Rafe pursuing just as blindly. Both men applied their whips with savagely vigorous strokes. Manes flying, barely under control, the terrified mules were more runaways than driven. The shelling was building to a crescendo, which meant it would soon end. Neither driver paid attention.

Pursued and pursuer seemed strung together by a piece of cable. The first caisson swerved to avoid a shell crater, and the second swerved moments later. Anthony kept mules to the far side of the street away from a burning building, and Rafe did likewise. Anthony turned right, Rafe somehow managed to follow him. Seconds later they found themselves heading down Clay Street toward the river again. This time Rafe wasn't going to be denied. His eyes fixed on Anthony, he whipped his mules into even more of a frenzy.

And as Rafe's whip fell for the third time, in the eternity of that small portion of a second when the leather tip arched and curled back on itself and made a satisfying small pop, the end of Clay Street erupted in his face. A blinding flash hit the night. A devastating concussion lifted Rafe out of the seat and sent him flying through the air. Slivers of wood filled the air like a million whirring deadly darts. Mortally wounded, the mules reared and fell back screaming into their own harness and caisson, streaming blood and entrails.

Rafe's arms, providentially raised at the moment of the explosion, took most of the splinters that otherwise would have struck his face. Rearing, the mules took the rest. Rafe felt himself flying and hitting, tumbling and skidding in the shell-churned earth, almost lost consciousness, and somehow managed not to. He found himself face down in the street. His face was cut, his uniform ragged from his slide. His forearms looked like pincushions. He crawled to his knees, vomited, and only then was hit with sickening realization that he had lost Anthony.

"You okay?" a soldier asked, running up and helping Rafe to his feet.

Rafe's legs started to give, he willed them to lock. He started to wipe his face with his sleeve, and only then noticed the fabric was full of splinters. "What?"

"C'mon. Run for it!" the soldier shouted, pushing Rafe ahead of him into a doorway, which was better protection than nothing.

Rafe tried to talk but his tongue felt thick and his jaw hurt. Zombielike, he sat propped against the doorway and pulled splinters out of his coat sleeves as the shelling gradually diminished. "Must've been carrin' a right good load a'powder," the soldier who had helped him out of the street said. "Durn caisson took a direct hit an' blew all ta hell over the place." He shook his head in wonder. "Ain't *never* seen the like. They'll be scrapin' the leftovers off'n the walls for days to come."

One of the mules was still screaming, but Rafe's ears rang so the sound seemed thin and very distant. Still dazed, it took a moment for him to realize that the broken, shattered pile of scrap in the middle of the street was the caisson he'd been riding. Luckily, it hadn't been loaded with powder, or the blast that obliterated Anthony would have set off his load as well. Someone was yelling something about shooting a mule. A gun fired, the sound ridiculously small compared to the rolling thunder that had only moments ago engulfed the city. The mule stopped screaming. Rafe staggered out of the doorway and walked uncertainly toward the hole. A few other soldiers stopped to stare at the crater, which was at least twice as large as any of the others.

"Jeee-sus!" one said, in a hushed whisper. He pointed at a chunk of horsemeat. "'At'ere's all that's left a' two mules, Bubba. Ah mean, *two* mules!"

"*Two* mules?" Bubba asked, not really believing. "Gaw-damn!"

Rafe saw their lips moving, turned away and saw, at his feet, what he assumed was one of Anthony's shoes. He reached down to pick it up, only to discover that it was smeared with a kind of gray slime. His stomach turning, Rafe stood and took a deep breath. When he was sure he wouldn't pass out, he kicked the shoe into the crater and covered it with dirt.

And that was the burial of Anthony Rutledge.

The material evidence of guilt is easily destroyed. Celia tossed the last piece of her uniform, the cap, into the roaring fire she'd built to consume the threads of her deceit. The pungency of burning wool stung her throat, the heat unbearable on a summer night. Gathering her gown around her, she fled the study and walked down the hall to the cooler, airier sun parlor. What time it was she had no idea. The clocks had chimed, she knew, but the passing of time meant little.

What matter an hour or two, a day or a week? Clocks were superfluous. Clocks were a waste of time.

A waste of time? she wondered, amused by the idea. She opened the sun parlor door and, glad for the cool darkness, felt her way to a wicker chaise in the hopes that she might, just might be able to doze a little before dawn. The hopes died abruptly when a match flared behind her and, in one of the windows, she watched Rafe light a lantern.

"I sent Broussard away," he said, rounding the bottom of the chaise to stand in front of her. His coat was missing, his shirt and trousers in tatters. What flesh was visible was streaked with blood.

Celia started to go to him, but quickly and wisely decided not to move.

"The boy was puzzled," Rafe went on, setting down the lantern on an end table. "I told him you'd been helping at one of the hospitals and didn't want to attract attention to yourself on the streets. No telling, after all, what might befall an innocent young lady out at night alone with ruffians out and about."

The sarcastic emphasis on innocence made Celia wince. "I don't expect you to understand," she began, "but—"

"Thanks. You have no idea how that lets me off the hook."

Celia closed her eyes. She hadn't expected this to be easy. "—But you might allow me to explain. Just a word or two in my defense?"

"A word or two?" Rafe walked to the wine cabinet, found the bottle they had opened together the night before and shared as they had shared their love. He poured the last of the wine into a single glass for himself. "You really think a couple of words would make a difference?"

"If you listened—*really* listened—they might."

Rafe snorted and then drank off half the wine.

Celia fought the urge to tell him about Micah, decided that she couldn't for Nathaniel's sake. "That's an absolute brilliant responsel" she flared, watching Rafe drink. "Give a disdainful snort to show how far above everything you are, and then drink something, as if either one helped in the slightest. Well, I'm sick and tired of it."

"Sick and tired of what?" Rafe snapped. He drank the last of the wine and, with a trembling hand, set the glass on the cabinet shelf.

"Men thinking that war is only for them."

"Well, it is, isn't it? You want to go out there and count all the women in the trenches? Count the women's names on the grave markers at Shiloh? Or anywhere else, for that matter?"

"They don't give the women graves any more than they give them uniforms. The men get the uniforms! The men get the graves! And what do the women get? To sew the uniforms? To weep at the graves? To raise more fodder for your stinking cannons?"

"I think you're mad," Rafe said quietly, drawing himself up. "Everyone knows that honor dictates—"

"Honor? And you think honor's just for men?" Celia interrupted, her voice deadly cold. "My father was an honorable man who didn't believe in your cause and tried, honorably, to remain aloof from the war. He died for his convictions. I tried to avenge his death in the only way open to me. For honor men died! For honor, I became a spy!"

"Oh, come on, Celia, no one killed Hal. You know that as well as I," Rafe lamely replied in the face of his own argument.

"Really?" Celia hissed. "How *do* you know? You weren't here, remember?"

"I didn't have to be here!" Rafe shot back. "There's a big difference between a man dying of a heart attack and a man getting killed. As big a difference as between a soldier and a spy. My God, Celia, we hang spies! That's one of my jobs. To turn you in!" He ran a hand through his hair, finally shook his head, and went on a little more calmly. "Hal knew the risks, Celia. He could have sold out at any time, moved North a rich man, and remained aloof from this whole bloody mess. But he didn't. And that doesn't mean I'm condoning plundering or beatings or anything to do with corn liquor patriots. All I'm saying is, that open *betrayal* of—"

"My father owned no slaves. My father decried secession. My father never voted for war. This was never his cause, nor is it mine!" Celia shrieked in Rafe's face. And then with deadly calm, emphasized each word. "*So what have I betrayed?*"

Rafe gripped her arms, drew her toward him and half off her feet. "Me!" he roared, his fingers digging into her flesh.

As suddenly, as if mere contact with her sapped his strength, Rafe's hands let go and dropped listlessly to his sides. "Stupid of me. Stupid," he mumbled, dropping into a chair. "I heard you'd gone out," he went on quietly, tiredly. "I came by here. Lights were burning, no one home. I checked outside, went down to headquarters to line up everything for the night, and came back here. That's when I found the letter." He shook his head sadly. "As you said, in case. Just in case you didn't make it back. I wish you hadn't, Celia. I wish to God you hadn't."

"I never meant to hurt you, Rafe."

"That's very comforting," came the bitter retort. "Only now what? Jesus God, but what in hell do I do now?"

Celia braced herself. She wasn't about to crawl. Not even to the man she loved. "Arrest me?" she finally asked, unable to bear the silence any longer.

"And see you hang? They'll want to, you know, as sure as black cats and bad luck go together. There'll be those who'd have you walk to the gallows." Rafe rubbed his forehead. God, his head hurt. He pictured Celia's neck in the hangman's noose. He couldn't let that happen. He loved her too— No. Not love. Once, but not after . . . what he'd learned. Impossible to love her, but to save her? Somehow . . . "Did you burn the letter?"

"Yes. And the uniform. But don't worry. I'll write you another letter, and Anthony can always verify my confession."

"Anthony is dead."

Celia blanched, steadied herself. An image of Anthony came to mind. Anthony young and fresh with the excitement and fervor of the coming conflict. Anthony so debonair and elegant. Anthony so . . . "Dead? You killed him?"

"A Yankee shell, fittingly enough. Almost took me with it. Then your problems would have been solved."

"What a horrid thing to say!"

"Sorry." Rafe looked at the wall behind her so he wouldn't have to meet her gaze. "You were in the Yankee camp tonight, weren't you?"

"Yes."

"And told them about the percussion caps."

"I wasn't going to tell Anthony, but he found out anyway, from a clerk in the quartermaster corps. If I hadn't gone out, he would have, and the shipment would've been intercepted."

Rafe's laugh was a hollow bark. "It won't now, of course. Now that *you* told them."

"No," Celia said matter-of-factly. "Because I gave them a very precise route and timetable."

"Oh, great!" Rafe threw up his hands in disgust. "Beautiful, Celia! That's just—"

"Saturday or Sunday night, from Flat Lake to Hart's Bayou and then down the river."

"Sure. And—" He regarded her with a quizzical expression. "And I'm supposed to believe that?"

"They did, I think." Celia shrugged. "It's the truth."

"I doubt your ability to recognize the truth anymore," Rafe said, advancing on her. "You lied to me and to all your friends. Maybe you're lying now as you lied when you left two years ago. Maybe lying has become a way of life with you. Every smile, every kiss, every endearment. Every laugh and every tear. Even your virginity was a lie."

Celia's hand caught him full on the cheek with enough force to twist his head around. Rafe raised his hand to strike her in return, then let it drop. Eyes locked in silent combat, they stared at each other. Finally, Rafe nodded and stepped past her to the door. "I'm going to have Broussard keep on watching you. So far as he'll know, it'll be for the same reason as before: that I'm worried about someone breaking in. He'll be your shadow. Your . . . protection."

Celia shut her eyes. Her shoulders sagged with a fatigue too great for mere sleep to allay, and her lips trembled.

"Just one last question," Rafe said from the door. "I can't imagine they needed you here any longer. There must be greener pastures, places where a lady spy would be more effective. So, why, Celia? Why didn't you just keep on going? Why'd you come back?"

"You," Celia answered in a tiny, broken voice. "Just . . . you."

Rafe's laughter rang hollowly. Utterly devoid of mirth, it was the devil's laughter—or Micah's. Celia glanced over her shoulder to make sure Rafe had not undergone some awful transmogrification. But Rafe was gone. Or the man that had been Rafe—what was left of him after she'd finished with him.

Celia almost ran to try to stop him, but the sound of the front door slamming brought her up short in her tracks. Her vision blurred, but she swore she wouldn't cry. By all the stars of heaven, she would not allow herself . . .

She made it as far as the stairway. There, sobbing bitterly, her knees buckled, and she slumped over onto the steps and gave herself to sorrow.

Sleep is a gift the overwrought mind gives itself. Physically and emotionally exhausted, Celia slept until a violent banging and rattling disturbed her dreams. Dazed, she struggled to sit up. The hall was dark. Her back hurt where the stair tread had pressed against her spine. She tried to breathe, but found her throat congested from weeping.

The front door rattled again, a fist hammered against the wood, and someone called her name. How much more, this night, she wondered, struggling to her feet. She stumbled to the door and released the catch. The door opened to the gray light of dawn and a figure at the edge of the porch steps.

"Jonathan?" Celia called. "Is that you?"

Jonathan Hays turned and looked back at her. He didn't wear his fear well. He looked sickeningly pale and his movements were clumsy and sudden. "Miss Bartlett . . . Thank God, you're here." His hands were shaking, his eyes wild. "I didn't know where else to go. I can't keep her in the carriage."

"Can't keep . . . Who?" Celia asked, a sudden premonition chilling her to the bone.

"Lynna. Oh, God, Celia, she's bleeding!"

Together Celia and Jonathan ran to the wagon drawn up in the drive. Her hair red against a pillow, her body covered with a blanket, Lynna lay in the back. Her face was white, and she looked still as death.

CHAPTER 22

It was the end of time. At least so Reverend Lundquist proclaimed from the fragments of his pulpit. He had preached against the war, he had preached for the war. Now, his hair askew and his eyes glazed, he stared over the empty pews of his fire-gutted church and called down the wrath of God until Father Razzoni and two soldiers led him away to a cave in the hopes of sparing his body the damage his mind had already sustained. Yet, in a fashion, Lundquist was more of a prophet than his bedraggled, shell-shocked state indicated.

Soldiers in gray still manned the redoubts and forts and trenches that ringed the beleaguered city, but with orders not to fire their weapons unless absolutely necessary. Every grain of powder, every percussion cap, was a priceless commodity to be used only to repulse a direct attack. Likewise, the artillery had long ago expended the last of its heavy shot and was forced to watch helplessly as Union gunboats plied the river unchallenged and turned the city they attacked into a living hell. A grim humor pervaded the trenches. Men bet on whose socks would rot first. Meal worm races were staged, with the owner of the winning worm getting to eat all the worms. When all else failed, there was sleep, for with sleep came wondrous dreams—nightmares to some—of plates piled high with food.

A similar lethargy gripped the civilians of Vicksburg as conditions in the city deteriorated daily. For the most part confined to their caves, men and women and children emerged to stagger among the ruins of their homes or walk aimlessly about on futile quests for food and clean water. Of meaningful employment there was none, save for the business of putting out the fires started by the nightly bombardment, and even that soon became just something to do to cope with boredom, for there was little left to save.

So perhaps Reverend Lundquist in his madness approached the truth. For it was, if not the end of time, certainly approaching the end for Vicksburg.

But not yet, for Vicksburg was the Rebel soul. Outnumbered, outgunned, wearing its scars and wounds proudly as the days of its drama drew to a close, Vicksburg represented the enduring, indomitable defiant spirit of the South, and was not to be easily or quickly vanquished.

Not just yet.

Sunday, the fourteenth of June, the twenty-seventh day of the siege of Vicksburg.

Rafe glanced at the lantern, turned the screw, and fed more wick into the chimney, went back to the unfinished report beneath his elbows on the desk. Reports, he thought dully. Reports and more reports, none of which would probably even be read. Poems once, but poems no more. Verse for lovers, and he didn't know any . . . lovers. The ticking of the clock on the bookcase sounded ominous in the stillness, like the footsteps of a man on his way to the gallows.

He was alone in the office and thankful of it. His mind was a turmoil of suppressed guilt, of rage held in check, of love he labored to bury. He stared at the bottle of bourbon he had taken from his father's house when he'd gone to check on Nathaniel the night before, and saw his reflection in the glass. A distorted, amber Rafe stared back at him out of the source of his brother's affliction. The image he saw looked almost like Micah. "That's right, little brother. Take my way out. Take my way. There isn't much difference between us. Just a bottle to stoke the anger and outrage. Not much difference. Two peas in a pod . . ."

The bottle went spinning across the room to strike neck first against the wall. A brown smear of liquor streaked the wall and puddled on the floor.

"Hell of a waste. That there would've bought you a nice parcel of land. Maybe even a small bag a' gold, if offered to the right gullet."

Rafe shaded his eyes from the lantern, saw Snag Parken, riverboat captain and pilot par excellence, coming through the door. Their paths hadn't crossed since the run into Vicksburg, almost exactly a month earlier. It seemed like forever and a week. "I thought you went down with the *Bayou Belle*," Rafe said sourly.

"I was sore tempted," Snag admitted, a line of bright white teeth lightening his grin. "Not much glory in goin' down at dockside, though. 'Sides, better sense got the best of me. Lucky. If it hadn't, then I wouldn't have been able to salvage enough to build *Little Sister*." He looked around the stuffy, airless office whose windows, long since broken, had been boarded up. "Christ, you make this place like a damned prison on purpose?"

"The *Belle*'s little sister?" Rafe asked, ignoring the last comment.

"One an' only. And a sweet little girl she is, too, though a mite cramped. She'll carry her share, though. Ten or so stout hearts an' what they need to start a new life."

Rafe indicated a chair across from him and leaned back with his hands behind his head. "Carry them where?"

"Montana Territory."

"Montana?" Rafe whistled in amazement. "That's a long, long way on what they say is a mean river, Captain Parken."

"Righto, my boy!" Snag looked as if nothing would please him better. "Far from Yankee shells and Yankee soldiers. Confederate ones, too, for that matter. The only battle a man needs fight is the one for his life. No generals to tell him when an' where to die, by God!"

"Sounds to me like running away," Rafe scoffed.

"What the hell from?" Snag hooted. "Look around ye, Rafe Lattimore. I mean to say use the eyes in your head. I give it my all, boy, done my share an' more. Startin' over, I call it. Makin' a new beginning!"

Rafe eased the front legs of his chair off the ground and balanced on the rear two, much like teetering on the brink of a decision. "Why are you telling me all this, Snag?"

The riverman chuckled deep in his chest. He heaved out of his chair, squatted by the broken bottle, and ran a finger across the drying stain. "I figured a man desperate enough to waste good bourbon," he said, raising one eyebrow in disapproval, "might just be fool enough to listen to what I had to say."

"I guess you knew when you left wherever you came from," Rafe said dryly, "that you'd get here just in time for me to throw that bottle."

Parken straightened and reached inside his coat. He slapped a weathered, hand-drawn map on the desk in front of Rafe. "My route, lad. Follow the Mississippi up to St. Louis. Then into the Missouri and, by God, plumb all the way into mountain country. And beyond, too, with a good horse 'neath your bones. All the way to Oregon. It can be done, lad, if a man's willin'. There's gold there, and room to grow and carve out your own dream. Gonna beat hell outta this poor ol' South we know, once this God-forsaken war's over."

"Easy on paper, Snag. Only one thing. Sounds to me as if you've forgotten about all those Yankee gunboats."

"Forgot, hell!" Parken's eyes gleamed. He raised one hand and tapped one temple. "They're gonna let us go right on past 'em."

"Oh?"

"'Cause the fightin'—here, at least—will be over. I'll wait until the surrender."

Rafe snorted in derision. Despite his own doubts, he was determined to keep an optimistic front no matter what the odds. "You don't hold out much hope, do you, old man?"

"Should I?" Snag asked, his fists planted on the desk, his eyes burning into Rafe's. "I spied some folks on the way over here. They was dirty, wore out, hungry, an' roastin' some meat on a spit. I thought they had 'em some mule meat like everybody else, but no, sir! It was rats. God-damn rats! For pity's sake, what do you soldier boys need to make you open your eyes an' read the handwritin' on the wall? Hell's bells, boy! You sit around waitin' for reinforcements from General Joe Johnston, and what does he send? A handful of God-damn percussion caps!"

"What's that?" Rafe asked, his chair legs hitting the floor.

"Caps, damn it. Hundred thousand or so."

"When?" Rafe demanded. "Where?"

"Last night around midnight, little later. Come through down where I got *Little Sister* stashed, in one a' them little side bayous that runs off'n Gum Creek. Yanks wasn't even lookin' for him, he said."

"She was telling the truth, then," Rafe muttered.

"Huh?"

"Nothing," Rafe answered with a wave of his hand. "Damn! A hundred thousand rounds! And not even looking for him!"

Snag shook his head in disgust. "Yeah. Ain't it excitin'? Four rounds for each of them twenty-five thousand skeletons we got strung around this whole city. 'Course they wasn't lookin' for him. Why should they waste their time? They know we're beat. We can all shoot four times, but we can't eat. Hell, man!" Snag grabbed the chair, sat down opposite Rafe, and leaned forward intently. "Listen to me, Rafe. I'll steer a straight course with you. As soon as these generals call it quits an' things quiet down some, I'm gone. There's room for a young fella who knows how to handle himself on the water to come along with me. You don't have to decide now, but just remember. Gum Creek when the last shot is fired."

"You sound awfully sure of yourself," Rafe observed sourly.

Snag folded the map and returned it to his coat pocket. "I put no claim to bein' a high-an'-mighty general like some, but I know that when the Yanks take Vicksburg, the Confederate States of by God America is cut right down the middle. I been around a long time, Rafe, an' never seen man nor beast live when they been sliced in half. The time's come to face facts. The old days're gone, an' we might as well forget 'em. But that don't mean there ain't never gonna be new days. Not for me, anyway." His face gnarled and tough as driftwood,

Snag sauntered to the door. "Nor for you, if you're willin' to take the chance," he added, and was gone.

Rafe started to rise, then sat back and stared at the report. The words were meaningless, though. He couldn't concentrate, not with Celia on his mind. While the courier had succeeded in delivering the caps didn't prove that she had told the truth, it certainly gave credence to her story. On the other hand, the fact was that she had been a spy, and honor required that he have her arrested. Honor was everything. Without it, a man was . . . what?

An ogre? A man? What did he expect of himself? Too much, evidently. Loving her too much in spite of himself and her perfidy, he had used his wounded pride like a whip to flay her. Now she surely hated him, and if he tried, if he really tried, someday his love for her might turn to hate, too. Tired, his thoughts hopelessly muddled, Rafe turned back to the report, which required no more than a straightforward description. The ink on the pen had dried. He dipped it in the well and, willing his mind to the task at hand, wrote.

Sunday, June 14th. The city has been under siege for twenty-seven days. Morale everywhere is extremely low. In the trenches, men fall listlessly to their duties. In town, civilians do what is necessary to survive, and with the setting sun scurry back to their caves and cellars, for night brings the terror of bombardment. Our work goes on, however great the obstacles placed in our way. It is impossible, for example, to search every hovel and abandoned building for deserters. I have too few men to stop the ruffians and looters who venture forth under cover of darkness to prey on the misery of honest citizens. I do what I can, though, and will until this dreadful matter is resolved.

The numbers of my men diminish daily. Last night's bombardment claimed two . . .

June 15, 1863.
Another boring day. We slept in the cellar again last night and have sat about the house all day with nothing to do. Lynna improves, I think, or at least holds her own. I wonder, how, sometimes, after watching her pain and anguish, why I still succumb to the urge to bear children of my own. Life for the men in the trenches must be intolerably hard, I suppose, but I am no longer so naive as to believe that being a woman and bearing a child is any easier.

I dreamed of Rafe again last night. It is so difficult to think of being without him. I am at a loss. I will continue, of course, even though I am haunted by the pain written on his face. His words to me were like daggers whose deadly draw cut to my heart. I hated him for his anger because I hated myself for causing it.

I find myself wondering, from time to time, how I shall remember these terrible times twenty years from now. If fate is kind and Rafe is at my side, I suppose I shall shudder and thank my lucky stars that our love prevailed over all the obstacles thrown in our way. If I am alone, or with some other man, I hope I have the strength of character to look back and remember the wonderful, shining moments we had together . . .

Celia closed the diary as Immelda rounded the corner. "Ain't nobody ever sits in here if they can help it," the black woman said, staring coldly around the formal parlor.

"The room fits my mood, I suppose," Celia replied, leaning against the back of the horsehair couch.

"Well, you're makin' things mighty hard on yourself, is all I got to say," Immelda chided, busying herself with a dust rag. "An' us as well," she added after a moment. "Tobias an' me just don't know *how* to feel. Plumb happy to see you back here, an' just as sad 'cause of that man an' the sorrow look you carries about with you."

"I'll try to smile more, if that'll make you happy," Celia snapped a little peevishly.

Immelda stopped dusting and stared angrily at Celia, then sighed and went to sit by her. "Guess we all gots a touch of the tempers, honey."

"I'm sorry, Immelda. My tongue—"

"Ain't your fault, gal. Mine neither, maybe. It's the worryin'. The longer you stay hereabouts, the more dangerful it gets."

"I know."

"But you still ain't gonna leave, right?"

"How?" Celia asked. "He has Matthew watching, and—"

"That's right!" Immelda exclaimed, slapping her thigh exuberantly. "I plumb forgot! You want I should brew up some tea?"

At a loss to understand the black woman's sudden change of mood and subject, Celia looked up at her as if she'd lost her mind. "We've been using the same leaves for nearly a week," she finally said, deciding Immelda had changed the subject merely to cheer her up. "You're the eternal optimist, Immelda."

"No, honey, I'm a Christian woman," Immelda retorted indignantly. "Had my eyes set on heaven's pearly gates since I can remember."

"Very well." Celia laughed. "I stand corrected, but will forgo the tea."

"Best think twice, honey. That Broussard boy done brought by a tin for you, an' I got some steepin' in a jug in the sun."

Fresh tea was a treat to cheer up the most morose. Her mouth actually watering, Celia placed her diary aside and followed Immelda down the hall to the kitchen. "Needs another few minutes," Immelda said, moving the jug into the direct sunlight. She jabbed a finger toward the back porch. "The boy said he didn't want none. I was thinkin' maybe you could change his mind."

"I can try," Celia said, moving to the door.

The back porch was shaded and cool, the air fresh and sweet smelling. Celia had become quite fond of the quiet, unassuming Matthew in the week he had been her guard and guardian. Smiling, she approached him where he sat on the floor at the far end of the porch, rifle propped against the wall, hands free for the more important task of whittling. "Thank you for the tea," she said, sitting on the swing. "That was very thoughtful of you."

Matt looked up at her and grinned. "Don't ask me how I come by it, Miss Bartlett, an' I won't have to tell you no tall tales."

"Why ever should finding a tin of tea have to be a secret?" Celia asked.

"Mr. Lattimore wants us to take anything like that to one of the hospitals 'stead of usin' it for ourselves. But I figgered this was as good as a hospital, what with Miz Hays laid up an' all. Anyways, I come across this here fella riflin' a dead man's corpse an' scared him off. Turned in the rest of the stuff I found there, 'ceptin' the tea. Figgered it'd get pilfered anyhow."

"I can't imagine Mr. Lattimore would mind that."

"Don't know, ma'am. He gets his mind set . . ." Matt slapped his whittling stick against his thigh. "Well, now, pshaw! I've gone an' told. Pa always said I could talk a cloud to rain. Said I took after Ma's kin. Reckon he was right. You won't tell Mr. Lattimore, will you?"

When she hadn't seen him since that horrible last Tuesday night when Anthony was killed? "No," Celia assured him. "It will be our secret. Will you have a glass with us?"

Matt thought about that a moment, finally shook his head. "I'd 'preciate it, ma'am, but my tongue's sort of got convinced that bark and chicory coffee's about all there is and has got used to makin' the best of it. I'd hate to let my taster know there's somethin' better in the world."

"Well, if you say so . . ." Celia started back into the house, stopped when Tobias came around the corner carrying a knife and a chunk of wood. "Tea, Tobias?" she asked. "There's fresh."

"I know. Seen it on the windowsill." A look of embarrassment crossed his face, and he held up the wood and knife. "Not much to do," he explained lamely. "Ain't nothin' growin' this summer but Yankee bullets."

"That's all right, Tobias. Papa always said whittling was better with company."

Tobias nodded. Many a summer afternoon he and Hal Bartlett had spent sitting together in the shade and carving deer or rabbits or horses. Sometimes they just whittled a stick away to nothing for the pure love of the way a good steel blade bit into the wood, big shavings from soft pine, tiny, delicate slivers from hard hickory. Good thing about young Broussard, Tobias thought, his eyes twinkling despite the gnawing hunger in his belly. Good that he had the appreciation, too. Wisdom was a rare trait in one so young. "Yes'm. Well . . ."

By the time Celia got back inside, Immelda had taken the jug from the window, strained the tea into a pitcher, and added fresh mint. The aroma was heavenly, the taste the perfect balm for a hot and humid summer afternoon. "He was just being modest," Celia explained, taking the glass Immelda handed to her. "I imagine that both he and Tobias will be tickled pink if you bring them each a glass. I'll take some for Lynna myself."

A glass of tea. It was hard to think that such a simple treat could mean so much.

Lynna's bedroom had once been the dining room. Celia had chosen the dining room because it was on the east side of the house and didn't get the afternoon heat, and because it was closest to the cellar stairs and hence to safety when the shells started falling. It was Tuesday afternoon, the sixteenth. An early morning rain had left the day muggy and close. The week was crawling. It should have been at least Friday.

"How is she?" Celia asked.

Tom Stewart closed the door and sagged against the wall. "Better. Much better."

"Thank God!" Celia smiled, took the doctor by the hand. "Come. There's fresh tea. It'll perk you up."

The sun parlor was still a cheerful room despite the broken and missing windows that had been blown out on the night of the party a week and a half earlier. Tom eased himself into an easy chair that, as Hal's favorite, formerly had sat in front of the windows but had now been pulled aside. A writing stand and paper were close at hand, and several books which Tom glanced through while Celia disappeared to get the tea.

"Oh, my, oh, my," Tom said, and sighed after he'd taken his first sip. "I've not tasted anything this good in—" He shook his head in wonder. "Isn't that strange? I can't remember when I drank my last cup of fresh tea!"

They drank in silence, savoring the taste and wondering when the next cup of tea or coffee or slice of white bread would come their way. They drank in silence broken only by the *whirr* of an exploring bumblebee that circled the room once and left a starker silence in its wake. "Nice," Tom finally said, his voice soft against the afternoon stillness. "Not doing anything but sitting in the company of a beautiful woman."

Celia blushed and sipped her tea. She wanted to know more about Lynna, but Tom had leaned back and closed his eyes. He looked so tired and haggard. His hair was shot through with gray and his sideburns were almost totally white. Age had assailed him overnight. No, Celia thought. Not overnight. Over the long month of siege.

"Solange is a beautiful woman," he said, opening one eye to look at Celia. His gaze traveled up the simple homespun gown, across the high breasts to the clean line of Celia's throat and neck, and the soft smoky topaz of her eyes. "We seldom . . . sit together." The eye closed and he shrugged. "Hell, we *never* sit together. Not anymore. Not since . . ."

The sentence dangled unfinished. Tom sat motionless for a long moment, then abruptly finished his tea and leaned forward intently. "Have you seen?" he began, then stopped and shook his head. "I mean, have you ever wanted to?" No. Not that either. He could no more ask Celia if she'd seen Solange with Micah than he could ask her if she'd ever considered killing a man.

Thoughts, thoughts. Thinking was too great an effort. And like lifting a boulder to drop in a well just to hear the splash, equally useless, too. "No bleeding or cramps for two days is a good sign," he went on, switching back to the easier subject of Lynna. "I've seen nothing to make me change my opinion that the baby's simply in the wrong position. Transverse lie is the technical term. I'd rather not risk trying to reposition the fetus until it becomes absolutely necessary. Each day we wait is another day the infant gains strength."

"But she's due—"

"I know. A couple of weeks. Still, time is her best ally. That and fresh air and rest and the best food you can find. You have been taking her down to the cellar at night, haven't you?"

"Of course. Jonathan and Tobias—"

"That's about all we can do, then. That and thank our lucky stars that Immelda's midwifed before." Tom shoved himself out of the chair. "Well, so much for peace and quiet, I guess. Thanks for the stimulant."

"There's more, Tom," Celia offered, wishing he would stay and talk.

"No, thanks. Maybe another time. By the way, the next time you see Rafe, would you tell him I'd like to speak with him?"

Celia looked away, out the window and to the dead garden. "I don't think I'll be . . ." She glanced back and smiled weakly. "Yes, certainly."

Tom nodded, took up his hat and bag. Celia walked him to the door and out onto the porch. Tom's carriage waited at the bottom of the steps. Beyond the front lawn, the empty street was bathed in sunlight. "Didn't see another carriage all the way down Monroe," Tom said, tossing his bag in ahead of him. "A few folks on foot. They looked at old Daisy here as if she were a meal on the hoof."

"She would be, for a lot of people," Celia pointed out.

"I know." Tom climbed wearily aboard, touched his hat before driving off. "Try to find me if anything changes. I'll do my best to get here if there's an emergency. If I can't . . ." His voice cracked, and he wiped a hand across his face. "I'm tired, Celia. So damned tired." The horse moved off and, strangely disembodied, Tom's voice floated back. ". . . My best . . . all I can promise . . . my best. . . ."

Wednesday the seventeenth was hot and muggy, too. Celia and Lynna spent the day in desultory chatter. It was late in the afternoon when Lynna took Celia's hand in hers and said, "We'll never be able to repay you, Celia. Never."

Celia thought about that a minute and realized that if she hadn't had Lynna to worry about the empty days might have driven her mad. "You already have, dear," she said, gripping Lynna's hand in return. "You already have."

One indistinguishable from another, the days ran together in a straight, featureless line. The only thing that made Thursday any different was the number eighteen on the calendar. Tom scrubbed his hands in the basin. When the water turned pink and then red, he lifted his hands free and dried them on a linen petticoat the surgeons were using for a towel. He sat on a stool and, utterly drained, stared at the wall. He tried to remember what good bourbon tasted like, but couldn't, and quickly sank back into the somnambulant daze that surrounded him during the rare quiet moments he used to cherish but no longer even noticed.

"Stewart?"

Tom jerked as if awakened, looked around to see a bald, middle-aged man in a blood-smeared frock poke his head through the doorway.

"I say, Stewart."

"Yes, Dr. Butler?"

"How about leaving things here for the time being and heading over to the Sisters of Mercy Convent. Rex Porterfield has sent word he's got his hands full over there. The change of pace might do you good."

Tom stared at his hands. He tried to imagine them caressing Solange's milk white flesh, thrilling to the subtle swelling of her breasts, circling . . . her throat and . . . squeezing . . .

"Tom!"

He spun around. Eyes like saucers, mouth rigid, lips pale with terror at the plaguing, maddening thoughts, he half rose, then sat again.

"For God's sake, man," Butler said. "What's the matter?"

"Nothing's the matter," Tom snapped, forcing himself back to reality. "A little tired, perhaps, but nothing more. I heard you. The convent. I'm going." He brushed past his fellow surgeon and crossed through the wasteland of hospital cots and their burdens of hewn flesh. A soldier waved a bandaged stump of an arm at him and called his name, but Tom ignored him and rushed out the door into the growing dusk.

Three blocks away, the convent had been converted to a civilian hospital the day after the siege had begun and all other spaces filled with military personnel. As he walked, Tom tried to count the days since he had talked to Solange. One? Two? Three? Strange how elusive days became. He could remember other things, though. Clearly and precisely. Opening the front door. Sitting across the table to confront Solange with her infidelity.

He had wanted to kill her. That he remembered. The almost unbearable urge to . . .

Maybe he would after all. Maybe later . . .

Or Micah! Yes! Why not Micah! Why not forget his oath to preserve life for just a few moments, just long enough to find the two of them together. He stopped in front of a storefront piled high with the assorted accoutrement of warfare, among which he spied a holstered revolver. Mesmerized, he reached through the broken window and, noting the loaded chambers, pulled the gun out of its holster.

Strange how little he knew about the weapons that gave him employ. This one was a little heavier than a bone saw, but with a similar grip. The discovery of other similarities intrigued him. The gun was a tool like many of Tom's, one that dealt in blood and pain. Normally, he liked to think his tools saved lives. But saved them for what? To make beggars of once whole men? To fill more trenches, defend more battlements, face more cannons, and to suffer even more frightful wounds?

No. Better death than that. Better this other tool that gave final, total surcease for all pain, including his.

Eyes blank, unable to stop the sickening, horrifying fantasy, he saw them. Saw the sweat gleaming on their bodies, heard their grunts of ecstasy and animal heat, smelled the pungency of their lust. Solange writhing, Micah rising above her, sinking into her. Solange's nails clawing Micah's back, Solange's features contorted in the throes of beastly orgasm. And not once! Not for one second does Solange think of Tom Stewart, not once of her husband until she opens her eyes and peers past Micah's shoulder to see her husband standing over them both.

"No!" she gasps as she sees the revolver rise.

"This is my last gift to you, my darling. Dishonest though you were in life, I leave you an honest death."

His thumb pulls back the hammer. The gun is an awkward weight, extended so. Micah's torso is twisted so he can better see from whence cometh his death. Solange's pretty mouth is rounded in a silent scream. One first, the one on top, and then the other . . .

The gun explodes in the stillness.

"Tom?"

A hand touched his shoulder. Tom jerked violently as if struck, and dropped the revolver. Dr. Butler drew back, taken by surprise as Tom turned on him. "I . . . ah . . ." Butler, too, had had his days of crisis. They all had. That day, that hour, that minute, when a single scream or moan or drop of blood, like the proverbial straw, broke a man's spirit and sent him spinning into darkness. Wisely, he said nothing. "A messenger just arrived. Porterfield's in a bad way. A shell brought in the room on Moll Evans and her kids. All the girls and two of the boys were injured. They've been carried to the convent." Butler held up his bag, the large one with the surgeon's tools. "Thought maybe I'd better give you a hand. Mind if I walk with you?"

"Mind? Mind?" The shadow of madness flitted across Tom's face. Then, as if awakening from a nightmare, he shuddered and turned his steps toward the convent. "The men are bad enough," he said, a half a block down the road. "The children are almost too much to bear."

"I know," Butler said, hearing the pain in Tom's voice and remembering his own anguish. "I've never admitted this to anyone, but sometimes, when I see them, the only thing I can do is—just sit and cry."

Tom stopped abruptly. His knuckles white, he gripped Butler's arm. "You, too?" he asked, his voice an awed whisper. Relief washed through him. In this misbegotten, satanic world of pain and death, in this nightmare of humanity gone mad and turned against itself, others cared, too, and were not afraid to admit it. He was not alone, he was not a freak. The world was not lost—yet: men still knew how to cry. Eyes closed, he let his head fall back, and breathed deeply. "I thought I was the only one," he finally said. "I was so afraid I was the only one."

"So was I once," Butler said.

Two men of medicine, saviors of a sort. Tired feet, bags heavy in their hands, they trudged up the road toward the convent and the torn children. *The children,* Tom thought, his steps quickening. *Think of the children. I have something to give the children.*

Behind him, unfired, the forgotten revolver lay in the dust.

At four o'clock, Sunday morning, June 20, a Negro named Mose Rivers died when a shell exploded and a blast of flames lifted him high in the air and, with hurricane force, blew him and a section of Jackson Street through the front of Rafe's office. Within seconds, more explosions followed to deafen Rafe as he struggled out from beneath the debris. Coughing, half blinded by the dust, his stomach churned in horror at the smoking remains of blistered meat clinging to the walls and furniture.

"Captain Lattimore! Captain Lattimore!"

What was left of Rafe's hearing identified the voice of Matt Broussard as the farm boy dug through the wreckage looking for him. "What the hell're you doing here?" Rafe yelled.

Matt and another homeguardsman named Jubal were clawing at a beam that blocked the door. "Jonathan's at the house," Matt explained, reaching in to give Rafe a hand as the beam fell aside. "Jee–sus!"

The ceiling of the office groaned, cracked, and collapsed behind the three men as they dove out from under the porch and landed sprawling in the street. They had thought, three hours earlier when the nightly shelling failed to materialize, that perhaps the Federals had changed their tactics. Now, as more and more shells inundated the city, they realized how wrong they'd been. The ground shook, the sky glowed with sparkling trails of arching fuses.

"Where the hell we gonna go?" Matt yelled, crawling to Rafe's side.

"That shell hole!" Rafe bellowed. "Ready?"

A few yards away, Jubal, normally a shy, taciturn man, suddenly stood and clamped his hands over his ears. "Stop it, damn your black souls! Stop it!"

"Get down!" Rafe shouted, dragging himself with his elbows toward the distraught man.

Matt didn't even try to crawl. Rolling, he covered the intervening yards and grabbed Jubal by the leg. "Get down, Jubal!" he shrieked. "For the love of God, get down!"

Too little food, too little sleep, too many deaths, and now the thundering hell of too many shells and explosions. Jubal kicked free of Matt's hand and started running. Rafe and Matt scrambled to their feet and tried to chase him down, but madness gave their quarry abnormal speed. Before they'd gone twenty yards, Rafe saw a fuse heading almost directly toward them. Diving, he caught Matt with his shoulder and sent him rolling behind a dead mule. A fraction of a second later, an explosion cast Jubal in stark relief against the brilliant glare and threw him high in the air, flying over their heads and into the darkness behind them.

"Oh, shit, shit, shit!" Rafe moaned, huddling against the still warm flesh of the mule. And then, more practically, "Well, you ready to find a nice deep shell hole?"

Matthew's grin was sickly, but determined. A minute later they were sheltered in a deep hole, safe from everything but a direct hit. They had survived the first five minutes.

They had moved her into the cellar at midnight, then back upstairs at two when the shells failed to fall for the first night in almost two weeks. Now, shocked, they stood in the hall and tried to figure out what was happening, why time was so out of sorts. An explosion rocked the house. Chips of plaster and dust showered down through the stairwell from the upstairs hall ceiling. Glass in the chandelier tinkled briefly.

"I don' understan'," Tobias said, still only half awake.

"Lynna!" Celia gasped. "We've got to get her back downstairs again!"

Tobias, Immelda, and Celia ran to the dining room, ducked inside the door just as another explosion outside sent a splinter or a piece of stone through one of the windows. "Jonathan! Lynna! Are you all right?" Celia called.

The candle that Immelda carried guttered and almost went out, then flared to reveal Jonathan covering Lynna's body with his own. "The chair!" Jonathan roared over the din.

In the hall, a flower vase toppled from its pedestal and crashed to the floor. Tobias grabbed the chair they used for carrying Lynna up and downstairs, and hurried to the bed. Jonathan waited for a moment of relative calm, then climbed off Lynna and the bed, and reached over to pick her up and place her in the chair. "Easy now," he told Tobias as the two men leaned over to pick up the chair, and then, feeling moisture on his cheek, shouted, "Wait! The candle!"

She was hurt! A piece of glass, a sliver, something had cut her. Horrified, Jonathan grabbed the candle from Immelda, held it close to his wife, and saw that she was unscathed. The moisture had been tears. Hand trembling, he passed back the candle to Immelda. "It's all right, honey," he crooned, almost sobbing with relief. "We'll have you downstairs in a minute. It's all right . . . Tobias? Let's go."

Immelda led the way with the candle, and Celia took up the rear. Down the hall into the kitchen, then to the cellar stairs. Twin explosions bracketed the house. The china in the cupboards rattled. A door swung crazily. An iron skillet jumped off its hook and snapped in two when it landed on the stove. "My poor kitchen!" Immelda wailed.

"The hell with your kitchen!" Jonathan shouted. "Get the damned door!"

Slowly, carefully, the tiny procession disappeared through the cellar door and gingerly descended into the dark depths. Last to go through, Celia stopped for one last look and then, as if drawn by some uncommon magnet, retraced her steps through the front hall to the front door and stepped onto the porch.

Outside, the world was being torn asunder. Trails of fire crisscrossed the sky. Shell after shell after shell erupted into tiny volcanoes that spewed fire and shrapnel. The concussions buffeted her, left her ears ringing. Smoke streaked her face, save where the tracks of tears cleansed her skin. The Cartwright's home was a ball of flame. As she watched, she felt first shame and then hatred. Shame that she should have been so weak as to succumb to her own petty ills and become a spy: hatred for the vipers who had chosen to utterly and needlessly destroy her city. And in that moment, she understood the look in Rafe's eyes the night he had discovered her perfidy.

How long she stood there she couldn't calculate. At last, though, when the sky began to turn gray in the east, she slowly turned her back on the growing devastation, and stepped unperturbed once more into the house.

Behind her, the shells continued to fall.

"Hey, sweet!" Micah called, virtually diving in the doorway. Panting, he leaned against the wall to catch his breath. "One hell of a storm out there," he said, wiping a piece of ash from one of his eyes. "Fella could get hurt, he wasn't careful. Dead, for that matter." Death. Wouldn't that be a pitiful end to all his plans! The irony amused him the more because deep in his soul he expected to live forever. "You here?"

A light bundle on the bed moved just enough to draw his attention. Micah crossed the room and stripped back the single sheet to see Solange curled up in the corner. She was naked and her pale knees were drawn up to her forehead, her arms wrapped around her legs. He nudged her with the toe of his boot. "What the hell are you doing?"

"I don't want to die. I'm afraid."

"And that sheet's going to protect you?" Micah threw back his head and laughed. Then, as always excited by danger, kicked off his boots and began to strip. "You won't, sweet. Someone else maybe, but not you. Not me either," he added, dropping down to join her on the bed.

And the shells continued to fall.

"Mommy!"

"She isn't here," Tom Stewart said, holding the boy whose shattered arm he had tried to set only the night before. Other children clung to the gentle women in black habits whose cloistered home had been opened to the suffering injured.

"I'm scared."

"So am I," Tom whispered. "Go to sleep."

"I can't. It's morning."

"Try. You were awake all night long."

"Will you sing me a song?"

Tom affectionately tousled the boy's hair. "My voice might bring down the roof. You wouldn't want that, would you?"

"I'm afraid," the little boy wailed, burying his face in Tom's coat.

Insanely enough, the only song he could remember was "Yankee Doodle." So he sang, crooning the words like a lullaby. And felt useful holding a child, whose arm he hoped he had saved.

And the shells continued to fall.

At ten, on Sunday morning, the shelling ceased. At exactly ten. Two men covered with dust and debris stirred and climbed out of the shell hole in the middle of the street. Knees weak, thirstier than he could remember being even at sea, Rafe brushed off his coat and shook out his hair. Next to him, Matt Broussard checked his rifle first, and then his clothes.

All the other nights had been a Sunday outing compared to the one just past. Rubble lay in every direction. Only here and there, miraculously spared, did a whole building stand. There was work to be done. Massive amounts of work. People to be dug out of premature tombs of wood and masonry. Streets cleared. Dead animals to be butchered and the inedible remains carted to the river and thrown in. Food and water to be found, somewhere, and distributed as best possible. Work enough for a whole city, and more.

"We're still here, you bastards," Rafe said, his look made more grim by the streaked soot and dust. "Matt."

"Yessir?"

"I'm going to start things going down here. Check on Miss Bartlett and my father's house. If anything's wrong either place, come back and find me."

"Yessir!"

"We're still here," Rafe repeated as Matt limped away. "Still here, you bastards."

And then he went to work.

CHAPTER 23

Listen to the Parrot shells
Listen to the Parrot shells
The Parrot shells are whistling through the air
Listen to the minié balls
Listen to the minié balls
The minié balls are singin' through the air.

Rafe trailed the sour melody to its source, the foremost line of trenches manned by Vicksburg's resolute defenders.

"Who the hell are you?" a voice to one side asked.

The singing stopped as Rafe scrambled the remaining few yards and rolled into the trench.

"Sir," the soldier added hurriedly, just to be on the safe side.

The singer sniggered in disgust. "Elwood, you are about as much sentry as piss is hot coffee."

Elwood, a dark, swarthy individual muscled his way past his smaller friend. "Which is as good a description of coffee as you'll find these days. But that's all right, Jonesy. I don't mind them harsh words, 'cause your singin' reminds me of my pa. Only difference was, when Pa stood on the porch an' caterwauled like that, hawgs come a runnin'." Elwood propped one foot on an empty powder box and leaned forward on his musket. "If you're a Yank," he went on to Rafe, "I hope you brought some vittles with you."

"Sorry, men. I'm from over yonder in Vicksburg. Captain Lattimore, Home Guard."

Elwood and Jonesy made a half-hearted attempt at standing at attention.

"Formerly of the Confederate Navy," Rafe added.

The men relaxed. Protocol didn't require them to pay deference to anyone not in the army. At least not that they knew of, never having been around the navy before. "Navy?" Jonesy asked, perplexed. "We got a navy in Vicksburg?"

"Christ, you're dumb," Elwood growled in disgust. "Vicksburg's on a river, ain't it? Hell, yes, we got a navy in Vicksburg. It's just sunk, is all."

"Well, if you're from Vicksburg, then you didn't bring doodly squat," Jonesy said. More disappointed than angered, he sank back to the ground and covered his eyes with his hat.

"So what the hell you come here for?" Elwood asked, leery of any man, much less a purported officer, who was insane enough to enter the trenches of his own free will.

"You ever get tired of being here?" Rafe asked in return.

"That's the dumbest question I heard in all my born days," Jonesy volunteered from under his hat.

Rafe picked himself up and brushed off his trousers. "Well, I'm tired of being there. I've spent better than a month dodging shells in town." He began to climb the steep slope to the top of the fortification. "Figured the time had come to send back a few."

"All well an' good to be lookin' now, but show your head above 'at'ere wall come daylight an' some Yank sharpshooter'll splatter what brains you got left, Captain sir," Elwood warned. "Only thing that'll get sent anywhere then'll be you straight to hell."

"Thanks," Rafe said. "I'll keep that in mind." Another half hour to daylight. Rafe squirmed the last few feet and carefully poked his head above the line of dirt. In the faint light, he could see another extended line of earthenworks somewhat less than twenty yards away from the one behind which he lay. Only twenty yards! To his left, perhaps a hundred feet away, the two lines almost touched. He'd had no idea they were so close together. And there, less than ten paces to his right, he could discern the dark maws of a battery of cannon aimed point-blank at the Rebel lines. "I'll *damned* sure keep it in mind," he added, sliding back down the incline.

He might as well have been there forever, for all the attention the soldiers paid him. Ignored, so quickly a part of the scenery, Rafe took time to look around. Jonesy was snoring quietly. The one called Elwood stood slumped over his musket and appeared to be asleep on his feet. The earth in all directions looked as if it had been stirred and left to dry in the sun. Gradually, Rafe realized that many of the brown lumps were sleeping men who, after a month in the trenches, blended perfectly with the dirt. The Third Missouri, someone had told him just before he'd undertaken the last few hundred yards of his trip to the front. The backbone of the defense blocking what had once been the Jackson Road. The likeliest place to see action, in this siege which had ground down to a test of staying power and will.

Which was why he'd picked it, of course, Rafe reminded himself, hoping that there would be action. He leaned against the mounded dirt and stared up at the stars. Night was on the wane. Daylight soon.

The world lay at peace. An uneasy, false peace to be sure, but one he relished as he often had the calm that preceded a storm at sea. There was time to relax, then, time to ready oneself for the test that surely followed, to set one's mind in order, to contemplate. . . .

Celia. No. Not her. Almost anything or anyone else. His father? Honor, duty, the Home Guard he was supposed to be leading? Words, words, words. He no longer cared. For four days he'd run himself ragged trying to restore some sense of order to the city after the terrible bombardment, and now all he wanted was a chance to fight back, to shoot at someone, to personalize the conflict that had become such an integral part of his life.

An unfamiliar noise, a soft but persistent scratching, cut his thoughts midstream. Tense, not yet knowledgeable about which noises meant danger and which could be ignored, Rafe checked his revolvers, made sure the loads were dry and the barrels and chambers free of dirt. Neither of the guards had moved. Rafe decided he was overreacting and sat down. It certainly was quiet, he thought, studying the terrain and the guards. The one named Jonesy, now asleep, was a slightly built man who appeared much too emaciated to lift a rifle, much less actually fight. Elwood, for all the breadth of his shoulders, had walked with a slow and measured, almost shuffling step, the result of quarter rations of pea meal biscuits and tainted meat. If the others, as yet unseen, were in similar shape, it certainly didn't seem as if there was any reaon why the Yankees shouldn't simply walk over them with impunity.

He'd find out more about that when daylight came, Rafe decided, closing his eyes and trying to rest. The smooth spot he'd found wasn't as smooth as he'd thought. Squirming, he lay on his back, then his left side, finally his right and, head cradled on his open left hand, tried to talk himself into sleep.

And heard the noise again. This time more clearly. Metallic noises, coming from the ground itself. Curious, he moved his hand, pressed his ear directly to the earth. There it was! Clearer, sharper, more ominous. "I heard something!" he whispered.

Jonesy snored, rolled over, and kept on sleeping.

Rafe got to his feet and roused Elwood. "I hear something," he repeated.

"What?" Elwood asked, coming awake.

"I hear something. Sounds like digging."

Elwood yawned and pushed a crink out of his back with the flat of his hand. "Just Yanks. They're tunnelin' under the redoubt yonder. We got men workin' on another tunnel comin' in from our side. Hopin' to catch Billy Yank afore he can blow up the dad-blamed redoubt. Kind of a race, I reckon you could call it."

"And the winner?" Rafe asked, not able to imagine exactly what would happen when two groups of men met face to face twenty feet underground.

"Gets to blow the other up, I 'spect," Elwood said, not really knowing himself. "All I know is, you wouldn't catch me diggin' underground. No, sirree, Bob!"

"Just one big grave, you ask me," Jonesy chimed in unexpectedly.

"I thought you were asleep," Elwood snapped. "But since you ain't, you can quit talkin' like that anyway. I've had 'bout all the talk of graves I want."

"You don't like it, you can always up an' quit," Jonesy snickered.

The idle banter spun itself out quickly, and a desultory silence soon reigned. Rafe eased back, fit bones and sore muscles into the soft dirt, tried counting stars and then, his mind drifting idly, thought of the times he'd counted stars. Rafting the river as a boy. Sitting on a quiet veranda. Hunting during the insect noisy nights. On the deck of a quiet ship at sea. All the easy nights of his youth, when trouble was measured in the failure of fish to bite or the begrudged imprisonment of rainy summer nights.

He woke under a high, hot sun, squinted, shaded his eyes, and studied the calloused hand offering him a strip of dark, stringy meat.

"If you close your eyes and chew an' try real hard, you can almost make it taste like somethin' other'n what it is," Elwood said with a grin.

Rafe's stomach growled, and he warily accepted the strip of half-jerked meat. "What is it?"

"Search me. A fella down the line was handin' it out."

Jonesy took a sip out of a mud-caked canteen, gargled, and swallowed. "I ain't the type to complain," he said, his head bobbing as he tried to make whatever it was he'd swallowed go down easier, "but I seen a passle of them wounded boys goin' barefoot an' holdin' up their trousers with rope as they was on their way back. An' the commissary, I hear tell, is right behind one of them field dressin' stations."

"What the blue blazes you gettin' at," Elwood growled, reinspecting his piece of meat.

"Nothin' special," Jonesy allowed. "'Cept I was gnawin' on one chunk for over an hour yesterday afore I realized it was a buckle. Damn near chewed off the C.S.A. writ on it, when I took a look."

Elwood wagged his head dolefully. "You're full a' shit," he snorted, manufacturing a reason to turn his head aside. He fished the by now gummy chunk of meat out of his mouth and inspected it, then put it back in. "Full of shee-it," she drawled as Jonesy and a half dozen of the other Missouri Regulars started laughing.

"Damn!" Rafe exclaimed. He held out a piece of meat and stared at it in disgust.

"What?" Elwood asked. Alarmed, he swiveled around to see what Rafe had discovered. "What'd you find?"

Rafe looked down distrustfully at the lump of meat in his hand. "Looks like part of a boot heel," he said in all seriousness, and then, sputtering, joined Jonesy and the others in laughter.

"You, too?" Elwood scowled and, forgetting his whereabouts, stood straight and started to walk off.

"You dumb ass!" Jonesy yelled, scrambling toward him. "Duck!"

Caught by surprise, Elwood spun around as if to see the bullet that surely sped toward him.

Jonesy and Rafe reached him at the same time. Both started to haul him down, but Elwood pushed them aside. "Wait a minute," he said, a strange tightness in his voice.

"C'mon, Elwood," Jonesy pleaded.

"I said, leave me be."

"Just because we was funnin' you is no reason to get your head blowed off."

"That's what I'm talkin' about," Elwood said, his square-jawed features turned full front to the Yankee lines.

Someone whistled in surprise. Another man put down his canteen and crawled up the embankment to take a careful look.

"Why aren't you dead already?" Rafe said, voicing the common thought and joining the general movement to peer, more carefully than Elwood, over the protective earthworks.

No fire greeted them. Not a single Yankee head showed. Only an unnatural, eerie silence. "Maybe we surrendered," one man off to the left mumbled.

"Don't bet on it," another replied.

"Maybe *they* surrendered." Everyone laughed, their voices without amusement.

Rafe looked to his right and saw the cannoneers and soldiers manning the defenses staring over the breastworks.

"I don't like it," Elwood whispered, still frozen to the spot. "'T'ain't like 'em not to potshot us."

"Listen," Rafe said, waving a hand to shush them.

The silence grew. "Navy," Jonesy finally said, "I don't hear a damn thing."

"That's what I mean," Rafe answered, pointing to the ground. He pressed his ear to the dirt. "The digging has stopped."

Heads up and down the line ducked and became still as the men listened. The awesome quiet permeated the air, and weighed it down with a sense of dread. "What's today?" Elwood asked, startling those to either side of him. "Anybody know?"

"Thursday, the twenty-fifth," Rafe replied. "Why?"

Elwood sat down at last and lay back, his hands behind his head. "Got me a feelin' today's gonna be a real scorcher," he said solemnly. "A feelin' things're gonna get almighty hot."

They did. Gunmetal, wood stocks, ramrods, cannon barrels, clothes themselves baked beneath a cloudless sky and brutal sun. Men invented what shade they could and waited and sipped stale, murky water. Noon passed. Stomachs growled. Throats grew dry.

"Captain Lattimore?"

Rafe felt his leg jostled. He pushed his hat off his face, raised a hand for shade, and studied the offending foot. When he looked up, he saw the wide-brimmed hat of an officer. He stood and saw lieutenant's bars and, in the deep shadow of the hat, a young face. At least he outranked him, Rafe thought. "Yes?" he asked, curious.

"My name is Allard, sir. Lieutenant Allard. Are you Captain Lattimore?"

Rafe studied the boyish, freckled face, bright with dignity and self-importance beneath a shock of red hair that his hat couldn't hide. The red fringe covering the boy's jaw was an unsuccessful attempt at maturity. "I'm Lattimore."

The young lieutenant saluted crisply. "Colonel Martin's respects, sir. He has directed me to ask, 'Captain Lattimore, what the hell are you doing up here?'"

The enlisted men waited to hear the answer, hoped they'd hear the real one.

"I'm on vacation, Lieutenant."

"Sir?" Allard asked, confused.

"Vacation, Lieutenant Allard. I got tired of putting out fires and needed a little rest and relaxation." Aware of the effect of his speech on the enlisted men, he concocted a wry, contorted grin. "I think I'm a little addled."

"I can see that, sir," the boy lieutenant replied seriously. "Colonel Martin has requested me to request you to report to him immediately."

Rafe sighed. "With all due respect, Lieutenant, I request in turn that you inform Colonel, ah, what is it? Martin, that he may need every man he can find up here before long."

All morning the quiet had grown in intensity. Not a single shot had been fired. None of the usual obscenities had been exchanged between the opposing armies. Lieutenant Allard looked around as if everyone had gone stark raving mad. "And with all due respect to *you*, Captain Lattimore," he responded, stiffly polite, "nothing has happened up here for weeks except the usual sniping and shelling, which we are used to. Nothing has happened and nothing will."

The world exploded. Rafe never heard the blast that lifted the center of the redoubt a hundred yards to their right high into the air and reduced the hill to an immense crater into which a deadly rain of rubble fell. One moment he was standing, trying to find an excuse to get the lieutenant out of his hair, and the next, kicked and flung about by unseen furies, he was thrown into the air, flung to earth, and half buried by he knew not what.

He was suffocating! Then breathe, a tiny voice in his mind told him. Frantic, he tried to remember how, and found himself focusing on a field. He was a boy lifting his grandfather's shotgun and then firing. The gun roared and knocked him off his feet. Flat on his back, mouth open like a fish, he tried desperately to suck in air, but none entered his chest.

"Help, Granpa!" he tried to say.

"Breathe, boy. Just breathe. Comes natural to us Lattimores."

Rafe squirmed beneath dead weight. Numbed fingers clawed a space for his mouth and nose. The ringing in his ears gradually subsided, only to be replaced by gunfire and the screams of men. The weight returned.

"Hey!" a voice gasped.

"I'm blind!" Rafe yelled, panic-stricken.

"Open your eyes," the voice ordered. "Open your eyes, mud for brains . . . uh, sir."

Rafe tried, saw a glimmer of light and then blinding sunshine as Elwood hauled the remains of Lieutenant Allard off him.

"Thanks," Rafe wheezed, realizing with relief that he was not only free, but alive and unharmed. "What the hell happened?"

Elwood's answer was a shrill scream. A point, then a full six inches of crimson steel poked through his chest. Crimson gore spattered Rafe as the attacking Yankee soldier tried to drag his bayonet free of Elwood's back.

Rafe kicked and rolled out of the rubble as Elwood's body took his place. The Yankee placed a foot in the center of Elwood's back. The dying Rebel grunted once as the bayonet jerked free. Rafe grabbed for his revolver and felt his heart sink as he realized the gun was somewhere in the dirt, at long last—it seemed like an eternity—he noticed a wooden grip protruding from Allard's holster just as the Yankee gave a cry and lunged at him. Rafe rolled and twisted. The bayonet sank into the dirt, skewering the spot where he'd been. Everything was a blur. Dirt, sweat, and blood stung his eyes. His chest still hurt from trying to breathe. His left arm was numb but functioning. Rafe half fell, half threw himself at Allard's bloody corpse and clawed for the pistol. He rolled again to dodge a second thrust and, while the Yankee was still trying to pull his bayonet out of poor Allard, fired upward into the blue uniform. Plucked from his musket, an expression of bewildered surprise on his face, the Yankee flew up and back and slammed into the dirt embankment.

"You stupid bastard! You stupid bastard, Elwood. Gone an' got yourself killed."

Rafe shook his head to clear the cobwebs, wiped his eyes, and saw Jonesy cradling his friend. Scrambling on all fours, Rafe reached him and pulled him away from Elwood's body. "He's dead, Jones," he said in a dry, raspy voice. "C'mon. There's fighting."

"Dumb bastard," Jonesy sobbed, reluctantly letting Elwood go. "We hung together like summer pig turds all this time, an' he gets himself killed. Dumb bastard. Dumb bastard!"

There was no time to mourn. Staggering over shattered timbers and broken bodies, Rafe and Jonesy gained the lip of the enormous crater torn out of the earth by the explosion and looked down at a scene of utter bedlam. The redoubt, a heavily reinforced fortification where the Rebel line made a sharp jog, had quite simply disappeared. In its place was a gaping breach in the Rebel line, into which poured men in blue uniforms from one side, and men in tattered gray uniforms from the other.

Men killed other men with rifles, pistols, bayonets, and sabers. When these were empty or lost or broken, they fought, as had warriors of eons past, with club and stone, with fist and tooth and nail. Bloodlust. That madness when men kill not for country or even self, but simply to let blood, to strike out, to kill like the animals they have become. Bloodlust. Trampling the dead and dying underfoot. The primal scream that tears the throat, that sends the hot blood coursing, that imbues the arm with unnatural strength, that overrides pain.

Reinforcements poured in from all sides. Already, men in butternut were running from the rear to fight in the bloodied trenches inundated by men in blue. Wide-eyed, mesmerized by the seething cauldron of men below him, Rafe watched in fascination and felt a growing elation fix him. This is what he had wanted! To fight! To kill! To spend himself and leach the torment from his heart and soul!

He took a step forward on shaky legs. One step toward the billowing dust, the howl of screams too loud to be drowned out by the clang of metal on metal and the sharp roar of firearms. The numbness in his left arm forgotten, he reached for and drew the revolver holstered at his left side. Stupid not to think of it before. Now he had two again. Minié balls whizzed past him. Death plucked at his sleeves. Two revolvers! A man without a face ran past him. Another man fell at his feet and, dying, grasped his boot. All along the line, to left and right, the firing had increased, but still paled in comparison to the carnage in the crater below.

And then he was laughing. Laughing insanely and striding forward.

"Where the hell're you going?" Jonesy shouted, unheard, and then ran to the rear.

Rafe didn't hear, didn't answer. Revolvers bucking and roaring in his hands, he descended into the violent melee, the awesome hell. To fight. To kill.

And perhaps, though he couldn't have cared less, to be killed.

CHAPTER 24

Solange stared at the mess on her plate. One soggy pile was reheated rice covered with a dirty white gravy. Another was of boiled peas that were still faintly and nauseatingly green. A third was a thin, dark piece of fried meat that, she had discovered when she tried to cut it, was much too tough and stringy for a common table knife. Next to the dinner plate, on a small bread-and-butter plate of its own, lay a rectangular piece of dark gray pea meal bread. Without butter, the bread would be dry and tasteless. That such slop was served on a table set with fine china, sterling silverware, and elegant crystal was ludicrous, frustrating, utterly revolting, and entirely unacceptable.

"No!" she wailed. A manicured hand with painted nails slashed out and swept the table clean. China, silverware, and crystal crashed to the floor. "No!" she screamed, and in a flurry of purple skirt, stalked through the low, dimly lit cave to the side room where the servants cooked and ate. "Zenia!"

"Yes'm?" Zenia jumped up from the table and swallowed quickly. Next to her, Harmon put down his fork and waited tensely.

"Where's Jesse?"

"Gone, Miz Stewart."

"Gone? What do you mean, gone?"

"Gone, ma'am. Soon as she fixed dinner she lit out to see 'bout her mama."

"Well, I won't eat that . . . that slop she served me," Solange shrilled. "She can't fool me. How dare she serve me that abomination?"

Zenia picked at her apron string. "You hasn't et anything 'cept bread for days, now, Miz Stewart," she finally said. "Jesse, she figured you needed somethin' else." Eyes wide, she dared look directly into her mistress's face. "Yo gots to keep up your strenth, Missus."

"*Strength*, damn you. I can't *stand* that talk."

"Yes'm. Strenth."

Solange almost screamed. Furious, she picked up Zenia's plate and held it under the black girl's nose. "What is this? Mule meat? And slops? It makes my stomach turn."

"But that's all they is, Miz Stewart," Zenia said. Her knees were weak, her hands shook. "I spent half the day findin' that rice an' a little molasses to put in the bread. As for the meat, everyone's eatin' it, an' it's rationed, too."

The plate spun across the room and hit the rug draped dirt wall. Food dripped down to the floor in a gray puddle. "I won't stand for it, do you hear? Living like animals burrowed into a cave. Animals! And nothing to eat. Someone has food. I'm just being made to suffer. My husband is a doctor. I deserve better than this."

Still ranting, Solange whirled and stalked out the door, yelling over her shoulder for Harmon to help her with the carriage. Behind her, the old Negro lifted his eyes to heaven. Silent prayer was the safest form of relief when Solange Stewart was on the rampage.

Because she belonged to a doctor, the mare was one of the few remaining privately owned horses in town that hadn't found its way to the table. Skittish because she seldom got out, she fought Harmon as he threaded her through the congestion clogging Mulberry Street in front of the hospital. Solange held a sachet to her nose and didn't wait for Harmon to assist her down from the carriage when they stopped. Neither did she pay the slightest attention to the wide-eyed, hungry stares of the emaciated, begrimed souls, the walking wounded, who waited for treatment outside the building. A late afternoon sun slanted across the recessed doorway of the hospital where an orderly stopped her. The orderly wore what had been a white coat but was now stained from red to brown, depending on the age of the blood that had soaked into it. "Yes'm?" the orderly asked.

"My name is Mrs. Stewart. I want to see my husband."

"Well, ma'am, uh . . ." The orderly looked uncertain. "I don't reckon—"

"Is he or is he not here?"

"He's *here,* ma'am, come back from the convent this morning when all them men from the fight in the Jackson Redoubt got brought in. But . . ."

"Then let me in immediately!" Solange demanded, imperiously sweeping past the orderly.

Caught by surprise, the orderly hurriedly caught up to Solange just inside the main door where she had stopped to stare at the canvas partition that separated the anteroom from the rest of the hospital. "You shouldn't be in here, ma'am," he said nervously.

"Please go and bring my husband to me."

"But he's probably busy right now!" the orderly sputtered. "You can't just—"

"I *insist.*"

The orderly sighed, wished he had someone available to tell him what to do, and finally threw his hands into the air and gave in. "All right, ma'am. I'll find him and tell him you're here. No harm in that, I reckon, but it might be a while if he's in the middle of . . . something."

Solange was left alone in an anteroom formed by sheets of canvas hung from sticks suspended from the ceiling. The air was still and stifling, saturated with the smell of chemicals, body wastes, and the sickly odor of infections. At first, she thought the silence was absolute, but as the seconds passed she recognized the soft rustle of men moving about on beds and an occasional subdued moan or groan. Once, from somewhere deep inside the hospital, a scream rent the air and sent her cringing back against the stone front wall.

Time became a hollow shell into which she retreated and sat alone with her anger and her fear, fed by the odors and sounds and the presence of death, mixing confusedly. She'd been mad to go to the hospital. Totally mad! What did Tom care, anyway? He was her husband in name only. Probably knew all about her and Micah, as if she really cared anymore, and was ordering the servants to feed her slop in revenge. That was it. Of course. If she had any sense, she'd just ask Micah. He was the logical one. If he couldn't take care of her, no one could. Convinced she was wasting her time, she turned to leave when the canvas wall at her side parted and Tom stood before her. The very sight of him infuriated her. Micah forgotten, she advanced on him and then just as abruptly stopped. He looked terrible. His coat glistened with drops of fresh blood that, as she watched, were starting to crust and dry around the edges to a deep, dark reddish brown. His eyes had sunk into his face, and looked hollow and empty. His left hand trembled, even as he held the hem of his coat to keep it from trembling. He looked at her as if seeing her from a great distance, as if he were a man seeing someone he thought he recognized.

And then he did recognize her. "You shouldn't be here," he said in a voice as dark as the circles under his eyes. "The streets are dangerous." That seemed to amuse him and he laughed hollowly, then choked back the tears. There was something about Solange he was supposed to remember. She was his wife, yes, but other than that. Ah, yes. He'd lost her. That was it. He tried to care, tried desperately to care, but simply couldn't find the strength. He was too empty, too far gone in fatigue, too drained of emotion. Perhaps if he was just nice to her she'd go away and give him time to rest. Tired as he was, a hint of sarcasm tinged his voice. "I ought not to scold you, oughtn't I? It's so seldom we see each other, my love."

The tone of his voice frightened her. Solange almost ran from him, but at the last minute remembered why she had come and felt the anger surge anew through her. "That's not my fault," she snapped. "It's yours. Yours and this stupid war."

A voice rose in a wailing crescendo and faded to a whimper.

"We ran out of chloroform days ago," Tom explained apologetically. "But not perforated abdomens and chests, or shattered limbs. The abdomens and lungs we can't treat very well. The lucky ones die quickly. The limbs? If a man is lucky, the pain of the saw causes him to faint. If unlucky, he dies or is tough enough to remain conscious. But then we need to tie him down."

Tom sat on a bench that ran along one of the canvas walls. They'd lost two doctors during the past week and he'd had to fill in for them. He blinked his eyes to clear them. "I'm very busy, Solange," he said, rubbing a hand across his face.

Solange gasped. Tom stared at his hand, still wet from the operation he'd just completed, and realized he'd inadvertently smeared his face with blood.

"We . . . we need food!" Solange blurted, desperately clinging to her anger. "At the house." Her knees felt weak, and she backed away from Tom and into the canvas, then rebounded with a shriek of alarm. "At the cave, I mean!"

"I left off a packet of meat this morning. And money so Zenia could find a little something extra."

"You?" Solange asked, her face contorting as the anger rose to a fine pitch. "You are responsible for—"

"Of course. They slaughtered early today. My orderly brought me some of the choice cuts."

Choice cuts of mule meat. Filthy rice. The horrid, dried peas. Blood on Tom's face. "I don't understand this," Solange said, paling. "I don't understand . . . know . . . you. What is happening? We must have proper food. The others . . ."

"Are lucky to get as good. And often get less."

"But I refuse!" Solange shrieked. She stamped her foot and beat her fists on her thighs. "I refuse to be reduced to such a level!"

"You refuse?" Tom asked, anger finally burning through fatigue. "You refuse? Damn you, woman! There's a hill of legs and arms out back higher than I can see over. Our corpses rot unburied in the sun! We have a man stationed there to chase away the carrion birds, but we tell him not to trouble himself too much because the birds and the rats make less work for our burial details. And you want me to concern myself with the fact that we're out of champagne and smoked pheasant? Well, I'm sorry. I've done the best I could, and I'm sorry it wasn't good enough. Maybe someone else can help you. Maybe Micah Lattimore can help you!"

The name jolted her. "I . . . I don't know what you mean," Solange stammered.

"Don't lie to me, woman," Tom warned. He had lived with the knowledge of her infidelity for almost a month. Most of the time he could blot out the pain by keeping busy, but now it overwhelmed him and spilled out of him like pus from a lanced wound. His bloodied, open hand quivered in front of her face and his voice shook with rage, malignant, hateful, delicious rage let loose at last. "Don't lie to me, do you hear? I could endure only so much gossip and whispered innuendos before I followed you. Just once. I prayed I was making a fool of myself by taking such talk seriously, but it appears you and Micah had beat me to it. So if you're hungry, my dear, if you're not satisfied with your fare, why not ask your rutting lover to find you more or better?"

Solange started to retort, but hurriedly reconsidered when she realized she had no defense. "So be it," she finally hissed. "I will not be home when you return. Do not bother to come looking for me."

Tom stepped near her. Solange felt compelled to hold her ground despite the horrid crimson smear across the face and the smell of suffering that permeated his clothes. To her complete surprise, he leaned forward and gently kissed her on the mouth, in the process smudging her cheek with the still damp blood. "My dear Solange," he said, "I quit looking for you a long time ago. A lifetime ago. Goodbye."

Stunned, Solange watched him walk away, push through the canvas wall, and vanish. The canvas swayed back and forth. Through the expanding and contracting slit, she could see a long double row of pallets, each with its silent wounded. She felt paralyzed, as if she were in a vacuum and pulled so many ways simultaneously she didn't know which way to go. Absentmindedly, she wiped her cheek with the sachet.

"Pardon me, ma'am. Pardon."

She jerked around, stepped back to let two stretcher bearers carrying a wounded soldier pass, looked down to see a mere wisp of a boy whose head was wrapped in a mud-and-blood-stained bandage and whose right arm dangled over the edge of the stretcher. Not until she felt a tug at her skirts did she realize that the arm ended in a blood-soaked, bulbous bandage where his hand should have been.

It was too much. Too much! Gagging, Solange whirled and stumbled through the front door. Outside, the waiting soldiers catcalled and cheered her progress through their ranks. One, bolder than the rest, dared place a hand on her arm. "Please, ma'am, would you have a soft, cool touch in you for a fevered brow?"

"Get out of my way!" Solange shrieked, jerking her arm free. "All of you! All of you! Stay away from me!"

Alarmed, the soldiers gave way, made no move to impede her progress, watched in awe the radiant fury of the beauty. Solange swept past them and, half running, almost collapsed at Harmon's feet before recovering enough to let him help her into the carriage. Then, before the black man could round the carriage to take his place, she grabbed the whip and reins.

"Missus Stewart?" Harmon called, perplexed as the carriage started to move away from him.

"Walk!" Solange snapped, and slashed the whip across the mare's rump.

The carriage skidded on the gravel. "The brake!" Harmon yelled, not wanting to be left alone but afraid the mare would strain herself. He saw a hand release the brake lever, and then watched as the carriage rolled away and left him to fend for himself.

"*Oo-weee!*" one of the soldiers called, laughing. "You better off without that one, Uncle!"

"Yassuh," Harmon agreed, already hurrying off down the street. "Yassuh, I sho'nuff is!"

Solange had stopped at the cave long enough to pack three carpetbags, a trunk, and two hat boxes, the latter with her jewelry secreted among the hats. She had taken longer than anticipated. Now, night and fog spilled ominously off the river and enveloped the lower parts of the city. The buildings on the waterfront, stark and tomblike, punctured, battered, burned, disfigured, loomed like ghosts out of the mist as the carriage clattered past in close proximity, then disappeared again.

Solange knew the way by heart and, her mind on other matters, drove without paying attention. Tom's weary renunciation had stirred the guilt that she had striven so hard to deny and cut her to the quick. He had humiliated her and, in a clumsy attempt to deny his own inadequacy, had as much as accused her of being a slut and a whore. How dared he! The fault was his. His! *He* had forsaken her. *He* had left her to starve. *He* had abandoned her and set her adrift in a terrifying world not of her own making. And in the end, he had driven her from his home and into the arms of another man.

The Bartlett warehouse swam out of the fog and shadows. Solange pulled back on the reins and the mare slowed to a stop. The whirlwind ride down the dangerously fog-shrouded streets had left the mare skittish and frightened. Solange swore softly in French and, fearing the animal might bolt, kept hold the reins for a moment after she set the brake. Orange yellow cracks showing through the shutters announced that Micah was already there, and a mental image formed. As clearly as if she were inside, Solange could see the bed and the floor, the single desk they used for a table, and the boxes Micah had scavenged to take the place of chairs. She could smell the sharp odor of whiskey as well and the heavy musk of sex, primal and without pretense.

She wanted Micah Lattimore, needed him every bit as much as she needed food and water and air. Why then did she hesitate, allow herself to consider the inexplicable urge to return to Tom? Suddenly unsure of herself, Solange looked back the way she had come into the blank wall of fog. Tom had been so vibrant and alive when they married. He had loved her, as she had him, without reservation. He was, she knew deep inside herself, a man driving himself to desperate limits in the service of others.

But ultimately, he was just a man, one who was unable to give her what she wanted and needed. Still, she was struck by the intriguing notion that if she were to return, and devote herself to him, she might share in that illumination a priest might have called salvation.

"You gonna sit out there all night?"

Solange looked to her left to see Micah wreathed in a halo of orange light. Tom faded into an illusion of might-have-been. "No," she said, climbing down. "I was waiting for you to help me carry in my bags."

She had made her choice.

After the last breath, the last spasm, the final seconds of spent lust, the darkness returns. The darkness always returns because the darkness never totally goes away. The darkness is emptiness of soul. The void can be filled again when the urge and the energy return, but there is still the knowledge of the void. The void which in the darkness is a blank space, a cavern for the heart. It numbs. It takes the shape and sound of love for a time, but after a while the smooth becomes rough and the melody sours as the notes of delight slide off key. Masks crack and crumble, and are not enough. Masks are not enough.

"What?" Micah said, stirring. He sat up and touched Solange's face. "You crying?"

The darkness and the void are worse at night when they form a dread bond with the soul and time laughs. "No," Solange said. "Yes. A dream. I was having a nightmare."

Micah laughed. "Is that all?" His hand slid across her buttocks. "Roll over and I'll give you something better to dream about."

"I'd rather sleep."

"Well, shit! Just like a woman. The minute you move in, you'd rather sleep,'" he mimicked.

"You ridicule me," Solange said, on the verge of crying openly.

"No," Micah replied. "Me. I'm a fool. A blasted fool for letting you move in." He swung one leg over her and straddled her thighs. "I should've known better."

"I'm tired," Solange protested, wiping her eyes. "Please, Micah?"

"Please, hell," Micah snorted. He reached down to part her flesh and, finding her dry, muttered his contempt and climbed back off her. "You got wet enough earlier. Hot and wet enough for a damn bull!"

"Why are you so cruel to me?"

"Because, my sweet, you like me cruel. But never mind. I've other things to do."

"You're going to leave me alone?" Solange asked, cringing against the wall.

"That's right, sweet." Micah stood in the center of the room and dressed quickly. "You mind your manners," he added, reaching across the bed to give her cheek a pinch, "and I'll take you with me next time."

"I love you, Micah," Solange said as he walked away from her. "And I hate you."

Micah sighed. "Which is precisely the reason we get along so well . . . *ma chérie.*" He paused at the door to tie on his pistol belt and check his knife. "Sleep tight," he said, and disappeared into the night.

Solange curled into a little ball. Outside, she heard the receding clatter of hooves and wheels. Micah had taken Tom's carriage.

The end was near, as any deaf, dumb, and blind man could tell. Micah didn't know exactly when the Confederate defense would finally crumble, only that it would, and soon. If he didn't prepare right then, the chaos of capitulation would come and go, and he'd lose his one best chance to escape with enough gold to set him up in the fine style he wanted and deserved. The choice of Celia's house as a diversion was a stroke of genius, he thought. Assuming Rafe believed Fancy and took the bait, he'd be waiting there, one man against six, to die alone far away from Micah's real objective. As for Celia, the bitch's humiliation would be complete, if he knew Cairo and his boys.

A stroke, all right. Both of them, Rafe and Celia, repaid with interest.

The amber-lit windows of Celia's house were barely visible in the mist. Micah lifted a gloved hand and pointed toward the house. "That's it."

"Yeah," Cairo snorted. He spat a glob of phlegm in the street. "I remember 'em now. One of them Goddamned Abolitionist nigger-lovers."

"None other," Micah said.

"Just take a better look, you don't mind," Cairo said, loping off into the mist. He felt uneasy being away from the familiar alleys and derelict buildings of Vicksburg Under the Hill, so he kept to the shadows as he made a wide, cautious circle around the house. There appeared to be no problem. Easy access from the rear, easier from the front. There would be a basement, of course, as evidenced by the fact that the house was still occupied. The basement only made things easier: everyone living there would undoubtedly sleep downstairs, which meant he could look around upstairs at his leisure. "And you're sure there's gold?" he asked, materializing at Micah's side again.

"Plenty of it. Probably in the cellar," Micah said, not really knowing or caring if there was. "Food, too, I imagine. You don't see Miss Bartlett lining up for rationed mule like everyone else."

"Hell with the food. Gold's more to my taste," Cairo said with a wide grin.

The breath from Cairo's mouthful of rotted teeth would have stopped a cavalry charge. Micah grimaced. He held no affection for Cairo or his kind, but they were useful under the right circumstances. "You'll have to bide your time," he cautioned.

"How long?" Cairo asked dubiously.

"Trust me. I'll tell you when."

"Ain't much for waitin'."

"How does dying sound?"

Cairo considered that. "All right, Blueblood," he finally conceded. "We wait."

"As soon as the surrender takes place. While the generals are busy talking and everyone else is sleeping by their guns, we let your people loose. You can tell them the truth—that it's the one chance any of them will have to salvage something from this godforsaken war and escape with their lives."

What Micah had up his sleeve, Cairo didn't know. Some thievery of his own, no doubt, but that was all right. As long as Cairo got his share, he was more than willing to cooperate. "They'll do what I tell 'em," he promised. "Them buildin's we set afire to draw folks away from you will draw 'em away from us as well. We'll get in and back out with that old man's gold before anyone can figure out what's happened."

"His daughter's gold now," Micah pointed out.

"Mine, in a few days," Cairo chuckled. "You got a head on your shoulders, Blueblood. Yes, indeedy."

Moving swiftly, the two men slipped down the street to where the mare waited. Whether or not there was gold in the Bartlett's basement didn't matter so long as Cairo believed there was. Micah knew where he could get his hands on enough gold of his own: in a safe behind a portrait in his father's house. He even knew the combination. And while Cairo was busy setting fire to buildings and looting Celia's house, and while Rafe was busy defending Celia, Micah intended to go calling, to pay the home of his youth one last visit. Alone.

The trek back from the trenches had been exhausting. Now, night obscured the identity of the man who slogged down Clay Street as, earlier, it had the men in the carriage. Rafe paused to rest and then, the effort of moving sapping what remaining strength he had, stumbled down the last block. He finally came to a halt at the rear gate to Celia's house, and there stared dully at the dim light coming from the sun parlor. They were still up. Lynna must have been having a rough night.

"That you?" a voice asked.

Rafe sorted through his mind, attached the voice to a name. "Yes," he said wearily. He slid through the partially open gate and stopped at Jonathan's side. "I didn't expect you out here. Where's Broussard?"

"Sent him off to get some sleep. Where've you been? We've been looking all over for you."

"In the trenches."

"Trenches?" Jonathan asked, surprised. "You mean you—?"

"I thought I'd go take a shot at someone for a change. Got more than I bargained for, I guess."

"I don't follow you."

"I was at the Great Redoubt. Up on Jackson Road."

"Jesus!" Jonathan swore softly. "Was it as bad as they say?"

Rafe considered that, finally shook his head. "Worse. It went on forever, and then I fell asleep." His voice sounded dull and heavy, even to himself. "I guess, anyway. It is Saturday, isn't it?"

"The twenty-seventh. Around eleven, I suppose."

"Feels like the middle of July," Rafe said, bone tired. "Had no idea

I'd gotten back so soon." He glanced at Jonathan, hesitated, and then asked, "She doing all right?"

"The last time I looked," Jonathan reassured him. "Why don't you go in and see her before you fall asleep again?"

"The last thing Lynna needs," Rafe said with a yawn, "is me paying my compliments."

"I wasn't talking about Lynna, and you know it," Jonathan snapped.

"Don't play teacher and student with me," Rafe snapped back, just as peevishly. "I'm too old. Besides, this is none of your business."

"It isn't?" Jonathan asked. "Why not? I'm the one who gets to watch her every day. She pretends nothing has changed, but her eyes fill with tears when she laughs. You're not around to see that, of course. You stand outside in shadows, like one of the thieves you instruct me to apprehend."

Rafe opened his mouth to retort, but then decided he was too tired to argue. Sighing, he eased himself down and sat with his back against the wall. "No problems while I was gone?"

"Quiet as can be," Jonathan said, joining him.

Rafe pulled a pair of cigars out of his pocket and offered one to Jonathan. The teacher accepted it and produced a light. "God, but I'd forgotten what a good cigar tastes like," he said dreamily.

"Found them on a dead Yankee."

"Virginia tobacco. I can tell." Jonathan puffed contentedly. "Makes a man feel, well . . ."

"Quiet?" Rafe hinted sarcastically.

"Not exactly. You'll need more than a bribe to still my eternal quest for truth." Jonathan wished he could see Rafe's face, then decided it was just as well that he couldn't. Some things were better said in darkness. "I'm glad you finally came back," he went on quietly. "I try not to worry about Lynna, so to take my mind off her, I worry about you and Celia."

"Don't," Rafe said shortly.

"Is that an order, Captain Lattimore?"

"It's anything you want."

They smoked in silence, enjoyed the murky stillness that had brought relief from the bombardment. In the distance, a smattering of rifle fire increased, then was topped by a pair of explosions that made the earth tremble.

"Assault beneath the cover of darkness?" Jonathan asked.

"Who knows? The war might be over by morning. Then you won't have to worry about killing anyone."

"It's over for us, anyway, isn't it?"

"We repulsed them yesterday," Rafe said. "They didn't get through." Suddenly, the cigar tasted terrible. He scrubbed off the burning end and tucked the butt away in his shirt pocket. "Yes," he said tiredly. It was time to face the truth. They had fought well, but would inevitably lose. "Yes," he repeated. "For us, it is."

CHAPTER 25

Nathaniel emerged from his bath and found the gray suit, his favorite, laid out for him on the bed. "Any word from my son?" he asked as Robert held his shirt for him.

"Down in the back parlor, suh. He come in sometime last night, 'pears. Slept in the chair. When I walked through he was sittin' an' starin' out across the fields like he was watchin' the trains, only there ain't no trains."

"He say where he'd been the last few days?" Nathaniel buckled his belt, held out one foot so Robert could help him with his shoes. "Any explanation at all?"

"No, suh."

"I can't fathom it. Something's eating at him, and not just the general sad state of affairs, mind you." Nathaniel tied his own tie, stepped back from the mirror while Robert helped him with his coat. "Well, I'll see to him. Bring my coffee, or what you like to fool me into thinking is coffee, to the parlor."

"Ain't never made no claims for it, suh. Anyhow, we done used the last of that chicory an' barley."

There were levels of injustice in the world. Nathaniel was sure he'd sunk to a new low. "I suppose that means we're down to hot water then, eh?"

"No, suh. Lucy found some sprouts she says makes a right nice tea. Strengthens the innards, so she says."

"I'll try anything once," Nathaniel said with a sigh. "A man ought to have a warm drink in the morning. Sets the world to right."

"If this brew does, Mistuh Lattimore, you let me know, an' I'll drink a whole kettle full." Robert's laugh turned into a reedy cough that shook the older servant's wisp of a body.

Nathaniel looked on in concern, for the first time noting the black man's watery eyes and the faint trembling in his hands. "What have you gone and done?" he asked, Rafe forgotten momentarily.

"Took ill, I reckon, Mistuh Lattimore."

"Well, have Lucy bring her tea to the parlor, then drink some yourself and get to bed for the rest of the day. The girls can take care of the house. Parlor, dining room, and my room as usual for the time being. I'll talk to Lucy about the next few meals myself."

None too steady on his feet, Robert hurried around his master and opened the bedroom door. "I ain't never laid down when there was work to be done, suh."

"You will today, and for as long as you feel poorly." The hall was dark, for all the morning sunshine. "Soon as I talk to Rafe, I'll see if I can find a doctor to take a look at you."

"Just so long as he don't do no cuttin' on me, Mistuh Lattimore. Doctors gettin' too used to cuttin' these days."

"No," Nathaniel said, patting the old man's hand. "No cutting."

Nathaniel followed the servant down the stairs and hall to the parlor, where Rafe was stretched out on the sofa with his feet propped on one arm rest and his head on a pillow at the other end. "What happened to you?" Nathaniel asked, taken aback by his son's appearance and the ragged state of his clothes.

Rafe found himself recounting, for the second time in less than eight hours, the tale of the explosion and battle at the Great Redoubt.

"Thank God, you came back in one piece," Nathaniel sighed when the story ended.

"Yeah," Rafe said, making a face as he finished Lucy's concoction. "I wouldn't have missed *this* for all the world."

"Look a gift horse in the mouth," his father said with a scowl. "If I were you, I'd be damned glad I was alive."

Lucy, the youngest of the servants, a bare slip of a girl, entered the parlor. "There be someone to see you, Mister Rafe," she announced, her bare feet padding softly over the throw rug. "A woman. Out back."

Celia? Rafe's expectations soared. Rising quickly from the couch, he hurried to the window. Gaudily attired in a full-length purple gown, Fancy Darren stood on the other side of the low wall that separated the lawn from the fields.

"Isn't that—"

"Yes," Rafe said, cutting his father off.

"Well, well, well."

"Well, well, well yourself. You seemed to recognize her quickly enough."

Nathaniel coughed discreetly. "I've lived in this town a long time," he said, as if that explained everything. "Just because I know *who* she is doesn't mean I ever—"

"Okay," Rafe interrupted again. "I believe you." Perplexed, he tried to recall his meeting with her. "But what does she want?"

"You, to begin with," Nathaniel snorted, covering a laugh. "And here I thought she was more Micah's type. Lucky for us the Reynolds and Laughtons have taken to caves."

"I imagine she couldn't care less about the Reynolds and Laughtons."

"And why should she? Her reputation isn't at stake."

A pained expression on his face, Rafe strode out the door and across the lawn. Fancy smiled as he approached. Her gown, Rafe now saw, was of heavy wool which must have been unbearably hot even at that hour of the morning, for sweat beaded her lip and streaked her rouged cheeks. Off to one side, the Negro piano player waited in her carriage. Rafe studied the prostitute a moment. "You're ill," he said by way of greeting.

"Not a very romantic remark," Fancy rasped, "for when a lady comes calling."

Rafe shrugged. "It's too early in the morning for romance. Besides, I've seen too much of the fever not to recognize the symptoms. Have you seen a doctor?"

"Hundreds," Fancy said with a knowing leer. "Be that as it may, though," she went on in spite of Rafe's obvious disapproval, "I came here to discuss your business, not mine."

"Oh?" Rafe asked. He combed his fingers through his hair and, arms folded, leaned against the wall. "And what business of mine would you know about?"

Fancy started to answer, then noticed Nathaniel staring at her from the parlor window. She waved to the older man who started and, embarrassed, ducked out of sight. "Sweet old dear," she said sarcastically.

"He'd have an apoplectic fit if he heard you call him that."

"Even though it's not half as bad as what he calls me?" Fancy asked, knowing full well the names the Nathaniel Lattimores of the world called her. She opened a purple velvet handbag and removed a slim silver flask, from which she drank deeply. The home brew washed her throat with liquid fire. Eyes watering, Fancy replaced the cap and returned the flask to her purse. "Nice place," she wheezed, looking around at the still intact house and outbuildings.

"The Yankee gunners probably have orders to avoid shelling the tracks, if possible. Makes our position luckier than most," Rafe answered laconically, biding his time until she was ready to reveal the real purpose of her visit.

"Indeed!" Fancy replied with exaggerated sweetness. "But that's the way it always is. Them that has get to keep what they has, no matter what."

"You're not being fair. Father has shared everything from food to bedclothes. He eats the same peas and mule meat as everyone else. The same could be said for many others. Well off before the war won't necessarily mean well off after the war."

Fancy's eyes narrowed and she leaned closer to Rafe. "That's not the way your brother and some of his friends see it."

So now they were getting down to business. "That lot will always complain," Rafe said laconically, not wanting to show too much interest. "It's in their blood. They find failure in everyone but themselves."

"Which doesn't make them any less dangerous, does it?" Fancy asked.

Rafe waited. The wind stirred. The brim of Fancy's hat bobbed up and down.

"All right," Rafe finally said. "I'll ask. What are you getting at? Why are you here, Fancy?"

"Micah has plans. He came by a couple of nights ago, real late. He wanted me to pleasure him, but I told him he'd never have enough gold to buy his way into my bed again. Which made him madder'n I've seen, except that day you were there when I kicked him out in the first place. Anyway, being drunk, he bragged about having enough gold to buy and sell me as soon as this surrender talk came true. What it sounded like was that him and Cairo and the rest of their gang have about ten places lined up where they know there's gold. The night before the Yanks walk in, they plan to hit them one at a time in a row, starting," she paused for emphasis, "with the Bartlett house."

Rafe's skin prickled. Starting with Celia? Could Micah really be so crazed? Did he still hate her for rejecting him in favor of Rafe so long ago? More importantly, would he stop at the gold, or wreak some more terrible vengeance? "Why do you tell me this?" he asked, suddenly suspicious.

"Why?" A faraway look came into Fancy's eyes as she remembered why. Fancy had no illusions about herself. Once a whore always a whore, as the saying went. But her son had been a far different matter. By the time he was twelve, it was impossible to keep him isolated from her place and business where he took the worst kind of riffraff imaginable for his heroes and ideals. At thirteen, she could no longer handle him, and for the first time in her life, Fancy knew the meaning of despair. Her dream had been to launch him in some honorable way of life, but no established businessman would take the son of a whore in any other than the most menial capacity. Until she spoke to Hal

Bartlett, who saw through the whorish exterior and saw within the fears and hopes and aspirations of a mother, and out of the kindness of his heart signed on her son and promised he should have a chance to rise. "I owe Hal Bartlett a favor," she finally said in a voice that was barely audible. "Owe him a favor I never repaid. This ain't much, but at least I can see they don't take the gold he left his daughter, and maybe save her life in the bargain."

Rafe started to ask another question, but Fancy cut him off with a wave of her hand. "Which is all you need to know, Blueblood, so don't be asking more." She took a deep breath, squared her shoulders. "Well, I told you," she said, and abruptly turned toward her carriage.

"Fancy . . . Miss Darren," Rafe called.

The prostitute paused.

"Thank you. Thank you very much. Now I . . . owe you a favor."

Fancy laughed harshly and let the piano player help her into her carriage. "Ain't that something," she cackled. "Mr. Rafe Blueblood owing the likes of Fancy Darren. Oh, they'd get a laugh out of that one, was I to tell them. They'd get some laugh."

"Are you going to be all right?" Rafe asked as the black man popped his whip and set the emaciated horse into motion.

"Of course," Fancy replied over her shoulder. "Men are men, whatever the color of their uniforms."

Her laughter could be heard after the carriage turned the corner of the fence and disappeared on its way back to Levee and Vicksburg Under the Hill. Alone, Rafe looked out over the green growing fields that held the memories of childhood and the rolling meadows where he had spent so much of his youth. At that time he had wished desperately to be an adult. Now he wasn't at all sure why.

So Micah had finally gone completely beyond the bounds of sanity and decency. Why Fancy Darren had been so compelled to divulge this information was a mystery, but Rafe felt equally compelled to believe her. Slowly he walked back to the porch and sat on the top step, his elbows on his knees, his chin in his hands. His stomach growled, but that had become a way of life. He stared out at the far rolling distance and tried to think, he told himself, constructively.

Trouble never seemed to come alone. First had been the dilemma of whether or not to arrest, or at least report, Celia. Honor and duty had dictated he do so, but his heart had rebelled. Luckily, no actual harm had been done because of his indecision. Micah was a different matter entirely. Harm *would* be done if he wasn't stopped. But how? Was he to confront his own brother? Perhaps even kill him?

His father's shadow crossed him and then Nathaniel was sitting next to him, sucking in his breath and easing his leg out straight to alleviate the pain in his hip. "What was that all about?" he asked.

Rafe considered lying, and then realized his father deserved the truth. "It's Micah," he said, carefully keeping his eyes from Nathaniel's. "He's brought together a rough lot to take advantage of the situation when the city surrenders. They're going to start at Celia's. They're after gold, among other things."

Nathaniel closed his eyes and exhaled slowly. "That boy," he finally said, shaking his head. "No. Not a boy. Not any longer. A man. Who has made his own choice."

"But why?" Rafe asked, anguished. "Why this one particular man? And why does he have to do this to *you?* What kind of a choice—"

"Maybe it isn't his fault," Nathaniel interrupted dolefully. "I like to think it's more like a fever, a destructive illness that comes on many boys, but one from which Micah never recovered. One that left him somehow . . . sick and not responsible. Somehow, that makes it easier."

"Easier?" Rafe asked ruefully.

"That's what I tell myself." Unsure of how to express what he needed next to say, Nathaniel stared at the tips of his shoes and, for the first time in his life, admitted to himself that he might be getting old. "The job is mine," he finally said, almost choking on the words, "but I'm too old and he's too strong. If he does go to Celia's, you'll have to be the one who stops him."

"I guess so," Rafe said, his stomach knotting.

"He's your brother."

"I know that."

"Of course. Of course." His hip was on fire from sitting that way. Gritting his teeth against the pain, Nathaniel struggled to his feet and held onto the railing. "Your mother spoiled him," he explained. "She always made him feel special. Maybe that was the trouble. Micah was never able to accept anyone as his equal, never able to understand that he couldn't do anything he wanted when he wanted." Slowly, pensively, he nodded in acceptance of all that had gone before. "Well, I am thankful she has missed all this."

"And what am I supposed to do, Father?" Rafe asked when he could no longer stand the silence between them. "Shoot him?"

"A man has two duties," Nathaniel said cryptically. "To be true to his honor, and to be true to his heart."

"And when these two duties conflict?"

Nathaniel looked at his son for the first time since they had started talking. His eyes were steady and his voice firm. "Then you must choose, my boy. You must choose one or the other. And that, Rafe Lattimore, is what we call being a man." Head high, Nathaniel hobbled down the last two steps and limped across the lawn toward the stone wall, then continued through the gate and stood alone in the field beyond.

A man. He'd been a man for some time, Rafe thought, watching the cloud shadows move over the land. Or had he? If, as his father had said, being a man meant among other things the ability to make the difficult choices, he'd been doing a poor job of it. For almost three weeks he'd vacillated between arresting or reporting Celia, and keeping her role as a spy a secret. Not deciding, he knew, was a decision of sorts, but only by default. He had never forced himself to choose between condemnation and forgiving. And if he couldn't do that, how did he hope to have the courage to face Micah, and if necessary take his life?

Honor or heart? Patterns of shade formed and dissolved and took on new shapes. Forgive or condemn Celia, somehow stop and if necessary permanently end Micah's threat. Answers were no less elusive than clouds. No absolute right, no absolute wrong. The choice was his, though.

His and his alone.

CHAPTER 26

A deathbed pall hung over Vicksburg. Isolated from the world beyond its boundaries, ignorant of all save its own agony, it languished torpidly under the relentless Mississippi summer sun. All but the most rabid diehards admitted the city was gasping its last. Perhaps that was why, on Sunday the twenty-eighth of June, the fortieth day of the siege, the churches, or what was left of them, were filled. From all walks of life, the citizens of Vicksburg flocked to be comforted, to have their fears allayed, and to reaffirm their faith that all was not lost forever and that life would go on.

Fortunately Reverend Lundquist's madness had been of short duration, for he was, if overly sensitive perhaps, also blessed with uncommon strength. On this Sunday, his ruined church to one side, he stood in a makeshift pulpit set under a shell-shredded oak tree and preached to a congregation of such great size that the sanctuary would not have held it had the church remained intact. Enough pews had been salvaged from the building for the old folks. The young and the multitude of attending soldiers gathered in rows and clumps as the spirit moved them. Two soldiers, their clothes so tattered as to be virtually nonexistent, perched in a magnolia tree and listened.

A strange quality permeated the day. One of peace and fellowship, and of time suspended. For this one moment there was neither war nor siege. Men did not lie dying a bare hundred yards away in a cramped hospital. No trenches lay over the horizon. There was no North, no South, neither did fiercely bearded generals dictate the course of each hour. Life had transcended maps and battle plans and logistics and tactics. Life was once again the song of birds, the whirr of insects, the lifting of voice in praise, the calm tone of the Lord's representative, who spoke of love and healing and redemption.

All this was true, and as surely as it was true, was false. Nathaniel dozed lightly at the end of one of the pews. Celia, uncomfortable in his presence and fearing he might inquire as to the problem between her and Rafe, took a seat next to the old man out of courtesy. This was the first time since her foray across the lines that she had left the grounds of her house, and isolation had heightened her perception of the changes that had taken place in the intervening three weeks. She had seen much of the damage, of course, from the upper story of her home, but the view from her carriage as she passed through the streets showed that the destruction had been even worse than she had thought. Buildings that appeared whole at a distance were mere shells. Mme. Cognaisse's dress shop was a rubble pit, Henry Schweicker's grocery store a shell. Clarke's Literary Depot, where women of leisure once had gone to read the latest novels, was a stable for mules. The corner of Washington and Jackson streets, once the busiest intersection in the city, was blocked by an enormous crater that, filled with rainwater and sewage, was a muddy brown, odiferous lake. Whole blocks of businesses were burned or shelled out. House upon house had simply disappeared as, blown up, the wood with which they had been made had been carted away to fuel cook fires or repair damaged but still standing buildings.

The effects of the siege were even more clearly written on the people who had lived through it. Normally tanned and healthy faces were pale and strained. Once energetic children sat listlessly, the hunger evident in their eyes and their little arms. Almost everyone had lost weight, and their clothes no longer fit. Privation had affected the old even more than the young. Men and women of her father's generation had aged remarkably during the tribulation of the siege. Many, she sensed from the vacant look in their eyes, would never recover fully.

And for what? Rumors were rife that Pemberton was almost convinced he should surrender. All hope for relief from Johnston or any other Confederate general had finally faded completely. Everyone knew that the soldiers in the trenches were half-starved, pitiful creatures who couldn't have held back a determined attack, and everyone both appreciated and resented the Yankee generals for not mounting that attack. Vicksburg was destitute. The city and army had run out of medicine weeks earlier. Of food there was little, barely enough to keep body and soul together. Water supplies were low and polluted. A pinch of salt was worth a king's ransom, and spirits, save for the few unbroken bottles in the caves of the rich, were virtually nonexistent.

And for what, one asked over and over again. To assuage the generals' sense of honor? Not really, for none of the dead cared about generals, much less their vaunted honor. To maintain the geographic integrity of the Confederacy? Not really, for not so much as a message had crossed the Yankee-controlled Mississippi for two months. To act as a symbol of resistance, even, to the South? How silly. The South didn't, couldn't, know what was happening in Vicksburg in the first place and needed symbols of victory, not defeat, in the second. For history? Ah, Celia thought. There was the real reason when all was said and done. So that men and women could, when the books were written, hold their heads high and say, "We did not give in! We did not give up! We persevered, we endured, we held!"

But ultimately surrendered, nonetheless. Ultimately defeated. As was she, Celia thought, unable to concentrate on the sermon. She was not unlike the view from her upper windows: the casual observer might think she looked intact, but she had sustained, in truth, far greater damage than met the eye. Her father's death had left a great gaping wound in her heart. That she had succumbed to the temptation of vengeance and become a spy was a festering ulcer that would not soon heal. Worst of all, she had lost Rafe, the one love of her life, and the loss had left her with an unbearable emptiness. She sensed that one day she would recover, but at the moment found herself incapable of caring when or how. It simply didn't matter.

She stood, she sang. She bowed her head as did everyone else. She greeted old friends warmly and chatted animatedly. She laughed, she sympathized. And when all was said and done, she hadn't the foggiest notion of how the hour had passed or how she escaped Nathaniel's solicitude and found herself walking the streets alone.

The city of a hundred hospitals, each marked with a yellow flag. A city of empty stores. A city of scurvy and measles and malaria and catarrh and typhoid and dementia. A city whose single remaining newspaper was printed on wallpaper. A city of caves and cave dwellers. A city where morning glories, jasmine, roses, and chrysanthemums grew out of dust and rubble. A city where, in spite of everything, a comical poster stuck to the single remaining wall of a building announced a menu that included Mule Rump Stuffed with Rice, Mule Ears Fricasseed à la Gotch, Mule Tongue Cold à la Bray, and Cottonseed Pie.

Perhaps all wasn't lost after all, Celia thought, oscillating between despondency and hopefulness. On a whim, she turned east up Grove Street and struck out at a brisk pace. The day was warm and still with an occasional light breeze that pressed her gown and underskirts to her legs, tugged at her bonnet, and cooled her face. She could hear the creek below the cemetery as she approached the fence and stepped through the gate. The last time she had been there . . . The thought threatened her reflective calm, and she hurried on to the Bartlett plot.

The cemetery was a shambles from soldiers who had bivouacked there for a time and moved on. Weeds had sprouted from her father's grave. Busying herself, she knelt and pulled them, consciously choosing to concentrate on that simple chore rather than on the multitude of troubles that had plagued her for so long. Doing something, anything, helped. The feel of earth on her hands. The sun hot on her back. Her father somehow close, his presence soothing and calming. But that was no surprise. He had always guided and advised her. Always helped her over the rough spots. He was gentle and kind, wise and thoughtful. He had never pushed her, rather had helped her clarify her own thoughts, and so steered her in the directions she knew to be best. If only he could speak to her now, she thought, the sadness rushing in with a violence that took away her breath. Numbed, she sat heavily, found herself staring at his name, at the straight-carved letters chiseled into the stone until, several minutes later, she realized that her fists were clenched so tightly that her hands had grown numb. Sighing heavily, she made herself get up and leave.

The creek drew her as a magnet draws iron. The sun glistened on the water as it rushed ever winding over smooth stones and making a grim world merry with its chuckling music. Creeks are the laughter of the planet. They were made to assuage the thirst of the spirit as well as the body. Celia descended the slope and followed the grassy bank as it curved behind a knoll that hid the cemetery from view. Soon she found a soft, dry spot of ground covered with long-stemmed grasses that made a comfortable bed from which she could view the world around her, a world constricted by trees downstream and a low hill opposite her, but full of the peace she so desperately sought. A squirrel scolded in the tree above her. A redwing blackbird flashed through the reeds, carved the air in a graceful arc, and disappeared. Honey bees lined paths to a large rock in the middle of the creek where they lit to drink and then dashed away to hidden hives.

Life did go on. Beauty did not cease at the crack of one man's death, was not diminished by one woman's broken heart. Tears rolling down her cheeks, Celia lay back and closed her eyes. The sounds around her, each rustle, whirr, cry, buzz, whoosh, murmur, and gurgle, mingled and melded to become a single, all-encompassing song. And at last, soothed by this great chorale that glorified life itself and healed the wounded soul, she slept.

His eyes woke her. Or perhaps it was her quickening pulse that told her she was no longer alone. The sun was a white fire in the middle of a painfully blue sky. Rafe was sitting a few feet away, his legs drawn up to his chest; his arms wrapped around his knees. Struggling awake, trying to make sense of his presence, Celia glanced around to set in place both earth and sky, reality and dream. The tingling in her hip where a pebble had dug into her flesh convinced her she was awake.

"Father said you'd gone off to be alone. I asked around. Someone had seen you heading this way. I guessed you'd come to the cemetery."

Celia sat upright. A blade of grass clung to her hair. Rafe stretched out a hand and removed it.

"I don't understand," Celia said haltingly.

"I do. It took me a while, but I do now."

He looked so calm, like the war within himself had at last come to an end. He was not in uniform, but he did wear a Navy colt revolver holstered at his left hip. And he was smiling.

"Why did you come after me?" Celia asked, thoroughly confused and not a little frightened.

Rafe half rose, rested on one knee, and took her hands in his. "Because I love you," he said simply. He looked down at her hands, then into her eyes. "I always used to say my father didn't raise any fools, but I was wrong. He raised a prize one in me. An arrogant fool, one who wouldn't blame you if you told me . . ."

Celia pulled one hand from his, put a finger to his lips. "No," she said, blinking back the tears. Her heart raced and her soul soared. "No, don't say it. Just hold me, Rafe," she whispered, going to his arms. "Just hold me, hold me, hold me."

Holding was not enough, is never enough after a painful separation. Starved, their bodies sought release. Each touch was ecstasy, each kiss a flame that kindled heightened desire. What fabric could keep such lovers apart? Shoes quickly shed. Buttons opened at a touch. Trousers and skirts and shirt and blouse magically removed. Fingers and hands and lips. What is more precious than an eyelash? What curves, what hollows more lovely? No glove fits more perfectly than lovers' bodies entwined. No touch is softer, more exquisite than a lover's touch. No moment surpasses that eternal second when bodies stiffen and souls melt and mingle in that perfect union of woman and man. Lovers always, lovers from the first roll and tumble of the sea to the last delicate architecture of a winter frost.

The sun melted down the long, languid afternoon. Dressed again—

"Madness," Celia had said, her face red. "What if someone had come along?"

"They didn't," Rafe said, but dressed quickly, too.

—They lay with Celia's head on Rafe's shoulder, his arms around her, their legs touching. "So far away?" Celia asked, tracing the worry lines aging Rafe's forehead.

"Planning," he answered, his voice very deep, as if he had just awakened. He kissed her forehead and, when she lifted her head, kissed her lips.

"Military strategy?"

"Our lives."

"Oh." She couldn't believe he was with her again. His fingers moved along her shoulder. She kissed his palm and placed his hand over her heart. "Father always said what will be, will be."

"After he made his plans, yes," Rafe said. "He knew as well as anyone that a man makes his own future. He chooses to eat, to sleep, to fight or not to fight. He chooses to stay or leave. The future is what we make it." Abruptly, he extricated himself from Celia's embrace and scrambled down the bank to the creek. He scooped water over his head and hair, splashed more on his face, drank deeply, then crawled back to Celia's side. Moisture dripped from the black streamers of his hair and ran down his chest inside his shirt. "Listen," he said, taking her hand when she reached out for him.

"What?"

"Shhh. Listen."

Celia listened. "I don't hear anything."

"I know. No gunfire from the east. The mortar boats have been quiet most of the day. The Federals haven't made a move, hardly fired a shot, since the explosion and battle at the Great Redoubt on Thursday."

"So?" Celia asked. "That's good, isn't it?"

"Depends on your point of view. I went by the courthouse this morning. No one wanted to admit anything, but there was talk of Pemberton and Grant exchanging letters. Grant's evidently going to demand an unconditional surrender. Pemberton will stall, they say. Probably ask for conditions of some sort. What he thinks he can get I don't know, but I don't have to be a general to know that when the food and medicine's gone, and there's no help on the way, and you're down to bricks and bayonets, there isn't much left to do but stack arms."

"Then it's over?" Celia asked softly.

Rafe lay back and stared at the tree overhead. "Pretty much," he finally said. "About as close as can be."

Celia lowered her eyes. "I'm sorry. I know after what I did that sounds like a lie, but it isn't. If I could undo . . ." She stopped, searched for the right words. "But I can't, can I?"

"It doesn't matter. There's no more sense in you wishing you could undo what you did than there is for me to be bitter. War drives people to extremes they'd never think of under normal circumstances.

What's left for any of us is to forgive the past and take the next step into the future."

"Can we do that?" Celia asked. "After everything that's happened, can we?"

Some questions can be answered. Two plus two equals four. Water runs downhill. Blood is red and sky is blue. Some questions are unanswerable. "If we believe," Rafe finally said, that being the closest to an answer he could find. "Only if we believe."

"Believe," Celia said, testing the word. "Believe." Her brows knotted in a frown. "I don't know what to believe, Rafe. I don't know what to believe *in* anymore. I just don't know."

He reached for her, drew her to him. "Believe in us, Celia," he said, his arms going around her. "Believe in the two of us."

"Very well, then," Celia whispered. Her head sank to his shoulder and her arm rested on his chest. "The two of us . . . together."

CHAPTER 27

And then nothing. Monday was quiet. Rafe told Celia, Jonathan, Matthew, Immelda, and Tobias about Micah's purported plans, and made plans of his own for the defense of the house. Nothing happened Monday night. Tuesday, Phillip Laughton showed up. Head bandaged and one arm in a sling, he had been hurt when his horse stepped in a shell hole, broke a leg, and fell on him. Rafe explained the situation once again and pointed out the Calders could very well be on Micah's list. The two men spent the day searching without success for Micah. Nothing happened Tuesday night.

On Wednesday, as the search for Micah continued fruitlessly, the Federals exploded another mine, but both sides broke off the engagement after a short action. Rumors flew as the status quo was quickly reestablished, but nothing happened Wednesday night.

Thursday was no different.

By Friday morning, the tension could have been cut and packaged. Admiral Porter's gunboats stayed out of sight around the bend in the river and shelled the city from a distance. The bombardment was ferocious, but for some reason mostly confined to the northeastern edges of town. The pressure to surrender had grown almost too great to resist.

The town waited. Red-eyed from lack of sleep, men, women, children, and slaves sat in the mouths of their caves and watched the sky for telltale fuses. Nerves taut, soldiers carried water to the hospitals and spoke in whispers. Tight-lipped officers arrived at the courthouse, disappeared inside, then emerged to ride back to their units without speaking. A few minutes after ten in the morning, a general accompanied by a colonel, carrying a furled white flag, strode down the courthouse steps. Eyes straight ahead, backs stiff, the two men rode north and slightly east, in the general direction of Grant's headquarters.

Gaillee had decided that if she stayed inside for one minute longer she would go stark raving mad. The minute Phillip had left, and against the express wishes of her mother and father, she had stalked from the cave and headed toward Celia's house in spite of the danger.

The morning was hot and she perspired freely, but the fresh air felt good on her face and arms. Even more refreshing was the greeting Celia gave her, and the feel of being in a real house again, even if only for an hour or so.

"Look who's here," Celia said, touching Lynna's arm.

Roused from sleep, Lynna opened her eyes.

"It's Gaillee Calder. She's brought you a present."

Gaillee stepped into the room. She carried a large leather case, which she opened and set on a chair.

"Your accordian?" Lynna exclaimed, rising on one elbow. "You shouldn't have, Gaillee. I can't—"

"Nonsense!" Gaillee leaned over and gave Lynna a little hug. "At least you can play it."

"But not now."

"One day soon, though. And your son or daughter will dance as you do," Gaillee said. "My playing is about as melodious as two alley cats fighting over a plate of fish. And you know that's true."

"But I feel so dreadful," Lynna wailed, sinking back on her pillow. "First I burden Celia and now I take your accordian."

"The world will be a better place." Gaillee laughed.

Celia noticed Gaillee had lost weight, that her face and neck and hands were pale with a sickly yellow cast. Her spirit was high, though. A little forced, to be sure, but nonetheless high, which was a good deal more than could be said of many others in Vicksburg in those dark days.

Gaillee leaned over the bed to give Lynna a quick peck on the forehead. "I can't stay long," she said, squeezing Lynna's hand. "Phillip doesn't know I've gone out, and he'll be upset if he finds out. His head—"

"Celia told me," Lynna said. "I've been praying for him. For you both. He'll be fine. I'm certain."

"I hope so." Gaillee turned her head before Lynna could see her tears. "I'd better . . . better leave. It's a long walk," she explained lamely, all but fleeing to the door.

Celia caught her on the cellar stairs, walked with her to the front door.

"Just look at me," Gaillee cried. "I was supposed to be comforting her, but she's the one lying down there in that dark cellar and encouraging me. What's the matter with me, Celia? I'm a spoiled, self-indulgent—"

"Hush, Gaillee Calder. Just you hush this instant," Celia snapped, interrupting her. "Let me tell you. Lynna's like that. One of the all-time grand worriers about other people's problems. One of the grand encouragers. Sometimes I wish she'd just wallow in self-pity for a while. It would make me feel a whole lot better. Now, you dry your eyes and get out of here. Tell Rafe I told him to walk you home."

"You and Rafe?" Gaillee asked, dabbing at her eyes with a kerchief.

"Are happy, under the circumstances. Under *any* circumstances, as long as we're together."

"Why, Celia Bartlett, you silly ol' thing!" Gaillee laughed, her old self again. "Gone and snatched up the handsomest man hereabouts. Except Phillip, of course." She hugged Celia in unspoken gratitude, and then, unable to keep up the brave front, sagged against the door. "Oh, God, Celia. I'm so frightened. I wish I knew what's going to happen to us when the Yankees . . . when they—"

"Nothing," Celia interrupted before she, too, was infected with Gaillee's fear. "Nothing at all. Life will go on as usual. They'll stay awhile and then they'll leave. Night will come, and morning will follow as always."

The line between bravery and bravado is thin. The fact was no one knew what would happen when the Yankees finally entered Vicksburg, and Celia was as aware of this as anyone else. For all her silliness, Gaillee was no fool, and appreciated Celia's fortitude. "I love you, Celia," she said, hugging her friend closely.

"And I you, Gaillee," Celia responded truthfully, returning the embrace. "But still, you'd best be on your way."

"I know. You'll send word when Lynna—" She stopped as hoofbeats pounded on the front drive and a voice called out. "That's Phillip," she said, blanching.

Celia and Gaillee ran outdoors in time to see Phillip sharply rein in his horse and jump to the ground and Rafe come running around the corner of the house. "What's wrong?" Rafe called.

"The word's out. They've done it! Surrender in the morning. Have you seen Gaillee?"

"Phillip?"

His head snapped around. "Thank God!" he exclaimed, running up the steps and taking her in his arms. "I had no idea—"

"I've been right here."

"I thought I told you—"

Jonathan and Matthew joined Rafe, and all three ran onto the porch. "Are you sure?" Rafe asked, interrupting.

"Grant and Pemberton are meeting this afternoon at three. No one knows exactly what will happen, only that some form of surrender is certain." Phillip wiped the sweat from his face, ran a hand through his unruly hair. "It's over."

"Good God!" Rafe sighed, sagging. "And on the Fourth of July."

Matt sank to the top step, sat disconsolately with his rifle between his knees. Jonathan stared into the distance, his eyes unseeing. Rafe took Celia's hands. "We all knew this day would come," he said quietly. "There's no sense in brooding. There'll be things to do, to take care of . . ."

"Beginning with Micah," Phillip said, voicing the common thought. "Assuming he—"

"He will," Rafe said darkly, "if I know him at all."

"Gather here about sundown?" Phillip asked.

"No. I've been thinking. There's a good chance he'll break his men into more than one group and hit two or three families at once. If he does, your place will be with the Calders."

"I suppose. Still . . ."

"We'll manage here," Rafe assured him. "Being ready is half the battle."

Reluctantly, Phillip took Gaillee's arm and started down the steps. "Those other men you took into the Home Guard," he said, pausing and turning. "Not a one has returned?"

Rafe shrugged. "Can you blame them? They have families of their own they'll need to look after. The way things are, I'd do the same." He grinned wanly. "Hell, I *am* doing the same."

"Right." Phillip unwound his horse's reins from the hitching post and prepared to lead the animal back to the cave where the Calders were staying. "We're close enough to hear. If the coast looks clear, I'll ride this way as soon as I can." He stuck out his hand. "Well?"

"Luck," Rafe said, taking the steps quickly and shaking Phillip's hand. "It's been some fight. Over after tonight. Gaillee, you do what Phillip says and everything will be all right."

All right. Empty words, Rafe thought, going back up the stairs and putting a protective arm around Celia as Phillip and Gaillee walked down the drive. Nothing was going to be all right in Vicksburg. Not for a long, long time to come.

Word traveled fast. Secrets were impossible to keep. So it was that everyone in the city knew within hours that a surrender was slated for the morning. So it was, too, that nine men gathered in a burned-out warehouse and, feral eyes gleaming like the gold Cairo promised that afternoon, listened to Micah go over the plan he had devised.

"So," he said, fixing each in turn with his eyes. "The fires are set, everyone's running to put them out. By that time you should all be back at the Bartlett house. While you attack in the front, Cairo and Hawkins and I will break through the garden gate and get in from the rear."

"You sure that gold's in the house?" one of the men asked. "Seems mighty easy pickin's."

"A Confederate bank wasn't exactly the place for an Abolitionist to keep his money," Micah explained. "Hal Bartlett was no fool. Once Jeff Davis conscripted his ships, he figured his gold might just be next, and put it away where he thought no one would find it." He scrutinized the faces around him to see if they bought the story he'd improvised a few days earlier. Truth or not, it must have sounded good, for no one seemed to doubt his word. "Any questions?"

"Mighty nice of his daughter to keep that gold safe all this time for us," another of the ruffians cracked, to the amusement of the rest.

"When do we make our move?" Hawkins asked. Shorter than Cairo, he was bald and solidly built. The empty left sleeve of his gray coat was pinned to his shoulder. "Don't want to wait too long."

"Around midnight," Micah said. "We'll leave here in threes. You three who are going to start the fires'll go first, Cairo, Hawkins, and me will go last. When we're finished, we'll break into our original groups of three and meet back here to divvy up what we get. Sound simple enough?"

"'Bout time I got somethin' but grief out of this damn war," a man named Andrews growled. "If it's all the same with you, though, I'd as soon divide it on the spot an' then head for my own hidey hole."

A rumble of agreement supported Andrews's suggestion.

"Fine with me," Micah said, not really caring one way or the other, but glad to allay any hint of suspicion. "Damned if I care where you go."

"You *sure* that gold's there?" the same man asked for the second time.

"I told you—"

"You can tell us again," Hawkins said, the first one of the lot brave enough to interrupt Micah. "I'd like to hear it, too."

Micah half stood, then sank back onto his chair. "I've seen it, Hawkins," he explained patiently. "My father and Hal Bartlett were close friends. I've been in that house almost as often as I've been in my own, and know it like the back of my hand. My father and old man Bartlett had the combinations to each other's safes in case anything happened to either of them, and one day I was in the cellar with them when Bartlett put a sack of gold in his safe."

"You know the combination?"

"No, but Miss Bartlett will. And will let us in."

"Be *more* than glad to let us in," Cairo chimed in with a wink and a leer.

Hawkins appeared mollified, as did the others. Micah went on for another minute or two about the house, then sent everyone off to eat and get some sleep before retiring himself to the bedroom he shared with Solange. "Hear anything interesting?" he asked, as she backed away from the door.

"Very," she replied, not at all embarrassed at having been caught eavesdropping. "Gold. Shared by so many," she added with icy sarcasm.

"Shared by no one but us," Micah corrected, cupping her chin. He moved well away from the door and spoke quietly. "Which brings us to your part."

"Mine?" Solange asked suspiciously.

"That is," Micah said, returning the sarcasm, "if you love me."

"I don't know if I love you, but I do need you, and that's enough. What am I supposed to do?"

"Nothing difficult. After we leave, you drive your carriage to the corner of China and Monroe and wait just east of the intersection. When Cairo and the others are occupied with little brother, I'll slip off, join you, and we'll pay my father a call."

"You'd steal from your own father?" Solange asked.

Micah laughed aloud and stretched out on the bed. "Let's just call it cutting little brother out of his inheritance," he said, reaching for her. "And coming into mine a little early."

"You've thought of everything, haven't you?" Solange said, avoiding Micah's grasp and moving to the table in order to dim the lantern. "I remember a man, long ago, who once warned me that when a person thinks of everything, that is the time to be the most careful."

"One of your lovers?" Micah sneered.

"Long ago."

Micah's boots hit the floor one by one. "And that's all he taught you?"

"No."

"What else?"

The shadows hid her face. "Ecstasy," Solange replied wistfully.

"Yeah. Well, maybe he left out a thing or two." Micah stood and kicked his trousers aside. "Come here and I'll show you."

"He was a great man," Solange retorted defensively. "Have some respect."

"We've a busy night or two ahead, sweet. It'll be a while before we get the chance again. I said, come here."

Drawn by the tension between them, entrapped by the insatiable desire she felt for him, Solange untied the ribbons at her neck, stepped out of her gown, and padded on bare feet toward his bed and voice. Even in the dark, she knew the way.

Ten o'clock came and went without so much as a hint of an alarm. For the third time since dark, Rafe slipped out the back door and circled the house. He checked on Jonathan, whispered to a well-hidden Matthew. He prowled the carriage house where his horse was stabled, quieted the animal with a few soothing words, and hoped there would be feed soon, for the gelding wouldn't be able to stand after another week or two of starvation. Everything was quiet. Clouds scudded across the sky, now covering, now uncovering the moon. Celia was waiting for him on the side porch. He could see her outlined against the silver smooth glass. Darting across the lawn, he joined her and escorted her into the house.

"You be needin' anything, Mr. Rafe?" Immelda's voice drifted up from the cellar.

"No thank you, Immelda. Everything's quiet." Together, he and Celia crossed the hall into the empty sun parlor. "We're as ready as can be," he said, sinking down onto the sofa. "Only thing left to do now is wait."

"Do you really expect him?" Celia asked, sitting next to him.

Rafe draped his coat over a ladder back chair. His gun belt followed. "I'd be a fool not to. Micah is capable of anything, it looks like. And desperate."

Celia lay on her side with her back pressed against the cushions. "I pray he doesn't," she said with a shudder.

"Are you that afraid of him?"

"I'm that afraid of what he might do to you."

"I can handle him," Rafe answered, stretching out at her side.

Celia lifted her head so he could slip his arm beneath her neck. "I wonder," she said, nestling against him. "You're different, darling. You'll hesitate because no matter what he's done, you still think of him as your brother. He doesn't have any such qualms, though. He could kill you and not think twice about it."

Rafe felt an icy tinge of doubt and fear course through his veins. But what was the use wondering what Micah might or might not do?

The readiness was all. Pensive, he traced the line of Celia's jaw with his fingers, turned his head, and gently kissed her forehead. In response, Celia turned her face to his and pulled his head down. Her mouth was damp and warm, her tongue a passionate dart, enticing, probing, hungry. His body was his master. Roused, Rafe rolled onto his side, heard Celia moan as his hardness pressed against her, and felt her thrust her body against him.

"Did anyone ever tell you you're a wanton?" Rafe finally asked, breaking off the kiss.

"Only you, now," Celia answered and, playfully pressing against him, added, "I can't help it if he likes me."

"Maybe so, but we'd both feel silly as hell fighting a battle stark naked. So for right now"— Rafe relaxed and lay flat on his back again — "I'm going to exercise a little judgment, and *he's* going to calm down."

Celia kissed his throat, then lay her head on his chest. Her left hand rested lightly on his swollen sex, not erotically but gently and familiarly. Nestling between him and the pillows pressing against her spine, she felt snug and safe, and wishing the moment might never end. "Rafe?" she asked, sleepily.

"Mmm?"

"About Snag Parken. Are you sure you want to leave? Vicksburg's your home."

"No." His head moved slowly from side to side, and his voice was soft and deep. "You're my home. Wherever we are together, that is home."

Stillness. And the full, life-giving knowledge of love shaping darkness and light, sorrow and joy into a single holy aspiration—to walk the wide, wide world, and always, always to be home.

"Satisfied?" Rafe asked, nudging her gently. There was no answer. He glanced down awkwardly. Her breathing soft and light, a smile on her face, Celia was asleep. At peace himself, Rafe repositioned his head on the pillow, shifted his arm under her slightly, so it wouldn't go to sleep, and listened to the house and the night.

Nothing. No sounds that didn't belong. That meant little, though. Micah was out there somewhere, waiting for the time he had set, making Rafe wait. Concerned, he lifted Celia's head, so he could free his arm, tucked a pillow under her, and let her go on sleeping. Waiting. Waiting for Micah. Would he hesitate that one fraction of a second too long? What man could predict that sort of thing in advance? Some men waited, some acted instinctively, brother or no.

Time and the night reeled out like cable from a spool, and Rafe saw

Micah and himself one day when they were boys. They were at the Country House, as their father called the mansion at their plantation just outside New Auburn. The green fields of cotton, waist high on boys, were tufted with puffs of white buds, but what should have been beautiful was not, for Rafe was lying in the dirt and blood was pouring from a cut in the corner of his mouth. Micah, just turned thirteen, was daring him to stand and fight.

"Get up!" he yelled, bracing himself for a rush. When Rafe wouldn't, Micah stamped his foot down on a toy horse carved by one of the slaves and given to Rafe as a present. "Nigger ain't got no call givin' you somethin' like that," Micah taunted. "Get up!"

Suddenly, their father was there and stepping between them. He yanked Micah toward the house, at the same time laying into him with a thick leather belt. Even then, Rafe couldn't stand. Micah was gone and being punished in the distance, but still Rafe lay in the mud of the field and cried.

Rafe stared at the night. Somewhere out there, Micah was moving, was stalking. Sometime in the next few hours, he was sure he would have to face him. Face his own brother. And this time, Micah wouldn't be drunk, and wouldn't walk away. This time was for real and for keeps. Suddenly, Rafe knew why the little boy he'd been couldn't stand. He didn't want to stand. He didn't want to stand because he was afraid. Afraid of Micah.

And deep down inside, he still was.

CHAPTER 28

The dream began, as do most dreams, innocently. There was a wide and lovely field covered with flowers. At the edge of the field stood a wall. She was walking toward the wall and the tall locked gate in the center of the wall, behind which she could hear children crying. The gate was made of metal and was slippery, unclimbable, but the wall was made of rough-cut stones. Without questioning, knowing only that the crying children needed their mamas, she began to climb. A fingerhold, a toehold. Her muscles strained and the protruding stones pressed into her abdomen. They hurt, but she had to keep climbing, because the children waited and cried and one of them was hers.

She couldn't cry out for some reason. Only climb. Only climb and accept the pain, for pain was part of the process. If she wanted to reach her child, she had to endure the pain.

Slipping! *Oh, God, I am slipping,* a voice in her mind said. She dug her fingers and toes into the stone and held on. The crying noises grew louder, and she could recognize one in particular that she knew was her child. Hers. Hers if she could hold on and climb. Hers if she could endure the pain.

Then climb. Climb! The edge was close. The top of the wall was within reach of her outstretched fingertips. If she could just . . .

Oh, God, no! One foot was slipping. Her foot was slipping off one of the rocks, and she couldn't stop it! Slowly, inexorably, the ball of her foot, then the toes. Her right hand flew back. The fingers on her left hand slid from the rock. Her body arched backward and plummeted, plummeted toward earth. And all the while she could hear her child—crying, crying, crying . . .

Lynna woke with a start. Perspiration beaded her forehead. The sheets and her gown were soaked. The contraction came swiftly. Pain dulled her thought processes, seared her abdomen and groin with white hot flashes. Immelda was asleep in the chair next to her bed. Her legs were splayed, her head cocked at an odd angle. She snored softly. Lynna tried to focus on her, but the light was dim and her vision hazy. Another contraction seized her and she bit her lower lip. "Immelda!" she gasped. It was happening. She'd bought her infant all the time she could. "Immelda!"

The black woman bolted awake. "Honey?" she asked, leaning over the bed. "What is it, honey?" And then, when Lynna's face contorted with pain, "Oh, my God! You hang on, honey, I'm gettin' help."

Pain cut through Lynna like a knife. "Don't leave me alone!" she pleaded. "Don't . . . Jonathan! Jonathaaaan!"

Immelda was out the door and beating Tobias awake. "That baby's comin'," she said, hauling her husband to his feet. "You go get Mr. Jonathan right now, an' come back with hot water. Move. Tell Miss Celia to get down here, too. Celia! Mr. Rafe!" she yelled, pushing Tobias up the stairs before rushing back to Lynna's side.

Dozing, Rafe was immediately awake and rolling off the sofa.

"What?" Celia asked, confused, only half awake.

"It's Lynna. Her time," Rafe said, strapping on his revolver. Tobias stuck his head in the door and shouted the same news, then disappeared out the back way yelling for Jonathan. "You know what to do?"

"Immelda does if nothing goes wrong," Celia said, slipping into her shoes. "Can you find a doctor?"

"I'll try, but Micah . . ." The kitchen door slammed and footsteps pounded in the hall. "I'll try. You'd better get down there."

Celia and Jonathan met at the top of the stairs. "What's happening?" Jonathan asked, terror-stricken.

"She's started, I think. Immelda's kept a kettle on the stove. You go on down, I'll get it."

"Jonathaaan!" Lynna's cry, thin and piercing, floated up the stairway.

"Oh, God!" Jonathan moaned, his face turning white in the amber lantern light. "Oh, God!" he roared, and leaped for the stairs.

Celia turned to go to the kitchen and ran into Tobias. "No," she said, turning him around and pushing him back to the kitchen. "We'll need more hot water. Get wood if we need it and get the fire going. Fast!"

Tobias loaded the last of the wood from the box into the stove, then disappeared out the door with the log carrier. Rafe reappeared in the kitchen after checking the front door and rooms. "I think we're still safe enough. I'm going to check around outside. If everything's quiet, I'll chance going for a doctor. Bolt the cellar door behind you and don't open it unless you're sure you know who wants down there."

Rafe saw Celia to the cellar stairs, waited to hear the bolt slide home, then ran back through the kitchen to the back door and out into the night. The moon was still bright and casting heavy shadows. To the south, more light flared where two or three buildings had caught fire. He caught a glimpse of Tobias at the woodpile, then struck out around the house to check the front and tell Matt what the commotion was all about. The side of the house was clear. He saw nothing suspicious near the carriage shed. Matt stood at the front gate and, as Rafe approached, turned and leveled his rifle.

Only it wasn't Matt Broussard after all.

Celia rushed into the storeroom where they'd set up a bedroom for Lynna and deposited the kettle of hot water on the bedside table. Jonathan was standing by the side of the bed looking sick to his stomach. Immelda had already turned back the sheets and was busy cleaning Lynna. "You take over cleanin'," she ordered Celia brusquely. "Just don't burn her with that water. Wash your han's first, like I tol' you t'other day," she went on, her speech reverting to a heavier Negro dialect under the pressure. "An' you, Jonathan. Stan' up dere at de top ob de bed an' gib her sompin' to hold onto." She showed him quickly what she meant and returned to the job at hand.

"Now, Doc Stewart said we gots to turn dat baby so he can git out." She placed her hands on Lynna's abdomen and started probing, eliciting a scream from Lynna. "I'se sorry, honey, an' I try not to hurt you more'n I gots to, but dis chile got to be turned."

"You can't," Jonathan wheezed. Sweat beaded on his forehead. "I mean, we have to wait for a doctor!"

Immelda's hands never stopped moving as she kneaded and molded Lynna's abdomen. "From the looks ob things, this young 'un ain't 'bout to set an' whittle 'til no doctor comes. We gonna have to do." She pressed hard and moved her hands sideways, trying to turn the baby. "Try an' rest easy, honey. Only gonna hurt a little while. Don't push 'til I say."

"I'm trying," Lynna gasped, blood on her lip where she'd bitten through the flesh. "Oh, Jonathan? Jonathan!"

"You've got to help her," Jonathan said, his eyes wild. He looked down at his hands, saw that her nails had cut through his skin where she held him. "God, Celia, tell her to stop!"

"You've helped calves an' foals," Immelda snapped, impatiently. "This is no different."

"The hell it isn't," Jonathan moaned. "This is my wife!"

"Which is why you gots to stay calm," Immelda grunted and pushed harder. "He's goin', honey. Goin' the way we wants, I think. Jes' a minute more. No. No! Don't push!"

Lynna spasmed and cried out. A gush of fluid rushed from her. "Her water," Celia said, using every ounce of her energy to remain calm at the same time she tried to catch as much of the bloody fluid as she could with a dry cloth.

"Good. Maybe we can move him easier." Immelda knelt on the bed next to Lynna. Sweat poured from her as freely as it did her patient. "A couple more pushes from me now, honey, an' it'll be your turn," she said as her hands tried to turn the baby.

It was then they heard the first gunshots.

Rafe didn't recognize the man. His holster flap was buttoned shut, but the revolver stuffed in his waistband was free. He grabbed for it and dove at the same time, hitting the dirt and rolling simultaneously. The man shouted "Hurry!" to his unseen henchmen, and fired.

The minié ball scarred the ground inches from Rafe's leg. His arm coming up, he fired from the ground. The man with the rifle grunted and staggered backward. Rafe fired again. The bullet caught him in the side, spun him around, and flung him in a twisted sprawl over the picket fence. "Zeke! Andy!" the man cried. "I'm hit!"

A figure raced across a patch of open ground. Rafe snapped off a shot, then held his fire and aimed toward movement to his left. "Don't shoot!" a voice called. "It's me. Matt!"

"Get down!" Rafe ordered. He jumped to his feet, darted across the lawn, and dove into the shadows by Matt. "What happened?"

"Snuck up on me," Matt moaned. "Never seen a thing." He touched the back of his head and groaned. "Jesus, that hurts. You get him?"

"I think so," Rafe said, firing at another moving figure. Chips of wood flew from the picket fence.

"Cover me," Matt said, crabbing away from the shadows. He pulled the wounded man off the picket fence, removed his revolver, and found his rifle, then scurried back to Rafe. "Thanks. Bastards. Never let nobody sneak up on me before."

"First time for everything," Rafe said, reloading.

"Last time, too," Matt commented dryly, ducking instinctively as a shot rang out. He fired in the general direction and heard a cry of pain. "That makes me feel a whole lot better. You got any idea how many there are?"

"Nope." Rafe finished loading, realized in horror that, with Jonathan in the cellar helping with Lynna, the back gate was unprotected. "Can you handle this?" he asked, searching the grounds before leaving the front.

"'Til hell freezes. I got me two extra cylinders full loaded, my rifle, an that'un's gun as well. They ain't about to get in this way."

Rafe didn't bother to reply, but was off and running. Someone saw him and fired, but other than the noise, the slugs were clean misses and dug into the side of the house. Changing direction, he hit the gap between the carriage shed and the house. Movement to his right. He darted left and headed for the cover of the shell hole near the remains of the gazebo, only to trip over a body and fall sprawling into the dirt.

"Damn," he grunted as a length of firewood dug into his back. He crawled back and recognized Tobias. Gunfire sounded from the front of the house. Rafe listened briefly, then put his ear to Tobias's heart and sighed in relief at the weak but steady beat. A quick inspection showed blood oozing from a saber slash that crossed the old man's chest and left a crimson slit in his thin shirt almost from the shoulder to the waist. The wound wasn't deep. Tobias must have fallen partly out of the way and either knocked himself out or fainted. If no one shot him by accident, he'd probably survive.

Rafe pushed himself to his knees and realized he'd lost both guns. There was no time to be spared looking. Grabbing the piece of firewood he'd fallen into, a stout club almost three feet long, he tried to figure his next move.

The backyard appeared empty. The gate stood open but he couldn't see anyone near it. The side porch was empty. He scanned the length of the house, stopped at the kitchen window where a light flared briefly, then settled down to a dull glow. Someone had lit a lantern. Cursing, he broke into a trot, rounded the corner of the house, and leaped silently onto the back porch before plastering himself against the wall and making himself wait a moment to catch his breath.

A faint cry! Lynna? Damn, he should have been looking for a doctor. Might even have found one if it weren't for Micah. His men threatened not only Celia, but may well have been costing Lynna's life and the life of her child! But not if he could help it. The back door was ajar. How many waited inside? Not enough, Rafe growled to himself. He hit the door with his shoulder and burst into the kitchen. There was no time to look, study, or evaluate. A one-armed man in Rebel gray, brandishing a saber, spun around in shocked surprise.

Rafe howled and attacked. Steel whistled in a deadly arc and clanged against the weather-hardened firewood, then bounced off uselessly as the club, not even slowing, caught the man in the chest. The man staggered backward and dropped his saber. Rafe swung again, struck him in the shoulder and sent him reeling into the hall, struck him from behind in the middle of the back. The man screamed and half ran, half fell into the sun parlor. Rafe followed him and struck again. The firewood caught the man in the back of the head and sent him flying through the rear windows.

Pieces of glass glittered in the moonlight. Rafe stood panting in the center of the parlor, at last staggered to the window and looked out at the battered, lifeless body. Then he remembered to count. He'd caught a glimpse of one man, and had seen two more clearly. Not one of the three had been Micah. He'd be somewhere near, though. Calmly, no qualms now at all, Rafe stepped through the broken window, over the man he'd just killed, and began the search for his brother.

Lynna's hands clutched Jonathan's. Her fingernails drew blood, but not nearly so much as flowed from between her legs.

Celia threw away one batch of soaked cloths and tried to stem the flow with fresh ones. She felt sick with fear. Not even on the night that Lynna had arrived had she seen so much blood.

"Turn here. Right here," Immelda mumbled to herself. "Now that's the head. Got to be the head. Got to—"

"Oh, Jesus!" Lynna shrieked.

"Our Father who art in heaven," Jonathan prayed.

"Push now, honey!" Immelda felt inside Lynna, encouraged her with a pat on her abdomen. "Push hard! An' you," she ordered Jonathan. "Hold her tight. Hold her!"

"Jesus God!"

"Hallowed be Thy name."

"It *is* the head, honey! Push, honey, push!"

"I can't," Lynna moaned. "Oh, please, God—"

"Don't give up, girl!"

"Thy kingdom come, thy will be done . . ."

"I can't!" Lynna panted, her eyes rolling back in her head.

"Push, damn it, and save your baby!" Celia roared. "Push!"

"On earth as it is in heaven . . ."

Lynna screamed. She screamed until her throat was raw, but she pushed.

Head, shoulders, arms, torso, umbilical cord, hips, and legs. A girl! A baby girl who as Immelda held her up, began to cry at first tentatively and then lustily. Lynna's screams faded, and she lay back spent. "My baby?" she asked hoarsely. "My baby?"

"It's a girl, honey bunch," Immelda told her. The black woman's hands moved surely and competently as she cleaned the tiny, red face, swabbed out the baby's mouth and nose. "You got the beautifullest little girl, honey. You can let go her hands now, Mr. Jonathan."

"Good," Jonathan said, and fainted dead away.

"Men!" the black woman scoffed. "Well, let him lie." She lay the child on Lynna's abdomen, and turned to Celia. "We still got lots to do here, honey. Now, there's the afterbirth coming, an' we got to—"

A shot roared and something hammered at the door at the top of the stairs. Twice more the sound reverberated through the basement. After the third the women could hear wood splintering. Jonathan was unconscious. Celia grabbed his rifle where it leaned against the wall and stepped out of the storeroom in time to see a man silhouetted against dim lantern light at the top of the cellar stairs. "Who are you?" she called.

The man faltered, took a tentative step down the stairs. "Don't matter," he said, searching the dimness of the cellar.

A scattering of gunfire sounded outside the house. Celia's hands were bloody from the delivery, but kept a firm grip on the rifle. Her aim didn't waver. "Get out of my house," she commanded, hoping she didn't sound as frightened as she felt.

"Ain't gonna, lady. I come for the gold."

"There's no gold here!" Celia lied.

"Is, too. Micah Lattimore told me about it." He took another step. "Might as well give it to me, miss. Ain't gonna leave without it."

"You get nothing from this house, do you hear?" Celia shouted. "Nothing!"

"Get what I come for, lady," Cairo said, raising his revolver. He started down the stairs. "Now you just put down that there gun, an'—"

Celia shot him. The rifle belched fire and smoke, and almost knocked her over. Cairo sat heavily on the top step, then slid and tumbled down the stairs toward Celia.

Numbed, her ears ringing, Celia backed away from him and into Jonathan, who stumbled out from the storeroom. "What happened?" he asked, groggy and embarrassed at having fainted.

Celia pointed. Jonathan moved quickly to Cairo and retrieved his revolver. "Who are you?" he asked, cocking the gun and pointing it at the wounded man's head.

Cairo's body had yet to register pain. A hole in his shoulder leaked blood. His legs were totally numb. "My back," he mumbled. "Somethin's wrong with my back."

"You aren't going to get— Hold it right there!" Jonathan shouted, raising the revolver to the top of the stairs.

"It's me," Rafe called. "Hold your fire!" He ran down the stairs. "What happened? Are you all right?"

"Celia shot this one," Jonathan explained, nudging Cairo with his boot.

"Who are you?" Rafe asked, kneeling to inspect the wound in Cairo's shoulder.

"I need a doctor," Cairo groaned. His head propped on a step, he looked up imploringly at Rafe. "I need help, mister. You gotta help me!"

"Where's my brother?"

"I dunno. My back. Somethin's wrong with my back. Shit, she shot me!"

"Where's Micah, damn you?" Rafe grabbed Cairo's arm and jerked on it. Cairo screamed with pain. "Next time is worse," Rafe threatened. "Where is he?"

"He run off!" Cairo panted. "Run off just as we was coming in the back gate."

Rafe glanced around the cellar, wished he could see into all the dark corners. "He can't be down here," Celia said. She pointed at Cairo. "This is the one who broke open the door. You're the only other person to come down the stairs."

Cairo's eyes pleaded for mercy. "Mister, please—"

"Shut up!" Rafe's hand moved so Cairo could see it, then rested lightly on his wounded shoulder. "This is going to hurt. One last chance. Where is he?"

"I ain't lyin'!" Cairo babbled, his eyes rolling from Rafe's face to his hand and back again. "I ain't. He run, I tell 'ya! I don't know why. He needed the gold as much as the rest of us. Yellow son of a bitch! Mr. High-and-Mighty Blueblood Lattimore, an' ain't got one cent of his own. Tol' us there was gold. But he run off, like he knew somethin' we didn't. Like he'd been holdin' out. Hell, mister, maybe he's gone after gold on his lonesome. But where he 'spects to find any, I don't know."

"Father's house!" Rafe said, shocked and no longer listening. The idea, mad at first, becoming perfectly reasonable where Micah was concerned.

The thin squawl of a newborn baby sounded from the storeroom. Rafe looked up at Celia, then Jonathan. "The baby came," Jonathan explained.

"Celia, honey?" Immelda called. "I need you in here."

Rafe stood, realized Celia hadn't heard, that she was still deaf from the gunshot.

"Immelda wants you," Rafe shouted, pointing to the storeroom. "Micah's gone to Father's house, I think. Go help Immelda."

"Want me to go with you?" Jonathan asked as Rafe turned to leave.

Rafe reached out and took Cairo's pistol from Jonathan. There were three rounds left. "No," he said at last, starting up the stairs. "It's something I have to do myself."

CHAPTER 29

"Hello, Father."

Nathaniel stared at his eldest son, saw in the hardness of Micah's face the failure of a father. What made it all the worse was that for the life of him, Nathaniel couldn't figure out how, or why, or what had gone wrong. At what precise moment had he not cared or loved or offered enough? Or was that the problem? With his firstborn son, had he cared or loved or offered too much?

"I'm leaving," Micah said. "Came to say good-bye and to collect what's mine by right." He brushed his father aside and strode into the house. "Where are the servants that my own father has to answer the door?" he bellowed. He heard a flurry of footsteps as the servants fled his wrath. Their fear inspired his confidence. "Well?" he asked his father, heading for the stairs.

"Robert is sick. Leave the others alone. Leave everyone alone," Nathaniel panted, trying to keep up with Micah. "My God, haven't you done enough?"

Micah didn't answer but continued up the sweeping spiral stairway with the strides of a man of singular, intense purpose. Nathaniel, his cane thudding hollowly on the stair treads, followed him to the master bedroom where Micah had already moved to the wall safe set behind the portrait of his mother.

"You go too far," Nathaniel warned, stopping by the bed.

Micah set aside the portrait, began twisting the large metal dial. "That's a matter of opinion, Father," he said, concentrating on the combination and not noticing Nathaniel stump to the head of the bed and open a mahogany box that lay on the nightstand. The tumblers clicked home and he yanked on the shiny metal handle. When the door swung open, he ignored the deeds and other legal documents and removed a foot-square iron strong box that was heavy with gold coins. "Ahhh," he sighed in satisfaction.

"Leave that alone. It isn't yours."

"*Wasn't* mine. Now it is."

The click of a hammer drawn back, the metallic rasp of a cylinder revolving to place a fresh charge beneath the strike. Micah turned to face his father and the ancient but lethal Patterson Colt the old man held. "Don't be ridiculous," he snorted derisively. "You probably haven't fired that thing since the Mexican War."

"Do you dare to take me so lightly?" Nathaniel fumed.

The strongbox was heavy. Micah tucked it under one arm, took a step, and then another. The gap between father and son narrowed until the muzzle of the revolver pressed against Micah's chest. Slowly, he reached up, took the weapon from his father's grasp, and tucked it in his belt. "Yes," he said blandly. "I have for a long time now. Any reason why I shouldn't?"

Nathaniel lowered his head. Tears of frustration and anger and shame and sorrow welled in his eyes, but he said nothing.

Micah patted the iron coin box. "I can't think of any, either," he said, and walked out of the room.

Behind him, alone, more a prisoner than the master of his own house, Nathaniel sagged against the bed.

A Lattimore carriage drawn by a dun gelding Rafe didn't recognize sat in front of his father's house. Rafe pulled his horse to a bone-jarring stop. Dismounting, he drew his gun before he realized that the driver of the carriage was a woman. "Are you with Micah?" he asked, not waiting to see who she was.

There was no answer. Cautiously, he approached the carriage. "Mrs. Stewart?" he asked, taken aback and remembering the day two months earlier at the picnic when he had seen her and Micah together in the woods.

"Yes."

Her face was harsher than he remembered. "Where's . . . uh . . . Micah?"

"Inside," came the curt and unfriendly answer.

"Oh. Well, ah . . ." Micah and Tom Stewart's wife. He should have guessed from that day he saw them at the picnic, and later when Tom had asked about her that day at Lynna's house. "Why don't you go on home, Mrs. Stewart."

"I can't do that."

"Then leave. Before it's too late."

"I think not."

He wasn't her guardian. Rafe shrugged and, careful to avoid the gravel, walked across the grass toward the front of the house. Images of the past, of children playing, laughing, shouting, flirted at the fringes of his consciousness. Children . . .

He'd forgotten to ask whether Lynna had had a boy or a girl. He wished he knew, now, but there was no time to wonder. He studied the wide, shadowed porch, the wicker chairs, and swing suspended by chains from the ceiling. Many a hot summer night as a little boy he had camped on that porch. Many a night . . . like this one . . . now.

Every nerve taut, he started up the steps.

Micah threw open the doors of the liquor cabinet and found it was empty. Not a single bottle remained. Not one.

"Gone," Nathaniel said from the doorway. "Every bottle, every last drop. What you didn't steal, I gave to the hospitals." His cane clumped on the bare floor. "But you wouldn't know about giving, would you? Only taking. And hurting."

"Spare me," Micah muttered, searching behind the sliding panels in the cabinet.

Nathaniel stopped with a sofa between him and his son. "But of course giving requires a sense of charity and implies a concept of mercy, which is another attribute utterly foreign to your nature. All you know how to give is pain and suffering. This . . . taking advantage of Tom Stewart's wife—oh, I've heard what you've been up to. Looting—you think I don't know about these things?"

"So?" Micah asked. "What am I supposed to do? Feel sorry? Hell, there isn't a one of them that didn't deserve what they got. A bunch of holier-than-thou—"

"And Celia?" Nathaniel snapped scornfully. "Did she deserve what you did to her?"

The liquor cabinet door slammed shut so hard the glass broke. "And you made me pay for that, didn't you? Through the nose," Micah sneered, bending to break open the bottom doors and rummage through the lower half of the cabinet. "Well, I've got news for you, Father. The damned little slut enjoyed herself."

"No woman enjoys rape, and you know it!" Nathaniel's cane slammed into the floor for emphasis. "An animal! That's all you are. You *bragged* about it! Jesus Almighty! To live knowing that the knowledge would cause Hal's death. Maybe that *is* what killed him."

"That's not the way I heard it," Micah snorted, scattering wine glasses in disgust. He stood, kicked the doors shut. "But what if it was? Hardly a woman around who isn't going to lose it sooner or later. The way I see it, I broke her in for Rafe. It's the least I could do . . ." Mouth open, he stopped and stared into the shadows behind his father.

Nathaniel turned slowly, gasped when he saw Rafe standing in the doorway. "You heard," he whispered, appalled. "I'm sorry, boy. I prayed you'd never learn the truth."

His face pale in the dim light, Rafe stepped into the room. "Micah?" he said, choking on the name.

"He was drunk," Nathaniel explained, fearing what came next. "So drunk he had to brag, but only after Celia had left and you were gone." The sentence trailed off and Nathaniel leaned wearily on the sofa.

"You raped Celia?" Rafe asked, choking on the growing rage that wouldn't be restrained.

The truth was out, and with it Micah tasted real fear for the first time he could remember. "Let sleeping dogs lie," he said nervously. "That's what I say. No real harm done. I'll be out of your life and you can have her to yourself." Micah edged toward the hall door. "Meanwhile, you don't mind . . ."

"Bastard!" Rafe roared, charging, throwing a chair out of the way, leaping the sofa.

Micah grabbed for the Patterson, but the hammer caught in his belt. Too late, he raised his free arm. Rafe collided with him and sent the coin box flying against the wall, where it broke open and spilled its glittering contents onto the floor.

The blows came too fast to parry. A fist caught Micah in the neck, another left his nose a bloody smear and knocked him off his feet. Rafe grabbed him and jerked him erect and, before Micah could find his balance, hurled him through the door into the hall where he obliterated a table and Greek vase.

Disoriented, Micah lurched to his feet and tried to find Rafe in the darkness. Footsteps from behind alerting him, he turned. Rafe buried his shoulder deep in Micah's stomach. The force of the blow propelled them both down the hall and sent them crashing through the window next to the door.

Glass flew like shrapnel, a jagged litter covering the porch. Micah and Rafe rolled free of each other and came to their feet. Micah reached for the Patterson again, then ducked when Rafe feinted and drew the knife from his boot instead. Crouching, the two men circled warily until Rafe's boot slipped on a piece of glass. Flailing, half falling, he fought to regain his balance. Seeing his chance, Micah lunged just as Rafe fell. The knife barely missed Rafe's head and plunged into the windowsill where it stuck.

His mistake was trying to pull the knife out of the wood. A second was all Rafe needed. Rolling, he came to his knees under Micah's outstretched arm and, with a flurry of short, savage punches to Micah's stomach, pushed to his feet. The last, with all his force behind it, lifted Micah off his feet and sent him reeling across the porch and crashing through the railing.

Micah was stronger, but slower. Micah was more experienced, but was fighting without the total rage that more than compensated for Rafe's inexperience. Gone was Rafe's deep-rooted fear, gone in the whirlwind of fury that consumed him. Bleeding from broken nose and butchered mouth, Micah staggered to his feet just as Rafe leaped over the railing, ducked a feeble blow, and replied with a backhanded swipe that blinded his older brother's right eye.

Micah was terrified. Screaming with pain, he clawed at his face and fell to his knees. Rafe's hand stopped, balled into a fist, and came crashing back to smash into the left side of Micah's face. Half unconscious, Micah felt himself lifted by his shirt and pushed across the lawn toward the carriage.

"Get out of here!" Rafe panted, pushing Micah again to keep him moving and off balance. "Get out, or so help me, God, I'll kill you."

Thinking the contest over was Rafe's mistake. The short reprieve was all Micah needed. Whirling, his eyes crimson cracks bordered by puffed flesh, Micah grabbed for Rafe, but not quickly enough.

Rafe stepped to one side and clubbed him on the back of the neck as he went by. Micah dove into the ground, and Rafe leaped astride him and, entwining his fingers in Micah's hair, slammed his head against the ground once, twice, three times.

The fight battered out of him, Micah groaned and lay still. Rafe pushed himself erect. He stood, gasping for breath, then reached down, grabbed Micah's shirt, and began dragging him toward the carriage again. When he felt his back hit against a wheel, he hauled Micah to his feet and propped him against the door next to Solange. The horse shied. Solange paled in horror at the bloody mask of the man with whom she had chosen to run away.

Rafe slapped Micah's face hard, twice. "Wake up!"

One eye finally opened and squinted at him in the moonlight.

"You hear me, Micah?" Rafe asked. "You hear what I'm saying?"

Micah nodded feebly and croaked something unintelligible.

"Don't *ever* let me see you again," Rafe gasped. "You hear? Don't ever let me see you again, because I'll kill you the next time. I'll kill you!" He glanced up at Solange. "You make me sick. Both of you. Get him out of here," he said, and then swung around and began walking shakily up the walk toward his father's house.

"You bastard!" Solange howled after Rafe, her heart sinking at the sight of her battered lover. "You do this to your own brother?" She grabbed Micah's arm and tried to help him into the carriage. "Your own brother?"

Micah pushed himself away from Solange and stood, weaving slightly, on his own. "We'll see," he rasped, his voice little more than a cracked whisper. He spat a glob of bloody phlegm and, using both hands, at last freed the Patterson Colt from his belt. "I'll send you to hell," he shrieked at the departing figure.

Rafe sensed the danger and, knowing he was too late, tumbled to the ground. There came a thunderclap explosion as the twenty-year-old pistol exploded in Micah's hand. A brilliant orange flash lit the night. Chunks of metal flew in every direction, ravaging already ruined features and blowing apart a hand. The hammer shot directly backward and, ripping through Micah's mouth, left a potato-size hole in the back of his skull as it exited. Dead without realizing what had hit him, Micah buckled and fell face forward in the dirt.

Solange screamed and fought the horse. Screamed again. Rafe slowly got to his feet, walked back to the carriage, and looked down at what had once been his brother.

His brother . . .

The words didn't sound right. "Micah?" Rafe said. His shoulders sagged. Blood dripped from his torn knuckles.

His brother . . .

Solange was quiet now, her hand balled into a fist she held to her mouth.

"Micah?" The rage drained from him, left his heart empty and heavy. It was over with. Finished. Done.

He glanced up at the sound of a whip and the creak of wheels, watched listlessly as the carriage rolled away and Solange disappeared into the night. Where she was going, he hadn't the foggiest idea and didn't care.

His brother . . . Over with, finished, done. Fighting an almost overpowering weariness, Rafe gathered up the still warm corpse and, cradling him like an infant, carried his big brother up the walk to the house and to his father who waited, his heart torn between sorrow and relief.

His brother . . . Thus did Micah return to his family, for the last time.

The house on Monroe Street bore the pale facade of death. Once white pillars, gray now and somber, fronted the scarred walls. Patches of blood darkened the ground near the fence. More could be found in the garden if one cared to look. Rafe didn't.

Celia waited at the front door. Celia, radiant in her torn dress and unbound hair, a smudge of gunpowder dark on her pale cheek. Rafe paused at the foot of the steps. "Micah is dead," he said.

Celia closed her eyes and nodded. "I'm sorry," she replied softly.

"You are?" he asked. "Even after what he did to you?"

He knew! Celia shuddered and cringed away from Rafe as if slapped.

"Father told me. He had learned from Micah. He'd kept that secret for over a year. It was what forced him to drive Micah from the house in the first place."

"Poor Micah," Celia whispered. "Poor sad Micah."

"How can you say that?" Rafe demanded, taken aback.

Celia seemed to have shrunk into herself. Rafe's words stung her. Why had she said that? After the pain and degradation, after the mind-wrenching shame and debilitating guilt, how could she say, 'Poor sad Micah'?

And then she knew why. Time had tempered her and left her with a core of such strength that, had she possessed it long ago, she wouldn't have had to fear Micah or anyone else. A core that could be touched only by love and by the man she chose to love. The answer was over two years in the forging, but one she would never forget. No matter what came her way, she could never again be harmed, never again be diminished. She was whole, she was complete, she was herself. She was free.

"Because," she said, her voice strong and resonant, "he hurt himself more than he ever could me. He destroyed himself, and I am here with you."

Rafe slowly, deliberately, walked up the steps to stand before her. His face was haggard but his eyes brimmed with understanding, and he felt as full as ever man has felt. And when he took her in his arms, his kiss spoke for him and her kiss answered. A kiss to say all the words, to sing all the songs of love and loving, from that day on.

At last, arm in arm, they entered the house where a baby was crying in the sunlight of its new life.

EPILOGUE

"Here, Reb. I know you are starved near to death."

Thus did the end begin as the Yankee soldiery walked past and under the white flags that flew along the line of trenches surrounding Vicksburg on that fateful morning of July 4, 1863, at ten in the morning. Thus did forty-seven days of siege end, not with cheers of exultation but with a deep and abiding respect for the Confederate men who had fought so boldly and held so long against such impossible odds.

By day's end the city swarmed with Federal troops. By day's end full for the first time in weeks, thirty thousand Rebel soldiers sat prisoner, waiting their fate and wondering. Fate was to be kind to them. There was no way the Federals could transport them all to northern prison camps. General Grant had decided he could not afford the men or munitions or provisions to cope with such a mass of prisoners. In the hopes that most of them were so tired of fighting that they would merely go home to their families, the Rebels were to be paroled—set free upon their promise not to fight again—and sent away from the city they would never forget.

So it was that four nights later, on Wednesday the eighth of July, Reverend Lundquist raised his right hand and said, "By the authority vested in me, I pronounce you man and wife. And now for heaven's sake kiss the bride before this thing sinks!"

"She won't sink, Parson," Snag Parken called from the raised, enclosed dais that passed for a wheelhouse.

Celia melted into Rafe's embrace and, to the sound of cheers and shouts of congratulation, felt her heart swell as his lips met hers.

"A strange wedding," the minister said, pumping Rafe's hand when the kiss ended. He blushed as Celia lightly kissed his cheek. "But a beautiful one, as all weddings are. May God bless you both!"

"He already has," Rafe said, escorting Lundquist to solid ground. "But watch your step. I'm not so sure if He paid much attention to this gangplank."

A whistle shrieked behind them. Snag had delayed his departure for four days and was anxious to cast off and be on his way.

Nathaniel cleared his throat. One hand clasping Rafe's arm, he embraced Celia and kissed her cheek. "I'll sell your house as soon as I can. Ought to bring a pretty penny, being one of the few left. The money'll be waiting for you. You or that son you promised me." He let go Celia and turned to Rafe. "You take care, boy," he said, his voice choking.

"I'll miss you, Father," Rafe said, not without having to clear his throat. "You'll be all right? Until we find a place to settle?"

"What is this?" Nathaniel grumped. "Think I can't take care of myself?" He clapped Rafe on the shoulder. "I'll be fine, and don't you forget it. Who knows? Maybe when this blamed war is over I'll even come looking for you. Little trip to the mountains will do me good by then, I imagine."

"I hope you do, Father." It wasn't a time for restrained emotions. Rafe threw his arms around Nathaniel and held him closely. "I hope you do. I'll miss you."

"Well!" Nathaniel pushed away from his son and took a swipe at his eyes. "Way out west! Think of it!" He cleared his throat, reached out and awkwardly touched his son's chest with a trembling hand. "Live your life, my son. Live it well!"

A baby squawled from the bow.

"Land sakes, woman," Snag hollered. "Plug that young'un's blow horn!"

"Just switching her from the starboard to port side," Lynna called. "Or is that port to starboard? One was drained dry of milk."

"Oh," Snag choked, embarrassed.

"Lines away up front—forward, Captain," Jonathan said, walking back from the bow and heading for the stern.

Nathaniel gave in, impulsively wrapped his arms around Rafe and kissed him on the cheek. Then, embarrassed himself, he turned and hurried to shore to stand by the minister.

"Haul in that gangplank!" Snag ordered.

Rafe untied the lines. Pulleys squealed and the plank rose from the bank and clanked against the supports that held it in a vertical position. "Gangplank secured!" he reported.

The whistle blasted. A cloud of white steam feathered in the light breeze. "Everybody ready?" Snag called.

A chorus of ayes answered him. "I wish Matthew had decided to come with us, too," Celia said, hooking her arm in Rafe's. "It doesn't seem right for him not to be here after all he did to help us."

"Can't have everything," Rafe answered a little wistfully. "I am going to miss that boy, though."

"We movin'?" Immelda asked, popping out from the deck level cabin just aft of the wheelhouse.

"On our way!" Snag called jubilantly.

Tobias appeared at Immelda's side. His chest still heavily bandaged, he moved stiffly to the rail and stood staring at the receding shoreline. "Can't believe it," he said in a hushed voice. "Can't believe we leavin'!" He turned tentatively to Celia. "You sure you don't mind us comin'?" he asked for the hundredth time.

"It's a free country," Celia replied for the hundredth time.

Tobias grinned and stood holding hands with Immelda. Both of them loved hearing those words.

The tiny stern-wheeler picked up speed and moved out toward the center of the channel heading for the Mississippi. Rafe waved to his father and then, taking Celia in arm, walked to the bow. The steam engine whooshed and rumbled. The paddle slapped the water and settled down to a steady, dripping rhythm.

Celia looked out over the water as they pulled away. The glimmering lights of Vicksburg, quiet and peaceful in the distance, were nothing compared to the canopy of stars overhead.

"It seems so far," Celia whispered, content in the warmth of Rafe's arms.

"What?"

"The mountains . . . the territories . . . the future. How will we ever make it?"

"The same way we made it through everything else," Rafe answered confidently. His arm tightened around her waist and his lips touched her forehead. Her hair smelled sweet. "With determination . . . and love." He looked up river, toward the future. "We'll make it."

And they did.